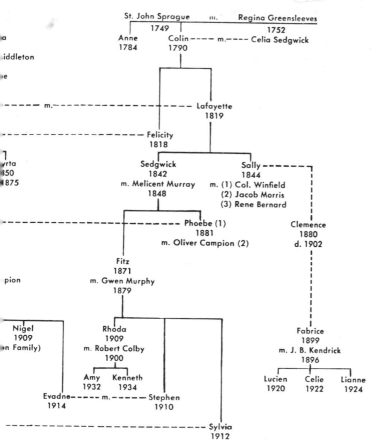

St. John Sprague — m. — Regina Greensleeves
1749 / 1752

Anne 1784 | Colin 1790 ---- m. ---- Celia Sedgwick

a
iddleton
e

---- m. ---------------- Lafayette 1819

---------------- Felicity 1818

yrta
350
1875

Sedgwick 1842
m. Melicent Murray 1848

Sally 1844
m. (1) Col. Winfield
(2) Jacob Morris
(3) Rene Bernard

---------------- Phoebe (1) 1881
m. Oliver Campion (2)

Clemence 1880
d. 1902

pion

Fitz 1871
m. Gwen Murphy 1879

Nigel 1909
n Family)

Rhoda 1909
m. Robert Colby 1900

Fabrice 1899
m. J. B. Kendrick 1896

Amy 1932 | Kenneth 1934

Lucien 1920 | Celie 1922 | Lianne 1924

Evadne 1914 ---- m. ---- Stephen 1910

---------------- Sylvia 1912

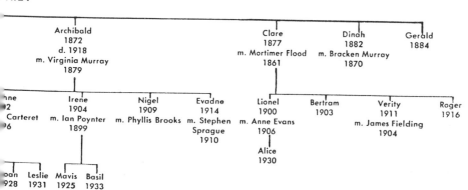

Archibald 1872
d. 1918
m. Virginia Murray 1879

Clare 1877
m. Mortimer Flood 1861

Dinah 1882
m. Bracken Murray 1870

Gerald 1884

hne
2
Carteret
6

Irene 1904
m. Ian Poynter 1899

Nigel 1909
m. Phyllis Brooks

Evadne 1914
m. Stephen Sprague 1910

Lionel 1900
m. Anne Evans 1906

Bertram 1903

Verity 1911
m. James Fielding 1904

Roger 1916

Alice 1930

oan
928 | Leslie 1931 | Mavis 1925 | Basil 1933

Dawn's
Early Light

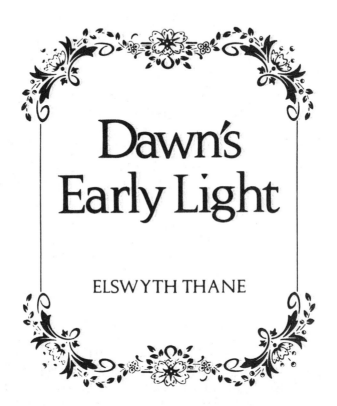

Dawn's Early Light

ELSWYTH THANE

HAWTHORN BOOKS, INC.
PUBLISHERS/*New York*
A Howard & Wyndham Company

DAWN'S EARLY LIGHT

Library of Congress Catalog Card Number: 73-9983
ISBN: 0-8015-1957-8
1 2 3 4 5 6 7 8 9 10

To

Frederic and Eleanor Van de Water

ACKNOWLEDGMENTS

A book with an historical background can seldom be accomplished without the patient assistance of experts. I would like to name with gratitude Mr. Bela Norton and Miss Mary McWilliams of Colonial Williamsburg, Dr. E. G. Swem, Librarian at the College of William and Mary, Mr. Thomas Pitkin, Park Historian at Yorktown, and Mr. William Brandon at the Guilford Courthouse National Park. I would like also to thank Mrs. Frederick Gore King of the New York Society Library for the advantages of a friendly and intelligent organization which rendered invaluable service. The end-paper was adapted and drawn by Edith Thane from a Colonial Williamsburg publication.

E. T.

CONTENTS

I

WILLIAMSBURG NECK. 1774-1779

1

II

THE CAROLINAS. 1780

167

III

VIRGINIA. 1781

225

Dawn's Early Light

Williamsburg Neck

1774-1779

I

He stood remote and alone amid the cheerful bustle of the dock at Yorktown. Around his feet in their silver-buckled shoes was stacked enough luggage for two men. Behind him rose the proud, sharp prow and slender spars of the *Mary Jones,* which had brought him across the Atlantic from Southampton.

The hot Virginia sun was in his eyes below the point of his tricorne. He wore his own brown hair unpowdered and tied with a black ribbon notched into swallow-tails. His blue broadcloth coat and knee breeches were London-cut, making the most of his rather overgrown height, his narrow waist and straight back. A black cloak lined with silk was folded over his arm. He would have, if he ever filled out a bit, an excellent leg. It was his twenty-first birthday.

Patiently in the pelting sunlight he surveyed the ambling colored longshoremen who threw ropes to one another, or passed heavy boxes from hand to hand in a sweating chain, or toiled past him under towering bales of goods, while good-natured white men bawled orders at them. To look at him, one would never have guessed at the hollowness of his inside.

He was not new to travel. He had seen Rome and Berlin and Paris and Vienna—to say nothing of Edinburgh, Bath, and his native London. The noise and excitement of a ship's arrival in port were familiar to him. Since childhood he was accustomed to see strange sights and smell strange odors and hear strange speech. But now, at the beginning of a new year in his life, he stood on the threshold of a new continent—

quite alone. He felt the way he had felt on his first day as a scholar at Winchester. He felt the necessity of a stiff upper lip.

Finally a man a little older than himself, with a thin, sunbrowned face, approached him through the confusion.

"You must be Julian Day," he said, and the tall boy bowed. "I have been wasting my time trying to find the captain to introduce me. I'm Sprague, from Mr. Wythe's law office in Williamsburg. Mr. Wythe did me the honor to send me down to welcome you and your father to Virginia."

"That is very kind. My father died at sea." The simple words fell gently into the clamor all about them.

Young Mr. Sprague's sympathy sprang quick and sincere.

"My dear fellow," he said, and set his hand briefly on the dark blue sleeve.

"They read a service and put him over the side three days ago."

"I'm sorry, I—can't seem to think of the right thing to say," Sprague confessed in genuine distress. "But perhaps the best thing I can do is to get you away from here at once. I've got a coach waiting, and I have engaged rooms for you at Williamsburg. That is—" He tripped on his own words, and his honest eyes were anxious. "That is, now that you are here, you will, of course, come on to Williamsburg?"

"I suppose so," said Julian Day. "I don't mean to sound ungracious, I just—" He made a little gesture with his empty hands. "—I just seem to have no plans!" The hot, overpowering scent of tar and tobacco and bilge and Negro beat upward from the baking planks under his feet. The hot southern sunlight beat down on his unprotected head. He turned rather white around the mouth, and felt Sprague's hand laid again on his sleeve.

"My dear fellow, anything in the world I can do— And I am sure Mr. Wythe will be most distressed to hear—and the people at the College too, of course—" He broke off to beckon to a young colored giant in livery who waited near by. "Joshua, put Mr. Day's boxes into the wagon," he said, and with his hand still under Julian's elbow moved down the dock towards the coach which stood in the road at the end.

"I shall have to decide something very soon," Julian resumed more steadily as they rolled away from the dockside followed by the baggage wagon, and took the road which led through the little town and along the shore towards the capital. "The *Mary Jones* sails again for Plymouth in a fortnight's time, and I—"

"Oh, come, now, Mr. Day, give us a chance!" cried Sprague. "You might like it here! Look!" He gestured through the coach window.

The glass was down, and hot dust rose from the horses' feet and settled in a fine powder on Julian's dark coat. Gripping the leathern strap which hung beside the window, he looked out into the glare with his grave, unrevealing gaze. The road ran along a high bank above the broad bosom of the river, whose surface was spiky with the masts of many ships.

"It is very—big," he said inadequately, and Sprague gave a shout of laughter.

"Of course it's big, man, it's America! It's so big we aren't quite sure where it ends! Think of it—Virginia has no western boundary line!"

"But—surely there are maps," Julian began. "I saw several maps in London—"

"Guesswork!" Sprague waved them aside. "West of the Cumberlands —all guesswork!"

"Yes, I suppose it must be," Julian agreed, and sat a moment watching the forest which now obscured the river for a space. West of the Cumberlands—boundless forest, boundless frontier, peopled by savages, bristling with unthinkable dangers, dreary with hardships impossible to conceive. And here on the fringes of that unpenetrated wilderness, along the great tidewater rivers, a precarious civilization hanging on by its eyelashes, only recently beginning to be sure that it would not be wiped out between sunset and dawn, only in the last generation able to feel secure in itself from one season to the next. How long, really, since the beat of Indian war drums had been heard in the very streets of the capital, he wondered. Something that was not fear, as fear, something that had little to do with his own personal safety, ran like a chill flame along his spine—a sense of the awful vastness to the west, crisping all his nerves. They weren't even sure where it ended. Thousands of miles of wilderness overhung him as though for a moment the continent had been stood on edge above his head. . . . "About the lodging you have found for me," he heard himself saying, "the fact is, we had very little money left after we had bought our passage. My father expected—that is, we thought that with his post at the College assured— The fact is,"

he said again, "I shall have to find some way of earning my passage
home before I can go."

"And a damned good thing too!" said Sprague. "By that time you
may decide to stay here—like me."

"You weren't born here?" Julian queried in surprise.

"I was born in England. But I shall take great care to die here, when
that time comes." Sprague's merry brown face was suddenly brooding
and grave. "Man, America is the greatest thing that has happened to
England since we beat the Spanish under Elizabeth! The New World!
Do you comprehend those words? A new world, just for the taking,
and enough of it for everybody! You have only to stretch out your
hand—" His lean brown fingers closed on the dust-filled air. "—grasp—
and hold!"

"There is certainly enough of it!" agreed Julian, dazed.

For twelve miles they drove through the forest, leaving the gleam of
the river behind them. Though Sprague was anything but homesick, he
craved news of London nonetheless. Was the King really a little mad?
Well, but one did hear rumors, didn't one! And what was the true story
behind Amherst's refusal to accept the governorship of Virginia? His
wife's objections, they said! Ah, women! Amherst would have been a
good man for the post. Not that one would say anything against the
present Governor, of course, Dunmore was merely the most obstinate,
tactless, narrow-minded ass the colony had had to put up with since old
Lord Berkeley a hundred years ago! One heard that Chatham was
rusticating in the country again with Garrick and his cronies—was the
old gentleman really done this time, or would he rally again? Nobody
in England appreciated Chatham, least of all the King. And what about
that new singer from Bath—Elizabeth Linley—was she as lovely as
they said? Married! To the fellow who fought that duel over her? *Two*
duels! Well, perhaps he had earned his luck. . . .

Julian answered questions as best he could, wondering at Sprague's
intimate knowledge of London gossip, even though in London it was
already months old. Diffidently he admitted to acquaintanceship with
Dick Sheridan, who had married the superb Miss Linley. Yes, as a
matter of fact he had attended the same fencing school at Carlisle House
—well, yes, he had crossed swords with Sheridan there more than once,
under Angelo's critical eye—yes, Sheridan was a good swordsman,

but impetuous, that second affair with Matthews over Elizabeth Linley had ended as just a hacking match with broken swords—yes, one of the duels had actually been fought by candlelight in a locked room— no, romance was apparently not dead, after all. . . .

Sprague's eager questions and easy laughter, the whole vital, youthful quality of the man, left Julian feeling somewhat old and staid and bewildered. Yet it was not as though Sprague had himself no knowledge of pain, for his compassion came warm and quick to another's sorrow. What a friend, Julian found himself thinking, what a friend to have at one's back these days! His itinerant boyhood, spent at the heels of a scholarly father always in pursuit of further learning abroad, had left him rather empty of friendships hitherto. Always one moved on. And now, at the back of beyond, one came upon this man Sprague, who in some mysterious way made one feel less alone in the world. . . .

Before he realized that they had emerged from the forest, the coach swung around a corner and into a broad tree-lined avenue, straight as a Roman road as far as the eye travelled ahead. Low, comfortable-looking white houses sat well back in green lawns behind neat paling fences, with now and then a rosy brick dwelling among them. There were gardens in early flower, and clipped box hedges. The arching branches of the mulberry trees nearly met overhead, their knobby trunks in cool shadow. Every wheel, every footfall, stirred the deep dust of the sandy road, and dust lay thick on the green leaves and powdered the grass.

At that hour of late afternoon the town was busy, and Julian received a swift impression of prosperous shops, liveried black servants ambling about their errands, a fashionable carriage or two with the gleam of silk and jewels inside, and fine saddle horses with well-dressed riders. "That was the Capitol," said Sprague, for the square brick building with its white columns was already behind them. "The Raleigh Tavern will be on your right—" He leaned across Julian to hang out of the coach window. "By Jove, there is a crowd at the Raleigh! That means more news. We heard yesterday that the Port of Boston is to be closed on June first, and British troops are encamped on the Common." He turned suddenly, fixing his level, uncompromising gaze on Julian's face. "Just where do you stand?" he inquired, and added belatedly, "if you don't mind my asking."

"Well, I—" Julian began, rather at a loss.

"You have heard, I suppose, about Boston's dumping all that tea into the harbor?"

"Yes—we heard about that before I left London."

"Well?" queried Sprague, watching him.

"We thought it was a pity in a way, as it seemed a needless affront to the Government. It must have been the work of a gang of ruffians. Nobody believes they were really Indians, you know."

"Of course they weren't Indians, they only wore paint and feathers as a disguise!" There was a brief silence. Then Sprague said, "You are bound to be a Tory, of course, with your background."

"You mean you personally subscribe to that Boston affair?"

"We can be pushed just so far," said Sprague darkly, closing it. "There is the Palace—it's quite a sight on Birthday Nights and Christmas and anniversaries, whenever the Governor gives a state ball—then the trees on the Green are hung with colored lanterns, and there are fireworks and free wine for the townsfolk. The Governor lives like a king, with a country estate he calls Porto Bello up beyond Queen's Creek—thinks nothing of forty to dinner—has his own coat of arms on a china dinner service, and six white horses to his coach!"

Julian leaned forward to look up the long Green which lay in front of the Governor's town residence—another square brick building with a tall white cupola and white dormers in the third story, a balcony above the door where the Governor could take his vice-regal bows, and imposing ironwork gates.

"That's very handsome," he said, impressed. "I had no idea. You say he is not popular?"

"He has a genius for putting people against him, from the Burgesses down. It was unfortunate, of course, that a man like Dunmore should have had to succeed Governor Botetourt, whom everybody liked. If Botetourt had lived—well, who knows? There is the church. They are very proud of the organ, be sure to admire it. And here you are—your landlady is a widow named Hartley, and rather a dear. She intends to mother you, so don't stand on ceremony—especially now that your father—"

They had turned another corner, to the right off the main avenue, and halted before a white house with green shutters and a graceful pillared doorway. Julian descended from the coach and looked about him with approval.

"Why, this is charming," he said. "There is even a garden."

"What did you expect, man, a circle of huts inside a stockade?"

"But there was a stockade," said Julian, as though glancing about for it.

"There was, when the Duke of Gloucester Street was a cow-path! The College is at the further end. We will walk up there this evening if you like."

The white panelled door with its shining brass knocker was opened to them by a fresh-faced woman in sprigged muslin, over which she wore a snowy apron and fichu. She welcomed them cordially and drew them into a square hall from which an oak stair angled upward. As Joshua and the colored lad who drove the wagon carried in Julian's boxes a trim black maid appeared to show them the way up stairs.

My father died at sea. Once more Julian said those five dreadful words, and Mrs. Hartley's sympathy was indeed motherly and tactful and comforting. Then Sprague accompanied him to his room where the luggage awaited him, and the smiling colored girl came in with a jug of hot water and clean towels which smelt of lavender and sunshine.

"Is that girl a slave?" asked Julian, when she had gone.

"She is. Would you prefer to be waited on by a bondservant whose skin is the same color as yours?"

"A bondmaid has at least the prospect of freedom," Julian reminded him.

"And of very little else as things are! We have had a rise in the slave trade lately. And with slave labor increasing, it is difficult for a bondservant who has worked out his time to find work to live by. That is the real evil of slavery, Mr. Day, and not man's inhumanity to man."

"I don't think I have a prejudice against slavery," Julian denied with a certain stateliness. "Doubtless out here one becomes accustomed to it. So long as they are well-treated," he added, and Sprague laughed.

"My dear fellow, we don't work them in galleys, you know! The second generation of blacks, born here, are very well off indeed, for the most part. The voyage out from Africa of the wild Negroes doesn't bear thinking about, of course."

"No, I suppose it doesn't," Julian agreed, and began to unpack the portmanteau Joshua had set on the chest at the foot of the four-posted bed. "I was surprised to hear Dr. Franklin say that not one in a hundred families in America owns a slave. One had the impression that it was almost a universal practice."

Sprague gazed at him from the window-seat with a mixture of awe and delight.

"You have heard Dr. Franklin?" he exclaimed. "In London?"

"Why, yes, and in Edinburgh. He and my father were friends. It was Dr. Franklin who was really responsible for our coming to Virginia. He got my father the post at the College here. He says there should be no politics and no national frontiers in learning. There is a man at Harvard who thinks the same way. My father wanted to make of himself a sort of link between the College of William and Mary and the universities at home, in the hope of a better understanding—" He turned away suddenly towards the wardrobe, and hung up a coat with care.

"Did you see Dr. Franklin often?" queried Sprague after a moment.

"Fairly often. There is a sort of club that meets every other Thursday at the coffee house in Ludgate Hill. I hadn't really any right to be there, of course, but my father always took me, and nobody objected, so I— sat and listened."

"There is something rather like that here too," said Sprague. "In the Apollo Room at the Raleigh. Tom Jefferson lets me go with him sometimes. You must meet Jefferson. He went straight into Mr. Wythe's law office out of the College, and they are old friends. They will all be glad to get hold of a man who has seen Dr. Franklin lately, we think very highly of him out here."

"We think very highly of him in London," said Julian quietly. "He is the best ambassador the colonies could have there, but he won't let you say that because the colonies are not entitled to have an ambassador."

"We shall see very soon what the colonies are entitled to," Sprague said grimly and rose from the window-seat. "I'll be off now, and leave you to settle in. But you haven't seen the last of me. I shall come back in about two hours' time if you will do me the honor to have supper with me at the Raleigh?"

"Thank you, I should be delighted," said Julian with a little formal bow.

For a moment they measured each other—Sprague's well-knit body poised as always like a duellist's, his blue eyes with their upward-curving lashes candid as a child's in his fine-drawn face; Julian's tall figure only just emerged from the boyish stoop of too rapid growth, his habitual gravity further clouded now by sorrow. They stood there, the new world and the old, one of them keen and ebullient, tiptoe to life, the other self-contained, conservative, and at present a trifle confused. Sprague was the first to smile.

"Injuns, niggers, or troops on the Common," he said, "let's you and I be friends!"

"By all means," said Julian with his slow, wide smile, and their right hands met.

At the door Sprague turned.

"I'm going back to the Raleigh now," he said. "It looks as though the House has risen. Jefferson said they were going to propose a day of fasting and prayer for Boston on June first. The Governor wouldn't like that!"

"Couldn't he forbid it?"

"Certainly he could!" Sprague's strange, innocent eyes were bright with laughter. "He could forbid it till he is black in the face, but that wouldn't stop it! You know, I've been thinking—somebody has only got to fire one shot in Boston now and—*pst!*" He made a little upward gesture of explosion. "Doesn't matter which side fires first. It blows the lid off!"

"But that would be civil war!" cried Julian in horror.

"Do you think such a possibility has never occurred to the King in London?" asked Sprague.

"I don't know, I—suppose it has. That is, we all feel—"

"Yes, Mr. Day? What do you all feel?"

"We do feel it is time these brawls in Boston were stopped, you see, somebody has got to take things in hand, that is—" He became wordless under Sprague's waiting, friendly gaze.

"Man, you're a gift of God!" said Sprague softly into the silence. "Dr. Franklin in his wisdom has sent us a link with the mother country. This will be a most welcome test case. Wait till I tell them you are here!"

"Well, now, wait a minute—" Julian began. "If my father were here you might have something to judge by, but I don't know that I qualify—"

Young Sprague was gone from the doorway.

Julian sat down on the nearest chair and put his head in his hands, while a wave of desolation engulfed him. If my father were here. . . .

II

About two hours later, composed, polite, and more than a little curious, he went out again with Sprague into the soft Virginia twilight.

Mrs. Hartley's house stood only a few doors down from the Duke of Gloucester Street, where they turned to their right and soon came to where the road forked, the lefthand way leading westward to Jamestown and the ferry, the other keeping on up the Neck and along the Chickahominy on the northward route to Richmond. In the crotch of the Y lay a broad green lawn and the three brick buildings of the College. A great live oak overhung the gate. When Julian saw the gracious façade of the main building, "It could have been designed by Wren!" he exclaimed, as though he had found a friend.

"It could have been," agreed Sprague, pleased. "And in fact we think it was, or by some one closely in touch with him. The house on the right is the President's residence. They will just be sitting down to supper, so we won't call until tomorrow. The other is Brafferton Hall."

"The Indian school," said Julian with interest. "We had rather hoped I might get some work there."

"The education of Indians is so far not a success," Sprague told him with a shrug. "They take on all the worst of Christian sin while they are here—and either die of it or revert to savagery when they return to their villages. Perhaps I should warn you that President Camm is a violent Tory and most of the students are equally violent Whigs. You can put your foot in it either way!"

"That can hardly make for academic peace," murmured Julian, as they emerged again into the Duke of Gloucester Street under the dark low boughs of the live oak.

They strolled back up the right-hand side in the gathering dusk. The town was indoors now for its evening meal, and the street was almost empty. Candlelight glimmered in the windows of the white-painted houses. And there were other tiny flitting lights in the shadows under the mulberry and catalpa trees. Fireflies. Julian had heard about the fireflies from Dr. Franklin, but he still could not believe he really saw them.

With a naive civic pride Sprague pointed out the octagonal brick Powder Magazine and its attendant guardhouse on the little green which faced the new Courthouse in the Market Square. And there was the apothecary's sign of the Unicorn, and the office of the *Virginia Gazette* which was also the Post Office, and the Ludwell house, an eccentric brick mansion whose present owners chose to live abroad—they might come scurrying home any day now!—and just beyond was the barber-surgeon, a Swiss named Pasteur who called himself a peruke-maker. The theater, said Sprague, was on the Palace Green, and had lately housed a rather good performance of *The Recruiting Officer.* Mrs. Hallam, the famous actress, had retired from the stage and established a school for girls in Williamsburg, where she taught deportment *à la mode,* music, dancing, and French conversation—a remarkably fine woman, they said, not at all what you might expect. . . . And here they were, back at the Raleigh.

The long, white-gabled building was a very hearty-looking place as they crossed the road to it, with the dust up over their shoes. Candlelight streamed from its many windows and through its open door, above which stood a lead bust of the great Sir Walter himself. Saddle horses were tied almost stirrup to stirrup along the hitching-bars in front of it, and the benches under the tap-room windows were full of talkative citizens.

Sprague led the way through a handsome parlor and the public bar to a dining-room set with polished round tables and fiddle-back chairs. A beaming black waiter seated them with a flourish, exchanging unself-conscious pleasantries with Sprague, who spoke to him with apparent affection as an old acquaintance.

There was a pervading friendliness in the atmosphere, and a lack of formality which Julian would come gradually to attribute to the cheerful colored service. The broad white-toothed smiles and loquacious greetings of the liveried slaves held no presumptuousness—neither was there room in their confiding natures for the tip-seeking self-importance of fashionable London butlers and footmen or the worldly impudence of cockney pot-boys.

As the leisurely meal progressed, the room filled with laughter and talk; sunburned men hailed Sprague as they passed by to their own tables; strange, fragrant dishes came and went—a sheepshead here meant delicious fish, and all the bread was hot. The effect of his surroundings was to Julian singularly gay and disarming. *Young,* was the word which would keep recurring to his mind during the days to come, when he was to know again and again the sensations of an elderly and somewhat disillusioned bachelor uncle in the company of his juniors. It was a young world he had come to, and Williamsburg seemed a toy town where politics and war and even learning were solemn games played by charming children. And yet, he would remind himself, these self-confident, free-and-easy folk were the sons and daughters of men and women who had toiled and suffered amid deadly dangers to carve this perilous paradise out of the wilderness which lay even now at their threshold.

Over the meal he learned more of Sprague's background. Orphaned as a child in England, Sprague was the sole heir of his Uncle Colin, who had been one of Virginia's many planter-lawyers, with a brick mansion up the James River and a white house in Williamsburg which he used during the Assembly times twice a year, when the whole colony descended on the capital for balls and races and shopping.

It was Uncle Colin who had sent his nephew to Harrow—Eton being a hotbed of Whiggery. When Uncle Colin died three years ago young Sprague came out from England to settle the estate and found it much involved in debt. Instead of being annoyed at the drastic curtailment of his prospects, he had fallen in love, as he said, with America and resolved to stay in it. He had sold the plantation and the slaves, except for three favorite maids and Joshua the butler-coachman and a lad for the chores, and established a modest household with his widowed Aunt Anabel in the Williamsburg house in Francis Street. Next year his sister Dorothea, just turning sixteen, would come out from her grandmother's home in London to join him. He had hoped to have a letter from her by the *Mary Jones.* . . .

Their exchange of views on the touchy question of politics continued without rancor. Each was too full of curiosity regarding the other's beliefs for nearsighted wrangling. Julian's impression that the Virginia colony was closer in thought and social standing to the mother country than the Massachusetts trouble-makers was confirmed by Sprague, who nevertheless seized the opportunity to point out that it would be a mistake to assume that Virginia did not ally herself with Massachusetts in the struggle. One must not, said Sprague, forget the complete unity which had existed between the colonies during the opposition to the Stamp Act nearly ten years ago—before either of them at that table, to be sure, was taking any interest in such matters at all. But men like George Wythe could remember. And even Tom Jefferson liked to tell how as a youngster in Wythe's law office as Sprague was today, but nevertheless a Burgess in his own right, he had heard Patrick Henry make his famous "treason" speech—

Julian had heard about that, at the coffee house in Ludgate Hill.

"Did he really say 'If this be treason, make the most of it?' " he queried skeptically.

"He really did! And those Liberty companies drilling all over New England now are electing officers and designing themselves smart uniforms—if that is treason! But don't think they won't find their counterparts, if need be, in the Virginia militia companies, under one of the best soldiers in the colonies—George Washington!"

"You have an *army* here?" asked Julian, astonished.

"We have militia. And we have officers trained in the Indian wars. It is easy to forget, here in Williamsburg, that only a few years ago every able-bodied man was liable to be called into the field against the Indians. The frontier has only moved westward a little. There is trouble now in the Ohio country."

"*Massacre?*"

"There is always massacre on the frontier, man! But it isn't the British army that keeps the Indians in order, you know. It is the settlers themselves, the fathers and sons with rifles in their hands, protecting their own homes. There is no British army except in Boston, these days!"

"But surely when Braddock—"

"Braddock was beaten, remember?"

"Yes, of course, he was killed in ambush at Fort Duquesne, but—"

"We call it Pittsburgh now. And he was killed by one of his own men."

"*What?*"

"Ask Colonel Washington, he was there! And Braddock wasn't ambushed, as a matter of fact, he fired first. He was caught in column and outflanked. The British in their red coats made fine targets, and they couldn't even see the Indians to shoot back at them. So they broke, and Braddock went amongst 'em with the flat of his sword, and they shouted 'We can't fight bushes!' and tried to hide. What Braddock wanted was to beat them back into platoons for an orderly retreat, and he was famous for his rages. That day he killed a soldier for hugging a tree, and the man's own brother fired point-blank at Braddock. It was when Braddock dropped out of the saddle that the real panic started. He wasn't dead yet, and one of his aides straddled him to save him from being trampled to death in the flight of his own men. Then Washington came up, very cool—just a colt he was then, in a hunting-shirt—and they made a sort of hammock of Braddock's sash, and they had to bribe men to slow down enough to carry him. Washington directed the rear guard action, fighting from tree to tree, and a few of them got away. Then Braddock died, and they buried him in the middle of the road he had made through the wilderness, and Washington read the burial service because the chaplain had been wounded, and they drove the wagons over the grave so the Indians wouldn't find it. And that, Mr. Day, is how the British army fights the Indians!"

Julian sat silent, a little stunned. It was not the way Braddock's defeat was spoken of in England.

"This—Mr. Washington," he began at last. "You say he is a militiaman?"

Sprague gave him a look of patient despair.

"Colonel Washington is a planter," he said, seeking words of one syllable. "He is one of the wealthiest men in Virginia. He is a member of the House of Burgesses. He was Commander-in-Chief of the Virginia forces when he was twenty-three. He resigned his commission when he married, but whenever Virginia needs a Commander-in-Chief again— she has George Washington!"

"You mean he would lead colonial militia against the King's troops?"

It had a very nasty sound, put baldly into words like that. Under

Julian's incredulous eyes, Sprague saw that somehow, with the best intentions, he had put the hero in the worst possible light.

"We must hope it won't come to that," he said rather lamely, as a hand fell on his shoulder and they looked up to see Captain Barry of the *Mary Jones* standing over them.

"Here ye both are at last!" roared the captain at quarter-deck pitch. "Looked everywhere for ye at the dock! What will ye give me, Mr. Sprague, for these two letters from London?"

"Whatever you'll have, Captain! Won't you join us?"

Captain Barry explained that he hadn't rightly started drinking yet, having a few more things to see to, but would take a glass of Madeira with them since that's what was going. Another glass was brought and healths were drunk, while the two letters lay beside Sprague's plate, the seals unbroken.

"So they're at it again in there, I hear!" said the captain, with a jerk of his head towards the closed door of the Apollo Room, and Sprague grinned. "Who's there tonight?"

"All of 'em," said Sprague. "Jefferson, Henry, two Randolphs, Wythe, Mason, Lee—"

"Colonel Washington?" queried Captain Barry, glass poised at his lips.

"Colonel Washington is dining at the Palace," Sprague stated flatly without a flicker, and the captain wheezed with laughter and slapped his thigh and drained off his glass.

"Ain't he a one!" marvelled the captain, and watched with satisfaction while the glass was filled again.

"In powder, and a new uniform," added Sprague, and the captain wheezed again, while Julian glanced from one to the other, aware of significances which escaped him. To an outsider like himself, the powdered presence of the Virginia colonel in what was apparently the opposite camp looked an odd subject for gratification.

"Nothing ketches *him* off balance!" said the captain, which he seemed to think covered everything, and set his empty glass on the table and rose. "Well, ye'll be wantin' to read your letters," he said kindly to Sprague. "And if ye'll allow an old married man to say so, there never was a prettier girl this side of heaven than that sister of yours, Mr. Sprague. Specially in a blue dress!"

He was off, with a broad farewell, to join sundry cronies round the tobacco-box on the bar.

Julian indicated the letters on the table with a smile.

"Don't delay longer on my account," he said. "You will be anxious to learn the news."

"This one is from Dorothea," said Sprague, and put the other away into his pocket. "Hers are always entertaining, I'll share it with you." He slid his finger under Dorothea's pale green wafer and read the closely written pages quickly, a smile on his lips. He finished with a chuckle, and looked up to find Julian watching him enviously. On one of his generous impulses, Sprague held out the letter across the table. "Here, read it yourself, it will do you good," he said.

"Wouldn't she mind?" Julian accepted it doubtfully.

"Of course not. It is just her usual nonsense."

My dearest Sinjie, the letter began, and Julian stuck there, characteristically unable to go on till all was clear to him.

"What does she call you?" he inquired, with a puzzled look, and Sprague laughed again.

"My name is St. John," he explained.

Enlightened, Julian read on.

My dearest Sinjie—

Captain Barry has just called with your letter and says he will bring you one back from me if I have it ready by Friday. I wonder how long he thinks it takes a fairly well-educated young woman to write to her brother. He seemed to feel I could just barely manage if I kept hard at it all this week!

I loved having one from you, the time gets very long, and I miss our foolish fun together as one misses the sun. Why is it that you are the only man I have ever known who makes me laugh. I mean really bellow, not just a polite simper! I shall never marry, alas, until I find another Sinjie, and I shall desperately envy the girl who gets my brother for a husband, no matter who she is. Shall I find you spoken for when I finally arrive in America? I think you had better not choose until I have looked over the field, you are such a kind-hearted motherly soul that dear knows how you may be wrought upon by some designing creature clever enough to be caught with tears in her eyes.

Lady Cathcart descended upon us yesterday and read Granny a lecture about the perils of the voyage to Virginia and prophesied that there will be fighting in America soon between the colonists and the British army. She said Granny was *mad* to think of letting me sail to join you at Williamsburg. Granny said Poppycock, and that if there *was* any trouble it would only be up in New England, which everyone knew was peopled by the scum of the earth, and that Virginia was civilized and delightful and I should be perfectly safe with you and it would be very broadening to my mind. She said if it weren't for her gout she would come with me herself and see Virginia—and incidentally you!—before she died. Lady Cathcart *bristled,* because her brother lives in Boston and writes dismal letters, not a bit like yours, all about what is the world coming to, and the King really must put his foot down, etc., etc. Lady Cathcart says there is a *feeling* in London that Governor Gage is entirely the wrong person to be Commander-in-Chief at Boston, because he married a lady from New Jersey—though not, she believed, an Indian squaw as some people said—and would therefore not *really* try to bring the people to their senses. So you see what will be said here if you do marry some Williamsburg minx—half London won't believe she is white, and of course there was Pocahontas, wasn't there!

Granny and I quite realize that there can't actually be a war, because the colonists are English after all, just like us here at home— much more English than the King, so far as that goes!–and old Lord Chatham is on the colonists' side, they say, though he has been terribly ill again down in the country, poor soul, and suffers agonies with the gout, and his sister has got *quite queer.* (I have just thought how awful it would be if you sat in Parliament one day, and made a brilliant speech, and people could say "You know, his *sister*—!" and then tap their foreheads! Well, I am sure you could make a brilliant speech if you tried, you are frightfully clever, and now that you are studying law with Mr. Wythe *anything* might come of it, so many great men seem to have begun at the Bar!)

If I don't stop soon it will be Friday after all. Darling Sinjie, I can hardly wait to see you again, couldn't I come out in time for Christmas, as a present to us both? I shouldn't ask for any other. My loving duty to Aunt Anabel, and all my heart to you.

Your devoted sister,

DOROTHEA

Julian finished the letter slowly, folded it with care, and returned it.

"She must be a most unusual girl," he said, and thought the words sounded stingy and unappreciative, and added, "I hope she will come while I am still here. Not that she would be interested in knowing me."

"She has a serious side," smiled Sprague. "You can talk to her about anything you like, I always have. I'll wager she knows more about the colonial situation than you do!"

"That wouldn't be difficult," Julian assented ruefully. "What did Captain Barry mean when he said they were at it again in there?"

"He meant the meeting in the Apollo Room," Sprague explained, with the same significant jerk of his head towards the closed door. "That is where the Burgesses go when the Governor dissolves 'em, which he did again today for that June first resolution. They met there when Governor Botetourt dissolved 'em during the Stamp Act trouble, and again last year when they started the committees of correspondence. Lord knows what they are cooking up now. That is the heart of Virginia beating in there. Those are the men I want you to meet."

Julian looked alarmed.

"I don't think my opinions—" he began.

"Your opinions are the sort they will want to hear."

"Opinions like mine have no weight with the King, you know," Julian reminded him drily.

"His Gracious Majesty!" Sprague made a rude noise. "Why, as Dorothea says, he isn't even an Englishman! He is a European tyrant, and Jefferson says his name will be a blot on the page of history!" As Julian's eyes widened at the heresy, Sprague realized that he had again given a wrong impression of a man he wanted Julian to admire. "Mind you, Jefferson doesn't go as far as Patrick Henry does. Jefferson feels that there could be a sort of Empire of free men under the British flag—"

"That is Chatham's idea," said Julian, relieved. "He calls it a friendly alliance within the imperial system."

"It's easy enough to say," agreed Sprague, "but things have reached a stage where the Government must either coerce Massachusetts or remove the tea tax. And now that they have landed troops in Boston, they have lighted a slow fuse. It is impossible to see how—" The door of the Apollo Room had opened on the scraping of chairs across the floor and men's voices making good-nights, and Sprague's head jerked up like a deer's to the wind. "Here they come! The meeting is over. You must be introduced to Jefferson, I'll try to bring him in here."

Almost the last thing Julian wished for was an encounter with the great men of Virginia, especially in his present bewildered frame of mind, but he watched helplessly while Sprague crossed the room and joined a group of men around the door.

There was a sudden alertness and curiosity in the air of the Raleigh, as the Apollo Room emptied. Heads turned, conversation dropped. Everyone was waiting, watching, trying to read on the disciplined faces of the men who represented them the results of that latest conference in the famous supper room.

"Tom Jefferson is pleased," said a lowered voice behind Julian as a man who had just passed through the little crowd in the doorway took a seat at a table near by. "They're up to something, no mistake! Tom has got that look on him again!"

"Patrick Henry is the man fer me!" an uneducated accent from the frontier broke in. "Nothing fancy about 'im! He says it will be war before we're done, and send it come soon, I ain't so young as I used ter be!"

"That's all very well for you, dad, but a war will ruin us in trade for years. The non-importation times were bad enough!"

"Ar, you *store-keepers!* The King wants to learn us a lesson, does 'e! Well, 'ow about us drivin' a little commonsense into 'is thick foreign skull? If 'e ain't too crazy altogether to be got at, that is! Let 'im send 'is lobster-backs down 'ere into Virginia, why don't 'e? *We'll* show 'em what's what—"

"All right, dad, all right, have another."

"Sure thing, I'll have another! And not to drink no 'ealth to George the Third, neither! *God save the King,* in a pig's eye! *I* say God save Mashachu—Massashu-shetts! Who'll drink it with me? Confu-shun to 'Is Majesty, and God save Masha—God save *Boston!*"

No one suppressed him, no one demurred. There was easy laughter and the clinking of tankard-lids and glasses, while Julian listened in chilled surprise. This was open anarchy, here in Virginia. Surely things were much worse in the colonies than anyone in England supposed. Surely it was time some one spoke a few plain words here, and brought men to their senses. Franklin believed that if war started now it would last ten years and he would not live to see the end of it. Chatham had said in the House that an hour lost now in allaying these ferments might produce years of calamity, but no one listened to Chatham any more. Most people in England felt that the opposition in America was a small faction in which most of the colonists had no part. That was apparently not so. From top to bottom, Virginia appeared to be in sympathy with the rebellious colony to the north who had dumped the tea into Boston harbor in protest against the principle of taxation by the home Government. It didn't matter to Massachusetts that the tea, if it had been brought ashore and sold as intended, would have cost them less than the tea they habitually smuggled in from the Dutch market. It didn't matter either that the tea tax as it now stood was of no consequence to the home Exchequer, and brought in less revenue than it cost the Government to maintain the machinery for collecting it. It only mattered that the King insisted on the tax in order to insist on the principle which Massachusetts denied. And for this abstract idea of resistance to what it considered obstinate tyranny, Massachusetts was inviting martyrdom and Virginia apparently stood behind her, heart and soul.

Some one ought to tell them, in London, how it was. There was also a conviction there that the colonists were cowards and would not face out a determined show of force. Some one ought to tell them about Patrick Henry, and George Washington, and St. John Sprague, and the man called Dad. These were not men who feared a fight. Equally, some one ought to tell these men in Boston and Virginia that the King and his councillors, right or wrong, considered the behavior of Massachusetts an intolerable insult to authority, and that people in England thought the Boston uproar out of all proportion to the possible injustice involved. And some one ought to quash this pernicious rumor that the King was a lunatic. . . .

Sprague was returning across the room, with three other men. Julian gathered himself together and rose, feeling gauche and conspicuous and very uncertain of himself, wishing hopelessly for his father's tact and presence of mind. Introductions were made. Mr. Wythe—handsome, elderly, gracious, reassuring; Mr. Jefferson—tall, straight as a gun barrel, sandy, a little appraising; Mr. Henry—gaunt, preoccupied, almost shabby in his dress.

More chairs were dragged up, wine and tobacco were brought, the talk was friendly and relaxed; the room hummed again with conversation and casual laughter as the other diners resumed their knives and forks. But Julian felt the eyes of Sprague's friends waiting on him, and strove against a tongue-tied shyness. Mr. Wythe was kindness itself. It was to him the Days had carried Dr. Franklin's letters, it was to him they had been directed to look for counsel and assistance. His sympathy for Julian's loss was simple and sincere. And he at once suggested that Julian call on him in the morning to discuss taking over at least temporarily a small boys' school whose dominie was recently too old and ill to continue. When that had been arranged—

"I have been hearing all the latest news from London," said Sprague. "The lovely Linley has sung herself into marriage with a lucky man named Sheridan—and the King is not mad at all!"

There was a silence. Julian endured it, their eyes upon him.

"Then what is this—mysterious illness one hears about?" Mr. Wythe inquired.

"I have heard a fairly reliable opinion that his illnesses have been exaggerated," Julian replied with some diffidence. "He is subject to fits of depression, they say—especially if his efforts to influence his Ministers do not have satisfactory results. They seemingly go in dread of bringing on one of his attacks by appearing to thwart him."

"Well, that is a new view of the Ministry!" exclaimed Jefferson. "Afraid to assert itself lest the sovereign go out of his mind! And here all the time I thought it was only because North was afraid of losing his place!"

"Perhaps Mr. Day will tell us," said Patrick Henry, fingering his glass, "what the feeling of the people in England is. Where do they take their stand on this matter of taxing the colonies?"

"I am afraid the people as a whole have very little idea what is going on in the colonies," Julian told them cautiously.

"Nor take much interest in it," nodded Sprague.

"They don't read enough, for one thing," Julian tried to explain. "In fact, there hasn't been enough written about America. My father and I found it very difficult to find books which would give us any idea what to expect here. Dr. Franklin urged my father to keep a journal from the day of his arrival in Virginia, as a foundation for a new modern history of the colonies—but that, of course, is all lost now."

"It need not be," Mr. Wythe objected, with his keen, kind gaze. "Why don't you undertake such a work in your father's place?"

"But I have no experience, sir, no—judgment, for such a book. I am —well, too young to express opinions, I—"

"This is a young country, Mr. Day," Jefferson reminded him, smiling encouragement. "You come to it fresh, with an excellent background."

"You will get older every day!" Sprague promised enthusiastically. "Why not stay here, Mr. Day, and carry out your father's work?"

"Well, I—" Julian looked from one to the other, a little uncomfortable as the center of their attention, for at those meetings at the coffee house in Ludgate Hill no one had ever taken any notice of him.

"It happens to be a favorite project of my own," said Jefferson in his husky, gentle voice. "But I shall never have the time, I am afraid. Please consider my library at your disposal, Mr. Day."

"And mine!" smiled Mr. Wythe.

The offers cheered Julian more than anything else they could have said. He knew his way around a library, and felt at home there.

"You make it sound very feasible," he told them, with his glancing humor.

"Then you mean the people of England don't really care what happens here." Patrick Henry jerked the conversation back to the only subject which interested him. "That is not just lack of book-learning, my friend, that is shortsightedness, to say the least! Even Burke has warned that proscription of a province will end in proscription of a nation! I hear that the King's private bill for bribery in the next election will keep his tradesmen waiting again!"

"There is nothing really new about Royal bribery," Julian objected mildly, noting that Mr. Henry called it "larning" and spoke altogether with a strange accent akin to that of the backwoods fire-eater called Dad. "Bribery is not a practice which originated with George the Third. He is more open about it, that's all."

Henry gave him a knife-like look.

"I see you have caught us a full-fledged Tory, Mr. Sprague," he said bitterly.

"No, I am not a Tory," Julian denied without heat. "That is, I am not necessarily in blind agreement with whatever the King chooses to exact from his subjects. But to me, as to most Englishmen, the King is a symbol. I am loyal to the King because I am loyal to England, because I believe in England's ancient principles of government—"

"Ah, but there is your paradox!" snapped Henry, levelling an accusing finger at Julian's nose. "George has turned his back on the principles of personal liberty and self-government which England has stood for since Runnymede! And therefore, under her present Government, England is driving us to extremities to preserve the very traditions we were bred in! She is driving us to war!"

"But the colonies have no fleet—no exchequer—no army—" Julian argued forgetting his shyness in bewilderment. "You could not hope to stand up against a British regiment, you would be wiped out: You could even be blockaded—"

"Does it look as easy as that, Mr. Day?" Patrick Henry inquired very low, and his smile was sinister. He glanced over his shoulder and leaned across the table, his long face white and tense. "I myself doubt whether we would have a dog's chance alone against England. But where is France while we are being wiped out? What about Spain? Have you forgotten Holland? The natural enemies of Great Britain—what would they be doing all the time that England was busy fighting a war with her colonies? With their help we can establish our independence of Great Britain and take our place on an equal footing among the nations of the earth!"

Julian wet his lips. This was treason—a hanging matter. They were putting their heads into the noose just to listen to it. In the presence of Patrick Henry's angular blasphemy the New World speedily became less Arcadian, and its lighthearted inhabitants seemed children who played with fire. He conceived a swift abhorrence of the man Henry, who in all likelihood would hasten its destruction.

"*Independence!*" he repeated, just above a whisper. "You would join a foreign alliance against England? But that is worse than civil war! That is matricide!"

The ugly word lay there, on a silence. Jefferson's eyes were downcast, resting on the fine lace which fell across his clasped hands. Mr. Wythe took snuff, deliberately. Sprague watched Patrick Henry's face.

"We contemplate nothing so drastic, I assure you." Mr. Wythe's suave voice slid smoothly into the tension, as the lid of his snuff-box clicked. "Tonight we have drawn up resolutions instructing our committees of correspondence to propose the election of an annual Congress, convening at Philadelphia—to direct the future measures required by the general interest. We are still hopeful of making the Ministry realize that an attack on any one colony will be construed as an attack on the whole thirteen. There is still time, we hope, to avert an open rupture."

They all relaxed a little as he finished—all but Patrick Henry, who sat in brooding silence and would not meet their eyes.

Again there was a stir around the door, and Sprague, who faced it, sprang to his feet.

"Here is Colonel Washington!" he said, and Julian looked searchingly at the man who came down the room towards them—a man of commanding height and military carriage, wearing powder and a sword, a dark blue uniform with scarlet facings and buff underdress, white silk stockings and dancing shoes. Heads turned towards him as he passed, voices sang out greetings, his big hand gave a free gesture of response, his smile was benignant and ready.

Everyone at the table rose except Mr. Wythe, for Washington set both his hands on the older man's shoulders with an affectionate familiarity, holding him in his chair.

"Good evening, gentlemen," he said, and his voice was very quiet against the furore of his entrance. "I hoped you might not have dispersed." He accepted Sprague's proffered chair with gracious thanks, and rested kindly blue eyes on the face of Julian Day as the presentation was made. "Welcome to Virginia," he smiled. "You find us a trifle preoccupied today, but I trust none the less hospitable."

"Everyone has been most kind, sir. I have been having a history lesson about Fort Duquesne."

"Ancient history now," said Washington briefly. "We are writing a new chapter."

"You put some rather neat touches on the old one, sir."

Washington glanced round the table under his brows.

"Who has been talking too much?" he inquired.

"I only told him about Braddock, sir," admitted Sprague.

"Did you tell him about the pillow too?" asked Mr. Wythe, and chuckled, and Washington laughed outright.

"Pillow, sir?"

"Mr. Wythe refers to a very sore point," Washington remarked, and the joke went round the table over the heads of the two younger men. "A bout of dysentery and fever had left me so fence-rail thin that the horse was like to split me to the chin, so I rode that day with a pillow in the saddle—till horse and all were shot out from under me!" This too was very funny to his friends, and Washington shook his powdered head over the afflictions of his youth. "They kept pouring rum down my gullet to keep me going," he said. "It is no wonder that everywhere I looked I saw two Indians! I have never been so outnumbered in my life!"

Again the table rumbled with mirth, and Sprague laughed in his sleeve as well to see Julian's face, where admiration was already dawning. Julian's experience of military men and their unseemly levity as regards death and heroism was nil. He was unprepared to find that the memory of that terrible day at Fort Duquesne appeared to evoke only facetiousness from the soldier who had brought away the remnants of Braddock's tragic army.

This was the man whom nothing caught off balance, who dined punctiliously at the Palace on the night after a dissolution, who wore the blue uniform of potential rebellion into the Governor's complacent presence—this large, low-voiced, almost diffident man whom everybody in the room regarded with such patent affection. Except possibly Patrick Henry? Julian wondered what Colonel Washington thought of Henry's dogmatism, and heard the casual interchange of civilities between them with perplexity. But surely Colonel Washington would never countenance this fantastic idea of Independence? Surely his attendance at the Palace tonight indicated that he would take no part in the folly of insurrection if it came?

He was the first Virginian Julian had met so far who had about him a completely adult realism, so that Julian felt absurdly that at last he had come upon some one his own age, which was exactly half the Colonel's. There was a massive dignity about the man, a—yes, that word again—a *balance,* and a vital, physical magnetism which made it difficult for Julian to render due attention to the other men who sat at the same table.

Colonel Washington was making no appreciable effort to captivate the observant young stranger from overseas, being always without any consciousness of his own impact on the beholder. It was his habit to clothe his big body like a gentleman and carry it like a soldier, but he knew with due humility that his hands and feet were the largest in Virginia, and that he had never learned to make either small talk or public speeches. As a Burgess he always attended the House faithfully but sat in intelligent silence while other more fluent men debated.

Tonight in the informal company of his intimates, he was talkative enough, for him, and after being thoroughly quizzed on his evening at the Palace he announced mildly that he had engaged to ride down to Porto Bello tomorrow with the Governor to give an opinion on His Excellency's fruit trees, which had suffered from the late frost. Jefferson expressed concern over a possible shortage of peach brandy as a result of that frost, and Mr. Wythe said it was a great pity about Dunmore's trees, wasn't it, and they all looked at each other with blank, polite faces and the air was somehow bulging with unuttered laughter, while Julian watched them as though they spoke Lower Cherokee instead of English. He had again that baffling sensation of seeing a dangerous game being played by clever, reckless children who were bound to get hurt. Except Colonel Washington. Julian drew comfort from the essential honesty in that square, tight-lipped face lit by smiling ice-blue eyes. Surely Colonel Washington knew what he was about, and he also seemed to know how to get on with the Governor. Surely here was the man to save the colonies from their own madness. If Colonel Washington would only go to London. . . .

IV

Surmising that the other three Burgesses might have things they wished to say to Colonel Washington without listeners, Sprague soon made a tactful withdrawal from the table, and Julian followed him out into the soft southern night which was pricked by myriad fireflies and fragrant with early blossom.

The wide, tree-arched street was shadowy and almost deserted, and the voices of Negroes singing came from quarters somewhere in Botetourt Street. Charlton Inn across the way, where they said Colonel Washington stayed if the Custis house was not open for use, was brightly lighted still. A dog scratched himself placidly beside the Raleigh horseblock in a shaft of light from the open door behind them. A few saddlehorses tied to the hitching-bars waited with drooping heads to carry their masters home. A handsome coach went by towards the Capitol Landing on Queen's Creek, its lamps aglow.

Through the cloud of dust it left, an odd little group came across the road towards the Raleigh, its progress lurching and uncertain, punctuated by the rise and fall of a drunken monologue of abuse from the stocky baldheaded man who was its central figure. On either side of him walked a child, a boy and a girl, each striving to support his wavering steps without being trampled on.

Sprague paused with a laugh that was half a sigh.

"Oh, Lord, old Mawes has done it again! We had better lend a hand or they'll never get him home!"

"Who is it?" asked Julian, unaccustomed to being called on to assist drunkards home.

"That is the town disgrace," said Sprague. "It's quite a story. His wife is a respectable woman who does fine laundry and tries to bring up the twins decently, so we all do what we can." He raised his voice. "Hullo, Tibby, would you like some help?"

Still holding her father's arm with both hands, the girl gave Sprague a rather embarrassed smile.

"Good evening, sir." The words were jolted by a sudden twist of the thick body of the man as he sought to free himself, and the boy on the other side of him staggered from an elbow in the stomach, but hung on doggedly. "He's not fit to ride, if you p-please, sir—he'll fall off, sure, and break his neck—"

"Lea' me alone, I say, yer dirty little bastards—outa m' way, I say, azzo *you* cared if I break m' bloody neck or not—" The bald man's voice rose angrily and he tried again to shake off his escort. "Yeh, and it would be nothin' but good news to yer mother, an' I'm tellin' yer true, if anything happened t' me—leggo me arm, now, or I'll—"

"If you could persuade him to walk home with us, sir—" gasped the girl Tibby, as Sprague and Julian approached them at the edge of the road. "We have been trying to make him understand we could come back for the horse if he'll only—"

With a roar of rage and a heave of his burly shoulders the man wrenched his right arm free of the boy's hold and landed a swinging blow full in Tibby's face. She dropped like a rag doll at Julian's feet, hitting the corner of the horse-block as she fell.

"Why, you—!" Sprague's fist smacked home against the drunkard's jaw so that the fellow came to a sitting position on the ground, holding his head and groaning.

The boy was on his knees beside his sister, crying her name, tugging at her with ineffectual hands. Julian knelt beside him.

"All right, lad," he said gently. "Let me look at her—she'll be all right—"

"He's killed her!" sobbed the boy. "He *said* he would one day! Oh, Tibby, Tibby, mother was afraid—*he's killed her, sir!*"

"She's not dead, Kit, hush that noise—we'll soon fetch her round again." Sprague bent above them as Julian turned the child's thin body on the ground and gathered it into his arms. She was so small when he touched her, with bones like a bird's. . . . "Bring her inside," said Sprague, sounding a little shaken himself. "We'll send for a doctor. Come along, Kit, be a man—she isn't badly hurt."

Carrying Tibby Mawes, with the boy Kit sobbing and snivelling beside him, Julian re-entered the Raleigh and Sprague began calling for a doctor. In the tap-room beyond the parlor, a chair was pushed against Julian's legs from behind, and he sat down carefully with the unconscious child on his lap, and found Colonel Washington first of the men who left their tables and gathered round.

"Her arm is broken," said Washington, and laid his vast palm under the small tanned wrist where the break was clearly visible. "Dr. Graves was here when I came in. Somebody find Graves."

"Here I am, sir—let's have a look—m'm—that's bad, isn't it—where is Southall? I'll want some things at once."

The inn-keeper came running as Washington shouted his name. More candles, hot water, towels, bandages, and a makeshift splint materialized without delay. More men, the hard-bitten, soft-hearted men of Virginia, most of them with cherished children of their own, filtered out of the dining-room beyond and joined those who already clustered about Julian's chair, offering advice, shaking rueful heads, sweating in sympathy as the edges of the bone were drawn together by the doctor's skillful fingers.

Tibby had not moved or made a sound since Julian picked her up. Her face, between two brief pigtails tied with string, was hidden against his coat. And he, who had never before in his bookish life held a child in his arms, sat marvelling at the frailness of her, the lack of weight on his knees, the delicacy of the wrist and fingers in the doctor's hands. There was nothing to her at all. Her dark, smoothly parted hair was soft against his chin. . . . He raised his head suddenly.

"What became of that brute outside?" he demanded.

"He is spending the night in gaol, I saw to that," said Jefferson's husky voice beside him. He was sitting on the edge of a table with his feet in the seat of a chair and a wine-glass in his hand, watching the doctor.

"Too good for him!" said Julian, and his cramped arms tightened round his treasure. "She hasn't made a sound, do you think she is still alive?"

Jefferson reached to lay an experienced father's hand on Tibby. His thumb found the sturdy pulse in her throat, his fingers passed soothingly across her temple, and he nodded.

"Knocked out," he said. "Wants a dose of brandy and water when it's over. She has small bones, wonder it wasn't worse. Fellow ought to be pilloried and whipped."

"Well, why not?" demanded Julian angrily.

"On account of the mother," Jefferson told him, and rose from the table and began to make his good-nights.

At last the doctor finished with a sigh of relief.

"That's all. Give her some brandy now, somebody. You're a brave girl, Tibby, we're proud of you."

Julian stared at him over her head.

"But—isn't she unconscious?" he queried.

"Not any more," said the doctor, rolling down his sleeves. "Where is that brandy? I'll take a glass myself."

Julian shifted so that he could see the face against his shoulder. It was white and wet with tears, but her eyes met his—gray eyes, set wide, with straight dark lashes and fine winged brows. Julian felt for his big lace-edged handkerchief and wiped the tears away. There was a bruise coming out on her jawbone where her father's blow had landed.

Sprague leaned over them with a glass of watered brandy.

"Drink this, child, the worst is over now," he said in the voice he kept for Dorothea.

Still silent, she sipped obediently at the brandy as he held it to her lips. The doctor laid his hand on her head, bade her come and see him in the morning, and went away.

The room was clearing now, as the rest of them began to drift away homeward. A colored waiter was putting out the wall-candles. The barmaid was washing up tankards with a cheerful clatter. Tibby turned her head away from the brandy glass, and tried to see around Julian's arm into the room.

"Where's Kit?" she whispered.

"I sent him on ahead to tell your mother we would bring you home," said Sprague. "Your father has gone to gaol till he sobers up. The horse is still outside and you can ride it home, and we'll walk beside you to make sure you get there safe."

"I'll carry her," said Julian jealously, though his arms were aching now.

"It's too far, down by the Landing. She can ride if we hold her on. Can you stand up now, child?" Sprague offered steadying hands, and Julian set her feet carefully on the sanded floor.

"She needs a sling," he discovered, and knotted his white handkerchief around her neck to support the splinted arm.

"This is Mr. Day, Tibby," Sprague told her kindly. "He arrived today on the *Mary Jones*."

She was giddy from pain and unconsciousness, and her head swam with the brandy, and there seemed to be nothing between her stomach and a non-existent floor which receded from her feet every time she felt for it to hold her up. The branched candelabra on the table at Julian's elbow drenched him with light in the dimming room, so that she saw nothing clearly except his face with its long, sensitive chin and generous mouth, and the tenderness in his eyes. Standing before him in a blue calico dress made with a square neck and elbow sleeves in a tight bodice, and a limp gathered skirt that reached her ankles, her hair in those innocent pigtails and her arm in a sling, Tibby made a curtsy.

"Your servant, ma'am," said Julian gravely, and rose to his impressive height and bowed with the same formality, she was sure, that he would have accorded the most beautiful young lady he had ever seen.

She smiled at him in a solemn rapture, and felt St. John Sprague's guarding hands on her shoulders as she swayed above the wavering floor. A warm surge of something more than compassion swept Julian as he stood looking down at her. Her little chin was firm, her teeth were white and even. Now that he saw her standing, she seemed smaller than ever. He wondered how old she was, but felt that it would be an impertinence to ask.

"Shan't I carry you out to the horse?" he offered anxiously, and though she longed for him to do so a pride stronger than her childish need made her refuse with courteous obstinacy and walk, still between Sprague's hands, through the parlor and out into the street.

An ancient spavined horse wearing a disreputable saddle was the last one left at the hitching-bar.

"We call him Crowsmeat," she explained as they swung her up and she hooked her knee expertly over the pommel, "because he is so old and worthless nobody would own him but us."

One on either side, ready to hold her steady if the faintness came again, they walked through the warm dusk of the Duke of Gloucester Street. Lights were going out in the white houses along the way, and Julian thought of the return journey which must be made still latei, and again a sense of the wilderness to the westward crinkled all his nerves. But there were no Indians any more—not here. This was Williamsburg, where there was doubtless even a night watchman to call to hours as in London.

They turned to the left just short of the Capitol and took the lane which led towards the Landing. The moon was high and white, the scented air was without a breeze, the fireflies wove enchantment. There was a high, sweet singing in the air, more musical than crickets, which Sprague said was tree-frogs and Tibby said was peepers, and which grew louder as they approached Queen's Creek. They came at last to a lighted cabin, set low on sandy land, a bulk of dark trees behind it, the path which led to its door picked out with bleached white oyster shells. Crowsmeat stopped abruptly.

"I hope Kit didn't frighten mother," said Tibby, and Julian realized that she was leaning towards him to be lifted down. He received the small, confiding body in his arms again, and carried her down the path. Her good arm, he noticed, was close around his neck.

Sarah Mawes beheld them so in the light from the open door—the tall stranger in his dark London clothes, with Tibby held high against his shoulder, her arm around his neck, her eyes shining.

"Mother, this is Mr. Day from England," said Tibby, with a note of awe.

"Good evening, sir." But Sarah's anxious gaze sought St. John Sprague, whom she knew well and trusted.

"It is only a broken arm, Sarah," he reassured her hastily. "Tibby has been very brave, but she was knocked right out and ought to have some hot milk, I should think, on top of the brandy we gave her, and go straight to bed."

"You were very kind to get the doctor for her and all," said Sarah, and Julian was somehow not surprised that she spoke with a less provincial accent than Patrick Henry. "Won't you come in, Mr. Day?"

She backed before them into the room, and Julian ducked under the low lintel, guarding Tibby's head. Kit hovered near them, large-eyed and shy, as Julian stood a moment with Tibby still in his arms, observing her home in the light of the candles on the table in the middle of the room. It was a rough, bare little place, with furnishings that looked home-made. A few pieces of blue and white china adorned an open dresser. There were fresh white curtains at the windows. The hearth was swept and empty. Everything was spotlessly, painfully scrubbed and clean. He set Tibby down reluctantly.

"Are you all right now?" he asked her with his slow smile, as Kit came to her and she leaned against him gratefully.

"Yes, thank you, sir."

The warmth of her seemed to stay with his empty arms. He hated to leave her here and go away. He turned to her mother.

"You won't have to worry about her," he said. "She has all the courage she will ever need."

"Thank you," said Sarah Mawes, and her smile turned her worn face beautiful before his eyes. "And thank you both for bringing her home safe."

"It's lucky we were there," Sprague remarked from the threshold. "Let us know how she gets on, won't you."

"I will, sir. She'll be all right, I'm sure."

Julian lingered in the doorway looking back past Sarah into the room where Tibby stood with Kit's arm around her waist. They were, he saw, fantastically alike, even though Kit wore breeches and his hair was tied back in a queue. But Tibby stood somehow a trifle the taller and straighter in her limp calico gown.

"Good night," he said gently.

She smiled at him.

They walked away through the moonlit dark in a silence which the intuitive Sprague forbore to break. He did not know that Julian had forgotten about the Indians and the wilderness, but he had observed that the child Tibby had caught the heart of this strange, lonely man from overseas. At last—

"You know, I am not at all sure I could have done it myself," said Julian. "Had an arm set without a whimper, I mean."

"No, nor I!" Sprague admitted cheerfully and stumbled. "Damn. We should have brought a lantern."

"How old is she?"

"Nine or ten at the most. They are twins, as anyone can see! Everyone says Tibby should have been the boy. Kit goes to the dominie's school—the one you are to take over."

"That's good. I can keep an eye on them."

"My Aunt Anabel tries to do that. Sarah does our fine laundry."

"You said there was a story."

"There is. Jefferson got Kit into the school, because Sarah was so anxious for him to learn. She was a bondmaid out from England when she was a girl. She was with a Yorktown family and she was going to marry a sailor in the West Indies trade when she had worked out her time and he had saved up for a little boat of his own. They had only a few more months to go, and he set off on a voyage to Cuba, promising to bring her back a silk gown for the wedding. His ship was never heard of again."

"Then they are not Mawes' children," said Julian, divining it with relief.

"No, they're not. Sarah had her freedom, and the family at Yorktown turned her out, and she couldn't get work, the way she was. Mawes had been hanging round her for a long time—he started as a bondservant too. He swore he didn't care how it was with her, he would marry her anyway. She put him off as long as she could, but in the end there wasn't much else she could do. He has always hated the children, though."

"Naturally," said Julian quietly, and Sprague glanced at him in the moonlight.

"Well, naturally, perhaps. But that is no excuse for knocking Tibby down!"

"I only wish there was something I could do for them," Julian sighed as they came to the Duke of Gloucester Street again.

"You could let Sarah have your laundry."

"Yes, of course I will."

Julian was by now leaden tired, and in spite of his growing affection for Sprague he wanted to be alone to sort out his day. Most of all he longed to bring these new experiences before the sane and kindly judgment of his father, which could never be again. He must make his own judgments now, evolve his own sanity, alone. Tired as he was, uprooted, baffled, and almost penniless, it seemed a colossal undertaking.

"Tomorrow you must come and meet my Aunt Anabel," Sprague was saying. "She hasn't been very well, poor dear, and we can't offer you a cup of tea these days, she has locked it up—but come to dinner tomorrow anyway!"

"Thank you. Will she—"

"She will be charmed," said Sprague definitely, and held out his hand. "I turn off here for Francis Street. Good night."

Julian lighted the candles in his room at Mrs. Hartley's and looked about him gratefully.

Some one—the young slave girl—had turned back the covers on the high four-posted bed and lowered the mosquito-net which hung in graceful white folds from a hook in the ceiling, with no perceptible way in. His banyan was laid over a chair beside which his house slippers waited. There were fresh flowers in a silver bowl on the chest of drawers. Some of his belongings had been more conveniently arranged. The room was homelike and welcoming. He wondered if the dominie's school would pay enough for him to go on living here instead of trying to find a cheaper place, and decided that no matter what it paid he must save every penny for the homeward passage he had to buy. That is, if he ever meant to go back to England. . . .

It was indeed a new world he had come to. Already some one had taken thought for his comfort. Some one had offered him work to do, and a library, two libraries, had been placed at his disposal. A man had called himself his friend. He had held a child in his arms. . . .

He went to the writing-table where he had stacked his books and papers before going out to supper at the Raleigh, and where pens and ink had been provided for his use. He found the handsome leather-bound journal which had been a gift from Dr. Franklin to his father before they left London—the book whose virgin pages awaited the notes for a modern history of the colonies to be written by a man named Day. He moved a candle, and sat down at the table. He opened the book and dipped a new quill in the silver inkwell.

Williamsburg, Virginia, he wrote at the top of the first page. *May 25, 1774. . . .*

Julian woke to bright early sunlight and mockingbird song. His window overlooked the back garden and the quarters, and its frilled white curtains stirred to a scented breeze which was soft as the touch of a woman's hand.

From somewhere below came a Negro girl's laughter, rich and free, and the murmur of voices, among them the chirping notes of a small child. Then, in a sudden high-pitched call: "Jen-*nie!* You come in here now, like I tole you, or yore ma will shore nuff scorch yore draw's!" The child crowed. Small feet ran. There was the sound of a smart slap, and a wail, which subsided quickly. The voices went murmuring on, and a warm smell of cooking drifted up.

Julian lay still, staring at the ruffled tester of his bed and the white mosquito-net. In the precious privacy of his room, in the neatness and cleanliness of good housewifery, with a fragrant breakfast cooking somewhere, and cheerful domestic sounds, he felt hopelessly a stranger. The chintz and mahogany of Mrs. Hartley's best spare room spelled luxury to one accustomed to the Spartan life of a bachelor scholar, inured first to the severe routine of Winchester School and then to the inexpensive lodgings kept by landladies who had usually cheated his vague, uncomplaining father out of his eyeteeth. Small as their income was, the two of them could have lived more cosily than they had ever done, if they had only known how to go about it. They dressed well, if soberly, and bought nearly half as many books as they wanted. But except for a tenderhearted widow who ran a little *pension* at Passy and coddled them 'way back in '71 when they spent a year in France, and for rare visits in the houses of the great, they had lived like monks and hardly known how much they lacked of comfort. True, they had somewhat envied Dr. Franklin the delightful establishment in Craven Street where as a lodger he lived more like the master of the house, but that was Dr. Franklin, and anyway he had more money than they had.

Desolately Julian lay imagining his father's surprise and pleasure at this unexpected snugness at Williamsburg. Then would have come the inevitable question: Could they afford it? And the answer, almost as inevitably, would be No.

His eyes went round the gay little room again, memorizing it against some bleak garret of the future. There was—he could swear—a Wilton carpet on the floor. The linen against his chin was fine and white and smelled of lavender. The mantelpiece had a small marble bust and a black basalt vase for ornament. The brass fire-dogs and the brass bail-handles on the chest of drawers glinted with polishing .The china chamber set had a colored floral pattern, adorning the washstand like a nose-

gay. There was an armchair, and a needlepoint footstool. The candles—
fat white candles—had shining glass chimneys. On the wall above the
writing-table was a child's sampler worked in cross-stitch; *Dorcas Maria
Entwhistle, 1742,* it said, inside a border composed of the letters of the
alphabet. He decided that Mrs. Hartley wasn't old enough to have done
cross-stitch in 1742. . . .

It was like a home. It was almost the sort of room people like St. John
Sprague might sleep in, people who had womenfolk and money of
their own. Of course no Day could afford it, and he must tell them so at
once, he had no right to let them think. . . . But it was a pity his father
had not known what it was to waken here, just once, to tidiness and
laughter and appetizing odors. . . .

Strange, exotic new world, where the language, though English, was
different, and even breakfast smelled unfamiliar, and deft black hands
performed all the most intimate services, and slaves were well-fed and
merry. One always thought of slaves in chains. In Virginia, they wore
bright liveries which pleased their simple vanity, and sang in the twilight round their own doors in the quarters. Of course Sprague had said
it was far otherwise with the wild Negroes. . . .

Sprague was an anomaly too. *We can be pushed just so far,* he had
said. *We call it Pittsburgh now.* We. He and the colonists. Yet Sprague
was an Englishman born, unlike Washington or Jefferson, neither of
whom had ever even been to England. But Sprague had taken root
here, become one of them, and was bringing out his young sister to the
wilderness—

What wilderness? Julian asked himself coldly, his eyes seduced again
by surroundings which were much more civilized than those he was
accustomed to in England. He did not know, of course, that Mrs. Hartley had brought the black basalt vase, which was a wedding gift from
her mother in London, and the sampler, which she herself had worked
at the age of eight, from her own parlor to enhance the welcome she
felt was due her distinguished lodgers. He did not know that she considered herself less a landlady than a privileged hostess to learning. He
did not know that Sprague's smile and Mr. Wythe's prestige and Mrs.
Hartley's own warm nature had fixed a weekly rate so low even for
Williamsburg that none of them had any idea he would think twice
about it. He only knew a vast, inexplicable peace and laziness, tinged

with melancholy, which was due partly to the climate and partly to a
need for breakfast.

Some one scratched on the panel of his door—not a loud tactless rap
to startle a man awake in an unfamiliar room—and a soft voice said,
"It's Melissa, suh. I got you some hot water."

"Thank you," said Julian, somewhat at a loss, and the young slave
girl entered with a large copper kettle and a broad smile full of white
teeth.

"Mornin', suh. Did you sleep well?" There was real solicitude in the
question.

"Yes, thank you," said Julian, recalling with surprise that his rest had
been dreamless.

"Sometimes in a strange room you don't," she remarked, and set down
the kettle and came to stand beside the bed. "Mis' Hartley say tell you
breakfast can go in any time you say, and do you take coffee or ale, suh?"

"Well—neither, thanks," said Julian, forbearing to mention his usual
morning beverage, but Melissa, looking disappointed, had no such
scruples.

" 'Fraid we can't offer you no tea nowadays," she sighed. "Mis' Hartley
done shet it up till they take the tax off'n it. We could make you a nice
cup of chocolate—or maybe you'd fancy a julep to keep off the fever."

"A what?"

"Julep, suh. Made with rum and sugar."

"No, thank you," he said hastily.

"Nothin' *at all* to drink, suh?" She was prepared to go into it ex-
haustively, there at the bedside.

"I wonder," he suggested on a sudden whim, "if there would be any
fresh milk?"

"Sure is, suh!" Her face cleared. "With a smitch of brandy in it,
maybe?"

"Well—just a smitch," he conceded. "In about half an hour."

"Yes, *suh!*"

Melissa departed with a swish of her blue cotton gown, closing the
door behind her as though a baby slept in the room.

After breakfast, when his astonished palate had encountered corn
bread and fried chicken, Julian set off by appointment for Mr. Wythe's
house to see about taking the dominie's school. On the Palace Green,

Mrs. Hartley told him. Behind the church, to the left. Ask anybody, if he wasn't sure. She added that it was going to be a right hot day, but he would get used to it.

As he turned the corner into the Green at the churchyard and approached the square brick house with the white door where Mr. Wythe lived, Julian was seized with acute stage-fright. Sensitive and shy, and unused to relying upon himself without the benignant presence of his father, he was all at once convinced that he would be no good at teaching school, and that anyway the whole thing was trumped up to save his face, contrived out of Mr. Wythe's kindness. At the same time, his need was there for anyone to see, and refusal was out of the question. Ought he to let them know that he saw through them? Wouldn't that be less humiliating in a way than to seem a complacent dupe?

A smiling colored butler in green livery opened the door wide into a spacious hall from which a fine staircase rose. Another open door at the back gave on the garden and a breeze.

"Will you step right in, Mr. Day, suh, Mr. Wythe expectin' you," said the butler, before Julian had time to give his name. He had not yet learned that the well-trained slave always recognized his master's friends, either by instinct or the grape-vine system. He surrendered his hat to a deferential black hand. "Jus' come right this way, suh, Mr. Wythe and Mr. Randolph in the parlor."

Julian entered a room which was bright with flowered chintz and polished brass and freshly gathered blossom. After the introduction to Mr. Randolph—a handsome man of middle age, with the same courtly ways as his host—Julian began an apology for intruding which was gently brushed aside. He realized then that they had been discussing him, for Mr. Randolph at once mentioned the school.

"I—think I ought to say, sir, that I have no wish to take the post at the expense of some one better suited to it," Julian got out, rather stiffly in his embarrassment, hoping it didn't sound ungracious.

"But my dear boy, the dominie is ill," said Randolph kindly. "The school stands idle."

"But when he is well again—"

"The dominie's ailment is chronic, Mr. Day. He is ninety-one."

"I only meant that I have had very little experience in teaching, and —there must be some one else you would prefer—"

Wythe, after a penetrating look, read his mind with ease, and picked up a newspaper from the seat of a chair and unfolded it.

"You want to be sure you are doing us a favor, and not the other way round," he said. "Read that." His finger pointed to a small adver·tisement in the *Gazette*.

> WANTED. A sober person of good morals, capable
> of teaching Greek, Latin, and the Mathematicks.

"I trust that you qualify," said Mr. Wythe drily.

"Well, yes, I think so, but—"

"We have had only one applicant, and he smelled so high of spirits in the middle of the day that we were forced to turn him down."

"I can promise you satisfaction on that point, at least." Julian gave them his slow smile.

"Then you had better go to see the dominie and put his mind at rest," said Randolph. "He is fretting that his pupils will all grow up ignorant as Indians if something isn't done at once. I must get back to the office and see if the post-bag is in."

"We will walk along with you," said Mr. Wythe.

The black butler produced their hats in the hall with the air of an indulgent conjuror, and the three men stepped out together into the hot sunshine. They parted at the corner of the churchyard, and when Randolph was out of hearing Wythe said sadly—

"Poor John. If war comes, I think it will break his heart. In fact, I wouldn't be surprised to see him go home to England. But his son Edmund won't, he'll stay here and fight for Virginia. And his brother Peyton will probably be chosen to lead the Congress at Philadelphia."

"Suppose the worst does happen—the sort of thing Mr. Henry spoke of last night," Julian began slowly. "Won't a great many people go home to England?"

"No," Mr. Wythe considered the question with care. "No, I don't think so. I am sure I wouldn't. We call England home, just as you do. But we live here. We expect to die here."

"I suppose the war would never spread as far south as this, from Massachusetts?" suggested Julian.

"If war starts, England can't win it by overrunning Massachusetts,

Mr. Day. She will have to control Charleston, and Yorktown, and Norfolk, as well as Boston and New York. That means sending an army and a fleet of some size, as Amherst knew when he refused to touch the job of subjugating the colonies to the King's will. If war starts, we shall see pillaging and burning and gunfire from Canada to the Carolinas—a tragic, stupid blunder worse than anything the Stuarts ever committed, and we ousted two of them! Look at this city!" Wythe flung out his hands towards the shady, unpaved street, with its rows of white houses and flowery gardens. "Peaceful, industrious, sober citizens living in decent prosperity, most of them. But if the King goes on as he is, you will see soldiers drilling on the Palace Green!"

"What will the Governor be doing then?"

"Nothing useful, you can be sure! Well, this is the school."

It was a plain little building set in a dusty yard. Above the single classroom was a dormered attic where the old dominie lived. His quarters were a bachelor rat's nest, and the old man lay in bed in the midst of it in stifling heat, reading a book.

"Good grief, man, mind if I open a window?" cried Mr. Wythe, and did so, to Julian's relief. "This place wants a thorough turning out. I shall send in one of my maids this afternoon to tidy you up a bit. Anything special you would like for dinner?"

"Thank you, that is very thoughtful," said the dominie punctiliously. "I have a Negro boy to bring my meals, and he is supposed to sweep up every now and then—" He surveyed the dishevelled room vaguely.

"My black Sally will attend to things, if you will permit her. Mr. Day is here to take the school for a time, and I thought you would like to talk it over with him. With your approval I shall just post a notice as I go out that classes will resume tomorrow."

"Splendid," said the dominie. "Thank you. Splendid." When Mr. Wythe had gone, he removed his spectacles to peer at Julian. "Sit down, lad, I can't see so high. That's better. Mm. Not seen you before, have I?"

"I arrived from London yesterday, sir."

"Mm. I see. That foreign-speaking body from Hanover still on the throne?"

"Yes, sir. George the Third."

"What, *another* one? Well, now. Ye haven't by any chance been to Edinburgh lately?"

"I went there several years ago with my father, to see Dr. Franklin and Mr. Hume."

"Ye don't say. Ye've seen Hume? Well, now. Splendid. So ye're going to take my school."

"Well, sir, I don't—"

"Young blood. Mm. Splendid," said the dominie, paper-white against his pillows. "Makes me easier. Where were ye educated, then?"

"At Winchester, sir. After that my father and I were abroad a good deal of the time."

"Winchester, eh? That'll do. I'm a Bluecoat boy, myself. Know Greek?"

"Yes, sir."

"Write Latin?"

"Yes, sir."

"Splendid. Splendid. None of this modern language nonsense, I hope?"

"Well, sir, I had to learn French and German, you see, I—"

"Forget it," said the dominie, with a wave of his old yellow claw. "Ye won't need it here. Not in my school. Ever teach before?"

"No, sir."

"Make 'em read Aesop in Greek. Homer too. That way they catch on. They want to know what happens next. Never use the classics for punishment exercises. Turns 'em. When I was a boy I was made to memorize Plato by the page till I preferred a lickin'. That's wrong. Know Plato?"

"Yes, sir." He added quietly, "My father quoted Plato to me—just before he died. Λαμπάδια ἔχοντες διαδώσουσιν ἀλλήλοις."

"Mm. Very nice, too," nodded the dominie sympathetically. "*Those who have lamps will pass them to others.* Hand knowledge on." He lay back against the pillows, savoring the phrase. "Hand knowledge on. Well, well. What was I saying? Oh, yes. For punishment, use mathematics. Or spelling. Understand?"

"Yes, sir."

"I have seventeen scholars, all bad," continued the dominie. "Children are savages, remember that. Don't be afraid to switch 'em. Quince twigs are best, I find. Reach me that paper there on the table—no, further over

—that one—I'll show ye where we left off in things—*they* won't remember—"

Julian had no idea how long he remained in the stifling room under the roof, listening patiently while the dominie piddled with his papers and lesson books, and his records of the scholars' weaknesses and black marks. Each of the seventeen boys was stripped to the furthest dingy corners of his young soul by the dominie for Julian's inspection. Kit Mawes, he said, would never amount to anything even if his mother succeeded in raising him—a delicate, dreamy, exasperating boy, but truthful and unmischievous—which was more than you could say for some of them. . . .

When Mr. Wythe's black Sally arrived with a basket of goodies on her arm and a housewifely look in her eye as it rolled round the disgraceful room, Julian rose to go.

"I have kept ye overlong," said the dominie penitently. "Ye're a grrand man to talk to, it gets me running on." He held out a wavering yellow claw, which Julian took in both his hands.

"I have enjoyed it, sir," he said. "May I come up tomorrow after school, and tell you how we got on?"

"That would be kind." The dominie clung to the strong, warm fingers. "And another thing, lad—being just out from London, would ye have a new book, maybe, I could read?"

"I have several. You will get them yet this evening."

"Splendid," beamed the dominie, and lowered his voice. "Ye wouldn't by any chance have a copy of that *Tristram Shandy?*"

Julian grinned. He and his father had been much amused by the adventures of Mr. Shandy.

"I haven't one with me," he said. "But I will try to find one for you and send it along."

"I hear it's a right freevolous piece of work," said the dominie hopefully.

"It will be a nice change from Sallust," Julian promised him, and went away, determined to borrow the book from Sprague or Mr. Wythe for the dominie's delectation.

VI

St. John Sprague's white house in Francis Street was less pretentious than Mr. Wythe's little brick mansion on the Palace Green, but it gave out the indefinable welcome of homes which have been lived in a long time by people who are fond of each other. Julian, whose acquaintance with such matters was pathetically scant, did not reflect that an aura of kindliness and cordiality was not a thing which could be built into a house like a stairway—that it must accrue slowly during years of gentle laughter and small sorrows shared in mutual trust and understanding. He only knew that from the time he turned in at the white-painted gate and walked up a box-bordered brick path and passed between the slender pillars of the porch he entered a new enchantment.

Dinner was at three, and the shadows were still short and the clipped box was pungent under the sun when he rang the bell. Joshua opened wide the door. "Yes, *suh,* Mr. Day, it shore is good to see you here again!" was Joshua's greeting, as though Julian had been a favored guest for years. "Shall I rest yore hat, suh?"

It was indeed a hot day, and Julian's London broadcloth was not the wear for it. He envied Joshua the sleeveless brown holland waistcoat and breeches he wore with a white cotton shirt whose voluminous sleeves were caught into a tight wristband. Joshua looked cool and comfortable, and Julian felt as though he himself were steaming.

The drawing-room, on the shady side of the house, had blue-green walls and woodwork, and the fabrics were the color of old gold. It gleamed with polished mahogany and brass, and the many-paned windows stood open on the garden. Sprague was resplendent in white linen with fine Mechlin lace at his throat and wrists, and his Aunt Anabel floated in a pale blue tiffany gown with a white gauze cap and fichu. It made one cooler just to look at them.

Aunt Anabel was, as Sprague had prophesied, charmed to see Julian, and like Joshua contrived at once to make him feel as though he was an old friend long expected back from a difficult journey, instead of a stranger making his first shy bow in her presence. Aunt Anabel's hospitality was famous even in Virginia, where hospitality had been brought to a fine art.

The food continued to mystify Julian, but he found it hard to refuse second helpings. The Days had never thought much about food, except now and then in France; usually because the less they thought about what was served to them in English lodgings the better it would be. The meal which awaited him in Francis Street reminded Julian that he had a fifth sense called taste, hitherto unexercised. He ate experimentally for the first time, acutely aware of each separate course. The soup was jellied; the baked shad was hot, with potato balls and new peas and corn fritters on the side; the sliced meats—tongue, chicken, spiced ham, and some kind of loaf—were cold; the salad was a miracle of crispness in an enormous china bowl, and Sprague made a little ceremony of turning it for several minutes while Joshua stood at his elbow to add the oil-and-vinegar dressing from a silver bowl and ladle; there were three kinds of bread, all of them hot from the oven; there were watermelon pickle and three other preserves; the fruit shrub was frosted and accompanied by brown-sugar cakes crusted with pecans. Sprague and Julian drank ale from sweating silver tankards, and Aunt Anabel had a watered white wine.

It was Aunt Anabel who offered to provide the dominie with a copy of *Tristram Shandy,* and she laughed aloud when Julian stared at her across the silver and fine napery of the dinner table.

"Bless the man!" cried Aunt Anabel, whose naturally gray hair looked as though it had been powdered because her pretty face was still so young. "Sinjie, your friend is shocked. You will have to apologize for my taste in literature."

"Mr. Day is no Puritan, Auntie. He is just surprised."

Julian, who for the past twenty-four hours had been drowning in surprise most of the time when he wasn't asleep in the big bed at Mrs. Hartley's, struggled ashore once more.

"It is just that I had no idea that a lady would find the book entertaining," he explained.

"I find it much more entertaining than the sentimental fadoodle they put in novels for ladies," said Aunt Anabel briskly. "Now he thinks I am a bluestocking, no doubt!"

"He thinks you are charming, and you know it!" St. John smiled.

"She is fishing, Mr. Day. You are supposed to say something complimentary, man!"

"Don't tease him, Sinjie. He'll learn."

"I am afraid my drawing-room manners are very wanting, ma'am," Julian confessed gravely. "And there has been nothing in my limited experience to lead me to expect a lovely woman like yourself to be intelligent as well."

"Good gracious me!" gasped Aunt Anabel. "That sounded exactly like Dr. Johnson! We must teach you about women, then, Mr. Day! What would your mother say!"

"My mother died when I was born."

"Ah, poor lamb!" Aunt Anabel reached to lay a plump ringed hand on his. "That accounts for everything, no doubt! From now on, I shall be your mother, and Dorothea when she comes shall be your sister. And with Sinjie for a brother, presto! you are in the bosom of a family!"

Julian was solemn.

"I should like that very much, ma'am," he said, and lifted her hand to his lips before he let it go.

By the time they rose from the table he was fairly adopted, and had heard his Christian name on their lips more than once. The speed with which he had been inducted into their hearts he found very touching. Suppose he had been some sort of rascal, he thought, innocent of the difference between his honest humility and the usual manner of rascals —how easily they could have been imposed upon. It made him feel protective and responsible for them in the future. He did not reason that St. John was entirely capable of taking his measure at the Raleigh the previous evening before offering him Aunt Anabel's friendship.

He listened to their easy chatter almost as though he sat watching a play. Their open tenderness for each other moved him. St. John behaved towards his middle-aged aunt as though she were the queen of hearts, and she seemed almost to flirt with him. The happy self-confidence and pretty airs of a pampered woman were something Julian had had very little opportunity to observe before. He thought Aunt Anabel quite the most enchanting creature he had ever known, dainty and gay as a girl, witty and warm as a woman. It was a revelation to him that a woman could age so gracefully. The Fountain of Youth, it occurred to him to say, was truly in America, whether Ponce de Leon had ever drunk of it or not—but he doubted his ability to put the compliment adequately into words, and so Aunt Anabel never received it.

They spoke of Dorothea and their plans for bringing her out to Virginia in a year's time. It was asking too much of her, they said, to set out alone before her seventeenth birthday. "If only we had known you were coming," Aunt Anabel lamented, "she could have made the voyage with you and would be safely here!"

"She will be perfectly safe coming out with Regina, Auntie," St. John reminded her, and Aunt Anabel gave him an arch look.

"Ah, yes, our Regina!" she murmured. (They pronounced it with a *j* for the *g* and to rhyme with China.) "And it's no good pretending you haven't heard from her, Sinjie, because you have been looking like a cat with a saucer of cream ever since the ship came in!"

"I'm not pretending anything of the kind!" he denied, laughing. "I did have a letter from her, if you can call a dozen lines of nothing a letter!"

"Regina Greensleeves," Aunt Anabel explained to Julian. "She went home to England last year with her mother to be presented to society, if you please! And they will bring Dorothea with them when they return next summer. I only hope a London season won't turn Regina's head entirely, she thought quite well enough of herself as it was!"

"She has a right to think well of herself!" St. John took it up amiably. "She was the most beautiful girl in Virginia, and now she is the most beautiful girl in London. She can't help that."

"Does she say so?" queried Aunt Anabel in a small pert voice, and St. John laughed in her face.

"*Meow!* You are all jealous of Regina, even the best of you!"

Aunt Anabel looked down her nose.

"Well, all I can say is, if Dorothea is anything like her dear mother, she will have Miss Regina looking to her laurels!"

"I only hope they will be friends," St. John said more gravely. "Regina and her mother have not found time to call on Granny yet."

"I dare say," said Aunt Anabel, and St. John laughed at her again, and turned the subject.

There was gossip of the College too, which Julian found extremely interesting. Some people objected to the professors' habits, which sometimes included playing cards all night and being seen drunk in the

streets. Well, not *all* the professors, naturally, Mr. Wythe himself taught
Law there. But the Tory families were inclined to engage private tutors
rather than expose their sons to pernicious influences.

Julian remarked that he had hoped to pick up some tutoring at the
College to add to the family income, but now that his father— St. John
said that was a very good idea, and he would see President Camm about
it tomorrow. Aunt Anabel said mind, Julian was not to go trundling
about down there as an usher or anything like that, and St. John said
no, certainly not. "An usher," Aunt Anabel elucidated, "has to do all
the horrid pokey things the faculty want to be rid of themselves, and
he gets hardly any pay for it."

"I must do anything I can to help fill my purse," said Julian, and
found he was discussing his most intimate affairs without any embarrassment. "In fact, I am not sure I can go on living at Mrs. Hartley's, it is
much too—luxurious."

St. John looked bewildered.

"But, my dear fellow—would you mind telling me what she is charging you?"

"I don't know. I daren't ask. I can tell just by looking at it that I
can't afford it."

"Oh, Julian, of *course* you can—!" Tears stood in Aunt Anabel's blue
eyes.

"I am afraid you don't realize—" He looked from one to the other
with his grave simplicity. "—I arrived here with hardly enough money
in my pocket to buy a queue ribbon!"

"But the school pays sixty pounds a year and lodging," said St. John.

"Sixty—!" It seemed to Julian at that moment as though it was more
money than he had ever heard of.

"It is endowed, you know. Out of the Mallison estate. Mr. Wythe is a
trustee. Of course while the dominie lives you will have to find your
own lodging—he has nowhere else to go. But I should advise you to
stay on where you are until—well, we may as well admit it, the dominie
is a very old man! I shall ask Mr. Wythe in the morning to let you have
the first quarter now if you will feel happier that way. But Mrs. Hartley
would trust you, you know, and so would the tradespeople."

"But surely I am not entitled to the money either, while the dominie
needs it?"

"Julian, my sweet fool, do you think George Wythe will allow you to teach the school for nothing?" demanded Aunt Anabel. "Sometimes those old men live forever! Sinjie, tell George from me that he is to advance fifteen pounds tomorrow from the school funds. The very idea! Now, Julian, are you sure you are quite comfortable at Mrs. Hartley's? What did she give you for breakfast this morning?"

"Chicken, I think. And some kind of hot bread."

"No ham? No fish? Sinjie, what is the woman thinking of? Was the coffee good?"

"I had milk. I asked for it," he added hastily as she opened her mouth.

"Oh. Well, of course Colin preferred brandy-and-milk too. Myself, I am trying to get used to chocolate at breakfast. Now, mind, Julian, if ever you have the slightest feeling of fever, you must start right in with juleps in the mornings. And let me know at once, so I can mix you Colin's hot toddy at bedtimes. *Toddy,* dear, you call it punch in England—"

Fifteen pounds of his very own, tomorrow. It was as the wealth of Ind. Julian walked home through the fading light, marvelling. It would be the first money he had ever earned, barring a few shillings here and there on tutoring jobs. Fifteen *pounds.* . . .

Mr. Wythe's Sally passed him on her way home from attending to the dominie, and dropped him a curtsy in the street. Outside the Charlton, Colonel Washington was dismounting from his horse. He paused to make Julian a broad gesture of greeting, and stood waiting, a hand still on the saddle-horn, while Julian approached.

"You must get out of that coat, Mr. Day," he said without preamble. "Broadcloth won't do here in the summer."

"St. John Sprague has been saying the same," Julian admitted. "I have promised him to go to Prosser, down on the other side of the Courthouse."

"That's the fellow. Nankeen or linen is what you want. He will fit you out. Can't have you dying of the climate straight off, you know! Must give malaria a chance!"

"And how were the Governor's fruit trees, sir?" Julian asked gravely, and Washington's blue eyes glinted.

"Bad. Peaches ruined. No brandy from the Porto Bello trees this year,

I fear! Monstrous unfair of somebody, isn't it! Mind about that coat, now
—our summer heat is just beginning." He laid a fatherly hand on
Julian's shoulder, and passed on into the inn.

Julian continued down the street with a feeling of unreasonable pride.
Colonel Washington had remembered him, after just those few minutes
at the Raleigh, had noticed what he wore, and advised him for his health.
How kind people were in Virginia, he thought, mopping at himself
with a fine cambric handkerchief though the air was cooling towards
sundown; how simple and leisurely and open-hearted; like friendly
children, well-mannered but intensely personal. There was an absence
of British reserve, of French indifference, and of German arrogance.
Virginia thought objectively, from the heart outwards, perhaps as a
result of the times, not far behind, when life was a daily struggle to live
at all, and one's neighbor was often one's dearest possession. Virginia
was indeed its brother's keeper, from a not altogether outmoded necessity, perhaps, which had become a virtue.

To Julian, who had always lived on fringes and scraps of companion-
ship, it was a singularly attractive trait. But suppose war did come, now
that he had committed himself to the school. John Randolph would go
home, they said. John Randolph had money for the passage. And what
about himself? It would take at least two quarters of his salary, paying
for his living as he went. And had he any right to leave the school as
soon as it had served his purpose? What would have happened in
America, by the middle of next year?

As he approached Mrs. Hartley's house, two small figures detached
themselves from the step and stood awaiting him. The white sling
which supported Tibby's splinted arm gleamed in the lengthening
shadows, but it was a cotton square now and she held Julian's laundered
handkerchief folded carefully inside a bit of brown paper.

"Well, good evening," he said, and Kit removed his hat and Tibby
made a curtsy. He could see that they were dressed in their best for the
call. "How is the arm, does it ache much?"

"Yes, sir," said Tibby, and held out to him the little parcel. "Mother
did up your handkerchief, and thank-you-very-much-for-the-use-of-it."

"Thank *you*," said Julian. "I wasn't expecting it back so soon. Will
you ask your mother if she would have time to do some laundry for me?
Mr. Sprague said she might."

"Yes, sir, I'm sure she would be glad to."

"Good. I'll have it ready tomorrow."

The twins stood, not barring his way, but looking up at him with eyes full of questioning. Obviously they still had something weighing on their minds.

"Would you like to come in a minute?" he inquired at a loss, for there was little in his room to entertain them with.

"Oh, no, thank you, sir, we have missed our dinner, waiting for you," said Kit.

"I'm sorry about that. You could have left the handkerchief with Mrs. Hartley."

"We wanted to see you," said Tibby.

"We wanted to ask you—" Kit began, and lost courage.

"Yes?" queried Julian helpfully. "Is there something I can do for you?"

"Please, sir—" It was Tibby now. "There is a notice on the door of the dominie's school. We saw it when we came by. Are you the Mr. Julian Day it says is going to teach the school now?"

"Yes, I'm the one."

The twins exchanged delighted glances, as if they had told each other so.

"Go on," whispered Kit, nudging his sister. "Ask him."

"Please, sir—" Tibby raised anxious eyes to Julian's face and stuck again.

"Yes, Tibby, tell me what it is." He sat down on the top step, bringing himself more to their conversational level, and put out a hand to draw her to him.

"C-could I come to the school?" blurted Tibby, and held her breath.

"The school is for boys," he told her gently.

"That's what the dominie always said. But we thought—with you it might be different."

"Well, I am afraid not, you—"

"She knows as much as a boy, sir." Kit came to stand close on the other side of him. "Mother taught us both to read, out of the Bible. And since I have been going to the dominie's school Tibby has done all my lessons over after me when I get home. Everything the dominie has taught me—Tibby knows. She spells much better than I do, sir. And she can do vulgar fractions, and the number game out of Wingate, and—and—"

"But there must be some other school—" Julian began.

"There is the dame school, for babies." Tibby mentioned it with scorn. "And there is Mrs. Hallam's school, but that's for young ladies." It was plain that she did not consider herself a young lady. "Please, sir, couldn't I come with Kit?"

"But you are not a boy," Julian pointed out.

"She could wear my other suit," suggested Kit, and giggled. *"Nobody could tell us apart then!"* It was a prospect which amused them both.

"I am afraid that would hardly do." Julian suppressed a smile.

"It seems as though they ought to let a girl get some education if she wants to," Kit said, and Julian looked at him reflectively.

"Yes—yes, it does, doesn't it! It seems to me, Kit, you have got hold of a very sound idea there."

"Does that mean I can come?"

"No, Tibby. That is—I shall have to think about this. I shall have to—consult somebody. It does seem as though a girl should have an equal chance—"

"She could pass an examination, maybe, like for a scholarship," Kit offered hopefully. "She could recite something for you. She knows things by heart, from the Bible and all. Lots more than any of the boys at school. Tibby, tell Mr. Day the one you learned last Sunday."

Tibby looked shy.

"Go on, Tibby." Kit prodded her in the ribs. "Or else he will think you don't remember it."

"Go on, Tibby." Julian was smiling at her from the top step.

" 'Entreat me not to leave thee,' " Tibby began very low, " 'or to return from following after—' "

"That's not the one I meant," Kit interrupted, and she quelled him with a look.

" '—or to return from following after thee. For whither thou goest, I will go. And where thou lodgest, I will lodge. Thy people shall be my people, and thy God my God. Where thou diest, will I die, and there will I be buried. The Lord do so unto me, and more also, if aught but death part thee and me.' "

Julian sat a moment in silence, staring through the gathering dusk at the small white triangle of her face. It was pure coincidence, of course, he told himself. This weird child had no possible way of knowing that he meant to return to England as soon as he could. And yet— She looked back at him straightly, under her winged brows.

"Those are beautiful lines," he said, and added rather severely, for he was deeply disturbed, "Do you know who said them? Do you know the story behind them?"

"The story spoils it," said Tibby. "It sounds more beautiful if you forget it was just two women talking."

Julian regarded her speechlessly, and Kit's voice came a little too loud between them.

"Ruth said it to Naomi," announced Kit. "They were both widows."

"That's what I mean," murmured Tibby, without removing her eyes from Julian's face. "Good night, sir. God bless you. Come, Kit."

She made her brief curtsy and walked away from him into the shadows, Kit a shadow at her heels.

VII

"The summer heat of the Virginia climate is a thing very difficult to become accustomed to," Julian wrote in his journal towards the end of June. "They say the dews are dangerous and advise me to keep my windows down, but I cannot do this without panting. Several weeks of dry, scorching weather with the dust ankle-deep in the roads have been enlivened by the most violent thunderstorms which did no good beyond a temporary gladness of the greenery.

"I shall never again smell a rose garden that I do not remember the peculiar dusty fragrance which spreads through all the air of this town from countless arbors hung with pink blossom drooping in the sun but smelling sweeter than any roses I ever knew before. Box hedges have fragrance too when the sun is hot enough to bring it out. And as you walk through the streets mingled scents from the herb gardens waft out over the white picket fences, so that you seem to be living in a hothouse rather than a town, with a perpetual bouquet under your nose.

"The houses are built for the heat, with a garden door set opposite to the front door, so that a breeze blows through the large entrance hall, from which the staircase rises, making it the coolest place to sit. The kitchens, laundries, store-rooms, and slave quarters are all in separate buildings at the back. There is a contrivance called the shoo-fly which works with a treadle and has a hanging fringe which keeps the air in motion above the dinner table or the master's easy chair. Everyone who values his rest sleeps under a mosquito-net which is suspended from the ceiling above the bed. This is a truly wonderful invention, as the stings from these tiny insects can be torment.

"At the insistence of St. John Sprague I have got two suits of light clothes, which cost more than I intended but will make the heat bearable—also he alleged that the broadcloth made me look like a psalm-singing New Englander, and created a wrong impression. Since they came home from the tailor, we are in a most unseasonable spell of chilly, damp, funky weather, with gales, which is causing much sickness—dysentery and an endemical ague. Blankets and fires are needed for the first time since my arrival. I am assured that it will be hotter than ever within a few days.

"The anomaly of happy slaves continues to interest me. House slaves are as a rule treated with kindness and even affection, and seem utterly devoted to their owners, especially to the children in their care, who in turn regard their black nurses almost as second mothers. A fair, laughing child in the arms of a loving Negress is a common sight. The field slaves are not so well clothed and are meanly housed, but they look healthy and cheerful and in the evenings can be heard like their more fortunate brethren in the home quarters, singing to their guitars and banjos, with often a cockfight for amusement on Sundays.

"There is disappointment in Williamsburg that the 'trouble' has spoilt the usual gay Assembly season, though the Burgesses' ball for Lady Dunmore was held in spite of it and was well attended. The air was said to be somewhat febrile. The performance of *The Beggar's Opera* which I saw at the theater on the Green was the last to be given there. The race course behind the Capitol too will probably be closed. People are not in the mood for frivolities."

Later, during the early part of August, he wrote—

"Everyone was looking to the August first meeting of the Burgesses at

Williamsburg to clarify the situation, and Jefferson drew up instructions for the delegates who were chosen for the Continental Congress in September. He still insists on his hope of an imperial federation, but he was ill and unable to attend the meeting, which was run by Patrick Henry in his own way. Colonel Washington made what is said to be the first speech of his career as Burgess, to the effect that he was willing to raise one thousand men, subsist them at his own expense, and march at their head himself to the relief of Boston. I find it very hard to credit, but I have talked with men who actually heard him say it. Patrick Henry, who looks like a country parson and is supposed to speak with the tongue of an angel (and also, I notice, with some sort of backwoods brogue) calls himself an 'American' now, and talks of forming Virginia companies to the extent of five or six thousand men, with the Indian fighters as officers. This seems to me utter Gasconade, but it is taken quite seriously by St. John Sprague, who is no fire-eater, but a very sensible man.

"A non-importation bill is to be introduced, which if passed will work much hardship among the merchant classes both here and in England. Some people express the opinion that that alone will be enough to bring Britain to heel—an odd phrase to my ears, I confess, but the least hint of what is beginning to be known as *Loyalist* sentiment is considered tactless to say the least in most public circles, and I am careful to avoid controversy. A schoolmaster must be discreet in his utterances. Only the other day John Randolph was insulted by some unthinking children who followed him down the main street shouting, 'Tory! Tory! Get a rope!'

"The dominie died a few days ago, leaving his books and poor belongings all to me, along with seventeen pounds in savings, because he had taken a fancy to me. He had no family, so I am not robbing anybody. It is enough money, ironically, to buy passage home at once, but to accept it with a clear conscience I must teach the school a full year.

"The Spragues have forbidden me to take possession of the dominie's room over the school until after the hot weather, so I shall stay on at Mrs. Hartley's another month. St. John's aunt has expressed the intention of having the room 'scraped out' and refurnished with some things of her own from the attic in Francis Street, and nothing I can say will dissuade her from this kindness. She appears to have stored away many treasures from the big house they sold, which she says she would like to see in use again, and I am to benefit by her generous heart.

"All my efforts to interest Jefferson and others in extending the opportunities for female education are so far without fruit. Jefferson listens patiently and boils with enthusiasm both for free education and free libraries, but his hands are full with the coming Congress and everyone is preoccupied these days by more urgent matters. Poor Tibby was downcast when the Trinity term began and she was still excluded. Her memory and gift for repeating verbatim what she has read always amaze me, and her familiarity with the Bible is almost embarrassing to one who is not in Orders. Last week I let her look into my Dryden, and within an hour she had mastered the passage beginning:

> 'Happy the man, and happy he alone,
> He who can call today his own:
> He who, secure within, can say,
> Tomorrow, do thy worst, for I have lived today.
> Be fair or foul, or rain or shine,
> The joys I have possessed, in spite of fate, are mine.
> Not heaven itself upon the past has power;
> But what has been has been, and I have had my hour.'

"I have no idea how she came to make so hedonic a choice, and she only looked at me slantwise and became tongue-tied when I asked her. The child is half elf and wholly fascinating. There is no doubt that she is quicker and more retentive than Kit, and therefore more deserving of opportunity to cultivate her intelligence, but as yet I have found no way to bring regular instruction within her reach. I have made several friends here already who are dear to me, but I suspect that when the time comes for me to return to England I shall find it hardest of all to part from a child less than half my own age. . . ."

VIII

At the end of August, when Patrick Henry, Colonel Washington, and Mr. Jefferson set out for Philadelphia to attend the Continental Congress, Julian had eaten his first watermelon and his first figs fresh from the vine, and the strange sweet banana from the West Indies. Tibby had brought him a jessamine nosegay which he placed in a mug of water on his writing-table and cherished exceedingly, and the Williamsburg roses were well past their prime.

He had seen half-naked Indian traders leading their pack ponies down the middle of the Duke of Gloucester Street. He had seen newly arrived slaves, with the marks of manacles still on their wrists and ankles. He had noted with approval the cheerful Virginia Sunday when the street in front of the church looked like a horse fair, especially on rainy days when it was the custom to remove the saddles and pile them inside the coaches. Every one took part in the leisurely social life around the church door after the mercifully brief sermon, and drove off bearing guests home to dinner, and dessert never arrived before candlelighting, on a Sunday.

Tibby's arm had healed nicely, but the swelling from the break was still visible under the golden tanned skin, and she had a trick of rubbing it furtively with her other hand when it ached at a change in the weather. Kit volunteered the information that it was stiff and weak still, and made her clumsy, so that she dropped things—once she had spilt her father's persimmon beer all over him because the tankard was too heavy, and he had taken another swipe at her.

By the time torrential autumn rains had washed away the last of the summer sultriness, the living quarters above the classroom had been thoroughly scrubbed by the Spragues' maids, and a bonfire made of most of the ancient contents. The place stood stark empty for several days, smelling of soap and whitewash. Let it air, said Aunt Anabel, who had visited it more than once during the process with a permanently offended nose. Let it air.

Julian was absorbed in getting his class sorted out and had also undertaken some tutoring in Greek at the College. The school had increased to nineteen pupils of assorted ages and degrees of proficiency in the classics and mathematics. Kit Mawes seemed to be getting a better grip on things by fits and starts, and Julian laid it to the extra work Tibby made him do at home to keep her abreast of the lessons.

One day just as school was closing, the furniture arrived in a wagon from Francis Street, and Aunt Anabel proved to be just behind it with one of the maids.

Kit lingered, offering assistance in the arrangement of Julian's quarters, and was allowed to stay and make himself useful when the other scholars had trooped out. The maid Jerusha began to hang the curtains. Joshua was setting up the bedstead. Aunt Anabel, with her hair in a palisade cap and a flowered gauze apron over her lutestring gown, was sorting the linen into a chest of drawers, and Julian pottered with his bookshelf. Kit had taken his coat off and was making frequent trips up and down the stairs to fetch the smaller objects, when there was a loud crash below and they all rushed to the stairs to find the china ewer in smithereens on the floor while Kit stood above it rubbing his left wrist with his right hand and looking frightened.

"It slipped," he said. "I'm sorry, sir. I was going to bring it up for you."

"Well, so long as you didn't hurt yourself," said Aunt Anabel, relieved. "It sounded like the chimney falling in. Do be careful, child, and leave the heavy things for Joshua. Now I've got to send back for another chamber set."

"I'm s-sorry, ma'am, I—"

"Well, don't cry over it. It's not worth tears from anybody."

Aunt Anabel returned up the stairs, shooing the servants before her. But Julian stood still, looking at Kit with close attention.

"That was clumsy of you," he remarked. "Bring that pile of books from the bench next, they won't break. Can you carry them all?"

"Yes, sir."

Kit picked them up, while Julian stood watching. The top book on the pile met Kit's chin. Half way across the room his left arm failed and the books spilled in all directions to the floor. For once Julian was indifferent to his bindings and made no comment.

"I'm—so sorry, sir!" gasped Kit, dropping to his knees to collect the scattered volumes.

"Come here," said Julian in his schoolmaster's voice, and Kit froze where he was, his head down. "I am waiting," said Julian after a moment, and the child came reluctantly to stand before him. "Show me your arm—the left one." When there was no move to obey, Julian laid hold of it himself and pushed up the white shirtsleeve—the swelling from Tibby's break showed clearly. Simultaneously her other arm flew up to ward off a blow. "I'm not going to beat you—yet," Julian said mildly. "So you are wearing Kit's clothes after all. How long has this been going on?"

"It's only the third time, sir."

"Does your mother know?"

"Oh, no, sir! We only do it on the days when she is out working. Mrs. Thompson is having her baby today and we knew mother wouldn't be home for supper."

"Where is Kit? At home in your dress?"

"Yes, sir. He—he stays inside the house."

"I think you had better go home and change. And I want you to promise that you won't wear Kit's clothes again."

"Oh, please, sir—!" But his face was unrelenting and her chin quivered. "It's the only way I can come to school! And it's much better than trying to learn from Kit. Why can't we take turns? Kit is willing, and no one need know!"

"It won't do, Tibby. If it happens again I shall punish you. Both of you. Do you understand?"

"Yes, sir."

He watched the small, disconsolate figure out the door, and then gathered up the books from the floor and carried them upstairs, looking very thoughtful.

Several hours later he was seated at his writing-table at Mrs. Hartley's when the girl Melissa scratched on his door and opened it at his call.

"Please, suh, Kit Mawes is here—says he got to see you—somethin's scared that pore child 'most to death, suh!"

"Let him come up."

Kit ran at him, white-faced and breathless.

"Mr. Day—oh, please, Mr. Day, will you come to Tibby, sir?"

"Where is she? What's happened?"

"She's hiding in Mr. Barrett's slave quarters, sir. I couldn't get her any further."

"Hiding? Why?"

"Father found out we had changed clothes. It was my fault, I gave it away! He thought I was Tibby at first, and said things I didn't know the answers to. He was getting suspicious when she came home—she was late. He watched us. We both knew he knew. It was horrible—waiting. Finally he made us strip and change to our own clothes. He called Tibby names, and said she was w-wanton, like Mother! We thought that was going to be all. Then he began to unbuckle his belt, and —I ran outside, but he caught Tibby. She screamed and screamed!" Kit's face worked hysterically, and he put up one hand to hide it, and the breathless tale went on. "When he came out to look for me I dodged in the back way and got Tibby out into the bushes. It was hard to keep her quiet, but he was too drunk to find us, and it got dark. She goes on crying—her back is so bad she can hardly walk—but I got her away to Mr. Barrett's Susan, she has hidden us before when father was look-ing for us."

Julian picked up his hat.

"Take me there," he said.

Kit ran beside him through the dark streets showing the way, his teeth chattering while he tried to elaborate on his story. Julian heard nothing more. His mind had stopped a while back—*Tibby screamed and screamed.*

She lay face down on Susan's bed in the quarters, her sobs reduced to long quivering sighs. Her hair was still tied back with a worn black ribbon in imitation of Kit's queue. The bodice of her dress had been opened, baring the child's thin body to the waist. Julian looked, and drew back, feeling sick. Blood clots were forming along the edges of the weals on her shoulders.

"I'm 'fraid to tetch it, suh," whispered Mr. Barrett's Susan. "Poisonin' could set in."

Julian bent over the bed again.

"Tibby, I am going to carry you and you've got to bear it. Put your arms around my neck." She sobbed once when he touched her, but her arms came up obediently and he wrapped her in the blanket she lay on and lifted her from the bed. "She will be taken care of," he told Susan. "Come, Kit."

Once more he hurried through the dark with Kit at his side, bound now for Francis Street. He could have taken her home to Mrs. Hartley, or to Dr. Graves, but something in him insisted on Aunt Anabel. Tibby must have the best. And the best was in Francis Street. This was for St. John too. Something had to be done about Mawes. And St. John was the man for that.

Joshua opened the door to them and stepped back silently. When Julian reached the drawing-room threshold St. John sprang up with a cry.

"Oh, God, Julian, not again!"

"She has been beaten," said Julian through stiff lips. "Unmercifully. Will you go and get that man!"

"Yes. Where is Sarah?"

"Midwifing. Get him, before she goes home."

"It will be a pleasure," said St. John. "Twenty lashes, sixty days, all I can pile up!" He was on his way to the door.

Aunt Anabel led the way upstairs, giving efficient orders to Joshua as she went. Julian laid Tibby face down on the bed in the dainty room which awaited Dorothea. She was quiet now, with half-closed eyes, like some small patient animal.

"Go down and ask Joshua for a toddy, there is nothing more you can do here," said Aunt Anabel. "Where is the boy? Have them give him some hot milk to drink and make him lie down on the sofa, he has had a bad fright. Make yourself comfortable till Sinjie comes back, I will see to this."

"Will she—be all right?"

"Of course she will, young things heal quickly. Thank goodness you had the sense to bring her straight to me. Now go away, here is Jerusha to help me."

Julian sat down in the drawing-room, gratefully sipping his toddy while Kit consumed hot milk and grew drowsy on the sofa. His gentle, sequestered spirit shrank from the idea of what must have taken place in the cabin by the Landing. He blamed himself for forgetting that Sarah would not be there when he sent Tibby home alone, to be beaten like a sailor. The sight of the child's back had affected him like a kick in the stomach. Even now a wave of giddiness passed through him. *Tibby screamed and screamed.* . . .

When St. John came home some time later with Sarah Mawes, whom he had collected on the way, he found Julian sitting with his head bent and his hands over his ears, and Kit sleeping on the sofa.

"He has been locked up tight," announced St. John with satisfaction. "And tomorrow he will get as good as he gave, or better!"

Julian looked at Sarah.

"I'm sorry about this," he said. "I feel as though I could have prevented it if I had had my wits about me." And he told them how he had discovered Tibby's masquerade at the school.

"There was no way you could have foreseen what happened," Sarah said wearily. "He has always knocked them about, but it's getting worse. They are growing to look more and more like their father, and when the drink is on him Mawes can't stand the sight of them. You see—their father once gave him the thrashing of a lifetime."

"Well, now he will get another," said St. John. "Administered by experts. It's time."

Julian saw her flinch, and laid his hand on her sleeve.

"They call him father," he said.

"Yes. Sometimes I think I ought to tell them."

"I think you ought," he said.

"Perhaps I'm wrong to want to make something better of them. Perhaps I shouldn't encourage Tibby to learn."

"From now on I shall encourage her myself," said Julian. "Somehow I am going to get her into Mrs. Hallam's school."

IX

He went to call on Mrs. Hallam the next day. She was a stately, charming woman, and she listened sympathetically. She had seen the children and knew their story. She was willing to accept Tibby as a pupil, for the usual ten-pound fee, but she was in duty bound to point out that there might be objections from parents who would resent the presence there of a child whose parentage and background were—of a different class. Julian assured her that Tibby's speech and manners were irreproachable. Mrs. Hallam sighed, and said there was the father. And the mother, admirable as she was, took in washing and went out by the day to sew and nurse, and that not in the best families, who all owned adequate slave labor for such duties.

"Suppose the child were sponsored by the best families," Julian suggested. "Suppose I could get Mr. Wythe and Mr. Jefferson to say that in their opinion she deserves a decent start in life, such as your school would give her."

"That would make a difference," she admitted doubtfully. "It would give me an answer, if there were any complaints."

A plan was evolving in Julian's mind. Kit had suggested that Tibby might pass some kind of examination. Well, suppose he tutored Tibby and then brought her before a board of Williamsburg citizens and let them test her in any way they liked as to her fitness for association with their daughters. And suppose they agreed that she was exceptional and must have her chance. He put the scheme to Mrs. Hallam. Touched by his sincerity, she gave him an outline of what was expected of a young lady of Tibby's age—needlework, music, dancing, drawing, French conversation—she looked at him inquiringly, a smile lurking in her dark eyes.

"Needlework, no," Julian conceded smiling back. "Perhaps her mother can help us there. Music—I play a guitar if I can borrow one. Does that surprise you? Yes, and I know how to step a minuet and a reel, and French is my second tongue. You see, I spent much of my time on the Continent as a boy."

"Well!" said Mrs. Hallam, who knew a good thing when she saw it. "My French instructor is anything but satisfactory—it is second generation Charleston French. Would you have time to take a class here?"

"I think that would be possible," said Julian, recognizing a subtle form of blackmail, but resolving to see for himself the sort of thing Tibby would be in for, the better to prepare her. They discussed details to their mutual satisfaction, and Julian stood committed to the fee, which was by no means covered by the French class.

"There is only one thing," said Mrs. Hallam, as he rose to go. "Suppose she comes here and is a success. Suppose she becomes my star pupil,

for that matter. It will not open doors to her. She is still old Mawes'
daughter."

Julian considered.

"She could teach," he said. "I can make her the best French mistress in
Virginia. You might even find a place for her here."

Mrs. Hallam threw up her hands with laughter which acknowledged
defeat.

"You are a very persuasive young man," she said. "Very well, Mr.
Day, if you can get Mr. Wythe's approval and Mr. Jefferson's, I will
do whatever I can for your infant bluestocking. But by the time you
have done that, there will be very little left for me to teach her."

"On the contrary, ma'am—the things she will learn from a woman
like yourself have never yet been put between book covers."

"Oh, get along with you!" cried Mrs. Hallam, relaxing unexpectedly.
"What's more, I'll lend you a guitar."

Julian hurried home and spent the evening mapping out a course of
study for Tibby which would consume months of daily toil. It was not
just the intellectual and social requirements of Mrs. Hallam's school
which she must measure up to. She must be so far beyond them that
the most captious board of examiners wouldn't have a leg to stand on.
She must qualify for entrance to the lower school at William and Mary,
almost, to get past Mrs. Hallam's door. And he must work against time.
He must see her safely under Mrs. Hallam's wing—he liked the woman
—before his stay in Virginia came to an end.

Tibby was kept in bed in Francis Street and missed any further
participation in Julian's move from Mrs. Hartley's. He settled into his
new quarters with a wary sort of contentment. It seemed a very permanent arrangement, to possess a place he could call his own, without a
weekly score to pay, and with a quarterly salary ahead of him. He still
took his meals at Mrs. Hartley's, and once a week Melissa was sent in
to clean and put things to rights. She had already informed her mistress
that he was the tidiest man she ever did see, bar none; he changed his
linen not by the day of the week but by the weather and the accidents
of daily life, so it was always fresh—and he kept his window open at
night, and hated flies and mosquitoes, and he cleaned his teeth every
morning with a frayed twig dipped in salt, which was why they were so
handsome, and he washed himself all over every day in summer, as she

knew very well, carrying all those buckets of water—and he would ruin his eyes reading so much, and burning all those good candles too, and you'd think he'd get lonesome and give the women a chance. . . .

St. John had gone off to Charleston on business for Mr. Wythe, and Julian missed him keenly. They might not see each other for days at a time, but the knowledge of their friendship was a cosy presence at the back of his mind. To the solitary habits of a scholar Julian had now added the lonely trade of a writer. He had found Purchas, Hakluyt, John Smith, Hugh Jones, and Stith in Mr. Wythe's library, and besides keeping up his journal he was embarking cautiously on the first chapter of his history, which dealt with the voyages of discovery and the first settlements in America.

One night soon after his interview with Mrs. Hallam he went to bed with a simmering headache and when he woke sick and shaking in the small hours he knew that the dreaded fever was upon him. He reeled out of bed and took a dose of James's Powders, as he had been advised, but nothing availed against the pains and nausea and fits of chill which kept him awake until sunlight, when he again dragged himself forth and tried to dress by easy stages. He had lost all sense of time, and when he did not appear for breakfast Mrs. Hartley sent Melissa to see why. Melissa took one look at him.

"Oh, law, Mr. Day, suh, you got the seasonin' fever, that's what it is! Just you get back into that bed, suh, and don't try to do nothin' for nobody. You goin' to be laid up quite a spell, suh!" She plumped his crumpled pillows and smoothed the sheets with a practiced hand. "Now, then, suh, you come and lay down, while I fetch you over some break-fast. Did you take them Powders, suh?"

Julian said faintly that he had, and sank back into bed while the room went round and round.

"Well, you can't do much about it yet awhile, suh. Fever just got to run its course. You lay still now, like I tell you, I won't be long. Mis' Hartley come over and see to things, most likely, when I tell her how you look, and they shore have to shet the school till you get round and about again."

Followed days and nights of such abject misery as he had never known, when he had not the desire to live nor the energy to die. The news of his illness soon reached Francis Street, and brought Aunt Anabel with a basket on her arm. She found him alone—Melissa could not be spared except to bring his food and make his bed each day—and he did not know her, and babbled some innocent delirium to his father who seemed to him to be present, but inattentive. Aunt Anabel installed Sarah Mawes as nurse, day and night, and sent to Charleston for St. John.

Julian woke one morning, clear-headed at last, and lay listening to the ringing of the churchbell. With a great effort of will power he raised heavy eyelids to see where he was. Oh, yes. The room above the schoolroom. With a further effort he turned his head on the pillow. Sarah Mawes sat beside the window, a Bible open on her lap, her worn, beautiful face bent above the page. As soon as he moved she glanced up with a smile.

"Well," she said in her quiet tones which had kept Tibby's voice sweetly pitched and her vowel sounds pure, "that's better. You were having a good sleep, though, and the bell woke you."

"Is it Sunday?" he whispered, trying to remember what day he had fallen ill.

"It is. Is there something I can get for you?"

He tried to think. There was something he wanted. His father was dead, he remembered that at once. He recalled that he had left his room at Mrs. Hartley's and come to live here with Aunt Anabel's furniture. And he hadn't got to worry about money any more, he had a legacy, and a salary besides. He was a rich man. And there was a book he had to write, but that wasn't it. St. John had gone to Charleston. . . .

"Tibby," he said. "Where is Tibby?"

He followed the direction of Sarah's eyes. Tibby stood on the other side of the bed near the foot, looking down at him.

"Hello," he said, and his hand moved on the coverlet, towards her. Tibby came closer, and touched it timidly. Her fingers felt small and warm. He remembered everything now. He had been to see Mrs. Hallam. "I must teach you—to play the guitar," he said, and drifted smiling into another sleep.

The following afternoon St. John arrived literally in a cloud of dust and ran up the stairs to Julian's bedside.

"Good Lord, Julian, this is a fine way to treat your friends!" he cried as he entered. "You almost died, man! And *then* where would we be?"

"You have come in time for the funeral," Julian remarked, very flat against the pillow.

St. John turned on Sarah Mawes.

"Does he behave? Does he eat? Does he sleep? Is the fever gone?"

"Quite gone," she smiled. "That is why he is so weak. It's only a question of time now, and rest."

"Well, what can I do?" demanded St. John efficiently. "Please let me do something. Isn't there anything you want?" he insisted, sitting down on the edge of the bed.

"I want a shave," said Julian.

Sometimes it was Tibby who sat with him in the afternoons as he improved, and she begged again and again for details of his conversation with Mrs. Hallam, and itched to get on with her studies. Not yet, her mother said firmly. Not till Mr. Day was stronger. So Tibby had to be content with learning the French words for chair and table and window and *la plume de sa tante*. The rest of the time she read his books and answered his questions.

Julian had never before had the leisure to make her talk about herself, which she did with an engaging lack of self-consciousness and considerable humor. She hated her pigtails and limp calico dresses and longed for silk and curls—like Regina Greensleeves, whose mother had taken her home to London to go to balls and see Garrick act. Had Mr. Day ever seen Garrick act? Mr. Day had seen Garrick act *Richard III*—wearing the regimentals of George III's dragoons—and promised that she should read the play. Tibby demanded a description of London. It was a dismal place, he told her, she wouldn't care for it at all. Tibby wasn't sure. It wasn't dismal where Regina Greensleeves was. People wore silk every day in London, and lived in brick houses with enormous staircases and marble mantelpieces and red carpets in every room. And crystal chandeliers. Had he ever seen a crystal chandelier? Julian, who had seen Versailles, agreed that crystal chandeliers were beautiful. If she lived in London, said Tibby, with a sidelong glance to show she knew it was all make-believe, she would have curtains to her bed, and a sedan chair to go out in, and wear a hooped gown, with her hair powdered. And she would have a doll.

"Haven't you one?" he asked.

Tibby shook her head and the pigtails wagged.

"Pretty soon I'll be too old for dolls and then it won't matter so much," she sighed.

Julian turned it over in his mind. It was fantastic that a girl child should not have a doll. Especially now that he had enough money to buy one. It didn't matter what they cost, he hadn't got to save every penny now, he could afford a doll for Tibby. But it must be a good one. The best.

That evening St. John received an urgent summons, and Julian spoke almost before he was in the door.

"Where can I buy a doll for Tibby?" he demanded.

"I'll ask Dorothea to bring one out from London when she comes."

"That takes too long. Where can I get the best one this side of London?"

"At Philadelphia, probably. Or I might have got a nice one in Charleston if I had known."

"A fine time to tell me," said Julian peevishly, and raised himself against the pillows with difficulty, so that St. John bent to set an arm behind his shoulders, saying—

"What's the matter? Are you starting for Philadelphia tonight?"

Julian had demonstrated to himself again that he still had no strength.

"Will you write a letter to Jefferson in Philadelphia for me?"

"Now?"

"Now."

"He's only got the Congress," St. John reminded him, sitting down at the writing-table. "He must have time on his hands."

"He is the father of children," said Julian, who would never have dreamed of asking Jefferson to do an errand for himself. "He will know what she'd like. Tell him it must have a silk dress, and never mind what it costs, I will send the money."

St. John wrote, adding a line or two of his own about Julian's illness. Jefferson, with two baby girls of his own in the nursery at Monticello, found time and took trouble. The doll arrived by the Burgesses' own courier, and Tibby opened the box on Julian's coverlet without suspecting what it contained.

The doll wore a pink brocade dress, and what's more it had the most fashionable thing in hoops under a draped skirt. Its shoes were of pink brocade to match, and its taffeta petticoat had a deep lace flounce, and its stomacher was sewn with tiny beads like pearls, and its high-dressed powdered hair was real. Obviously, it was on its way to a ball. Tibby stared at it, and then at Julian, in silent ecstasy.

"Well, there is your doll," he said with some satisfaction. "I asked Mr. Jefferson to get one for you in Philadelphia. Lift it out and let's see it."

Tibby took hold of it in a gingerly way as though it might crumble at a touch. Its pink dress was smooth and cool to her fingertips. Its eyes were blue. It was all the way from Philadelphia, and Mr. Jefferson had chosen it. But all that was as nothing beside the fact that it was a gift from Mr. Day, whose friends called him Julian. She had never been so happy in her life.

She sat down with the doll in her arms, speechless lest she dissolve into foolish tears.

X

St. John was horrified when he discovered that the only heat in the room above the school was the dubious warmth of the chimney leading up from the classroom fire, and he removed Julian almost bodily to Francis Street and installed him there in sybaritic style in time for Christmas.

The tempo was quickening ominously as the year ran out. News of the Philadelphia Congress filtered back to Williamsburg before it adjourned and the delegates returned home around the first of November.

The city of Philadelphia, Williamsburg heard, was gay and hospitable. There were balls and elegant entertainments which opened the eyes of the simple-living New England representatives, but the Philadelphia women were reported to be plain and sour. The popular toast was: "May Britain be wise and America be free!" Washington attended daily at Carpenters' Hall where the Congress sat—six feet three of magnetic silence, clothed in the blue and scarlet of a Virginia colonel. He had made his speech at Williamsburg in August. The uniform was his only reiteration of his willingness to fight. Backwoods marksmen were rallying to his name, and it was plain that he would be unanimously chosen again as Commander-in-Chief of the Virginia forces— by buckskin-clad men whose test of good shooting was the neat removal of a squirrel's tail at two hundred yards without damaging the squirrel.

Everywhere troops were enrolling and drilling. The King had called them rebels rudely and prematurely. They were becoming rebels now in deadly earnest. Trade was almost at a standstill, and everybody seemed at a loss how to proceed, in view of the non-intercourse resolution—a ruinous measure born of the obstinate hope of a bloodless victory. Roads were under surveillance, and mails were likely to be opened en route.

News of Boston trickled south too. Food was scarce in the city. More troops arrived from England at the end of the year, and there was a sort of grim game going on in which Governor Gage tried unobtrusively to collect the colonists' scattered stores of ammunition bit by bit while the citizens and organized Minute Men stole it back bit by bit under the noses of the garrison.

New Year's, 1775, was heavy with foreboding everywhere in America. Tories were slipping away to England by every boat. Regina Greensleeves' father became alarmed that a declaration of war might catch his womenfolk in London and sent for them to return home on Captain Barry's next voyage. They were to arrive in April via the West Indies, and Dorothea would be with them.

Julian when he heard this immediately spoke of returning to the schoolhouse, but Aunt Anabel said Nonsense, there were four bedrooms, which was one apiece and nobody could do with more. Julian persisted feebly that too much soft living was bad for convalescence, to which St. John replied with certain vivid language of his own, and the subject died down, with a secret resolve on Julian's part to vacate his room in Francis Street when Dorothea arrived.

He was teaching school again before the first of the year. Tibby was progressing with gratifying speed in her private lessons, and could sing *Gentle Shepherd Tell Me Where* to her own accompaniment on the guitar so that, as St. John said, there wasn't a dry eye in the house.

In March the Second Virginia Convention met in the church at Richmond—removed from Williamsburg because of the Governor's belligerent attitude towards what was after all an assembly of the Burgesses without Governor or Council. Patrick Henry rose in his pew near the east door and made another of those flaming speeches of his which within a remarkably short time could be quoted by any Patriot in America at the drop of a hat. "Gentlemen may cry Peace, peace—but there is no peace!" he shouted, and the cords of his neck stood out white and rigid as his voice rose. "The war is actually begun! The next gale that sweeps from the north will bring to our ears the resounding clash of arms. Our brethren are already in the field! Why stand we here idle? Is life so dear or peace so sweet as to be purchased at the price of chains and slavery? Forbid it, Almighty God! I know not what course others may take, but for me—give me liberty or give me death!"

It was being said at the Raleigh the next night that his hearers were positively sick with excitement when he finished. Washington was chosen by the Convention to head the committee to prepare for enlisting and equipping the troops it had voted to raise, and Virginia stood pledged to war.

The *Mary Jones* was late into Yorktown from the Indies, and it was the afternoon of the twentieth when she was sighted. The Sprague coach whirled up to the door of the schoolhouse just at closing time, and St. John waded through the departing scholars calling on Julian to get his hat and come along.

"Aunt Anabel has decided not to tire herself with the drive," he said. "She will stay at home, preparing the feast. You are expected to supper, you know."

"Well, perhaps—at a family reunion—" Julian began, his old diffidence upon him at the thought of this unknown seventeen-year-old girl.

"God Almighty, man, since when have you divorced yourself from the family?" demanded St. John. "I believe you're *afraid* of Dorothea! You will soon get over that, come on, where is your hat, do you want her to think there is no one to meet her?"

The spars of the *Mary Jones* were tall beside the Yorktown pier when they arrived with the horses in a lather. St. John sprang out of the coach and ran through the noisy bustle of the dock where little groups of passengers mounted guard over growing piles of luggage among the black stevedores and brawny sailors. Julian followed more slowly with mixed emotions. It was nearly a year ago that he himself had stood here alone in this same confusion and seen St. John Sprague coming towards him. He wondered how it looked to St. John's sister, fresh from her grandmother's house in Berkeley Square. She must have courage, to set out into the unknown, even to such a welcome as that awaiting her in Francis Street.

Then he saw her, or at least saw something blue enveloped in St. John's brotherly embrace, from which she emerged pink and breathless and straightening her hat, to make him a schoolgirl curtsy on their introduction. She was dark and slender, with lips the color of a damask rose, and soft, nearsighted brown eyes, and a dimple in her smile. She was all that they had said she would be, and not a bit terrifying, and he smiled down at her without shyness.

"St. John said his sister was beautiful," he said, "but I thought that was just his usual brag. It seems for once he wasn't exaggerating."

It was a ponderous enough compliment, perhaps, but it brought more color to her cheeks.

"Regina is the beautiful one," she said. "Introduce him, Sinjie, I know you are dying to go and talk to her yourself."

Julian was led up to the Greensleeves family, who received St. John warmly. Fair as a lily, with pale golden curls under a chip hat tied with pink ribbons and eyes the deep blue of the Virginia sky, tall for a woman, with a proud high bosom and the carriage of a queen, Regina Greensleeves was quite accustomed to the look of dazed delight with which any man beheld her for the first time. St. John was obviously enslaved all over again. This Mr. Day with his slow smile was just another conquest completed with her own first smile in his direction.

"You are the new schoolmaster St. John has been writing to me about," she said. "I have been led to expect something exceptional, you know."

"That is unfortunate." Julian was embarrassed. "You should know by now that he is not to be relied on."

Her blue eyes had already measured his unusual height, his well-cut clothes, his quiet charm, his open bedazzlement.

"I prefer to form my own opinions," she said, and held out her hand to be kissed. "See that you give me an early opportunity, Mr. Day."

He made some formal reply which he felt as he spoke it to be half-witted. He stood beside her for a few more minutes, unable to take his eyes away. To find beauty like this in the wilderness, he was thinking—to find a creature made of pearl and roseleaves and spun gold, the sum and substance of a man's most wild and secret dreams—to have her look kindly on him, to hear from her own lips her wish to know him better—wasn't it for this that his destiny had brought him to Virginia, he wondered—wasn't it this woman, cool and laughing in the southern sunlight, he had travelled all his life to see. . . .

He came to himself slowly in the coach, with Dorothea's tabby silk skirts brushing his knees, her eager chatter requiring answers from himself as well as from St. John. Yes, he was better of the fever. Yes, he was still living in Francis Street, but must really go back soon to his quarters over the schoolroom, he had imposed long enough. Yes, he often felt homesick for London, but had set no date for his return, for he owed something to the school. No, they had not heard that Dr. Franklin was coming back to America. . . .

It was all a haze; a golden haze in which two deep blue eyes held a challenge and a promise. Julian had fallen in love.

Supper in Francis Street was gay and went on forever, with a few close friends invited to welcome Dorothea to Williamsburg. When they had all gone at last, St. John put another log on the fire, for the night had grown damp, and the four of them sat down, yawning, to sip hot milk—Julian's always had rum in it now, for the fever—and nibble sponge cake and hear the news of Granny and London. Julian had proposed tactfully to go to bed and was promptly squelched into his usual chair by the hearth. St. John lighted his yard of clay and put his feet on the fender.

"You ought to smoke, Julian," he observed, not for the first time. "It's very soothing."

"It stays on the tongue," said Julian—his usual answer—and Dorothea looked at him with added interest.

"I thought all men smoked," she remarked innocently.

"And do all the men of your acquaintance drink themselves under the table too?" Julian inquired, and St. John said he didn't see the connection, and there was laughter.

"There aren't really any men of my acquaintance, that is the trouble," she confessed. "Granny didn't like men, and I seldom saw any. Was Grandfather so dreadful, Sinjie?"

"Grandfather was a bit of a lad in his day," her brother told her comfortably. "He drowned himself in a butt of Malmsey when I was about twelve."

"*Sinjie!*" cried Aunt Anabel. "Your poor grandfather died in his bed of a stroke! I was there."

There was no argument. St. John only sat smiling at the fire through a cloud of pipesmoke.

"You always were a liar, Sinjie," murmured Dorothea with affection. There was a little ring of milk around her red mouth. Her eyes were heavy with sleep, her dark curls had loosened. She looked adorable, but Julian was still bemused by the fact that Regina Greensleeves had known who he was and wanted to see him again. "Were you lying when you said there was going to be a war?" Dorothea pursued, and Aunt Anabel sighed.

"I am afraid that is one time he was telling the unpleasant truth, my dear."

"There is a story going round London that the King has asked the Empress of Russia for troops to send to America," Dorothea remarked.

Everybody sat bolt upright and stared at her.

"Russian troops!" cried St. John. "Do you realize what you have said?"

"Well, it's only a story."

"But if it's true!" St. John was on his feet. "Hired mercenaries, sent against us! He would, would he! God Almighty, that is *too* much! If he does that I shall enlist myself! Julian, how can you sit there? Say something, man!"

"I—can't believe it is true," said Julian.

"No, of course not, why Russians?" asked Aunt Anabel sensibly.

"Because Britain hasn't got enough soldiers, they say. Mind you, I'm only repeating gossip Lady Cathcart brought." Dorothea looked distressed and uncertain. "*She* says it is difficult to find British officers willing to serve against the colonists, and the ranks don't like it either. Of course that only annoys her, because she thinks Massachusetts should have a good drubbing. But Regina knows General Burgoyne, and *she* says he stood up in the House of Commons and said he hoped that America could be convinced by persuasion rather than the sword, and he was howled down for disloyalty to the King. Of course Regina is a Tory herself, and she says Burgoyne is fascinating. A man named

Howe, who fought at Culloden, is being sent out to Boston with reinforcements for the garrison there, and they say it took a personal request
from the King to induce him to accept the command. Burgoyne may
come with him. Lady Cathcart says if *that* is the state of mind of the
men sent to establish order in the colonies, she would like to know what
the world is coming to. But of course her brother in Boston writes angry
letters about how the townspeople persecute the poor British soldiers
there. *She* thinks America is a rabble, but I'm sure from what I have
seen of it so far she has entirely the wrong impression." Dorothea beamed
round at them, her eyes resting last and longest on Julian.

"Russians!" said St. John, pacing the room. "Well, I'm damned! Wait
till Jefferson hears this!"

As he spoke there was a distant roll of drums. They listened, and the
air of the quiet room drew taut. The drums came again.

"*Indians!*" gasped Dorothea, white-faced.

"No, it's not Indians. Nor Russians, either," said Aunt Anabel firmly.
"Sinjie, what does it mean? Everybody in town must be in bed but us."

St. John turned from the window and laid down his pipe with a steady
hand.

"They are beating the alarm," he said very low, and the line of his
jaw was tight. "That calls the Independent Companies to arms. It sounds
as though it came from the direction of the Powder Magazine. They
had a guard there for a while, but I thought it had been removed. I'll go
and see what is going on." He rang for Joshua and asked for his hat
and sword.

"I'll go with you." Julian rose.

"No!" cried Aunt Anabel. "I won't be left without a man in the house,
you must stay here and protect us! Now, Sinjie, do be careful and don't
get into a fight!"

"Stay with them," said St. John. "I shall be perfectly safe, Auntie."

The door closed behind him.

They waited, while the drums swelled and receded, and there were
scattered shouts, and a spatter of galloping hooves down the Duke of
Gloucester Street. They waited for the sound of gunfire, and it did not
come.

"I suppose it must be at the Magazine," said Aunt Anabel. "I heard
Sinjie say that Dunmore had had the locks removed from the guns there,

and might try to take the powder next. That leaves us helpless if the
slaves should rise."

"The slaves!" Dorothea glanced over her shoulder with apprehension. "I didn't know—I thought it was only the Indians—"

"Now, don't be nervous of our people, child. Joshua and the girls
would lay down their lives for us. But there are always renegade slaves
hanging round the edge of town, and sometimes the wild Negroes
escape. Sinjie says they will never give any trouble unless they are egged
on by some one, but the surest way to encourage such a thing is to
take away our ammunition. Julian, put another log on the fire and light
some more candles, or I shall get the creeps!"

The drums went on, sporadically, and then were silent. Dorothea
drooped in her big chair, and finally dozed for sheer weariness.

Julian and Aunt Anabel spoke conscientiously of this and that, but
each was aware of the other's growing anxiety. St. John had gone out
into the small hours, wearing a sword. If there was a fight, St. John
would be in it. Nobody knew what the Governor might take it into his
head to do these days, he was a dangerous man to thwart. Perhaps the
King was landing troops in Virginia, as he had done in Boston. . . .
Drums in the night. But no guns. Not yet. It was difficult to sit still and
wait, while St. John— But by an unspoken mutual agreement that Dorothea must not be frightened, they went on talking, almost at random,
went on sitting still. . . .

St. John returned at last, very calm, but pale with excitement. The
Governor's marines from the armed schooner *Magdalen* lying off Burwell's Ferry near Jamestown had waited till the guard was relaxed at
the Magazine and then attempted to remove the powder to their ship
under cover of darkness, he said. They had been discovered, but the
powder was already gone. Drums had then been sent out to raise the
Companies, and a crowd had gathered in front of the Palace, which
he joined.

"They were growling that the Governor wouldn't admit a spokesman, and passing the word that he had armed his servants," St. John
reported. "I swear if it hadn't been for Peyton Randolph they would
have attacked the Palace and seized the Governor's sacred person! They
were ripening for it when Mr. Randolph rode up the Green—I don't
think they would have listened to him, either, if he hadn't been President

of the Congress at Philadelphia, but that gave him a new authority on top of the Randolph name. Anyway, he stopped them, single-handed—they're dispersing now, but they're in an ugly mood. He has promised to make a formal demand tomorrow for the return of the powder to the Magazine. It looks bad," added St. John, and his eyes met Julian's. "It looks like a real fight now. Dunmore has taken the bit in his teeth. If this is war, what are you going to do?"

"Why, I suppose I shall go on teaching school," said Julian slowly.

"You have decided not to go home, then."

"I can't go home yet. Apart from my obligation to the school, I have set aside the money for Tibby's fee at Mrs. Hallam's, and I can't buy passage with what is left."

"I'll lend you the passage money," said St. John, watching him, "if you really want to go while you can. But we would like you to stay, you know that, don't you!"

Julian looked round slowly at the three of them in the candlelight—St. John's brilliant, unwavering gaze and vital fencer's body; Aunt Anabel's china blue eyes full of tears; the girl Dorothea, leaning forward in her chair, her flower face lifted to help her nearsighted eyes to see him across the width of the room, her red lips parted—all awaiting his answer as though it mattered greatly to them. These people were his friends. He had never had friends like them before. Their world was smouldering into flame all around them, yet their concern was for him, the outsider. They refused steadfastly to consider him an outsider, even though he himself felt, with his Loyalist bias, like a cuckoo in the nest. Disarming, open-hearted children, all of them—and now gunpowder. Something closed his throat and almost choked him. His gaze came back to St. John.

"Thank you," he said. "I must stay the term out, at least. And besides, it wouldn't be fair to Tibby if I went now."

"Julian, dear, you couldn't feel any differently—about things here?" Aunt Anabel came to lay her hand on his sleeve.

"I could never take up arms against my King, if that is what you mean," he said gently. "Perhaps in view of that fact, you would rather I left your house at once?"

But Aunt Anabel held to him lovingly, and laid her cheek against his shoulder.

"How can you say such a thing? Especially now, when I feel so much safer with two good swordsmen in the house!"

It was an hour later, lying awake under St. John's roof, that J lian realized with surprise that he had never once thought of Regina Greensleeves when he made his decision to stay.

XI

"The situation seems to grow worse daily," Julian wrote in his journal early in May, "and now the first shot everyone has been waiting for has been fired, at Lexington in Massachusetts. An exhausted express rider with a very sore seat brought the news here within nine days of the event, and rode on towards Smithfield and the Carolinas. He might as well have carried a fiery cross, for all America will spring to arms now. There is wild talk of a siege of Boston, and Jefferson has been heard to say that the last hope of reconciliation will evaporate in a frenzy of revenge.

"Beside the battle of Lexington our own alarums and excursions seem rather tame, but there is a feeling that certain disaster here is only hanging fire, and that Virgina is all blown to pieces by gunpowder which never exploded. Incidentally, there wasn't enough powder involved to be much good to either side—some fifteen half-barrels is all, but the principle of its seizure is being bitterly disputed. The town authorities demanded the return of the whole amount, or its equivalent in cash. Governor Dunmore barricaded himself in the Palace, with muskets loaded and primed at every opening, and the streets were full of marines from Yorktown. Dunmore swore by the living God that if any violence were offered to him or his men he would free the slaves and lay the town in ashes.

"Some citizens began to send their wives and children into the country, and Regina Greensleeves, for one, was bundled off to their plantation, called Farthingale after a famous house in Gloucestershire. It lies on the north bank of the James near Westover, where the Byrd family lives. She offered to take St. John's aunt and sister with her, but they refused to budge, and St. John always allows them to make their own decisions. I confess if I had a young sister I should have sent her out of Williamsburg.

"Patrick Henry, whom I cannot but consider a mere rabble-rouser, was at his home in Hanover County on the night of April twentieth, and he immediately began a march on Williamsburg with one hundred and fifty men, to demand restitution by force. It was only by the utmost exertions of such level-headed men as Peyton Randolph that an armed clash was averted, for by that time Dunmore had set up cannon at the Palace. I cannot say that the Governor's conduct throughout has been in any way admirable.

"On the fourth of May a bill of exchange for the value of the powder was presented to Henry at his camp near Doncastle's Ordinary on Williamsburg Neck north of the town, and thus narrowly we escaped what could only have ended in a battle in the streets. Henry then returned to Hanover and dispersed his force and proceeded (as something of a hero) to the Second Congress, which went into session at Philadelphia on the tenth. Dr. Franklin has arrived from England just in time to take his seat there. Peyton Randolph is again President, and Jefferson and Washington are of course present, the latter as always in uniform.

"Philadelphia, they say, is sober now, in contrast to the gaieties of last September. War with Britain is no longer just a wilful possibility. It has become a grim reality. Independence—Patrick Henry's word—is now openly talked of, but only as a last resort. I have heard Washington speak calmly of resistance to the Ministerial Army, as a fine distinction, I suppose, to fighting England as a whole. Purists regard the present Government as unrepresentative and allege that it is behaving in an unconstitutional way; which seems to indicate that a change of Government might even now leave room for reconciliation. St. John says this is Stuff, because the King has got exactly the Government he wants. The Congress is drafting another petition to the Throne, but nobody seems to have much hope that anything will come of it.

"Since Lexington a great many people, including myself, find themselves in a dilemma. I have more sympathy for the colonists' cause than I would have thought possible when I left London. I suppose the schoolmaster in me objects to what seems unjustly harsh discipline on the part of the Government. One has occasional irresponsible impulses to throw in one's lot with these sturdy, lovable people who have a good deal of right on their side—but at the same time one would die thrice over rather than forswear allegiance to the King. As a consequence, one does neither, which looks like weakling indecision and gives rise to misunderstanding. I have given Mr. Wythe notice that he must try to find another schoolmaster for the next term, and as soon as I can complete my arrangements for Tibby, I must take passage home before my position here becomes intolerable. . . ."

XII

Williamsburg never forgave the Governor, and the officers of the British men-o'-war who had tried to intimidate the town were cut dead in the streets by the Virginian beauties with whom they had danced and flirted all spring. Members of the legislature, who had been threatened by Dunmore with prosecution for treason, went armed when they ventured from their up-river homes down the Neck to the capital.

On the first of June, Dunmore summoned the Burgesses to a special session to hear him read what he termed Lord North's conciliatory proposition, which had just arrived via Boston—too late by many months. Peyton Randolph and Jefferson returned from Philadelphia to attend the meeting, and Jefferson prepared the reply, which was in effect No, and resumed his seat in Congress.

North's offer had accompanied no less than three British generals into Boston harbor—Howe, Burgoyne, and Clinton found the British army shut up in the town living on salt rations, with a large and motley body of colonial militia encamped around the edges. The reinforcements they had brought with them, worn by a long voyage in ill-found, evil-smelling transports, raised the British strength in America to ten thousand men. It was not enough. And it could not get out of Boston.

A force of riflemen in hunting-shirts was mustering at Williamsburg, and they carried their arms ostentatiously when they went to stand in scowling, unfriendly knots on the Green looking up at the windows of the Palace and daring the Governor to show himself. There was another incident at the Powder Magazine, where a few remaining arms were stored. It was all too much for Dunmore. Before dawn on the eighth of June he fled to Yorktown with his family and took refuge on board the flagship, leaving the Palace closed and deserted. The King no longer ruled Virginia, and the capital was more orderly after the flight of his representative than before.

It was gayer too. Regina Greensleeves returned to town and went ahead with her plans for a ball, for which she had persuaded her father to take the Apollo Room at the Raleigh, with supper to be served in the Daphne Room about midnight. Everybody had ordered new gowns for the occasion, there was to be an orchestra of five pieces, and though the original glittering list of guests was curtailed by the departure of the Palace and Navy element, the local Tories scorned to be embarrassed by recent events, and still mixed freely with their Whig neighbors. Everyone was determined to enjoy the most elaborate social function the town had seen since the Palace entertainments had begun to fall off.

Dorothea was making her *début* at the ball, and Julian was to be her escort. St. John of course belonged to Regina, and some people even whispered that there might be an announcement of the betrothal before the evening was out.

It was an exquisite night in an exquisite Virginia June, with a moon. The Raleigh blazed with candles, and the windows of the ballroom stood open to the still air. In the shadows of the Duke of Gloucester Street outside the tavern the voices of the peepers in the trees could be heard above the violins. There was a steady procession of coaches from which beautiful women in filmy fabrics and men in light silks and satins emerged like butterflies, and the humbler Williamsburg citizens collected in knots around the entrance to hear the music and see the Quality go in.

Kit and Tibby were among them, but Julian, absorbed in making sure that Dorothea's and Aunt Anabel's small satin-shod feet found the coach step as he handed them down, did not see the children. They watched him with pride and affection as he escorted his lovely charges through the open door, and they agreed that it was much the handsomest group they had seen yet.

"Perhaps if we slip round to the back," Tibby whispered, "we could find a window where we could watch the dancing."

When Julian stepped out on to the waxed floor with Dorothea for the first minuet his pulse was quickened, for during the *cercle* and the *courvette* in the dance his hand would touch Regina's, and her eyes would rest on him, mysterious and smiling, with a glint of challenge to which all his manhood awakened. He was very new to this first flurry of love which had him in thrall, and very uncertain how to deal with it. He knew that it was madness, but he could not seem to care about that. At least—not yet. He drifted deliciously, for his had been a very barren youth, and allowed himself the luxury of boyish dreams. It was plain that she liked him. Each time they met, however briefly, it was plain. Her interest in him had gone to his head a little. For the first time in his sober life, he was conscious of his own good looks, his unusual height, and a certain quiet, almost diffident wit which had never been given play before.

Regina was deliberately bringing him out of himself. He was something new in her experience—a man without the London sophistication or the rather high-handed colonial masculinity—or St. John's fond, resilient impudence, which was neither, and which had already captured her own imperious spirit.

It was very warm in the crowded ballroom under the candles, and midnight found her pacing the bowling green behind the Raleigh, her hand on Julian's sleeve, her fan moving lazily in the soft air. Other couples strolled around them, the sound of laughter and talk reached them faintly.

"What a lovely night!" she murmured, breaking a silence which had endured between them long enough. "I missed our Virginia moons in London. Are you ever homesick for England, Mr. Day?"

"Not any more," he said, looking down at her.

"That is very gallant of you!" she laughed, taking it to herself as he had intended. "But apart from present company, do you like Virginia?"

"Since the first time I saw you," he told her solemnly, "it has been impossible for me to think—apart from present company." And he gave her his slow smile. "You are very like Virginia yourself, you know —gentle—blooming—kind—"

She sighed.

"If only Virginia stays that way! If only people like Patrick Henry don't talk us into war! It doesn't seem possible, does it—look around you here tonight—lights and music and laughter—this is civilization—

this is sanity and, as you say, kindness, and friendship. Why must we have a war? Mr. Day—you *are* on the King's side?"

"Yes—I'm afraid I am."

"I'm glad. Why should you regret it?"

"Because most of my best friends think otherwise. It makes things awkward sometimes. Take St. John, for instance—"

"St. John and I don't agree," she said, and tossed her head. "To hear him, you would think the King was some kind of monster!"

"I think the Ministry have handled the question badly," Julian conceded.

"They have done the only thing they could do! Massachusetts doesn't seem to understand anything but force!"

"Perhaps if they hadn't antagonized Boston in the beginning—"

"Well, really, Mr. Day, do you mean to tell me you *sympathize* with Boston?"

"N-no, I think they are wrong, of course. But at the same time, I can't think much of Governor Dunmore's attitude here, can you?"

She withdrew her hand from his arm.

"I thought you were loyal to the King, as I am!"

"And I am. But I still say that Dunmore has been—tactless. That is not heresy, that is only commonsense. But must we talk politics under the moon?" He replaced her hand on his sleeve.

"Evidently you are one of those odious creatures who think women shouldn't have political opinions!" she accused, still ruffled, but she fell into step beside him again. "I suppose you will call me a bluestocking now!"

"You are much too beautiful to be called anything so stupid as that," he replied soothingly. "Much too beautiful to argue with—too beautiful, in fact, for anything but dreaming of. Which I have done, very persistently, since the day I first saw you."

"They say dreams always go by opposites."

"I hope not. Because in my dreams you are always—kind to me."

Regina gave him a pleased and radiant smile.

"You know, for a schoolmaster you turn a very pretty compliment, Mr. Day!"

"Thank you. You are the first to say so. But then, you are the first to set me dreaming. My name, by the way, is Julian."

"Yes, I know. I was waiting for permission."

"That was unnecessary. Whatever you desire from me," he said, and laid his fingers on hers against his sleeve, "is already yours." And he added, with a long look down at her in the moonlight—"Even my name."

He saw the startled upward sweep of her lashes, and St. John's voice spoke just behind them.

"So it's *you*, Julian! I was about getting ready to call somebody out! This is our dance, Regina, the last before supper."

"Julian has been telling me I have no commonsense," she remarked as she accepted St. John's arm.

"Nothing of the kind!" Julian gasped. "I only said that the Governor could have handled a delicate situation better than he did, and I—"

"Oh, *that* again!" said St. John with a shrug. "When will you learn, Regina, not to mix politics with pleasure? Besides, you have been away in London too long to know what you are talking about out here."

"You needn't rap my knuckles before people, St. John," she told him coldly. "After all, we are not married yet!"

"Julian isn't people, goose, he is one of the family!" St. John laughed. "Are you going to dance with me before supper?"

They moved away together, both of them very handsome in the moonlight, Regina seeming to float like a swan in her hooped white tiffany gown, St. John erect as a flagpole except for the devoted bend of his head towards hers.

Julian stood and watched them go, with desolation in his heart. They weren't married yet, as she had reminded St. John. But they would be, and the sooner one got used to the idea, the better. St. John was her own kind, and they understood one another, and no matter how they quarrelled they always made it up and forgot about it—till the next time.

Remembering guiltily that it was his privilege to take Dorothea in to supper, he started back alone across the turf, and paused in the shadows beside where a square of light lay yellow on the ground outside a window of the ballroom. In the light, as on a stage, two small figures moved gravely—Kit and Tibby performing with childish grace the steps of the minuet he had taught her, to the music from within. At the *progression terminale* Julian stepped out behind them, and laying one hand on Kit's shoulder to move him aside while the other took Tibby's fingers from her brother's, he finished the measure in Kit's place, and his bow at the end was as deep and formal as any he had made to Regina Green-sleeves that evening.

Tibby rose from her curtsy with shining eyes, and Kit said, "There, Tibby, you got your wish! You wished on the star that you could dance with Mr. Day at a ball, and now you have done it!"

"Reckon it's about as near as I shall ever come to it," she said philo-sophically, and backed away into the shadows as though suddenly shy. "Come on, Kit, mother will be wondering where we are. Good night, sir—and thank you very much."

XIII

Julian had got as far as the Jamestown settlement in his history, and had long held the intention of visiting the site of the old town for a first-hand impression. It lay only six miles away on the bank of the River James. On a glorious hot morning that June of 1775, he borrowed a horse from St. John's stables and accompanied by the twins riding Crowsmeat took the road which led away to the left of the College, bound for a picnic among the ruins.

Tibby sang as she rode, for her heart was beating high. She had got the schoolmaster to herself for a whole day—Kit, her shadow, hardly counted as a third person. For Tibby it was always fair weather in Julian's company, and they had brought along a meal of bread and cheese and gingerbread and cherries. The doll had come too, travelling in its box under Tibby's arm.

They rode through the dense pine forest where the air was cool and fragrant, and emerged into a reedy marsh. Here the damp breeze itself seemed heated, with a stench of vegetable decay, and they were glad to reach the Back River ford and splash across it to Jamestown Island.

"You can see how unwholesome it would be," Julian pointed out. "But at the same time you can see why they chose to live here, in spite of Hakluyt's warning against swampy ground—it gave them some measure of natural defense against the Indians."

The streets of the burned-out town were a jungle of weeds and rank tobacco, cat briar, and vines, with now and then a patch of color from some long forgotten flower garden. The brick walls of the Ambler house seemed intact. The river had eaten away its banks till it washed the weed-grown mounds of brick where other houses once had been. The tide was low, and the remnants of the fort showed at the water's edge. Old sycamores shaded the broken church, whose brick tower still stood. They dismounted there, and walked about among the tipsy tombstones, and further along came upon the crumbling brick curb of a well.

"This is where they made the great experiment," said Julian, speaking as much to himself as to the children. "This is where they tried to live like the early Christians, without private property. The land they tilled was owned in common, and their crops were put into a common pool. It wasn't a success. They were all of them hungry most of the time, and the ones who had worked hard and faithfully were no better off and had no more to eat than the slothful ones who had done little to keep themselves, and so there was no incentive to industry. They quarrelled among themselves, and stole what was common property, and famine came, and disease, and pretty soon there were only sixty of them left, and all they wanted was to go back to England and forget the whole thing. But just then Lord De la Warre arrived as the new Governor, bringing new blood and supplies, and he persuaded them to try again, and abolished the community system, and it was every man for himself again, which is healthy and right and makes for generosity towards the unfortunate—which is a paradox—and the colony began to thrive."

The twins listened with the rapt attention they always bestowed on Julian's utterances. It gave them a feeling of awe anyway to be assisting however remotely at the birth of a book, and they never doubted that Julian's would be published between fine calf covers for them to read.

"Tell about the bride-ship," said Tibby, for it was a thing which had caught her imagination that a girl should sail across the ocean to marry some man she had never seen and live in a wilderness, and she heard the story over and over with renewed interest and the most searching questions. "But suppose one of them hadn't found *anybody* that she liked," she objected once, and Julian replied that one must of course assume that in that case she was permitted to live and die a spinster. "I wonder if one of them did," said Tibby, whose ideas about the sort of person one would want to marry were lately in very concrete form.

In the early afternoon they sat down in the grass above the pebbly shore, Julian with his back against a tree trunk and his notes on his knee, and Tibby opened the packet of food and spread it with house-wifely care on a white napkin. The doll, whose name oddly enough was Julia, was taken out of its box and allowed to look on. Tibby had made it a white apron from a bit of cambric and a calico capuchin dust-cloak which was laid aside on account of the heat.

"I'm so afraid she will spoil her dress," she sighed, propping Julia carefully against the box for fear of grass stains.

"She should have a summer morning-dress," said Julian, looking up from his papers. "We might buy her a length of dimity, if you think you could make one."

Tibby was sure she could make Julia a dimity sacque. Her mother would help her to cut it out. Julian promised to see to it.

"What was your mother like, sir?" Tibby inquired sociably over the bread and cheese.

"I never saw her. She was only seventeen when I was born, and she died. She was small, my father said, and had red hair."

"There is red in your hair too when the sun shines on it," Tibby in-formed him. "Round your ears, where it waves a bit. Mine is just brown and straight all the way. When were you in France, sir?"

"Mother said you were not to ask Mr. Day a lot of questions," Kit reminded her, and Tibby's hand went guiltily to her mouth as she re-membered the injunction.

"I was in France three times," said Julian, amused. "There is no secret about that."

"It wasn't because of secrets," Kit explained. "It's because she wonders about you all the time—like how old you are, and where you were when you were our age, and what happened when you were in France, and things like that—and mother says it is none of her business and she mustn't ask."

"Well," Julian began, rather flattered than not, and a little embar-rassed that he had been a hook on which to hang lessons in manners, "I am twenty-two, and at your age I was a scholar at Winchester, and the last time I was in France was in '71. The King has died since, and the Dauphin is King now."

"Tell about Paris," Tibby entreated.

It was a little difficult to describe the Paris of Louis XV to a pair of children from the chaste shores of Virginia. He told of pollarded willows along the Seine, of peach orchards in pink blossom at Passy, of primroses in the grass at Fontainebleau. . . .

The sun had swung over and now the midday stillness gave way to a whispering breeze that brought coolness. Kit fell asleep with his hat over his face. Tibby lay on her back in the grass beside Julian, her lips stained with cherries, her small brown arms locked behind her head, staring up at the leafy branches above her. The river murmured with the rising tide. Julian's mind was sorting out his new chapter, and she respected his silent preoccupation, content merely to be within reach of his hand.

At last he looked down at her and smiled. Her wide-set eyes looked green in the leaf-filtered light.

"Well, mousie," he said affectionately, "what were you thinking about?"

"I was wishing this day would never end."

"Yes, it's a good day," he agreed, and looked about him gratefully. "A day of peace and plenty. That is worth having, in these times. One doesn't like it to end." His eyes came back to her. "What have you learned lately? Isn't it about time I heard a new one?"

"Well, I found a piece in Matthew yesterday that I liked the sound of."

"What was that?" Her choice of pieces always interested him.

" 'Then shall the King say unto them on his right hand, Come ye blessed of my Father, inherit the Kingdom prepared for you from the foundation of the world; for I was an hungered, and ye gave me meat; I was thirsty, and ye gave me drink; I was a stranger, and ye took me in;—' "

Julian's hand came down hard on her shoulder.

"Stop it, Tibby—stop it! Who told you that I was going back to England?"

"N-nobody told me such a thing. It's not true!"

"I'm afraid it is. I thought you had chosen that text to shame me. I know that you have all been good to me here, and I owe Virginia a debt I can never repay. Since I can't repay it by joining in her fight against what she feels is tyranny—I have no choice but to go back to England as soon as possible."

"But schoolmasters are like clergymen!" she cried. "They don't have to take sides!"

"I can't stay here and be hated as a Tory by people I have grown fond of," he said obstinately.

There was a long silence, filled by the loud drone of a bee and the lap of water only a few yards from their feet. She had turned on her side away from him and he could not see her face.

"When—are you going?" she asked so that he hardly heard.

"As soon as I can arrange for your examination when Mr. Jefferson comes back from the Congress. Mr. Sprague says he will give a supper party in the Apollo Room that night. If things come out as I hope they will, you can start the Epiphany term at Mrs. Hallam's. Why, Tibby— are you crying?" He bent above her, leaning on his elbow in the grass. Her thin shoulder quivered under his hand, but she made no sound. "Child, you mustn't cry—you'll be happy at Mrs. Hallam's, it is what you've always wanted. I haven't had time to do all I meant to for you, but—Tibby, don't do that, you will be ill—!"

Kit woke with a start, and sat up.

"What is it?" he demanded with the false alertness of the newly wakened. "I must have been asleep. What happened to her? Tibby, why are you crying?"

Julian gathered her into his lap and sat with his back against the tree and his arms around her, trying to talk away her tears, trying to soothe her, trying to see her face. Her grief was silent and unchildlike and frightening. Her little body was tense and trembling in his hold. She seemed not to have grown much since he had first picked her up, outside the Raleigh, more than a year ago. Her bones were so small. . . . There was a nightmarish quality of repetition in the way Kit knelt beside her now, worrying at her inert shoulder with his hand, beseeching her to tell him what the trouble was, imploring her not to cry any more. . . .

"Be quiet, Kit," Julian said sharply. "Let her alone. Something came up about my going home to England soon, that's all. I thought she knew."

Kit lifted a shocked face.

"How *could* we know? Of *course* she is crying! We wouldn't know how to—how to get along without you now, sir!"

But she had to know some time, Julian thought helplessly—only he had meant to break it to her. Her uncanny prescience had tripped him up. Moreover, he was guiltily aware in his conscience that he had not told her the whole of his decision to go home. For the thought of Regina Greensleeves had become a fever in his blood, and the desire to see her again and again had destroyed his slumber and his peace of mind. He carried in an inner pocket her written invitation to visit Farthingale when the Spragues went for their annual stay at the plantation up the river later in the summer—when all day long, day after day, he could eat the lotus of her presence and involve himself always more hopelessly in what he knew was madness. And there were two reasons why that must not be. One was that he had nothing to offer her along with the marriage he foolishly dreamed of. The other was St. John Sprague, who had loved her first. So far, St. John did not suspect. But Julian knew that he could not sustain a house-party without betraying himself to them all. He was a Tory, yes, and it was becoming awkward with his friends. But he was leaving Virginia because he did not dare to see Regina Greensleeves again and again. . . .

"Tibby," he heard himself saying to the stricken child in his arms, "Tibby, don't, my darling, I can't bear it, I will stay in Virginia as long as you need me, do you hear? I promise, Tibby. I will stay in Virginia till I grow a long white beard, *now* will you stop crying?"

Her arm crept up around his neck. She curled herself closer against him, and relaxed with a long sigh, exhausted and content. He sat while shadows crept towards him, holding her and wondering. War or no war, Tory or Patriot, Regina or no Regina, he was a Virginian now.

Kit, who was always awed by Tibby's rare tears, lay down again and pulled his hat over his eyes to think things out. It did not seem possible that Mr. Day had changed his plans just to make Tibby stop crying, though it certainly sounded that way. He wondered what his mother would think, and supposed that this was one of the things he must not mention unless Tibby did. It was sometimes difficult to know, with Tibby, which things were not to be mentioned. But it was a safe guess that anything to do with Mr. Day was Tibby's exclusive property. . . . He drifted off to sleep again.

Tibby stirred in Julian's arms at last, and sat up. Her eyelids were heavy, her cheeks were streaked with tears, but she smiled confidingly into his face.

"You gave me *such* a fright," she said without reproach. "Were you joking all the time?"

"No. It wasn't a joke," he said, thinking how young she was, and how unconscious of power, to turn a man's whole destiny on a summer afternoon.

"But you promised to stay in Virginia," she insisted anxiously, and he nodded.

"Yes, child. It was a promise. I—changed my mind."

"Not just because I cried!" said Tibby, offering an absurdity with her unexpected humor, but he neglected to smile.

"Well, you see," he said slowly, his eyes on the small, vivid face with its honey tan, its finely-cut lips and wide-spaced, green-gray eyes, "nobody cried when I left England."

It was an explanation which had to satisfy himself as well as Tibby.

They rode homeward through the lengthening shadows, under the sycamores, across the marsh and the ford, into the tall pines where it was already twilight. At the edge of the town they passed a farm lad, driving in some cows.

"Have ye heard the news?" he hailed them excitedly, and Julian drew rein. "There's been a bloody great battle at a place called Bunker's Hill!"

XIV

On the day that Jefferson returned to Philadelphia from Williamsburg, Washington received his commission from Congress as Commander-in-Chief of the Continental forces, and set out for Cambridge. The news of Bunker Hill met him on the road. When he arrived at the headquarters of the American army, the British had removed their wounded into Boston and the militia had sat down outside, like terriers at a rat-hole.

Congress' choice brought forth some criticism even from Washington's own neighbors, partisans of men who, having seen active service on the frontier while Washington was farming at Mount Vernon, thought they could do better in the field than he. Some of his Tory friends regarded him as a traitor. His own mother, a steadfast Tory, said it would all end in the halter.

But with the appointment of a southern general, it was no longer just New England's war, and troops from Virginia and Maryland began to assemble. Volunteers were pouring into the recruiting camp behind the College at Williamsburg, where Patrick Henry with a new colonelcy made the grave social error of being seen among his men with his coat off.

Jefferson was back at Richmond for the Virginia Convention in July and August, and though he had illness and sorrow at Monticello he agreed good-naturedly to attend the supper at the Raleigh with Peyton and Edmund Randolph, George Mason, George Wythe, and a professor from the divinity school at the College—the evening which was to open the door of Mrs. Hallam's school to Tibby Mawes.

Pleading much to do in preparation with Tibby and little time, Julian had persuaded the Spragues to make the visit to Farthingale plantation without him, though Dorothea promised she would never in the world forgive him, and said Regina was sure to be furious. Regina, having discovered a young Marylander of strong Loyalist sentiments which matched her own, bore up very well, but Dorothea found him tiresome and nagged St. John into returning to Williamsburg two days before their time. Once there, she found it impossible to maintain any sort of grudge against Julian after all, and excused it by saying that she admired a sense of duty in a man, and found Julian's preoccupation with Tibby's welfare very touching.

It was a formidable group of gentlemen who accepted St. John's invitation that hot August night, to entertain themselves by an informal debate on the question of female learning and whether it was on the whole desirable; the evening to be topped off by a demonstration that it could be done, in the person of Julian's now famous infant bluestocking, Tibby Mawes. Jefferson alleged in his humorous husky drawl that even the barmaid, when appealed to, had said she would gladly learn her letters if Mr. Day was the one to teach them. And Jefferson's friend,

George Mason, had laid a frivolous bet with young Edmund Randolph that he could stump the little beggar in three minutes without recourse to her spelling book either. Mr. Wythe, overhearing, had come in against him with a guinea that said Tibby would face them all down and make them heartily ashamed of themselves.

"I would make it five," said St. John promptly, "only I never bet on a dead certainty."

Julian sat silent and a little apprehensive, while the chaff went round. They did not mean to be unkind, and indeed it was kindness itself that they had taken this evening out of their busy lives to hear a child, however remarkable, perform. He knew that it was partly St. John's hospitality he had to thank for that—and the Virginian's strong innate family sense and essential good will towards children, no matter whose —and also the Virginian's love of sport with an edge of gamble to it. For Tibby herself was gambling tonight—her chance of a decent, self-respecting future against the handicap of her birth. Placed under Mrs. Hallam's august wing at the recommendation of these genial, skeptical men, she could make a place for herself in the community far better than anything he could win for her without their aid. If she bungled it, or lost her head, he would have to start all over again. If they teased her, or frightened her, she might forget all she knew. Long before the end of the meal, he had begun to suffer vicarious stage-fright for her.

When the cloth was drawn and the fruit set out and the wine decanters were in motion and the air had begun to cloud with pipesmoke, Mr. Southall the inn-keeper opened the door and put his head in.

"The child is here, sir," he said to St. John Sprague, and there was a scraping of chairs as they made themselves more comfortable at angles round the long table.

Tibby paused on the threshold, looking small but self-possessed, with some books under her arm. She was dressed as usual in a limp calico gown to her ankles, and tonight her brief pigtails were tied with brave red bows. Her eyes went straight to Julian and rested on his face, awaiting his instructions.

"Come in, Tibby," he said quietly, and she advanced down the room towards his chair, walking well, with her back straight and her chin up.

"Don't be afraid of us, child," said Mr. Wythe. "We are entirely at your service."

"Good God, Mr. Day, it's not knee-high to a cricket!" exploded George Mason, who was one of those adults who seem to think that children cannot hear unless they are directly spoken to in a rather loud voice. "You don't ask us to believe that a scrap like that knows a Greek letter from a flyspot!"

It was Jefferson who rose politely from his chair and made her a little bow, and then introduced his confreres by name, one by one, around the table. To each of them Tibby made a grave curtsy, her eyes meeting theirs with childish dignity. George Mason, massive, swarthy, of a cynical humor, began to shake with indulgent laughter.

"How old are you anyway, missy?" he asked, with the general effect of having poked her in the ribs.

"I'm nearly eleven, sir."

"No!" he said in exaggerated surprise, and his bold dark eyes ran over her briefly. "You don't say! Come here, and let's have a look at you." When she approached his chair he uncrossed his legs and leaned towards her, took the books and laid them on the table, and then held her by one small brown wrist, deliberately testing her composure and her courage while the others looked on. "Eleven, eh! D'you get enough to eat at home?"

"Yes, sir. I have a twin. We're both small."

"Well, where is your twin tonight? Not so smart as you, eh?"

"Kit is a boy, sir. He is allowed to go to the school."

"Oh, so you wish you had been a boy too, eh?"

"No, sir."

"Not even in order to go to the school?"

"I think girls should have a chance to learn too, sir. Something besides cooking and sewing."

"You think, eh? Sure the schoolmaster didn't put it into your head?"

"It was the other way round, sir. I put it into his."

"Oho, so you teach the schoolmaster, is it! Bit young for that, aren't you?" He pinched her cheek, and she stood looking back at him clearly, without moving. "Well, what's your answer to that one, eh?" he queried, shaken again by his massive mirth.

"I'm not quite sure what you mean, sir."

"Bit young, I said, for the schoolmaster, aren't you?"

There was a taut second of silence. Now was the time for her to flinch, to hide her head, to burst into tears, to succumb in one way or another to the battery of embarrassment and confusion he had deliberately trained on her. And in repeating the question he had subtly altered its implication. Julian, engulfed in compassion at the other end of the table, restrained himself by main force from interference. She was too little—too inexperienced—too honest—he should never have tried it— it wasn't fair—he wanted to snatch her up and shield her from their bright, knowing eyes, their careless laughter, their heartless banter.

She stood, one cheek quite pink where Mason had pinched it, the other paler than before. It was impossible for any of them to tell by her face whether she followed the wilful intention of the query, though they all saw her chin come up a fraction higher, and the throbbing pulse in her throat was visible to them in the candlelight.

"But it is Mrs. Hallam's school, sir, and not Mr. Day's, that I want to enter," said Tibby.

There was a shout of laughter, Mason's loudest, and Tibby looked round the table gravely till she came to Julian, who wore a small tight smile. She knew without any doubt that they were aiming at him as well as at herself, and her protective instinct was up in arms. This was no matter just of Latin verbs and Wingate's Arithmetic. They were trying to make her disgrace Mr. Day. They were trying to show him that she was not as clever as he thought she was. They were trying, through her, to embarrass him. She would die first.

"George, I'll trouble you for that guinea which I have already won," said Mr. Wythe, and held out his hand across the table.

Still rumbling with merriment, Mason dropped Tibby's wrist and laid the money in Wythe's palm, and flipped another coin at the grinning Edmund Randolph.

"First round to the challenger," he said cheerfully. "And well worth the price!"

Jefferson's long fingers closed next on her arm and he drew her on down the table to face him where he sat sidewise in his chair, his elbow on the back of it. Peyton Randolph was next to him, his fine eyes shining with a very kindly amusement, his pipestem between his teeth.

"My turn now," said Jefferson and smiled disarmingly as she stood braced and ready for him, the racing pulse in her throat. "Tell me, child, in as few words as possible, why it seems important to you that women should be educated—besides cooking and sewing."

Tibby thought it over while they waited. But the atmosphere was subtly different now. Besides Jefferson's characteristic gentle ways, she felt an increased cordiality all round her, and in their expectant smiles encouragement lurked.

"A fallow field isn't much good to anybody, sir," she said. "You might as well plow it up and plant something there."

This time a murmur ran round the table, and Jefferson looked towards Julian, who shook his head.

"I never said it, so help me," he denied.

"I am beginning to doubt," said Jefferson to Tibby, "that Mrs. Hallam's is going to meet your requirements." He paused. "You don't ask me why," he said.

For the first time a smile touched Tibby's lips.

"I am not supposed to ask the questions, sir," she observed, and St. John winked at Julian above his glass.

"True," Jefferson nodded. "Well, for one thing, there is no Greek or Latin at Mrs. Hallam's, and very little mathematics, I should think. I am wondering exactly what you expect to learn there."

"Deportment, sir," said Tibby, and again Jefferson glanced towards Julian.

"It's a laconic child, isn't it!" he murmured admiringly.

"You asked for as few words as possible, Tom!" Peyton Randolph reminded him, with satisfaction.

"You want to learn to be a lady, is that it?" queried Mr. Wythe, who sat beyond Randolph, beckoning Tibby on to him as Jefferson relinquished her.

She stood a moment looking into the delicate, finely-drawn face. Mr. Wythe was already a legend in Williamsburg. Everybody loved him, everybody was proud to be recognized by him, everybody looked up to his learning and his wisdom. She was not afraid of Mr. Wythe, she was more enthralled at this near view of him, and the fact that he bent his friendly smile upon her. Ever so little, Tibby relaxed under his hand.

"You have to be born a lady, sir. But you can learn not to make mistakes, and how to do the right thing."

"God bless my soul!" exclaimed Mr. Wythe, impressed. "And what will you do then? Marry some lout and waste it all?"

"No, sir."

"Marry into the peerage, more likely, and serve 'im right!" said George Mason, who smarted still. "How about a duke, young un? Would that suit you?"

"I should have to go to England to do that, sir."

"Well, why not?" demanded Mason. "Wouldn't you like to live in London and wear a duchess's strawberry leaves in your hair?"

"I shouldn't like to go and live in England, sir."

"Why on earth not?"

Tibby considered warily. They were waiting.

"When you are born in a place like Virginia," she said, feeling her way among things she had never put into words before, "you belong to it, inside you. Especially now, when it's in trouble."

There was a silence. They looked at each other, instead of at her.

"George," said Mr. Wythe solemnly, "I rather think you owe me another guinea."

St. John Sprague spoke unexpectedly from where he sat at the end of the table next to Julian, and reached for the books Tibby had brought with her.

"When you gentlemen have quite finished your bear-baiting," he suggested with some sarcasm, "Mr. Day might be allowed to proceed according to plan."

"Must we listen to Latin verbs now?" asked Mason plaintively. "I'm satisfied. I'll vote her in."

"We may all be satisfied," said Jefferson, pouring himself another glass of wine. "But I, for one, am vastly entertained. I don't want to miss anything. Proceed, Mr. Day."

There was a general shifting of chairs and a lighting up of pipes which had gone out. Tibby fell back step by step to Julian's side, as he accepted the pile of books St. John handed on to him. For the first time she dared to take a quick glance around the Apollo Room. Her mother and Kit would want to know what it was like when she got home. Cherry-colored damask hangings framed all the windows from ceiling to floor. There was a handsome wainscoting which came half way up the white-washed walls. A harpsichord stood in one corner, with a cluster of music-racks round it—that was where they played for the dancing. The big fireplace, empty now for the summer, was at Mr. Sprague's back—there were some words carved over the mantelpiece—hard to see in the candle-light—*Hilaritas.* . . . *Bonae Vitae.* . . . Something about laughter and good living. It pleased her that she knew the meaning of Latin words now, if only she could see them clearly. Her eyes came back to the school-master. They might even ask her to translate what was written over the mantelpiece—

"Have you got money on me too?" she whispered.

"I am not a gambling man." He smiled at her anxious face.

"Will they laugh if I answer wrong?"

"Possibly. But in any case, I have had my laugh already."

Her gaze lingered doubtfully on his face, for she had not heard him laugh. It seemed to her that she had never heard him laugh aloud in her life.

"I have here," Julian was saying to the rest of them in a matter-of-fact classroom voice, as he took a folded paper from an inner pocket, "a list of questions. Tibby has not seen them. For that you must trust my own integrity." He glanced briefly round the table. "In order that there may be no question of my assisting her in any way, I would like some one else to read them off to her."

Mason held out his hand and Julian passed the paper to him. Mason adjusted his spectacles and scanned it carefully, Edmund Randolph leaning over his shoulder.

"Gad, this is pretty stiff!" commented Mason midway. "Half the time we ourselves won't be quite sure whether she's right or wrong, will we, eh?"

"In case there is any—doubt as to her answers, I have here—" Julian touched the books on the table before him as his glance flickered once more across their faces. "—the sources."

Mason cleared his throat portentously. The whole thing was still a parlor game to him, in which he joined indulgently to amuse the children.

"Well, hold tight, here we go," he said. "The first thing out of the bag, Tibby, is a passage from, I believe, a fellow named Virgil. Who was Virgil, do you know?"

"He was a Roman poet, sir, born in Cisalpine Gaul in 70 B. C."

"Mm," said Mason, who could not have produced the date himself. "Quite so. Good Lord, Mr. Day, you don't tell me the little witch can construe stuff like this by ear!"

"She has read it," said Julian. "She should recognize it again."

"*In freta dum fluvii current,*" Mason read out and looked at Tibby over his spectacles inquiringly.

"*While the rivers shall run to the ocean,*" she supplied at once, and added, "Perhaps that one is hardly fair, sir—I liked that bit so I learned it by heart, but Mr. Day didn't know I had."

"*Dum montibus umbrae lustrabunt convexa,*" Mason pursued inexorably, refusing to be deflected, and she capped it patiently—

"*While the shadows shall move in the mountain valleys—*"

So much for Virgil.

"And now," said Mason, warming to his work as they progressed, "you are next required by this paper I hold in my hand to render into Latin the following phrases. Such as—and a very good choice too, if I may say so—*On behalf of their country, their children, their altars, and their hearths,* and who said it, if you please?"

"*Pro patria, pro liberis, pro aria atque focis suis.* Sallust."

"And are we to understand, Mr. Day, that this child has *read* Sallust?"

"Excerpts," Julian explained. "I chose certain passages. I made a sort of bird's-eye Latin text-book for her."

"Took a bit of time, didn't it?"

"It was interesting," said Julian. "It would be interesting to prepare such a book of exercises for general use in the lower schools. So much of the original is beyond them."

"Interesting, no doubt, but very unorthodox, eh, Tom? Encourage them to skip, what? *I* always skipped," murmured Mason, but Jefferson's eyes as they rested on the new schoolmaster were speculative and friendly.

"A book of exercises," he repeated slowly. "The best, culled from the best, all in one volume. I don't know, it might catch their attention. I should like to see the selections she learned from, Mr. Day."

"Thank you, sir. It is a very incomplete compilation. If there had been more time at my disposal—"

"Still, it's a beginning," said Jefferson. "And certainly a departure. I should be interested."

With ever-increasing aplomb, Tibby took her hurdles one by one, and they came to the mathematics, and played the number game out of Wingate, which they could all do on their heads and which never failed to amuse them anyway; and they listened soberly to her conscientious explanation of the phenomenon—"If to the double of any number, a second number be added, the half of the sum must necessarily consist of the said first number and half the second, and therefore, if from the said half sum the first number be subtracted—" and so forth.

By now the whole table was agrin, and Julian saw that he had won. Or rather, Tibby had won. Each and every one of them would have taken her into the bosom of his family and held her there with the most lavish affection, if such a thing had been possible. It was only for their own delectation that they pursued his examination paper to its end, watching with covert glances of glee while she took a pen and paper and thereon reduced seven shillings sixpence to the decimal of a pound sterling, and divided a hundred and ninety-seven by five and a half, explaining that to do so you must double both your dividend and your divisor. They didn't want to miss anything now.

But they came at last, with regret, to the bottom of the page, and Julian said—

"Well, gentleman, that concludes the test I had prepared. There remains the matter of religious instruction, in which I have had no hand. But if you, sir—" He bowed to the divinity professor, a silent, pleasant-faced man with humorous gray eyes. "—if you care to put your own questions—?"

"Thank you," said the Church, and smiled benignly on Tibby, who returned the smile with something almost like confidence. "I have been thinking that at this point I should like to hear certain verses of the Fifty-seventh Psalm. Do you happen to know that one, my child?"

"I think so, sir."

"How does it go?"

" 'Be merciful unto me, O God, be merciful unto me—' "

"Quite. I see that you do know it. The fourth verse, if you please."

" 'My soul—' " Tibby began, and hesitated, and her eyes grew round.

"That's right," he smiled. "Go on."

" 'My soul is among lions,' " Tibby went on, and sent an uneasy glance at Julian, and thereafter kept her eyes fixed on the clergyman's face.

" 'And I lie even among them that are set on fire, even the sons of men, whose teeth are spears and arrows, and their tongue a sharp sword.' "

George Mason was heard to chuckle. The lid of Mr. Wythe's snuff-box clicked.

"And the sixth?" prompted the divine, and by his very gravity beneath twinkling eyes struck an answering spark in the wide green-gray gaze which met his.

" 'They have prepared a net for my steps,' " Tibby recited obediently. " 'My soul is bowed down; they have digged a pit before me, into the midst whereof they are fallen themselves.' "

"Thank you," said the clergyman, and glanced in gentle triumph round the shouting table. "Gentlemen, I am satisfied."

XV

Governor Dunmore had sent his family home to England at the end of June, and when autumn came he was established at a naval base at Portsmouth in Virginia, pillaging and burning and harrying along the coast with a flotilla of small boats. His force of marines and sailors was augmented by a rabble of renegade slaves and servants and a few fanatical Tories. The King could hardly have found a man better fitted to ruin his cause in the colonies.

Therefore when business took St. John to Charleston again, Aunt Anabel insisted that she was nervous without a man in the house, and that Julian must stay in Francis Street to protect them, with Dunmore behaving the way he was. St. John laughed at her sympathetically, but made Julian promise not to leave them alone in the house at night.

Many families were moving out of the coastal towns of Norfolk and Hampton and even Williamsburg, for what they considered greater safety in their up-river houses. But Mr. Greensleeves declared he was tired of false alarms and brought his family back to the capital for the winter, alleging that he would not allow his children to grow up uneducated heathens just because Dunmore was playing the fool. He had been unable to find a satisfactory tutor for the younger ones, and offered

Julian the post at Farthingale. Julian had declined as tactfully as possible, urging the prior claims of his other work. The life of a resident tutor in the river mansions was likely to be an easy one, but he had no wish to meet Regina daily as a hireling in her father's household, however much pleasure the sight of her gave him.

Her outspoken Loyalist tendencies, fostered by that year in London, would have made anyone but a woman, and a beautiful one, very unpopular, and they caused her father some vexation. But most of Williamsburg, who had known her all her wilful life, smiled at them as part of her English affectations which she would grow out of in time, along with riding side-saddle in a tailored mannish gown, and saying *eyether* in the German fashion. They formed an intimate bond between herself and Julian, which he found perilous and sometimes a little uncomfortable, for she rather threw it in St. John's face that she and Julian thought alike, whereas he, as a Patriot, was quite beyond the pale.

As the autumn went on, the constant mustering and drilling of colonial troops on the parade ground behind the College filled Williamsburg's wide streets with rough characters, and the noise of their practice firing at a target became a trial to the once quiet town. Julian began to take his guardianship of St. John's womenfolk more seriously, at least during St. John's absences.

They had given him the small family parlor at the back of the house down stairs for his own study, and shifted Aunt Anabel's favorite armchair and Dorothea's embroidery frame into the drawing-room, which they decided was an improvement anyway, as the harpsichord was already there. Aunt Anabel maintained that without a man in the house one would never know what to have for meals, and Dorothea remarked that without a man in the house there was no point in having meals. Julian said it was all very flattering to him, and didn't they know it was wicked to tell lies, and everyone was more than pleased with the arrangement.

St. John on his return endeavored once more to make it permanent.

"Mr. Wythe is all taken up with the Congress now and I'm likely to be in and out of town all the time," he said. "They need some one to fuss over, women get bored shut up together. What is your objection, man, to calling this house your home from now on?"

Julian hesitated.

"How will your friends feel about it," he inquired, "if you take a Tory to live under your very roof?"

"Oh, stuff!" said St. John. "My friends aren't as rabid as all that. Besides, it is none of their business."

"I'm not sure," said Julian. "Feeling is rising everywhere. You might come to find me—embarrassing."

"You have a right to your own opinion! I'll wager half my friends don't know how you feel anyway, so far as that goes. And while you are under my roof it's not their place to ask."

Julian gave him a straight look.

"You are doing it for my own protection, then," he said quietly.

"Nothing of the kind!" St. John denied it with heat. "Damn it, man, I happen to like you, no matter what your politics are! Aunt Anabel likes you, Dorothea likes you. You are one of us. If you leave now it will feel like a funeral in the house! Besides, that room over the school isn't fit for a dog to live in. It's too hot in the summer and too cold in the winter!"

"Your aunt went to a lot of trouble with it."

"Yes, and you almost died in it! Place gives me the shudders. Don't be a pigheaded ass, Julian!"

That seemed to settle it.

Julian paid Tibby's fee at the beginning of the autumn term with sensations which he supposed approached the paternal, and laid out more money on a new dress and hat and shoes. Her utter lack of a sense of inferiority or self-consciousness, all buried under her eagerness to learn, at once endeared her to Mrs. Hallam, and when Regina's little sister Lucinda, obeying orders from Regina, took Tibby under her wing, the other girls accepted her without snobbery. She was far ahead of them in French, far behind in music, dancing, and the other stylish female arts. But she was quick and observant and good-tempered, and it was soon the fashion to encourage Tibby rather than discountenance her.

So for an hour every Monday, Wednesday, and Friday, she went to school to Mr. Day after all, in Mrs. Hallam's French class, and felt just the least bit superior when some of the girls sighed romantically after the tall young schoolmaster, for Tibby knew him better than any of them.

On an evening in December Aunt Anabel's Jerusha tapped on the
door of the back parlor and put her head in.

"Mr. Day, suh? That Tibby child is here, says can she see you about
somethin' important?"

"Certainly, let her come in." Julian laid down his pen without re-
luctance.

Tibby's eyes were enormous and shining above her curtsy, and she
obviously held to her courage with both hands. She had come, she explained, to ask him to do her a favor, please, if he wasn't too busy.
Julian leaned back in his chair and drew her to him with an arm around
her waist and suggested that she tell him all about it.

At Christmas time, said Tibby, at Mrs. Hallam's school there were
exercises, and everybody's parents came and there was a collation after
the program. This year the dancing-master had arranged to bring his
pupils from a boy's school in Yorktown and they would all do a minuet
with an orchestra to play for them. Lucinda Greensleeves was going to
play a solo on the harpsichord, and another girl was going to sing, and
some of the little ones were going to recite. Julian at once inquired what
she herself was going to do, and Tibby wilted within the circle of his
arm. They had asked her to be in the minuet, she confessed, but it meant
a fancy dress which she hadn't got, and so—

"And so we must buy a new dress, is that it?"

"N-no, sir. I told them I couldn't do it."

"Oh, nonsense, Tibby, we can run to another dress for Christmas, I
think. Maybe a silk one, though it isn't supposed to be patriotic to wear
silk nowadays."

"Thank you, sir, but that wasn't what I came about. There is something I would rather have than the dress, if it isn't too much trouble."

"Well, say what it is, monkey, or have I got to guess?"

"Please, sir—the other girls have all got families to sit in the gold
chairs and look on. Would you come—just for a little while—as though
you were my family?"

Julian was touched.

"Well, but Tibby, surely your mother—"

"No, mother can't come there. She is right not to come, don't you see,
Mrs. Greensleeves will be there, and Mrs. Randolph, and people like that.

You see, they might not understand. But you, sir—everyone would be pleased if *you* came, being a man, and all. And anyway, without you *I* wouldn't be there, and so—"

"Well, if you think I won't be cast out for not being a bona fide parent, I'll come and gladly," he said at once, and Tibby gazed at him in delight. It was as easy as that, and she had nearly died of fright to ask him. "Isn't it lucky I have ordered a new suit of clothes," he was saying. "Otherwise I might disgrace you."

"Oh, sir— Oh, Mr. Day—I never thought you would really come—!"

"Well, why not?" he demanded. "All I need is to be told about these things, I can't see through a board. Look here, how would you like to invite the rest of them? Mr. Sprague's Aunt Anabel doesn't like Mrs. Greensleeves to get ahead of her, you know. Then you would have a real family, and we might all go down in the coach in style. Would you like that?" Tibby was speechless. He rose. "Let's go and ask them now," he said, and led the way to the drawing-room.

Aunt Anabel was knitting by the fire. St. John sat near her, in a fragrant cloud of tobacco smoke, with his feet on the fender and read a book. Dorothea was at the harpsichord, playing softly to herself.

"May we come in?" Julian asked from the doorway, and St. John rose at once with his friendly grace and greeted Tibby as though she was a lady grown, to her boundless pleasure.

Julian explained about the exercises, and how they were all invited as Tibby's guests for the evening, and they all accepted enthusiastically— St. John inquired gravely if she would like him to wear powder, and she replied as gravely that she didn't think it was as formal as that but she would ask Mrs. Hallam if he liked.

"Behave yourself, Sinjie. What about her clothes?" said Aunt Anabel, who always thought of everything. "She will want a new dress for the night, Julian."

"Yes, I was coming to that," he began, but Aunt Anabel was in charge. The dress was her gift, her Christmas gift to Tibby, and it would be made by her own dressmaker, and she would go in and see about it in the morning.

"Then—perhaps I could be in the minuet after all!" cried Tibby, and Aunt Anabel said Bless the child, of course she could, and listened to details with remarkable insight and sympathy, and then inquired minutely as to Tibby's preferences in color and material, while Dorothea played Boccherini softly at the harpsichord. "That is the one they are going to dance to!" cried Tibby, drawn to the music as if by a magnet. She stood at the end of the keyboard, watching Dorothea's slim fingers. "You play it beautifully. I can only do scales so far!" she sighed, and Dorothea laughed and ran scales lightly, comprehendingly, and slipped again into the minuet.

"I know!" she nodded. "I've been through all that! And then one day, all of a sudden, lo and behold, you can play! Like this."

"Sing something, Dolly," commanded Aunt Anabel from the fire. "There is no danger tonight of disturbing Julian."

"But there never is!" he said in surprise.

"She never will sing when you are working in your room," Aunt Anabel explained.

"But I should work all the better!" he assured them earnestly.

So Dorothea played *Low Down i' the Broom,* which was one of Miss Linley's songs, and sang it almost as well as the divine Elizabeth herself. Julian, who thirsted for music always, came and leaned his elbows on the harpsichord, watching Tibby's enchanted face.

Dorothea played without notes, because her lovely nearsighted eyes could not read them as far away as the music rack, which was what gave her that trick of lifting her face like a flower in order to see better. She did it now, looking up at Julian, so that Aunt Anabel put out a satin-shod foot and kicked St. John smartly on the shin, and nodded towards the group at the harpsichord, illumined by the candles in brackets at either end of the empty music rack.

St. John screwed round in his chair and saw them from a slightly different angle. St. John saw his sister's soft look fixed on Julian while she sang, saw that Julian watched Tibby, saw Tibby's eyes go from rapt contemplation of Dorothea to meet Julian's waiting gaze, saw the intimate smile they exchanged. And a chill doubt ran down St. John's spine. Dorothea and Julian, yes, he would never object to that, you couldn't but love the man. She would be safe with Julian, safe and cherished and protected. And yet—how old was Tibby? A child, of course. And yet—and yet. . . .

"Play *Drink to Me Only*—," St. John demanded when the music

paused, and he took up the air in his own clear tenor. "Come on, Julian
—*Or leave a kiss, withi-in the cu-up*—"

They all sang it heartily to the end, even Aunt Anabel, and then ap-
plauded themselves heartily too, and sang *Blacked-eyed Susan*, and
Tibby had never had such a good time in her life.

When at last she must tear herself away from the firelight and the
music and the loving laughter that made a home like this one, Julian said
it was very dark and he would walk along with her. They set off together
towards the cabin by the Landing, their footsteps crisp in the frosty air,
and Julian found her rather silent and inquired why.

"I was thinking how lovely she is," Tibby confessed with a sigh.
"And how she sang. It must be wonderful to be like that. Don't you
think she is beautiful?"

"Yes, I suppose she is," he said matter-of-factly, as though he had
never given it much thought.

"How old is she?"

"Well, let's see, she must be all of eighteen by now."

Tibby trudged on, deep in her own reflections.

"What is the matter with you?" he prodded at last. "Are you by any
chance breaking the tenth commandment?"

"Yes, I am. I covet her family."

Julian forebore the perversity of pointing out that Tibby had a family
of her own. He knew only too well what she meant, judging by what
the household in Francis Street had come to stand for in his own lonely
life.

"And I covet her beauty," Tibby went on fiercely beside him in the
dark. "And the way she can play and sing, and the lovely clothes she
wears, and—and the way she looks at you!"

"Now, whoa!" said Julian firmly. "That will do. I can't have anything
like that, do you hear?"

"Yes, sir."

"If you said that to anybody but me, it might be misunderstood, you
can see that."

"Yes, sir."

"That is the way false impressions sometimes get started, by some
one imagining something as harmless as that, and mentioning it to the
wrong person. Besides, she is very nearsighted and can't see beyond the

end of her poor little nose, so you can't really tell how she is looking at anything. About the last thing I expected from you is thoughtless envy of Miss Dorothea."

"I don't envy her now. I feel sorry for her."

"Well, I don't see that either," he objected severely as they reached the sagging wooden gate and the path edged with oyster shells which ran down to the cabin. "How can you be sorry for her?"

"Because you are not in love with her," said Tibby. "Good night, sir. Thank you for seeing me home."

She made him a curtsy and left him, surefooted in the darkness down the path.

XVI

Mr. Greensleeves was away in Philadelphia and Mrs. Greensleeves fell ill of a pleurisy two days before the Christmas exercises. Lucinda wept at the prospect of missing her opportunity to perform a solo on the harpsichord, to say nothing of missing the collation—so Aunt Anabel offered to chaperone both Lucinda and Regina that night. "It will be a bit of a squash with all our dresses in the coach," she remarked cheerfully. "The men will have to ride."

But St. John was detained in Richmond when the night came, and Julian was their sole escort.

The coach was sent round early for Tibby, and she arrived in Francis Street to find her adopted family awaiting her in the drawing-room. The new dress was a success. Aunt Anabel's dressmaker had fashioned it of pale green damask over a buff quilt, with short *panniers* looped high towards the back. The neck had a white lace fichu and there was deep lace at the elbows. Green damask shoes went with it, and little green bows for Tibby's hair. She made them a curtsy on the threshold, and Aunt Anabel rustled forward to kiss her on both cheeks, and Dorothea made her turn round twice, bestowing sisterly pats and tweaks here and there, and an affectionate spank behind.

And then Julian advanced—looking very splendid in his new wine-colored broadcloth, with a formal black *solitaire* cravat above a froth of Mechlin, and a swinging triple-caped riding-cloak that nearly touched the floor and was lined with white silk—advanced to present her with a small painted fan which had carved ivory sticks and a tassel. Outside, he handed her into the coach with as much ceremony and care as he lavished on Aunt Anabel. All the way to the Greensleeves house, sitting with her back to the horses, she could watch him through the window where he rode beside the coach. He owned his own horse now —a dainty bay mare who lived in St. John's stables and had cost more than a schoolmaster could afford.

When they came to the Greensleeves house in England Street, Julian dismounted and went inside to fetch the two girls. Regina was coming down the broad staircase as he entered the hall, which was bright with candlelight. Her hair, nearly as pale as though she wore powder, was dressed high with a smooth curl on her neck. Her intricate gown was of creamy brocade draped over a high hoop. The bodice was cut square in front, with a ruching and a jewelled breast-knot. Filmy lace fell free from her elbows to the diamonds on her wrists, and diamonds lay around her white throat.

He stood waiting at the bottom of the steps, his hat in his hand, the lining of the cloak framing his slim height to his heels, and it crossed Regina's mind not for the first time that he was the most striking young man in Williamsburg, and that they went rather well together. Her blue eyes approved and encouraged him as she gave him her hand to kiss.

"You look very solemn this evening," she remarked when he raised his head from her fingers. "Shall we be everlastingly bored, do you think? Lucinda is quite beside herself with excitement, and I sent her on ahead ten minutes ago with one of the maids, just to be rid of her!"

Julian said it was a great occasion for everybody concerned, and inquired politely after her mother.

Regina paused to look up at him in the hall, while the Negro butler laid a white velvet capuchin around her shoulders and opened the door.

"Some time," she said, "you will fail to say exactly the right thing to me, and then I shall know that you are human, after all. Provided, of course, that you are!"

Julian winced visibly.

"I don't see what I have done to deserve that," he objected, but she picked up her hoop and swept past him through the door without replying.

He wondered as he followed her to the coach if he should have stammered out something banal about her beauty as she descended the stairs. He wondered if she guessed the rapturous agony the sight of her always produced in him and had perhaps determined that he should so far forget himself as to show it—or if she thought him the dull, inarticulate clod he seemed to appear. He wondered what would happen between them if ever just once he said the things he was not entitled to say and set his lips to hers as he had done in his dreams. The question then would be, how human was Regina?

They settled themselves on the frail gilt chairs in Mrs. Hallam's drawing-room and the program began. Some of it was pretty embarrassing, and some of it, like the minuet, was delightful. Regina, on his left hand, smiled up at him ruefully as the children circled and dipped and pointed their toes with exquisite gravity.

"It all makes me feel very matronly," she complained. "How many little darlings have *you?*"

"I am just the bachelor uncle," he smiled back, and caught himself thinking that Regina's child might look very like Lucinda, even if its father's hair was dark. . . .

On his right hand, Dorothea tilted her flower face towards his profile because she could not see as far as the dance floor, and allowed her mind to wander. If Tibby were really his child, his and hers, this is what it would be like. . . .

Beyond Dorothea Aunt Anabel sat wishing that St. John could have been there—first because he would have enjoyed the children, and mostly because Regina was flirting outrageously with Julian and only St. John could put a stop to that. Everyone knew that Regina would marry St. John some day when she had had her fling. Everyone except perhaps Julian. . . .

Later, when the company stood about in talkative groups with plates of scalloped oysters and cups of chocolate and punch, and Aunt Anabel had explained over and over again where St. John was, she found Tibby at her side and asked her with a smothered yawn if she wasn't ready to go home now. Tibby said she was, and Aunt Anabel glanced at her sharply, for all the sparkle had left the child, and she stood quietly among her elders with an air of patient waiting.

"Now, you haven't gone and eaten something that disagreed with you?" she entreated, setting down her cup.

"No, ma'am."

"Have you got a headache, then?"

"No, ma'am."

"Well, what is it, child, haven't you had a good time?"

"Yes, thank you," said Tibby politely.

"It is getting late. We must go now, before you fall asleep on your feet." Aunt Anabel looked about efficiently for her family. "There is Dorothea, with the Randolphs. Where are the others?" Tibby was silent in an unhappy sort of way, and Aunt Anabel gave her another searching glance. "Tibby, do you know where the others are?"

"Miss Regina wanted to see where Mr. Day taught us French. So he is showing her the schoolroom."

"But good gracious me, there is no one in the schoolroom at this time of night!" Aunt Anabel rustled towards the hall, across which lay the closed, deserted room where lessons were said each day. Tibby followed at a reluctant distance.

Regina had surrendered to a perverse impulse to get Julian to herself for a few minutes. His impervious good manners, belying with every breath he drew the ardor of his honest eyes, challenged and exasperated her. He had never learned the London fashion of easy flirtation, the lingering kiss which fell not on the fingers but in the palm, the lightly uttered impudent word which brought hot blood to a woman's cheeks, the ruthless pursuit of a chosen quarry which lent zest and sometimes a thrill of actual fear to the life of a reigning belle. He was altogether too respectful to suit Regina, now that she had been to Bath and Ranelagh, and had had a duel fought over her good name, which of course was thereby handsomely vindicated when the right man walked off the field unscathed. Nor had he St. John's headlong masterful ways which made of her sudden assumed submission after a wordy quarrel an amusing game.

Regina was spoilt, there was no denying. She meant to marry St. John when she got round to it, but she could not for her pride's sake allow his conquest to look too easy. Meanwhile the world was full of charming men, none of whom had the level, worshiping gaze and self-contained humility of Julian Day. She had, in fact, never known anyone else quite like Julian Day, which in itself was dangerous. She had set herself wilfully to shake his composure or perish in the attempt.

They found the schoolroom dark and empty, stripped of its chairs and musical instruments for the program in the drawing-room, its books and work-baskets in temporary disarray. It was chilly too, for the fire had been allowed to go out. The candelabra in Julian's hand made a patch of light which wavered in the draught from the hall, and the door swung shut behind him with a click, under Regina's hand.

"What a dismal place!" she said, and shivered.

"It's not quite itself tonight, as I warned you." He stood holding the candles until it should be her pleasure to return to the party in the other room. "Why don't you come some time when we are in session and hear us recite? Tibby's French is really remarkable."

"You know, I think I am a little envious of Tibby."

"Of Tibby?" He was lost.

"She has found the way to your heart."

"Well, that's—not difficult to do, is it?"

"Isn't it?"

She came to stand before him, looking up, all cream and crystal in the light from the candles he held. The brass candelabra was heavy, and he moved to set it on the desk, and she moved with him so that when his hands were free she still stood within his reach. The light shone upward on her now, into her eyes, catching her round chin and the delicate lines of her parted lips.

"You have very little mercy, Regina," he said gravely. "When I have counted ten, we had better go back."

"And in the meantime—?" she whispered, looking up.

His hands closed hard on her shoulders, but his height still kept his mouth from hers.

"Are you going to marry St. John?" he asked, very low.

"Well, Julian, *really*—!"

"Because if you are, what do you want with me? And if you aren't—"
The words caught in his throat.

"If I am not—?"

"I think it is time you told him so," he said.

"But I have never told him that I would," she whispered, and just then the knob turned under Aunt Anabel's hand.

Julian stepped back quickly, picking up the candelabra as the door opened. They were not directly in front of it. It was possible to hope that he had moved in time.

"Regina? Come, my dear, it is time to go home," said Aunt Anabel crisply, and stood on the threshold waiting until Regina had passed her through the doorway; then, lifting her hoop, Aunt Anabel turned her back on Julian and shooed her charges towards the cloakroom. Of course, if he had been holding a five-branched candelabra the whole time. . . .

When the coach stopped again in England Street and Julian escorted Regina to her door and they waited for it to be opened to them—

"I'm afraid we are in disgrace," she said confidentially, raising her face to his. The cold moon rode high, and the shadows of the portico were black around them. She stood so near he could see her breathe, and he felt her hoop against his side. Her eyes were shining, her teeth showed white between her smiling lips. "I should not have asked to see the schoolroom," she confessed.

"It seemed a harmless enough request at the time," he said briefly.

"To anyone who knows you as well as I do!" she laughed, her face upturned to his. The hoop pressed his side.

"Some day," he whispered, "I shall forget to count ten, Regina."

"By then I shall be too old to care, no doubt!"

The rattle of the chain inside the door startled them both, and they drew apart as the widening shaft of light from within fell between them. He bent formally over her hand. The door closed behind her. He was in the saddle again, an angry singing in his ears. She had no right to laugh at him because he had tried to remember St. John, among other things.

Then it was Tibby's turn to be escorted to her door, down the narrow path which led to the cabin.

"Well, Tibby, we were all proud of you. I hope that next time you need an extra family you will let me know," he said affectionately.

"Thank you, sir. It was very kind of you all to come."

She sounded tired and deflated. He looked down at the straight little figure beside him, and with a rush of tenderness remembered Cinderella and the ball.

"The fun isn't all over yet, you know," he said gently. "For you it is just beginning. I shall see to that." His cloak swept the path as he bent and kissed her cheek. "Good night, sweetheart."

He was gone, tall in the moonlight, his step so light it died away at once.

Dorothea, who could not see beyond the end of her nose and was spared a great deal as a consequence, had enjoyed herself at the party and was still all achatter when they entered the hall in Francis Street.

"Sinjie would have loved the tot who tried to say the Seven Ages of Man," she chuckled. "She couldn't have been more than four, could she, and she said 'snatchel,' did you hear? It was a silly thing to set a child to learn, anyway. Our Tibby is amazing, she carried the whole thing off to the manner born, while we're quoting Shakespeare! Julian, you *are* proud of Tibby, aren't you?"

"I am, very."

"It must be such a satisfaction to you, after all you have done for her, to see her learn so fast. And I'm proud of *you,* too, for being so kind."

"Well, thank you, but I only—"

"You only took trouble with her," she said warmly, and laid her hand on his sleeve as she passed him towards the stairs. "And I do think it is good of you, Julian, that's all. Good night."

"Good night, Julian," said Aunt Anabel, following her niece, and the look she gave him over her shoulder was not quite as fond as usual. "I'm sure Tibby was a credit to us all. Will you see to the drawing-room fire, please, before you come up?"

The drawing-room was cold, but Julian stood quite a while with his elbows on the mantel-piece staring down into the embers. She had no right to laugh at him, because he tried to keep his head. Or was it possible, by some miracle, that she didn't intend to marry St. John anyway? Even if she didn't, there was no miracle to change his own meager prospects into a suitable future for them both. He felt again the pressure of her hoop against his side. . . .

But it was Tibby, sliding into innocent sleep under the eaves of the cabin by the Landing, who had his kiss.

XVII

St. John was still in Richmond when the news arrived there of the fight at Great Bridge near Norfolk, which drove Dunmore off to a British warship in the harbor and restored Virginia's largest commercial center to the possession of the militia. The first Virginia blood was spilt at Great Bridge, but the British losses were said to be much heavier, and their commander was killed. Once again as at Lexington the colonists had won a small victory. And in view of passing events the grandiose colonial proclamations referring to the need of an army "to defend women and children from the butchering hands of an inhuman soldiery" seemed to Julian just slightly ridiculous. The soldiery, after all, consisted of very manifest Englishmen, not sanguinary naked savages.

St. John's Richmond client had possessions in Norfolk on which he desired a reliable report, and so with a sigh St. John set off on a ride southward which would keep him from home over Christmas. It also brought him to Norfolk in time for the New Year's Day bombardment, when Dunmore's ships set fire to the town by shells from the harbor— a three days' conflagration which left four-fifths of the city in ashes, and many of its wealthiest inhabitants without shelter in midwinter. Some people said it was a blessing in disguise, having at the same time smoked out a nest of Tories. There was even a report that the inhabitants had let it burn, to destroy a possible headquarters for future operations by Dunmore. But in any case, the talk of Independence increased materially thereafter in Virginia.

St. John saved his horse but nothing else, and arrived home late in January in a quiet rage, to be wept over by Aunt Anabel and Dorothea because he was safe after all, when they had somehow convinced themselves that he had been instantly killed by the first shot. St. John had now seen war at first hand, and it seemed to him both hideous and infuriating. He began to talk darkly of offering himself as a gentleman volunteer or a cadet, serving without pay on the chance of a commission—a prospect which left Dorothea white-faced and silent, and reduced Aunt Anabel again to tears.

Tragic John Randolph had slipped away to England with his wife and daughters, as Mr. Wythe had prophesied, while his son Edmund remained behind to join Washington's military family at Cambridge. From there he wrote St. John what Aunt Anabel called unsettling letters, since they encouraged St. John in his belief that he too had a call to enter the army.

Washington was established in a convenient house near Harvard, Edmund wrote, and the militia (now known as the troops of the United Provinces of North America) were encamped in the town and in the College buildings and *à la belle étoile,* so that Cambridge had rather the look of a county fair. Washington was wearing an official blue and buff uniform now, with rich epaulets and sword-knot, a light blue ribbon, and a black cockade. Owing to a general lack of regulation clothing, his officers had all resorted to colored ribbons worn slantwise across the breast between the coat and waistcoat—pink for major- and brigadier-generals, green for the aides, pink cockades for the field officers, yellow for captains, and so forth. Some of the men in the ranks, sick of shabbiness amounting to near nakedness, deserted to the British, were outfitted with pretty red coats and white breeches, and deserted back again, which then caused some confusion more or less amiably borne. Washington was known to favor the hunting-shirt costume he had worn in his youth in the Indian wars, as being both durable and inconspicuous, for the rank and file. A new flag had been raised at headquarters—a rattlesnake with thirteen rattles, and the arm and clenched hand of a man holding thirteen arrows.

The hardest task of all before the American Commander-in-Chief, according to Edmund, seemed to be to collect sufficient powder and ball for his army. Most of the men possessed about nine cartridges apiece, whereas the British regulars carried sixty rounds each. An appeal was sent out to Patriots to donate every ounce of pewter and lead—even clock-weights and those from window-sashes were gratefully received, along with eavespouts and tableware. There was talk of issuing pikes in a desperate effort to cope with the deadly British bayonet.

The British in Boston cannonaded the Cambridge camp almost every day, with trifling result. The balls sometimes passed clean through a house, filling it with plaster dust which choked its cursing occupants, and the grenades rolled harmlessly along the grass while the colonists chased them and pulled out the fuses with derisive laughter. Riflemen and gentlemen volunteers were coming in from Virginia and Pennsylvania via Reading, where they were issued knapsacks, blankets, and ammunition. A man who brought along his own horse or gun was a minor hero.

Late in March the Williamsburg churchbell rang and the Raleigh buzzed with excitement and everybody stood everybody else drinks, because Washington had taken Boston away from Howe. It sounded better that way than to say that Howe had evacuated Boston for Halifax by sea, taking his army with him and all the Loyalist population which could find water transport to accompany him. Washington hadn't exactly won a battle, maybe, but it came to the same thing, didn't it?— he had occupied Dorchester Heights and fired shells into Boston till it got too hot for Howe, hadn't he?—and of course while he hadn't marched in until after Howe's ships were slipping down the Bay, still he was in Boston, wasn't he, and what more did you want, after all?

Then Edmund wrote of a rumor that the King was negotiating among the German princelings for mercenaries in an effort to eke out his overseas forces, and St. John said that if the King were sufficiently crazy to send a pack of paid Hanoverian swine against his own people, he, St. John, would personally go and shoot a few of them just for luck—at which Aunt Anabel cried out in despair that she wished Edmund Randolph would keep his stupid firebrand letters to himself. But Julian, sitting silent and unhappy in the family circle, had to acknowledge in his own troubled mind that the German troops were after all much more the King's own people than the rebellious colonists, and that in the King's possibly unbalanced point of view it was an entirely logical move; which did not, of course, cancel out the logical reaction in America. He felt that if St. John went away to the army, his own position in the community deteriorated, no matter what Aunt Anabel or Regina Greensleeves might say, and in spite of the schoolmaster's traditional exemption from politics.

The Virginia Convention met at Williamsburg in May, led by George Mason and Patrick Henry—Jefferson was at the Congress in Philadelphia—and passed a unanimous vote: "*Resolved:* that the delegates appointed to represent this colony in general Congress be instructed to propose to that respectable body to declare the United Colonies free and

Independent states, absolved from all allegiance to, or dependence upon, the Crown or Parliament of Great Britain. . . ."

That evening Williamsburg made carnival, all the bells were rung, guns were fired, and the British flag was hauled down from the cupola of the Capitol and the new rattlesnake flag of the United Provinces was run up in its place, to the acclaim of a delirious citizenry. Independence. Revolution. For Julian Day, the end of a world.

He stood alone in the swirling crowd before the Capitol, with the bells loud in his ears, feeling sick. *Dies irae—blow the trumpet in Zion —and the sun and the moon shall be darkened, and the stars withdraw their shining*—this day's work would bring war indeed—civil war, which is always more terrible than when whole nations go out to fight each other. . . .

A hand was laid on his shoulder and he turned blindly to find St. John at his side.

"By God, we have done it!" St. John cried, almost inaudible in the din, and his eyes were clear and fierce like an angry child's. "By God, we can't look back now! The other colonies are bound to fall into line! It's Independence, man! We have damn' well got to win now!"

Independence. Just two years ago at the Raleigh, the night he arrived in America, Julian had first heard that word, on Patrick Henry's tongue. Two years. He had thought then of getting away before it happened. He had never wanted to stay and see it happen, any more than he would have wanted to witness a hanging. Then he was a stranger without ties and sympathies. Still less now, did he wish to be present at Virginia's doom. But things were different now. Now he could not turn his back on the holocaust to come. He had made his decision last summer on the riverbank at Jamestown. These people, reckless, headlong, defenseless, were his people. His life was here, his work was here—for presumably education must be kept alive even during a war.

"Does this mean you will join the army?" he heard himself asking, and saw St. John's face cloud over.

"You know how women are," he said. "Aunt Anabel hasn't been well. I have said very little so far, but—I must talk them round, perhaps now they will be able to see—"

There was a scuffle in the crowd and the twins appeared, dusty and panting, from among people's legs.

"Here he is!" cried Kit, and they fell upon Julian and clung to his hands, looking up at him with eyes full of faith and confidence.

"Oh, Mr. Day, isn't it exciting! Does this mean we are a country like France or Spain? Who will be King of America, sir?"

Their voices overlapped so that it was impossible to tell which was speaking. St. John laughed aloud.

"There won't be a king in America, that is the whole idea!" he said.

"No king?" They stared at him. "But then who will rule?"

"Ah," said Julian, and caught St. John's eyes. "That is the question— one of them!"

"Why, Congress, of course," said St. John promptly.

"Mr. *Jefferson?*" Tibby's eyes grew round, for Mr. Jefferson was just like anybody. One could almost say she *knew* Mr. Jefferson.

"And Mr. Randolph," said St. John hastily. "And Mr. Wythe. All the delegates from all the colonies together."

"But there can only be one king at a time!" insisted Kit.

"There isn't going to be *any* king!" St. John reminded him with impatience. "For the Lord's sake, Julian, have you never implanted in their infant minds any conception of constitutional government?"

"I am not allowed to teach modern history," said Julian with an odd smile. "Nor modern languages. You might take it up with the board!"

In June Virginia elected Patrick Henry as its first governor under the new régime, and he was at once invited to give up his military command and establish his residence in the Palace—which seemed to some a slight incongruity.

At about the same time that the Declaration of Independence was passed by the Third Continental Congress at Philadelphia in July, the British generals Cornwallis and Clinton joined forces off the coast of Carolina and bore down by sea on Charleston, where Colonel Moultrie had thrown up a palmetto fort on Sullivan's Island. Most incredibly, the British were driven off at Charleston with heavy losses, and were last seen headed northward—presumably for the comforting vicinity of Howe, who had left Halifax during the summer and established himself on Staten Island off New York harbor.

It was a brilliant and decisive victory for the colonial forces at Charleston. The south had been preserved from the invader, and everyone's spirits soared, and Williamsburg drew its first long breath in days.

They were not to have any more good news from the field for a long time.

XVIII

It was not pleasant hearing in August that Hessian troops had been landed on Staten Island and presumably would soon be used against Washington's fortified positions at Brooklyn Heights and New York. St. John and his womenfolk had gone for their usual summer visit to Farthingale, which had been the major part of his Virginia inheritance. In settlement of his uncle's debts he had sold it to the Greensleeves family, old friends of Aunt Anabel's, who urged her to regard the place still as her home, and received her young nephew from England on the same terms. Julian sat down with a heavy heart to report to St. John by letter. This Hessian intrusion would be the last straw; it seemed to Julian that now, unless a miracle happened, the colonists were done.

With German man-power to draw on, the King was going to win his war. And that meant ruin for America, and disaster for the brave men who had staked everything on their belief that man was born with the right to mismanage his own affairs as he saw fit, and—quaint, endearing phrase—to pursue happiness. Only a people piteously young and strong under God could incorporate in the solemn declaration of its wrongs, its principles, and its intentions, its determination to be happy too.

If the colonists were beaten now there would be anything but happiness for Jefferson, who had written out that amazing document which Wythe and the Lees and Nelson, the Adamses and Franklin and the rest, had all signed at Philadelphia; that cool indictment of the sovereign which had shaken Julian more than anything which had occurred so far.

If the King won, and it seemed as though he was bound to, the signers of the Declaration would all be sent to England for trial, and it was doubtful if any of them would ever see his native shore again. George III with his narrow, belligerent, pompous personal conceit would exact a heavy toll for what could only seem to him unsurpassed impudence. And Washington? It was within the King's royal prerogative to hang

Washington, and Greene, and Putnam—officers who had organized and drilled and led into battle a ragged, unseasoned army of Patriots who could only face the British regulars from behind trees and walls and inadequate earthworks. As for St. John—if he became one of those officers in the American army now, and it lost the war, the least that could happen to him was confiscation of his property, if he escaped capture and a brutal imprisonment.

Julian sat a long time over a half-filled page. At last he folded and sealed it with a sigh, and took it down to the *Gazette* printing-office to find the post-rider for Richmond, along whose route Farthingale lay.

Aunt Anabel, all smiles, brought the letter to St. John in the airy drawing-room which overlooked a lawn shaded by tulip trees and fragrant with summer blossom above the river's broad bosom. Regina sat by an open window with the breeze stirring the lace at her neck and elbows, a piece of embroidery in her hands—St. John was astride a chair near by, his chin resting on his clasped hands on the back of it while he teased her for being too bone-lazy to set foot in the garden with him, and David Allen, the Loyalist Marylander who found such favor in Regina's eyes, watched them moodily from the window-seat. At the other end of the long room, Dorothea's fingers whispered on the harpsichord keys.

"Guess what I have brought you!" cried Aunt Anabel, waving it at them, and they guessed instantly that it was a letter from Julian, for she loved the bits of gossip he always inserted for her special benefit. "It seems a very short one," she remarked wistfully as she surrendered it to St. John's outstretched hand.

"You needn't all pretend to look the other way," he said as he broke the seal. "I know I'll have to read it to you!"

But he didn't read it to them. He read it swiftly to himself, while they watched him with a growing uneasiness. Then he folded it shut again, and rose from his chair without looking at them, and turned away, down the room.

"Sinjie, is it bad news?" gasped Aunt Anabel, thinking of fire and fever and sudden death.

He told them what it was, briefly, looking rather green around the mouth. "And that settles it," he added, through his teeth. "From now on, this is my war!"

Regina, whose obstinate Tory bias might have been considerably lessened by this introduction of foreign mercenaries into what was after all a purely family quarrel, took fright at the disproportionate fury in his face and spoke sharply herself.

"What do you mean, St. John? What are you going to do?"

The harpsichord was silent now, for Dorothea knew only too well what he would do. Aunt Anabel gripped a chair-back and prayed one of her private, hysterical prayers to a benevolent personal God—*Don't let him—oh, dear God, don't let him say whatever he is going to say—!*

"I am going back to Williamsburg at once to find out how I can be of most use," said St. John more calmly. Too calmly. "If Virginia has enough officers, or if there is going to be a delay about commissions, I shall go straight to Washington at New York and offer to ride express —copy dispatches—carry a musket—dig earthworks like a nigger— empty slops—what in hell does it matter what I do, so long as I am *in* it, and not sitting round on my backside talking about it!"

"There is no need to be vulgar, St. John," said Regina coldly, for there was terror in her heart now lest he be killed, as well as anger at his lust for this unseemly war.

"I feel vulgar!" he snapped. "I have left it too long as it is. Too many other people are going to get a shot at those meddlesome German bastards before I do!"

"Sinjie!" murmured Aunt Anabel feebly, with a glance at Dorothea.

"I'm sorry. I apologize for my language," he said briefly, and David Allen rose with lazy grace from the window-seat, feeling that at last the Lord had delivered St. John Sprague into his hand.

"I quite agree that we have left it too long," he said in his insolent drawl. "Personally, I shan't waste time waiting for the King's com- mission now, I shall just get into one of the Loyalist regiments as soon as possible."

"Why, you damned, impertinent, interfering young blackguard," said St. John softly, and they stood very still, looking into each other's eyes across the room.

"I consider that provocation, sir," said David through quivering lips. "My friends will call upon you tomorrow to arrange a meeting."

"Boys, boys, that is quite enough of that!" said Aunt Anabel with unexpected authority. "There is bloodshed enough in the world without adding a nonsensical duel. You are not to fight him, Sinjie, do you hear?"

"It will have to be now or not at all," said St. John to David, as though she had not spoken, "because after today I shan't have time for sport."

Neither man was armed. David made a formal bow. He was younger than St. John, with a longer reach, and he had been schooled in France, whereas St. John's solid London training was enlivened by a personal flair for sword fighting which had given Julian plenty to think about in their friendly practice bouts in the garden in Francis Street.

"My sword is in my room," said David. "I will meet you on the lawn by the river in five minutes' time."

"If you do," said Regina calmly above her embroidery, "you need never come here again—either of you."

David paused on one foot on his way to the door, his fine manly impetus all gone awry.

"But surely you would not have me tolerate an insult!" he pleaded.

"But surely," said St. John softly to Regina, and his smile showed his teeth but did not reach his strange, brilliant eyes, "you will allow your guests to amuse themselves in their own quiet way?"

"I would have you both behave like sensible people," she told them, and threaded her needle with a steady hand. "And I really must refuse, St. John, to have my lawn turned into another battlefield. You will doubtless have ample opportunity to settle it elsewhere before the war is over."

David glanced uncertainly at St. John, who still wore that chilly smile.

"If you are prepared to waive the privilege of this house for the privilege of being run through on the lawn, I am prepared to accommodate you within the next five minutes," St. John told him. "Though I confess that the pleasure would be for me inadequate compensation."

"Perhaps as Regina says we shall find a more opportune time and place," said David, and added picturesquely, "We shall meet again at Philippi!"

"Very well, then—until Philippi," St. John agreed with a perfunctory bow, and turned to his hostess. "Regina, will you do me the favor to ask them to bring my horse around at once, I am leaving for Williamsburg."

"Don't trouble to ring, dear, I'll—tell them myself, and see to the saddle-bags. Come, David," said Aunt Anabel firmly, and though she failed to catch Dorothea's eyes she left the room with her hand hooked through David's unresisting elbow.

Dorothea still sat limply at the harpsichord, her fingers resting on the keys. The silence of the room drew taut around her, and neither of the other two would be the first to break it.

"Aren't we to go home with you?" she asked quietly.

"No. It would be too much of a scramble. I will send back word as soon as I know, and you can travel down comfortably with Joshua."

"That might be too late," she said, not looking at him, her voice under careful control. "Too late, I mean, for us to see you again before you start north."

He went to her with compassion, lifted her passive hands from the keyboard, and found them cold in his.

"Child, I'm sorry it had to come upon you like this. But you knew very well it was bound to come, didn't you."

She nodded speechlessly, unable to raise her brimming eyes above their clasped hands.

"I shall be perfectly safe, you are not to think about that part of it at all," he told her. "If I see a cannon ball coming I shall get behind Washington, nothing ever hits him, you know!"

With a sob she threw herself into his arms and clung convulsively round his neck. He held her tenderly, his cheek against her wet one.

"Now, now, you mustn't cry, either, you know it makes wrinkles!" he soothed her. "I have been on bad terms with myself for some time, you could see that. I would like to think better of myself, if possible, and that is why I'm going north at last."

"You can doubtless think very highly of yourself," said Regina, pulling viciously at a knot in her embroidery silk, "when you are at the end of a hangman's rope!" And she went on, while Dorothea stared at her in horror from St. John's embrace—"That is what it will come to, you know. Because it is treason, as Washington himself may yet find out!"

"Regina, I have had about enough of your damned Tory nonsense!" St. John left his sister and descended on the woman he loved, terrible in his righteous wrath. "If it weren't for your petticoats you would have been gaoled long ago. It's not fair to your father, for one thing, nor to me, if that matters to you at all!"

"Strange to relate, it doesn't matter to me in the least," she said, and her voice and her fingers shook above the embroidery.

He mastered a flaming retort with a visible effort.

"I shall be leaving in a few minutes, for I don't know how long," he said instead. "Let's try, before I go, to look at this thing calmly."

"I prefer not to look at it at all. I prefer to dismiss it."

"Then by God you must dismiss me with it, once and for all!" he cried, and cast an unhappy glance at Dorothea where she stood paralyzed in the middle of the floor.

"I—I'll go," she whispered, and fled from the room.

St. John resumed where he had left off, but with a change of tone.

"You must make up your mind, my dear," he said, and set his hands on the back of Regina's chair and leaned above her from behind, till his cheek was near her hair, and his voice dropped low and fierce into her ear. "You must choose now, between me and the King, because you can't have us both any longer."

"Then I choose the King!" she announced quickly, and her stitches were crooked and crazy in the pattern she could no longer see.

His hands came down over her shoulders and captured her hands and his lips were against her neck where the smooth curl lay.

"The King is a long way off," he reminded her softly. "The King doesn't hold you fast in his heart, as I do. You wouldn't care for the King, my girl, not when you want a lover. He has got a bit paunchy, for one thing, and he is much too heavy-handed, for another, and not, I should think, very imaginative when there is a chair in the way—" His lips, hard and sweet, crept upward to her cheek, and she slipped into delicious laughter in his hold.

"Oh, St. John, you *are* a fool—why must I love you so—!"

He caught the words on a kiss.

Then, while he knelt beside her chair with his arms around her waist and hers across his shoulders—

"Let them fight their war," she whispered. "It's nothing to us—is it!"

"I'm afraid it is," he sighed, and turned his face gratefully into her bosom.

She held him there.

"St. John," she whispered. "Don't go."

He made a little sound of amusement and regret, without moving.

"Don't go," she whispered. "Choose between me and Washington."

Again the same sound came from him, almost drowsily, against her neck.

"I'll give up the King," she whispered, and kissed his ear.

"I should damn' well think you would!" he laughed, and raised his head, and his eyes with their candid curving lashes were very bright. "Has anyone ever even *tried* to tell you how beautiful you are?"

"And so you must give up Washington," she persisted, and took his face between her white hands. "That's only fair."

"Kiss me," he commanded, and she obeyed him sweetly like a woman wed. "Never waste that on a king," he murmured, and hid his face in her palms.

"Say you will give up Washington," she whispered, bending over him.

"But I won't," he said, into her hands, and felt her stiffen in the chair, and looked her in the face with a rueful smile. For a long moment their eyes held, and she could not but recognize the unswerving purpose in his.

"You beast!" she cried, but it was the protest of a child who has been duped with a sugar plum.

"Because I saw through you all the time?" he smiled, still kneeling beside her chair, and every word as he spoke it was an impudent caress. "Oh, Delilah!" he said. "You with the seven green withes that never were dried, afflict me some more!"

"I hate you!" she cried, and believed it.

"You love me, thank God. And when I come back, I shall prove it to you, all the rest of our lives."

"If you go today," she said passionately, "I hope you never come back!"

His face whitened, and he rose abruptly from his knee and turned away from her.

"I wish you hadn't said that," he said, and she rose too, to her full height only a couple of inches less than his.

"Understand me, St. John, I will never marry a man who has borne arms against the King!"

"I thought we had finished with the King," he remarked, and for the first time, remembering that kiss so freely given, she flushed under his possessive gaze. "Besides, the Prince of Hesse-Cassell is not my king, and the scum and scrapings of his gutters and pigstyes are not my countrymen. Don't you see, my dear, the quarrel is no longer between the colonies and the mother country! It has become a contest between Magna Carta and a gang of unenlightened ruffians from the middle of Europe who never have known the meaning of liberty or acknowledged the rights of free men!"

"You sound exactly like Patrick Henry!" she gibed. "You will meet British soldiers on any battlefield you come to, and you know it!"

"Yes, and with their hearts not in it, you may be sure!"

"And so you would shoot them down, because they are brave men doing their duty!"

He looked at her with affectionate despair.

"They will have an equal chance of shooting me first," he reminded her, and saw her lips tighten. "I know this comes very hard for you, my dear. You are used to having your own way about everything. And if you can't catch your flies with honey you must lay about you till they are all dead on the floor. But that's no good either this time, Regina. You can't come between a man and his conscience."

"If you leave this house today," she said deliberately, "I never want to see you again as long as I live!"

He made a small, polite, ironical gesture of acceptance.

"But mark my words, you were not designed for spinsterhood, my girl," he said, and she gave an angry little laugh.

"Well, really, St. John, one would think you were the only man in the world!"

"I am the only man for you," he told her very quietly. "I am the only man who can bend that damned domineering spirit of yours and make you like it, Regina, and if while my back is turned you marry some one else, may God have mercy on him because you never will!" He walked away from her towards the door, moving with his splendid carriage by which she could always recognize him down the length of the Duke of Gloucester Street, long before she could see his face. He turned in the doorway, with the room between them, and his look was all tenderness again, as though he held her in his arms. "You will forgive me," he said. "Some day." Smiling, he kissed his fingertips to her, and was gone.

When she heard his horse's feet in the drive she ran to the library window to watch him ride away, and knew that her heart hung at his saddle-bow. I shall marry whomever I please, she told herself, dry-eyed, and began to cull over, in cold blood, the available Tories she knew. There was David Allen, handsome, sulky, and beside St. John very immature, who was going to join a Loyalist regiment to please her. And there was Julian Day. . . .

XIX

Because Mr. Wythe had been away in Philadelphia signing the Declaration, St. John found a great deal of unfinished business awaiting him when he returned to Williamsburg. Before he could get clear of what even in his desperation he recognized as inescapable responsibilities, Washington had retreated from Brooklyn Heights and was preparing to abandon New York, which could not be held without command of the sea.

The Patriots' cause looked hopeless. After the arrival at Staten Island of Clinton and Cornwallis from their Charleston failure, Howe had something like twenty-five thousand men, equipped and disciplined. Washington's tattered army was a scant eighteen thousand, and a large part of it was next to useless under fire.

It seemed a form of suicide to pin one's fortunes now to what might prove to be the Commander-in-Chief's last stand, at the Harlem River, but in mid-September St. John was off to the north—grim and quiet in his new blue uniform with Virginia's scarlet facings, a handsome sword at his side, his boots a miracle of polishing by Joshua's black hands. Dorothea said he looked beautiful, which made him laugh, and Aunt Anabel tried to say that he made her feel very proud, and puckered into helpless tears against his buff waistcoat.

Julian had moved back into the room above the school and would not be dislodged from it. Dreading the interview, but determined to behave as though there was no shadow across their friendship, St. John stopped at the schoolhouse on his way out of town. It was a Sunday morning, and Julian was at his desk writing up his journal. He beheld St. John's uniform without a change of expression, and offered him a chair rather formally. St. John stood still in the doorway with a quizzical smile. Then he held out his right hand and said simply—

"I have come to say good-bye. Let's get it over."

Julian's clasp was quick and hard. For a moment they stood there without words, and Julian was the first to turn away.

"I suppose you will never understand why I can't go with you," he said.

"I don't need to understand. You are right not to go if you have no wish to. And you are wanted here, you know."

"Am I?" The question came listlessly, over his shoulder.

"You will keep an eye on them for me, won't you—in Francis Street. If anything goes wrong, I mean."

"St. John, in heaven's name, what becomes of them if you—if Washington loses this war?"

"He isn't going to lose it."

"I wish I could believe that."

"I wish you could. And you will—later on."

"It isn't just because I can't believe it that I—that I am not coming with you. I know it must look that way—as though I held back from a forlorn hope."

"Why, no, it doesn't have to look that way." But the words came without the usual ring of St. John's speech.

"If I could be sure of meeting only Hessians in the field—but it's fighting your own kind, St. John, men whose job it is to preserve the Empire, officered by fellows you might have been at school with! And they must feel the same way, they know we are kith and kin here, it's inconceivable! How do you face it?"

St. John's jaw tightened.

"I don't face it," he said. "I just know I've got to do it—like giving your own brother a bloody nose for the good of his soul. This lunkheaded death-and-destruction on the throne needs a kick in the seat of his breeches. The British army can't do it, that would be mutiny. So the American army will do it in spite of 'em. Somebody is going to get hurt, that is inevitable. Meanwhile, I am just a little easier in my mind about those two in Francis Street with you here, than if you were charging round Harlem waving a sword—if that is any comfort to you!"

"I'll do the best I can for them," Julian promised solemnly.

"Thank you. And there is one thing more," said St. John, and paused a moment. "Regina will make your life a hell on earth if you let her. I can master her. You can't. Never say I didn't warn you. Good-bye, Julian."

He sketched a salute lightly. His scabbard struck the door as he turned, his spurs clanked on the staircase, the street door banged. His horse went at once to the gallop.

Julian waited till the hoof-beats died away and then sat down with his head in his hands.

It was an altogether dismal autumn everywhere, and things looked more and more as though St. John had wilfully run his neck into the noose.

All through October and November the post-riders who swung stiffly out of their saddles in front of the Raleigh or the *Gazette* office brought news which got worse, as Washington retreated from Harlem to White Plains, and then lost Fort Washington and evacuated Fort Lee, and began to fall back across New Jersey—Newark, New Brunswick, Princeton, Trenton, all were abandoned one by one, until at last the dwindling army had scrambled across the Delaware into Pennsylvania, and people at Philadelphia began to hide their valuables and send their wives and children into the country.

The saddle-galled express who said that Congress had fled to Baltimore was nearly mobbed by men who swore he was a liar, men who knew in their sinking hearts that they might have done the same, as the shadow of the halter crept towards Carpenters' Hall. Williamsburg Tories walked and talked less guardedly now. When Howe issued a proclamation offering protection to all citizens who took oath of allegiance to the Crown within sixty days, and the Jersey population fell over itself to comply, the Patriots of Williamsburg cursed them roundly and then took sidelong glances at each other, wondering who among their number would have had the conviction to hold out in similar circumstances. When word came that Howe was to receive a knighthood with appropriate festivities at Christmas time in New York, as a reward for his triumphant campaign, the taprooms jeered and swore and jeered

again, and speculated coarsely as to what title that would confer on the
obliging American woman now known among his officers as the
Sultana.

At last a letter came from St. John—written to Dorothea, with a request that she share its contents with Aunt Anabel and Julian. She read
it aloud to them after supper in the candlelit drawing-room in Francis
Street, her gentle voice making fantasy of the disasters he had set down
so matter-of-factly. . . .

". . . There is no denying we have been weeks on the run and our
reputation is no longer all that it might be," he wrote. "The army
is melting away, companies at a time, partly because terms of service
are up for the militia, partly by out-and-out desertion. We lack tents
and blankets and even shoes for the ranks, and the men are sickening fast and becoming contentious. You cannot blame them for
losing heart. Neither can you blame the Commander-in-Chief for
their predicament, and he preserves a sort of leonine calm, to say
nothing of a titanic resolve—but I suspect that he feels as strongly as
the rest of us that the game may be pretty nearly up. Nevertheless
he goes on hoping, appealing, and I think praying for reinforcements. If only we can get recruits to fill the ranks and help us to
last the winter out—

"Howe has garrisoned Trenton with his Hessian bastards—forgive me—under Generals Donop and Rahl, together with a handful
of Scots under a so-and-so named Grant, who I hear has boasted
that he can hold all Jersey against us with a corporal's guard—and
Howe has gone off to New York to get his damned knighthood.
The German troops are pillaging in the customary European manner, taking whatever they see that they fancy, and most of them
haven't got a word of English to argue in. If only—our conversation here is conducted almost entirely in the subjunctive—if only we
could scrape together a few stout hearts and a half dozen rounds
of ammunition each, and if only the enemy could be taken by surprise, and if they all fell over their own feet and lost all their bayonets
in the snow, we might just possibly contrive to dislodge them from
one or two Jersey towns and capture some of their stores for our
own use. I suppose there must have been a time when my thoughts

were not occupied almost exclusively with food, and when I would
not have been willing to part with my hope of heaven in exchange
for one of Jerusha's chicken pies. . . ."

Dorothea raised stricken eyes from the page at this point.
"You don't suppose he is really *hungry?*" she entreated.
"Of course he is hungry!" cried Aunt Anabel impatiently. "He is
starving, and cold, and discouraged, and *beaten,* and we sit here helpless, stuffed with food, and for the first time in my life I am glad my
poor Colin is safe in his grave!"
"Oh, Auntie, don't let's talk about graves!" Dorothea felt for her
handkerchief. "It is three weeks since he wrote this letter. Julian, you
don't—don't th-think anything will *happen* to him up there?"
Julian came out of a reverie to search hastily for any form of comfort
to offer.
"The fighting is over for this year," he said. "We can be reasonably
sure that he won't be under fire again before spring. Washington should
be able to sit the winter out where he is—"
"Sinjie doesn't say a word about coming home for Christmas," she
lamented. "He could have had all he wanted to eat, and taken back some
things, like hams, to the rest of them."
Christmas was to find St. John otherwise occupied.
On a frosty day early in January of 1777 all the bells in Williamsburg
began to ring, and the streets and taprooms were soon full of hysterical
citizens who pounded each other between the shoulders and bought
each other an endless succession of drinks to celebrate the news that
Washington had recrossed the ice-choked Delaware and attacked Trenton in a snowstorm, thus ruining the Hessians' Christmas carouse. Rahl
was killed in the street fighting, the British line was cut at Princeton,
and the redcoats were indeed dislodged from all but a precarious foot-
hold at New Brunswick and Amboy.
The tables had been entirely turned, in an audacious postscript to a
campaign which had already been written off, and Washington was a
hero again. Julian drank the Commander-in-Chief's health willingly
enough more than once, deeply moved by the childish soaring of Patriot
spirits at what he could only feel was a fleeting triumph. He was able
to share their fierce local pride of a neighbor's courage and daring, but

he could not muster any sort of conviction that there was any permanent improvement in their prospects.

It was March before anxiety for St. John was relieved by a letter from him to Julian, delayed in transit, full of an unself-conscious satisfaction that he had been in the thick of the action at Trenton and had come off unscathed after taking *prisoners of war,* underlined.

"Besides the human specimens and the guns and drums and colors we took as trophies in the action," he wrote, "we brought back blankets, ammunition, and other supplies less decorative but decidedly more valuable. If we had only had a few fresh troops we could have captured all their stores at Brunswick as well, and indulged in square meals for days on end!

"Congress has returned somewhat sheepishly to Philadelphia, and Howe has withdrawn himself again to the fleshpots of New York— no doubt digesting with difficulty the fact that he has lost most of Jersey to a general he thought he had beaten. We are now ensconced at Morristown to sit the winter out more comfortably than we ever hoped, and recruiting is brisking up. If the British did not lack horses for their artillery they would certainly have come down on us again before now.

"Fortunately it is a mild winter so far, but there is smallpox in the ranks and we are inoculating the recruits as they come in. The medical service is pretty rough and ready, and equipment is as scarce as ever. One thing we realize here on the Jersey mud rounds— the army which could achieve an adequate hospital corps adequately supplied with drugs and lint and attendants for the wounded and sick would have a most incalculable advantage in this war. In any war. But herbs and simples are not all we lack! There is hardly a sound pair of breeches among us, and even the mighty, like General Wayne, go shabby and threadbare. . . ."

Dorothea was proud that St. John had gone north when things looked blackest. Anyone could join the army since Trenton. But St. John had taken the long view, and Washington had justified it handsomely.

After that letter from Morristown they were a long time without one, and what news arrived from other sources was disquieting. Howe left

New York again in the early summer by sea, presumably to attack
Philadelphia, but Washington wrote to Governor Henry to put the
Virginia militia on the alert in case the British should swing southwards
towards the Capes. Yorktown and Hampton promptly girded themselves in what they believed was the Charleston style and swore they
were ready for anything.

June was an anxious month. British troops were being shifted from
Jersey posts and there was marching and counter-marching, but nobody
could find out what Howe was up to. Burgoyne was coming down with
an army from Canada. The Continental troops evacuated Ticonderoga
as they could not hope to stand against him. July was full of suspense.
No one, not even Washington, seemed to know what was going to happen, or where. August came, and still Howe's intentions were obscure.

On a sultry afternoon in September, Dorothea appeared suddenly at
the door of the empty schoolhouse. Julian was in his room upstairs,
working on a pile of copybooks, when he heard her call to him, and went
down.

She was looking very lovely in sprigged muslin over a hoop, and a
wide chip hat tied under her chin with blue ribbons, and she stood peering uncertainly towards the stairs when she heard his footsteps there.

"Julian, is that you? I wasn't sure I ought to come, but we have had
news—I couldn't wait to tell you— Oh, Julian, Sinjie is coming home!"
She laughed, and her breath caught, and she reached for his hand, and
he saw that she still held St. John's folded letter against her heart. "There
has been a battle somewhere called Brandywine, and he got a ball in his
foot—he says it is nothing, really, but he can't ride or even walk for
some time to come, and— Oh, Julian, he is coming home!" Her soft
brown eyes were shining with happy tears. "Of course it is dreadful
that he has been wounded, but he *says* it will heal, and meanwhile we
shall have him here to nurse— I know I oughtn't to be glad, but when
I think of seeing him again, *alive—!*" The tears spilled over.

Smiling at her, saying small, futile, comforting things, he guided her
to the front row of forms and set her down, and pulled up a chair to
face her.

"It is very foolish of me to cry!" she struggled on, mopping at herself
with a damp bit of cambric. "But I am so happy— I hope he isn't in pain,
but at least he will have a good rest here and proper food again, and

Dr. Graves can see to the wound— Oh, Julian, you *will* be glad to see him, just like old times?"

"Yes, my dear. I shall be very glad to see him. Who won the battle?"

"The battle?" Joy died in her. "Washington is retreating—towards Philadelphia."

"Again?" he sighed. "That sounds bad, doesn't it."

"There is a new broadside tacked up at the *Gazette* office, but I didn't stop. Sinjie says Philadelphia would be no good to the British if they got it—but it's the capital so they will try to take it."

"Oh, yes—they will try to take it!"

"Julian—" She laid her hand on his sleeve. "Julian, what about Regina?"

"I haven't seen her for days. Why?"

"Well, I thought—I thought she ought to know about Sinjie being wounded."

"Yes, I think she ought."

"It might make a difference in the way she feels."

"Very likely it will."

"Julian—will you be the one to tell her—please?"

"But, my dear girl, surely it would be better if you—"

"No, no, don't you see, you are his friend—and I am only his sister. Whatever I try to say, Regina brushes it aside because she says I don't understand. But perhaps she would listen to you."

"What do you want me to say?"

"Just that he is coming home, wounded—and—he will want to see her, and she must be kind again—she *must!* And ask her not to tease him about David Allen—that Maryland boy—he is an ensign now, in a new Loyalist regiment under Simcoe—she will throw it in Sinjie's face if you let her!"

"My dear, I can't rule Regina. Nobody can."

"Sinjie can. But you must make her see him. Then everything would come right again. Oh, Julian, please try—"

"It is a little difficult for me too," he said slowly, and she leaned forward to see his face, and then drew back at what she found there.

"Julian, you aren't—you haven't—you wouldn't come between them!"

"God forbid," he said devoutly, and added—"There is not much chance of that, I assure you."

But Dorothea was on her feet, looking a little blinder than usual. "I must go," she gasped, and made for the door. "I'm sorry, Julian, I—didn't realize—"

"There is nothing to realize," he assured her patiently, following her towards the door. "My dear, you must believe that. It would be very embarrassing if you misunderstood. It's only—"

"I think I understand—quite well," she said breathlessly, and he caught her at the door.

"I will talk to her if you wish," he promised. "Dorothea, I will do my best to bring them together again."

"They belong together," she whispered. "Oh, believe me, Julian, they do!" And she was gone.

Julian got his hat and set out very thoughtfully for England Street, wondering how he was to go about his mission. As he passed the apothecary's shop, running feet overtook him and the twins flung themselves at him, one on either side.

"Oh, Mr. Day, have you heard? Congress has fled Philadelphia again! They are saying at the *Gazette* office that the British will march into Philadelphia this week! Does that mean we have lost the war?"

He paused in the broad shady street, Kit holding his left arm, Tibby panting on his right, her hat hanging down her back by its ribbons. In the waiting eyes of both was the same shining confidence in his wisdom —whatever he said, would be.

"We haven't lost the war until Washington surrenders," he said.

"But he'll never do that!" cried Kit.

"There, Kit, I told you! Washington will go on fighting! Philadelphia is only a town!" cried Tibby. "We've still got Norfolk and Charleston and Yorktown!"

"There is an express just in from the north, sir, and everyone is down at the Raleigh." Kit tugged at him. "Come and hear what they are saying!"

"I can't now," he said, wishing he could use Kit's invitation to postpone what was ahead of him. "I am on my way to England Street. Mr. Sprague has been wounded and is coming home to recover."

Kit and Tibby exchanged a knowing look.

"Brandywine," said Tibby. "Kit, you go back to the Raleigh and see what you can hear. I'm going to walk a ways with Mr. Day."

Julian shortened his step to hers. Tibby wasn't growing much, but she had a new dignity since her modest success at Mrs. Hallam's, and soon she would be allowed to earn a few shillings by helping with the younger children. He was very well pleased with what he had been able to do for Tibby, but he had not seen much of her lately. Her mother, always frail, had had a bout of fever, which made extra responsibility for the twins.

"Will they be married now, do you think?" Tibby inquired with her customary directness on the way to England Street.

"I don't know. It is possible."

"If I had been Miss Regina I would have married him before he went," said Tibby, and Julian smiled at her slantwise and said "Would you?" with some doubt. She nodded, and pulled up her hat to shade her face. "If the man I loved was going to war," said Tibby, secretly thanking God that he wasn't, "I wouldn't want him to go without—that is, I would want him to have—anything he wanted of me—while there was time. Suppose Mr. Sprague had got killed at Brandywine—*then* how would she feel?"

"Suppose he had lost his leg," said Julian. "Then how would *he* feel?"

"It oughtn't to matter to her—so long as she got him back."

"You are very wise today, Tibby. How would you like to come along in and give Miss Regina some advice?"

Tibby glanced up in surprise, for the ironical tone was not one she was accustomed to from him.

"Reckon I spoke out of turn," she apologized. "I was thinking if it was you. I mean," she floundered, getting pink under the hatbrim, "I didn't mean to criticize Miss Regina— I only meant that if you love a man *enough,* you can't bear to have him be without anything you can give him—I shouldn't think."

There was a pause, punctuated by their measured footfalls. At last—

"I'm sorry, sir," said Tibby humbly. "I'll go back now."

Julian, who had scarcely heard her, came to himself with a start.

"Tibby, I apologize. I'm afraid I wasn't listening. I was trying to think how to break it to her—wondering how she will take it."

"If she loves him she will be very ashamed of herself!" cried Tibby. "*I* should go down on my knees to him, if I were in her place, and promise to do everything he wished from now on!"

Julian set his forefinger under her chin and raised the flushed and angry little face to his sympathetic gaze.

"Why, Tibby," he said, "are you jealous of Miss Regina?"

"Sometimes I hate her!" she cried, and jerked her chin free and made him her curtsy and marched away from him, back along the way they had come.

He stood staring after her, his hat still in his hand. Poor Tibby, he thought—she was only a child, of course, and it was perhaps inevitable that she should apparently have come to idolize St. John, who was always so charming to her. But St. John belonged to Regina, and it would never do to have Tibby breaking her heart for him as she grew older—Julian could never remember the twins' exact age without counting it up; they had never reached an awkward stage and were small-boned and childish still. But Tibby falling in love—hopelessly—with St. John! He wondered if he ought to mention this curious prospect to Aunt Anabel, because after all, Tibby must be coming into her teens now. . . .

He entered Regina's drawing-room still bemused, and blurted out his news about Brandywine with less finesse even than he might have done. Regina was startled and unhappy, he could see that, but anything beyond the concern due to an old friend was quickly masked. Bunglingly he proceeded.

"Dorothea thought perhaps in the circumstances—you would see him again," he suggested.

"Dorothea is a darling—but just a little dense, isn't she, to send you on this errand?"

"She is only thinking of St. John," he said uncomprehendingly.

"It might be better for Dorothea if she thought of herself once in a while! Still, I should be grateful to her, I suppose, for this unexpected pleasure." The words, plus the smile which went with them, had a double meaning, and he stiffened defensively. "Must you avoid me so?" she asked, and made a small imperious gesture towards the sofa beside her.

"Our paths don't cross in the ordinary way," he said, and sat down at the far end, warily, and inquired in his punctilious fashion after the health of her parents, while their glances sparred and their smiles grew a little fixed, and the devil who lived in Regina's proud, undisciplined spirit possessed her again.

If St. John had written to tell her of his wound, and made a suitable plea for a sight of her to restore him to health, Regina would have condescended. But that would not have been St. John. He wrote to Dorothea, with probably never a word of her, Regina, in the letter, not even to send his love, and Dorothea sent Julian to plead for her brother, which was tactless, and just the stupid sort of thing a schoolgirl like Dorothea would do, and if she could not learn better she deserved to lose him. Not that he was hers to lose, so far, but it was plain enough she wanted him, thought Regina cruelly, her eyes on Julian's hands—big, but beautiful, with thin boyish wrists—hands very different from St. John's sinewy brown fingers, but nothing womanish about them, nothing soft. He would be very gentle always, very kind, very easily hurt. He would never hit back with a laugh, like St. John, who seemed actually to enjoy being trodden on, and always gave as good as he got. There would be some satisfaction, when St. John came home a hero, in telling him that one was going to marry somebody else. . . .

She had not noticed how long the silence was stretching, until at last Julian rose rather abruptly, towering over her, and said that he must go.

"But I never see you any more," she complained, and held out both her hands to him, rising as she yielded them to his clasp.

"Presumably that makes my life a little easier," he smiled, holding her hands.

"I think you are very unkind!" she cried, laughing up at him.

"Don't imagine I enjoy it, though—denying myself even the sight of you, while days I can never live again slip away empty."

Her fingers curled warm and close in his, for this was more the way she wanted him to talk. Backward lover though he might be, she knew by the quickening of her own heartbeat that these still waters ran deep. St. John's wound was not so serious but that she could bear to have her triumph anyhow, and Julian with his reticent but always tacit worship of herself was mysterious and enthralling and unlike any man who had ever desired her before. One could make him happy without ever being bored oneself, she was thinking, and at the same time teach St.

John that he was not the only man in the world. And the time was now, when Julian had for once made something more than a pretty speech.

"Then why do you deny us both our simple pleasures?" she murmured. "I have missed you, Julian. One hasn't so many friends these days one can afford to miss them. We *are* friends, aren't we?"

"Not exactly."

"You say very strange things today. What am I to think?"

"You know quite well what to think. We can't be friends because you go to my head like wine. And the only thing for a man who cannot carry his liquor to do is to shun the bowl."

"You are always full of moralities, aren't you, Julian!"

"Perhaps because I am a schoolmaster."

"Do you feel like a schoolmaster—always?" Her hands laid his behind her waist, he felt the yield of her hoop against him, her face was upturned to his. For a moment, with a roar of blood in his ears, he hesitated, and then said quietly—

"You quarrelled with St. John, didn't you? Are you using me as a stick to beat him with?"

It was so exactly the truth that she could not deny it. And anyway she had seen his hesitation, and thought she had won through his defenses at last.

"St. John made his free choice between me and Washington," she said, for it still rankled in her. "Let him abide by it. I warned him how it would be."

"You want me to help you teach him a lesson, is that it?"

"Oh, Julian—why do you make it sound so cold-blooded?"

"Because that is the way it seems to me. Because I think you still love him, in spite of yourself."

"But I don't. That is finished."

"Just to make sure," he said, "won't you see him?"

"No. Not even to please you. And I would like very much to please you, Julian."

A moment more he stood with his hands clasping her waist, while his gaze caressed her face and hair and throat.

"Then—let me go," he said with an effort, and stepped away from her and kissed her hands which clung to his, and walked out of the room without a backward look.

So she had nothing to tell St. John after all.

XX

St. John arrived home in a ramshackle dog-cart drawn by an emaciated horse which he drove himself—transportation was scarce in the north. His uniform was shabby and battle-stained, his wound was painful from lack of care, and the British were in Philadelphia—but St. John's spirits were high, he was full of hilarious stories, and referred to his bulbously bandaged foot as the gout. He refused to stay in bed, and got about the house rather precariously on an improvised crutch he had brought with him, thwarting whenever possible the ambition of Joshua to carry him and the pleas of his womenfolk to lean on them. Dr. Graves called every day and managed before long to reduce the pain and the size of the bandage.

All Williamsburg flocked to Francis Street to hear St. John's stories, and he was the first to admit that some of them were apocryphal. Such as the one, demanded over and over again, about the British sentry who caught an American militiaman near an outpost one night and called back to his captain: "I have taken a prisoner!" The captain replied, "Well, bring him in!" "But he will not come!" bawled the sentry. "Then leave him and come back yourself!" commanded the captain. And the sentry, plaintively: "But he will not let me go!" St. John told it well, and it always produced a crow of laughter from Aunt Anabel, who never tired of it. Aunt Anabel even permitted him to sing, more than once, certain verses of a very rude song about General Howe, including the one which ran as follows:

> *"Sir William, he, snug as a flea,*
> *Lay all this time a-snoring,*
> *Nor dreamt of harm as he lay warm*
> *In bed with Mrs. Loring."*

St. John said little about how he had got his wound, beyond remarking that the first he knew of it he had a bootful of blood. He was inclined instead to dwell on the coincidence that Lafayette had had a similar experience and had been carted off somewhere beyond Philadelphia to recuperate—which he, St. John, would not have cared for at all. According to St. John, the army surgeons were all too prone to amputate what could not be dealt with easily by the limited skill and resources at their disposal, and the best thing to do if you got hit in the arm or the leg was to keep out of hospital.

Lafayette? He loved to tell about the young French marquis recently added to Washington's official family—and a very different proposition from most of his countrymen now swarming to America in search of military fame and easy pickings. Lafayette's belief in the cause of freedom burned like Washington's own, and he was already regarded almost as a son by the Commander-in-Chief. He was as tall as Washington— barely twenty years old, and very unassuming. When the French Government had refused to permit the departure from France of so wealthy and prominent a member of the nobility, Lafayette had bought a whole ship and worn a disguise to escape in, and he left a young wife and family behind, asking only to serve as a volunteer without pay in the American army. St. John, who had been present at the Marquis' first meeting with Washington, said it was rather like that of Jeanne d'Arc and the Dauphin—in that Lafayette had selected and approached the Commander-in-Chief unerringly from amongst a group of officers surrounding him at a banquet in Philadelphia.

The drawing-room in Francis Street liked to hear about de Kalb too —the gigantic gallant German who had accompanied Lafayette from France and during the endless stormy voyage had labored patiently to teach him English. De Kalb had served so long with the French army he ranked as one of its officers, and he had been in America in 1768 as an agent of de Choiseul. St. John said the people who laughed at de Kalb were all wrong. True, he wore an odd Swiss hat, and his hair was caked with powder and had a ludicrous black pigtail sticking out behind—but Frederick the Great, no less, had praised his generalship, and his experience in the field with de Broglie during the Seven Years' War must tell. Besides, said St. John, he was the soul of kindness, and sensitive to the snubs and ridicule his appearance sometimes brought upon him.

St. John had seen the new flag, recently authorized by Congress and first under battle fire at Brandywine—thirteen stripes alternately white and red, with thirteen white stars on a blue ground—and he pronounced it very handsome and distinctive. There was nothing like it in the world, and its beauty was a great improvement over what he called the snake-and-muscle emblem. The stars and stripes made a flag as charming as a woman's gown, with which to clothe the new nation in its care. It was a feminine-looking flag, said St. John sentimentally, and the rough, homesick men who fought under it liked that. The color sergeants at once called it "she." "Ain't she the purtiest thing ever waved in a breeze?" one of them demanded of the circle of upturned faces viewing it for the first time. "Ain't she dainty and sweet? No snakes on you, is there, my girl!" And he patted the staff with a horny, affectionate hand.

Howe, St. John reported, was such an infernal gentleman about it all, he even returned unopened one of Washington's letters to Mrs. Washington, when a post-bag was captured. You couldn't, St. John pointed out, work up a murderous rage against that sort of fellow—not even, it would seem from the man Loring's behavior, when he appropriated your wife under your very nose! Speaking of letters—and then would come the tale of the other Howe, the Admiral, who addressed an official communication to "George Washington, Esq." only to have his messenger politely informed that there was no person in the American army with that address. A few days later the British adjutant-general himself arrived with another letter from the Admiral addressed to "George Washington, Esq., etc., etc." and attempted to explain to the Commander-in-Chief in a personal interview that the etceteras meant everything required. Washington agreed with a pleasant smile that they might indeed mean almost anything, and added that as the letter appeared to be addressed to a planter in the state of Virginia, it would be forwarded to him at the close of the war, and until then would not be opened. The requisite "Excellency" and "General" were never wrung from Admiral Howe, but his brother had finally resigned himself to the formality, to facilitate the necessary correspondence regarding the exchange of prisoners and so on.

Meanwhile, St. John's new uniforms with a captain's epaulet on the right shoulder arrived from the tailor and became him mightily.

He never mentioned Regina and for days her name went unspoken. He asked after Tibby, though, and when she came to see him he devoted himself to her for an hour and was much impressed with the change in her. Tibby was turning thirteen, and bore herself accordingly.

After nearly a year away, St. John was conscious of undercurrents. His precious Dorothea was quieter than he liked, and seemed inclined to leave him alone with Julian, and avoided the subject they had always spoken of freely—Regina's place in their future. Julian was quite himself, perhaps a little remote still, but with the exercise of tact they slipped again into the old easy ways. And Tibby? St. John pondered Tibby, staring into the fire with his foot on a hassock and a pipe between his lips—her direct greenish gaze and straight small shoulders, her gentle speech and obstinate chin—she could not be discounted as a child much longer.

Dorothea came in and laid a caressing hand on his shoulder and his went up to cover it.

"Oh, Sinjie, darling, I *tried* to make her change her mind!" she cried impulsively, for she supposed that he brooded over his wayward love. "I thought surely when she heard you had been wounded it would bring her to her senses!"

He smiled, and laid aside his pipe, and pulled her down on to the broad arm of the chair.

"That was subtle of you!" he said affectionately. "What did she say when you told her?"

"Well, I—I didn't tell her myself, I asked Julian to. You see—" She flushed before the amused quirk of his brows as he looked up at her. "I hope you don't think it was interfering of me," she apologized. "But you see, it had got so that she wouldn't pay any attention to me—because of my being your sister and naturally prejudiced—"

"Poor Julian," murmured St. John. "He couldn't have enjoyed it much himself."

"Well, you see, I was stupid, I didn't realize till after I had asked him that he was in love with her."

The strong brown fingers that caressed hers were suddenly still—and something in their stillness turned Dorothea quite cold, and then hot, and then cold again. Too late she knew that for once St. John had been taken by surprise—that she must have given something away. She sat paralyzed with her hand in his, waiting for the sky to fall on her. And St. John said nothing at all. It seemed to her that he had stopped breathing, under her hand, until at last she could bear it no longer, and slipped to her knees beside the chair, with her face hidden in her arms flung across his lap. "Oh, Sinjie, forgive me, I shouldn't have mentioned it, I didn't think what I said, I thought you knew, I— Sinjie, it's just as bad for me as it is for you!" she sobbed, all her defenses gone.

She felt his hand on her hair—it slid down, warm and comforting, to close on the nape of her neck in a way he had to ease a headache. But still he did not speak, and she raised her face, wet with tears, to look at him.

"Sinjie, *say* something!" she begged him.

"Yes, child—what do you want me to say?" His eyes were fixed away from her, on the fire.

"Sinjie, don't look like that! I don't think it has come to anything—yet."

"No. It won't come to anything," he said quietly, his eyes on the fire.

"You mean you can put a stop to it?" she asked, hopeful in spite of herself, for St. John always made things come right somehow.

He turned his head then, and smiled at her, looking deep into her trustful eyes. Put a stop to Regina's wilful whims, perhaps, he had done that before. But how to put a stop to his surging anger at her savage selfishness, her wicked, witless pride, which took no heed of anything but her necessity to make him sorry he had crossed her? And how to master that other anger, quick and hot, at Julian, who should have known better, who should have been too sensible to play moth to her flame? True, he had warned Julian before he went north, but only as a precaution, a crossing of fingers against the highly improbable thing which seemed to have happened after all while his back was turned. As for this soft, beloved creature in his arms, he would have given a year of his life for the answer. But you cannot challenge your best friend because he will not see your sister.

"You—won't ever let him know?" she pleaded.

"It is a thing a man likes to find out for himself," he told her.

"He has to look, first! Oh, if only this war would end, because with you here at home again she would never dare to lead him on!"

"Does she lead him on?" His smile was a little rigid.

"I don't know. I don't know what passes between them, or how often he sees her. I can only wonder and wait. Sinjie, it would be the wrong thing for him—even if I didn't love him so much myself, I should hate to see him marry Regina. She would only make him miserable, he doesn't know how to take her, she would *trample* on him, and he wouldn't know what to do—"

"I know," he nodded, still with that odd smile. "Regina wants beating every now and then, and I am the man for that!"

"Oh, Sinjie, you c-couldn't—!" She paused, round-eyed, for a short, hard laugh escaped him.

"She knows I could," he said. "She knows I *would*. It's the same thing!" He reached for his pipe, and she opened the tobacco jar and held it for him, and then lighted a spill at the fire. "I will go so far as to wager with you," he said between fragrant puffs as she held the spill to the bowl, "that Regina will not marry Julian. She would like to, just to spite me now. But it is very unlikely all the same, if I survive the war."

"If you—!" She threw the spent spill into the grate and knelt beside him again, holding him with jealous, loving hands. *"Must* you go back, Sinjie?"

"Very soon."

"Haven't you done enough?"

"No one has done enough. And there is another thing, my dear—if it goes on, and it will, you will see Julian in a uniform like this one yet."

She looked up at him from the floor, between hope that he was right and fear that he was—right.

"In which case," St. John continued, voicing her half-formed conclusion, "he too will be cast into outer darkness while the war lasts!"

"I suppose he will take that very hard," she reflected.

"He always takes things hard," said St. John sadly. And— "She does want beating," he repeated, lingering wistfully on the idea.

Dorothea showed a fleeting dimple.

"I dare you," she said.

"I would have to break down the door to get at her," he objected gravely. "It would make an awful mess, and a crowd would gather. You know how crowds are. Besides—I'm not sure it would help Julian."

"Sinjie—isn't there anything *I* can do to help Julian?"

"Not yet," he sighed, and laid his hand on her hair. "Not yet, sweetheart. He is going to take this war very hard. We must be patient."

"I never meant you to know," she whispered, leaning against him, obscurely comforted, and his arm tightened round her.

"I knew," he said. "But it is getting complicated."

Very complicated, he was thinking—with single-hearted Tibby growing up before their eyes.

He and Dorothea were still sitting by the fire, hand in hand in closest understanding, when Julian was announced and stood looking at them gauntly from the doorway.

"Burgoyne has surrendered at Saratoga," he said in a dazed sort of way. "His whole army. They are saying at the Raleigh that now France will come in on our side. That is good news too. But merciful God, St. John, will there never be an end to this thing?"

St. John was leaning forward in his chair, his eyes ablaze on Julian's white face. Burgoyne—yes, great news—and France—wonderful news, about France! But—

"On *whose* side?" he demanded unbelievingly. "On *whose* side did you say?"

"On ours, of course," said Julian. "America's."

XXI

When Dorothea had gone off to bed, they sat a long time with a bottle of wine between them, and their talk was desultory and intimate as of old. Something of recent constraint and caution and a skirting of certain topics was magically abolished tonight, not just because Burgoyne had surrendered, not because the French might come in, not because the tide might be turning—but because they both understood at last that they were after all on the same side. It was no *volte face* on Julian's part—rather it was a slow, inevitable growth, a gradual accretion of perspective. He was not yet ready to go out and shoot redcoats. But he knew now where his troubled heart lay. He had ceased to be a Tory.

St. John could talk to him tonight to ease his own laden soul, of things he had thought to keep locked within himself: of the privations and humiliations endured by his men in the ill-provisioned ranks before Philadelphia, dependent on the bungling, bewildered, incompetent Congress from which most of the stronger spirits had now departed to serve in their own State legislatures. Congress was full of bogies—it dreaded a powerful army, a powerful commander-in-chief, even a powerful organization of itself—so that for fear of any concentrated authority it seemed prepared to allow the whole war effort to fall apart of its own weight.

Looking worn and lean as a rake in the firelight, St. John told how one's senses were shocked with the sights and sounds and smells of fellow creatures perishing for lack of care and the bare essentials in what passed for hospitals and rest camps. The regimental surgeons were swamped, and useless wounded who could get about by themselves had to be literally turned out on the charity of the countryside, where people barred their doors against them, or feigned absence, in the effort to preserve their scanty comforts for the use of their own families. It was little wonder that enlistment lagged when broken stragglers returned home to tell of their own bitter experience in the army. Soap and vinegar and shoes were almost entirely lacking in the ranks. At Morristown men had sat up all night by the fires because there were not enough blankets to go round.

He told of the pathetic march of the Continental troops through Philadelphia on their way to what ended at Brandywine—at least a thousand men walked barefoot that day in the hot dust, and many had pieced out inadequate costumes with bits of blanket and flour bags and even British scarlet. Some were near to reeling with weakness, all were scraggy from an irregular diet—but every mother's son of them was as clean as he could make himself, and some with flour in their hair for powder, and for martial plumes each one had stuck a fresh green sprig into his hat, and they stepped out smartly to live up to Washington riding at their head on a sleek Virginia horse in his miraculously preserved fine raiment, and Lafayette, resplendent in the best Continental uniform money could buy, who rode at his side. It was enough to break your heart, cried St. John, to see the men that day and the brave show they made—only to lose the battle because of a muddle about fords and back roads, and General Sullivan in trouble again as usual! Washington was superhuman, exposing himself recklessly to rally the men, seeming to be everywhere at once. And Lafayette was very nearly taken, on foot and wounded among his troops—his aide, Gimat, threw him on a horse just in time. The men adored the Marquis. It was Greene, though, who saved them from an utter rout—a great lumbering lovable man who had been born a Rhode Island Quaker, and who showed now a steadfast genius for command. If anything should happen to Washington, which God forbid, Greene would be the next best general. . . .

And then, out of one of their companionable silences, filled with the ringing of bells in the town for the victory at Saratoga—

"It will be a long war, Julian—even with France's help—a desperate, bloody business, still—"

"Something must have gone very wrong with Burgoyne," Julian suggested. "Our man was Gates. Do you happen to know anything about him?"

"Lord God above!" said St. John blankly. "Are they saying *Gates* took Burgoyne?" He gave a loud, rude shout of laughter. "Who else was at Saratoga? Schuyler? Arnold? Morgan? Gates, my eye!" roared St. John, while Julian stared. "Gates is a summer soldier, hanging round Congress, trying to undermine Washington! I'll take my oath he had nothing to do with winning the battle! Schuyler was doing all the work up there the last *I* heard. How did Gates get in? I must get back to headquarters, things are really going to pieces! Well, anyway—" He raised his glass. "God give us France, and quickly!"

"I don't quite understand it," Julian ruminated. "Kings usually hang together, and Louis would hardly like to see a brother monarch defeated by his subjects."

"Revenge," said St. John. "Louis has no love for America, nor for free men. But he loves the English still less. Don't forget, we were so tactless as to win our last war with France! They have been waiting for this, hoping for it, ever since the Stamp Act trouble. Now is their chance! I don't say Louis' motives are lofty, but if he will send us a fleet, I won't ask why!"

He filled Julian's glass and his own, and reached for the poker to push a charred log further into the flame.

It was Julian who broke the pause this time.

"I have been a little worried about Tibby," he began, and St. John glanced at him humorously.

"I shouldn't wonder," he murmured.

"You have noticed the same thing, then," said Julian, assuming with some relief that St. John shared his own wrongheaded conclusion that Tibby's heart was set on the one man who was certain to marry Regina.

"For some time," St. John nodded, believing that Julian was aware at last that Tibby would never be even remotely concerned with any other man in the world save the schoolmaster.

"Did she—have you ever spoken of it with her?"

"Good grief, man, what kind of blundering fool do you think I am?" demanded St. John. "I couldn't speak of it, any more than I could strip her naked! Besides, it's all still in the bud. She hardly knows herself how it is with her."

"She knows enough to be jealous of Regina," Julian informed him ruefully.

"I shall take a cane to Regina one of these days," St. John promised darkly. "And when I do, don't you come trying to stay my hand, Julian! I have warned you before. Not just because I mean to marry her myself —not so much that as because I am devilish fond of you, old sobersides, and I don't want to see you driven right out of your mind, understand?" His eyes rested with their clear, childlike frankness on Julian's averted face.

"She has no use for the likes of us nowadays," said Julian. "David Allen is in New York with a King's commission."

"*The bastard!*" yelled St. John, leaping in his chair. "What regiment?"

"Simcoe's Rangers."

"Simcoe, eh! Well, it's a real fighting corps he has got himself into, even if they do wear pretty green hussar coats and tight breeches! So *that's* the kind of blankety-blank sons-of-so-and-so's she calls her friends now, is it!"

And in the flow of language which followed and the wrathful emptying of the bottle, Tibby was forgotten and neither one of them knew that they had been talking about her entirely at cross purposes.

Soon after Christmas St. John was off, still hobbling with a cane, to rejoin his regiment in winter quarters at a place in Pennsylvania called

Valley Forge, and the Francis Street household was empty and aimless again.

His letters were far between, and some of them got lost on the road, but there was a long one during May which described the celebration at Valley Forge of the French treaty of alliance—a full parade of the starving, ragged troops, he wrote, heartened as never before since the war began—and the *feu de joie* of musketry running along the lines, and the hoarse, glad shout: *"The American States!"*—and the officers' so-called banquet, and the toasts, and the new lift to Washington's chin.

He wrote that Clinton had succeeded the easygoing Howe in command of the British forces in America, and that no British general with a grain of sense would now attempt to hold Philadelphia, what with a French fleet due over the horizon any minute. And sure enough, in June Clinton began an elaborate evacuation of the city, with Washington's dogged, indomitable army at his heels.

Francis Street had to wait nearly a month for St. John's version of the battle of Monmouth, which had been fought to a draw in sweltering June heat.

"You will have heard that Clinton got away to New York," he wrote. "He had to leave his dead unburied to do it, and abandon most of his wounded. Admiral D'Estaing arrived with the French fleet just too late to be any good to us! The day of the battle was hotter than the hinges, and darkness fell too soon. Everything went wrong on our side, and Washington swore like an angel from heaven, until it was a privilege to hear him.

"I am whole and hearty and full of chagrin. It was our chance to trounce them, and we missed it. The British are now pretty well back where they started from, and there is still no end in sight."

No end in sight. And there the dreary prospect lay throughout the autumn of 1778 and until December, when bad news began to arrive from the opposite direction.

Having failed to smash Washington or to lead him into a trap and capture him, Clinton sent Colonel Campbell south by sea at the end of the year, and Williamsburg learned with a sinking sensation that the British had actually taken Savannah. By spring the invading army was spreading northward, gathering Loyalist forces as it went, and General Lincoln hurried down from the north, overland, to direct a second defense of Charleston.

The war was closing in on Virginia now. Portsmouth was defenseless. Norfolk was still in ruins. Yorktown lay open on the sea way to Williamsburg—where would the British be brought to a stand? Thomas Jefferson succeeded Patrick Henry as Governor of Virginia that summer, and on his urgent recommendation the capital and legislature were moved up the James to Richmond, where records, stores, and the governing body were less liable to capture by a sea borne army. With Palace and Capitol deserted, and people like Mr. Randolph and Mr. Mason absent most of the time, Williamsburg felt oddly naked and empty.

Dorothea received a proposal of marriage in June, from a dashing youngster who was off to join Lincoln in Carolina. She refused him with such kindness and confusion that he departed still hoping, and Aunt Anabel sighed and dratted the war, which was robbing her lovely niece of the swarm of suitors which was her due.

Georgia, disorganized and overrun, offered little resistance as 1779 rolled on, and a slave population less loyal and more numerous than Virginia's gave the enemy a terrible advantage. In the Carolina back country bitter feeling arose between Loyalist and Patriot neighbors, who shamelessly betrayed each other in the interest of the cause. The British were quick to profit by the internal strife in the South, and cruel reprisals began on both sides amongst the colonists.

"They say that Clinton himself has sailed from New York with nearly ten thousand men to take Charleston," Julian wrote in his journal, now in its third volume, early in 1780. "We have not heard from St. John since Christmas, when he wrote to say that this winter in the old camp at Morristown was worse, if possible, than last year at Valley Forge.

"There is a rumor that Washington is sending all his southern troops, including the Virginia regiments, down to reinforce Lincoln. They are determined to hold Charleston at all costs, and Clinton has failed there once before. This time, however, he has an active and organized land force already in the field.

"And so the war comes south at last, perhaps because Washington has proved too much for the English generals. Everyone hopes that if things get really bad—if, for instance, the British should take Charleston—Washington will come down himself to direct our campaign."

At this point his pen had come to a stop while he contemplated the echo in his written words of that first day in the coach, when St. John had said, *We can be pushed just so far.* We. He and the colonists. And Julian had learned with surprise that St. John was English-born like himself. Now, on the freshly written page of his own journal, *our campaign.* He realized that like St. John he had come to identify himself completely with the colonists. He too had taken root here, meant to live and die here, like George Wythe and the rest who only a few years ago had still called England home.

How had it come about, he wondered, while odd flashes of memory supplied odd, fragmentary answers: the dignity and magnetism of George Washington that first evening at the Raleigh and his tenderness for an injured child; *thy people shall be my people*—out of the twilight on Mrs. Hartley's front steps as Tibby stood before him with her arm in a sling; the peal of a churchbell penetrating oblivion in the room above the school, and the worn, sweet face of Sarah Mawes as she sat beside his bed; the dominie's little hoard, bequeathed without question to the Winchester scholar who had come to take his place—*hand knowledge on;* the strength and fire and lilt of St. John's nature, which had flung him headlong into this cause they both believed to be right; Aunt Anabel's gay, loving ways, and Dorothea's damask beauty; all the rest of them, from Mr. Wythe to the Spragues' black Joshua, friendly, openhanded, confiding, ready and willing that he should be one of them, withholding nothing from him just because he had come to them a penniless stranger, anxious only that he should at once feel at home among them and should lack for nothing which it was within their power to supply. His people now, holding his daily life in their warm, gentle hands, possessing all his heart. . . .

Well, not quite all. There was Regina Greensleeves, who preferred a man who joined Simcoe's Rangers. . . .

His pen was moving again, down the page.

"As soon as we can learn where St. John is, I will go to him, and leave it to his good sense to determine how I can be most useful henceforth.

I have never fired a musket in my life, and am not at all sure of my ability to lead men into and out of danger, though I presume I can stand fire myself. I can ride, and use a sword, and possibly if there is a cavalry regiment forming I could find a place in that.

"It is when I think of Tibby and Aunt Anabel and—the others, in the possible line of fire, that I feel I must somehow place myself between them and harm. The barbarous behavior of Campbell and Prevost since Savannah fell has pretty well eliminated my bone-deep prejudice against going to war against my countrymen. Henceforth I am truly a Virginian.

"If the British take Charleston they will take Norfolk, and soon after that they will be in the streets of Williamsburg. They must be stopped before then, somehow. This endless, indecent war between Englishmen must be stopped. It need never have begun but for one man, an outsider, and I think now more than a little mad, with the obstinate Guelph itch to dominate, and too much power. But it is a strange feeling, all the same, to have no king. Who takes his place? I suppose the answer is Washington. He has dignity and compassion, without which no man has the right to command loyalty from his fellow human beings."

XXII

Julian was dining in Francis Street that day early in June of 1780 when Williamsburg learned that Charleston was lost.

There was a brooding sense of unreality over the meal, though everything seemed exactly as usual—the gleam of polished silver and white napery, the soft-stepping service, the solicitous bend of Joshua's broad back above the proffered dishes. Julian sat between the two women, and they tried not to talk on and on about the war, which until then had been remote and a little hard to keep track of. Even with St. John away fighting, they did not quite realize the war—for he had been away before, on peaceful errands. One could forget, even with shirtmen drilling on the Palace Green, that America was at death grips, if one lived in Williamsburg and it was summer time, and the roses were in bloom. But the British in Charleston—a whole American army taken prisoners

—*at Charleston*—surely one would wake up soon and know it all for nightmare!

The dreadful story of Charleston's surrender had come up slowly, overland. They pieced it together in low voices while they ate, pooling rumor and hearsay—what Julian had heard at the College and the Raleigh—what Mr. Greensleeves had written his wife from Philadelphia—what Joshua had got from the Randolphs' coachman. General Lincoln was a prisoner of war, as everybody knew; Lord Rawdon, with British and Hessian troops, Tarleton's famous cavalry, and Cornwallis had all arrived at Charleston from New York with reinforcements for Clinton; there were hangings and confiscation and terror in Charleston among people alleged by the British to have broken their paroles, unwillingly given, not to take up arms in the Patriot cause, and inhabitants roundabout the city were flocking to take the oath of allegiance to save their skins and their property; Clinton was garrisoning Camden, Augusta, Ninety-Six, and other points in the Carolina interior; armed bands, both Loyalist and Whig, were plundering and intimidating the countryside; the British had turned brutal on this southern campaign, and were carrying off at will everything from silver to slaves, while Tarleton's green-clad dragoons became a byword for ruthless raiding. . . .

Jefferson as Governor at Richmond had admitted freely in a letter to Mr. Wythe that there was very little to oppose the British advance on Virginia except the ill-equipped, frightened militia and a small force of Continentals under General de Kalb who had been rushed south in an attempt to rescue Lincoln, and who were now at Richmond trying to accumulate supplies of food, wagons, and horses. And over the Francis Street dinner table, between alternate hope and despair, they speculated about what Washington would do to save his own beloved Virginia from Carolina's fate. They wanted Washington there with his army, and they wanted St. John. Then, they felt, they could face things.

Hating to rob them of the illogical comfort they drew from his own presence, in the way of women who see an able-bodied man within reach, Julian said at the end of the meal—

"I am going to Richmond tomorrow."

They stared at him, stricken.

"F-for long?" quavered Aunt Anabel, guessing the answer.

"Yes. I shan't come back till the war is won."

"Oh, Julian, I'm glad you said *won*," said Dorothea softly. "You used not to be so sure—"

"I used to be more of a fool than I am now," he confessed brusquely. "I don't know how or when—but it has got to be won. Else this country won't be fit for people like you to live in," he finished, and laid his hand over Aunt Anabel's with impulsive tenderness.

"But I thought at least you would wait till we heard from Sinjie," she objected.

"I can't wait any longer."

"Julian—" Dorothea leaned to look into his face. "—that doesn't mean you think we won't hear—?"

He gave her his other hand, and sat linked to them both, his heart wrung by their helplessness and their faith in his omniscience.

"No, it doesn't mean that at all," he assured them hastily. "If St. John's regiment is on the move he may not be allowed to send word of his whereabouts. Or if he did write, the post-bag has been captured again. There are a dozen good reasons why we don't hear from him, but you will get a letter soon, you're bound to."

"You could ask them at Richmond." Aunt Anabel discovered some consolation in the idea. "You could ask de Kalb, since he has just come down from Morristown."

"Yes, my dear, I could ask de Kalb," he agreed. "And while I am away, will you please keep an eye on the twins for me? See that they have whatever they need—I will leave some money with you to cover it."

"You will take your money with you," said Aunt Anabel firmly. "And be sure I will do everything I can for them, but Sarah is so stiff-necked and proud she smells charity in the very rain from heaven."

As they rose from the table, Aunt Anabel laid trembling lips against his cheek, murmured something about a parcel for his journey, and went away, blowing her nose. He followed Dorothea into the drawing-room and she paused beside the harpsichord, idly fingering the keys with one hand, fighting for composure. He came and stood near her, and took the slim, faltering fingers in his.

"You mustn't be unhappy about this," he said gently. "I haven't felt right about things since St. John put on a uniform, you know!"

"You aren't like Sinjie. He loves a fight—always has."

"I wish I were more like him," he admitted simply. "He is the kind they need to win the war. I shall just have to do the best I can."

There was a silence between them, her hand lying warm in his. She seemed to be waiting for something. Slowly she turned to him, lifting her face to see him better, and laid her other hand on his shoulder.

"Good luck, Julian. I—we will be thinking of you—praying for you —every day. Promise to come back safe."

"I shall come back safe," he repeated gravely, and looked away from her round the gracious room, the only home he had ever known. "And I shall always remember this house, no matter where I am. You have been very good to me, you and Aunt Anabel. You know," he smiled, "even before you came, they promised me a sister."

Dorothea snatched her hand away and stepped back, her chin well up. He had never seen her angry before.

"I am *not* your sister!" she cried, and stamped her foot at him. "I'm not even kissing kin to you, and I'll thank you to remember it!"

And she was gone, with a rustle of silk, into the hall and up the stairs, on flying feet. A door slammed.

Julian looked after her, astonished and rather hurt. He had had no idea of presuming to kiss her. He found his hat on the table in the hall and let himself out into the street.

When he told Regina he was going to Richmond she assumed that he would ask for a commission, and when he doubted his fitness as an officer, she opened her eyes and inquired if he had lost his mind entirely, and just what did he intend to do.

"What they seem to need now is a lot of men to carry muskets and shoot them off at people in red coats," he told her patiently. "I thought perhaps I could learn to do that."

"*In the ranks?*" cried Regina. "But that is even worse than St. John!"

"I am afraid it will be some time before I am as good as St. John."

"But, Julian, you can't serve as a common soldier! You would die of it in a week!"

Somehow her sureness of that caught him on the raw, and he answered with a spirit he seldom showed to her.

"I am getting into this war now, the quickest way I can! And if that means slogging along on foot and biting cartridges under fire, that is the way it will be!"

"St. John will be pleased!" was all she could find to say to that. "Why don't you go and take orders from him?"

"I should like to. But we don't know where he is."

"Haven't you heard from him?" she asked quickly, for as the war dragged on she was haunted more and more by a memory of her own voice crying, *I hope you never come back!* and a memory still more relentless of St. John's white face—and she too wished now that she hadn't said it, would have given the tongue out of her head to have the thoughtless, cruel words unsaid—and sometimes in the night another voice which came from her heart reiterated that it would serve her right if he never came back. . . . "Haven't you heard from him?" she implored quickly.

"Not for some time. He was at Morristown then, but it is time for the summer campaign. Washington will be on the move from there."

"He can't move far from New York! He daren't turn his back on the British there!"

"Regina, don't let's quarrel over Washington now," he pleaded.

"I'm not quarrelling over anybody!" she denied indignantly. "I hate to see my friends make fools of themselves, that's all! Even St. John has a commission!"

"Even David Allen has one," he reminded her.

"A better one than St. John's!" she laughed. "You might at least join the right army, Julian!"

"I am joining the right army—the one that is fighting for a man's right to his own opinions and the life he wants to live and a hand in his own government. It isn't England that sends a gang of bullies in red coats to dispute that right with us. It is a King and his minions, a King who speaks our language with a German accent—"

"Oh, Julian, you sound like a Continental Congress! I won't listen!"

"You don't have to listen. I didn't come here today to argue the Patriots' cause with you." He stood watching her sadly from across the room. "I only came to look at you once more—to hear your voice. I know I have no right, as St. John's friend, to say these things to you, but I know too that they won't matter very much, one way or the other, in the end. It is St. John you love, and that is as it should be." She started to interrupt him then, but he overruled her without raising his voice and went on. "Before I go I only want to say—I love you, Regina. Ever since that first day at Yorktown. You don't have to answer, or pretend to be surprised or say you're sorry. I love you. That is really all I came to say. And then, good-bye."

He went towards her slowly and she rose to meet him. Her breath came between parted lips, her blue eyes were wide and waiting. His simple sincerity moved her deeply as it always did, and there was more than her wilful coquetry in the warm surrender of her hands to his. He stood looking down at her for a long moment before he could speak.

"If things were a little different," he said, "I might be asking you to marry me."

"If things were only a little different," she whispered in all honesty, "I might be saying Yes."

He kissed her, his hands holding hers—a boy's kiss, gentle and undemanding.

"Thank you," he said, and went.

The sun was low behind the trees and the quick southern dusk was near when he came to himself, he had no idea how much later, in the lane beyond the Capitol. Not far ahead the oyster shells which lined the path leading down to Tibby's home were pale in the shadows. He paused a moment and stood staring towards the cabin in a daze. Yes, of course —he could not go away without seeing Tibby.

He crossed the lane. Kit was hoeing in the garden patch beside the gate.

"Is Tibby there?" Julian called to him.

"Yes, sir. Shall I fetch her out?"

"Please."

He leaned against the gate-post and it swayed drunkenly under his elbow. He waited for Tibby, his eyes on the last bright streaks of sunlight which caught the treetops along the Creek. He must talk to her alone. No more fuss. Tibby wouldn't make a fuss. . . .

She came to him swiftly down the path, with her greenish eyes shining. She wore her pigtails pinned in a tight knot on the nape of her neck now, and carried her head high on its slender stem. Her still childish body was clothed tonight in a faded cotton print gown with a white apron freshly tied on with hasty fingers when she saw him from the window as he crossed the lane. Mrs. Hallam had closed the school for lack of pupils, and now Tibby did the fine laundry and household jobs her mother was becoming too frail to accomplish alone. Julian was so accustomed to her scrupulous tidiness that it never occurred to him to wonder that she could spend a sultry day ironing gauze caps and fichus and then present herself to him looking as crisp and sweet as morning. She made him her curtsy just inside the gate.

"Good evening, sir."

He glanced behind him, where the lane ran on towards the Landing and the new stone bridge with a wooden railing above the sluggish water. It was not much used these days.

"Will you come with me?" he asked, and unquestioningly she opened the gate and came through it to walk at his side.

By the time they reached the sandy planks of the bridge the first fire-flies were gleaming in the bushes, and the twilight chorus of tree-peepers had begun. The Landing was deserted, except for an ancient Negro dozing in a rowboat which waited with its nose against the muddy bank and its painter knotted to a post at the bottom of the steps.

Julian took off his hat and leaned his elbows on the railing above the water, and stood looking down. Tibby hooked her heels over the bottom rail and hoisted herself up with the ease of habit, to sit facing him beside where his elbows rested. This brought their heads almost on a level, and whereas he stood gazing into the slack water below them, she saw nothing but Julian Day almost under her hand—preoccupied as he often was in her presence; in trouble, apparently, but seeking her company.

"You are going to the war," she said at last, and he smiled without meeting her eyes.

"How did you know that?"

"I knew you would go, sooner or later."

"You wanted me to go, then."

"No, I wanted you to stay here. But I knew you would think it was right to go."

"You might have said something about it a little sooner."

"It's soon enough," she sighed. "I have been dreading it. What will become of the school?"

"Closed, till the war is won. All the older boys have gone, anyway. And you will think better of me, all the same, when I am in the army."

"I couldn't think better of you than I always have."

"Weren't you ever ashamed of me, Tibby—for not taking sides?" He raised his eyes from the water to her face, and they seemed to her to be pleading for something she did not know how to give. "I wonder you didn't disown me, when Mr. Sprague went north."

Tibby looked back at him mutely, while her heart pounded somewhere at the top of her throat, and the piercing music of the peepers was drowned in the song of her own young blood in her veins. She had not been so close to him for a long time—years, maybe. Never before had she seen him levelly like this, eyes to eyes—the shadow his dark lashes cast, the way his hair grew reddish round his ears, the strong, generous curve of his mouth—Tibby gripped the railing on either side of her and struggled against giddiness. It crossed her mind to tell him that you can't disown God, but that would sound profane, so she said nothing and prayed instead that she would not topple backwards into the water.

"Poor Tibby," he was saying. "Why do you put up with me? No one else can."

"Was Miss Regina very angry," she asked astutely, "because you are going to the war?"

"According to Miss Regina, I am joining the wrong army," he confessed with a wry smile.

"Her and that David Allen!" Tibby lifted her nose.

"Now, how on earth did you ever hear of him?"

"Mr. Sprague. He laughed. He always laughs about David Allen, but it hurts him just the same. Is it true that she never saw him all that time he was here wounded?"

"Yes. It is true."

"She doesn't deserve him."

"She loves him, though, Tibby. We might as well make up our minds to that, you and I." He laid his arm across her lap to the rail on the other side of her. It was a gesture to comfort a child, and to steady her on her perch. It brought their left shoulders near together as he leaned a little towards her, holding the rail beyond. She wondered if he would notice her heart pounding a few inches away from his sleeve. She wondered what he would think if she bent forward and laid her cheek just once against his and begged him not to mind so much about Miss Regina, who deserved nothing better than David Allen anyway. *You and I.* What did he mean by that? It sounded nice. She was not within miles of guessing his obstinate conviction that it was St. John she had set her heart on. "All this about David Allen," he was saying, "that is just to save her pride. But if she married him—or anyone else—it would be only to spite Mr. Sprague, you know that, don't you? And you want him to have a chance to be happy with her when he comes back from the war—don't you, child?"

"Why, yes, of course," agreed Tibby, who would never have questioned St. John's right to happiness with whatever woman he chose. But anyone could see what the trouble was, just as she had long suspected. "Oh, Mr. Day," she cried, and laid her arms around him, "I'm so sorry you want her too!"

"We must try not to—not to grudge it them, mustn't we." And with an odd breathless sound he hid his face against her shoulder.

Tibby held him, sitting motionless with awe and amazement. He was breaking his heart over Regina Greensleeves, but he was here in the mothering arms of Tibby Mawes, where he had come of his own accord, seeking comfort.

It was quite dark now, with the moon still below the trees. The ancient Negro apparently slept in the bottom of the boat, the peeper chorus grew in volume, the fireflies were myriad. Intoxicated with her own daring in the fragrant, pulsing night, she laid her face against Julian's hair. He seemed not to notice. She racked her brains for anything to offer him in his need, for philosophy or consolation for his trouble.

"Would you like me to say you a piece?" she whispered dubiously, and he nodded against her shoulder while his arm tightened to draw her closer.

" 'Thou shalt not be afraid for the terror by night,' " said Tibby with her cheek against his hair. " 'Nor for the arrow that flieth by day; nor for the pestilence that walketh in darkness; nor for the destruction that wasteth at noonday. A thousand shall fall at thy side, and ten thousand at thy right hand; but it shall not come nigh thee. There shall no evil befall thee, neither shall any plague come nigh thy dwelling. For He shall give His angels charge over thee, to keep thee in all thy ways. They shall bear thee up in their hands, lest thou dash thy foot against a stone.' "

After a long moment he stirred, and lifted his head slowly, and leaned again on the railing, his arm still lying across her lap. She let his weight

go from her reluctantly, her fingers lingering on his coat. It was too dark
now to see his face.

"You're sweet, Tibby," he said. "You're sweet and strong and very
wise. How are you so wise at your age?"

It crossed her mind to tell him that she was old enough now, surely,
to work things out for herself and be of some use to people, if only they
would give her a chance—if only people would stop thinking of her as
a child, just because she stayed so small. It was no child's love she felt
for him any more, she knew, still tingling as she was with the warmth
and size of him in her arms, still dizzy with the pomaded scent of his
hair against her face. This was the lord of her world, she knew, and
there would never be any other. But how could one presume to point it
out to him, and he the schoolmaster—how could one say to him, even
in the shielding dark, that there was nothing he could ask of her that
was not already his? Take me instead, she might have said—I'm not
beautiful, I'm not a lady born, I'm not very old, but I'm yours, and maybe
I'll grow—take me, for your comforting, I'll never ask for more. But he
had left his heart with Regina Greensleeves, and so again Tibby was
mute, and the moment passed.

"You are a silent creature too," he murmured in the dark, and now
there was a smile in his low voice. "Be not silent to me, Tibby, lest I
become like them that go down into the pit."

"Oh, Mr. Day!" she gasped. "That's sacrilege!"

"Is it, my dear? To implore you, as I have done, to find me a ransom,
and bring back my soul from the pit where it seems to dwell along with
Job's?"

"I would do anything I could for you," she said, too simply for diffidence. "I would be the ransom, if you—if you—"

"You are braver than I am, Tibby," he said ruefully. "To hear you,
one would think you had nothing to bear yourself."

"I don't know what you mean," she said helplessly. "If only I were a
boy I would run away and go to the war with you. If only I were Kit,
you would not have to go alone!"

"If only you were a boy we might go and drown our sorrows in persimmon beer tonight!" he said with an effort at cheerfulness, and
straightened from the railing. In the dark his hands found her shoul-

ders and he lifted her down. Someone was coming along the lane with a lantern, a man's voice shouted for Bide, and the old Negro answered from the rowboat against the bank. "As it is, I shall now see you safely home. You had better take my hand, or we may both end in the ditch after all!"

"The moon will be up soon." Her small fingers slid gratefully into his clasp. "We could see our way home better then."

"We can see it now, between us." He moved towards the oncoming lantern. "They will think we are a courting couple," he remarked, and she would have said that she wished they were, but could not, because of Regina Greensleeves.

"When do you go?" she asked instead, as they picked their way along the dusty lane.

"Tomorrow morning."

"So soon?" she said faintly.

"The sooner the better now."

"And what will you do?"

"Whatever they tell me to, at Richmond."

"They need horses."

"Yes, I shall trade mine in for a musket."

"And will you wear a uniform like Mr. Sprague?"

"Mr. Sprague is an officer. I shall have to wear a hunting shirt, no doubt."

They walked in silence for a while, her hand in his, and the lighted windows of her home lay just ahead as the moon broke out, strong and golden, above the treetops. Just three minutes more, she was thinking— two minutes—one minute more, and he will be gone, and there will be nothing left but waiting and emptiness and praying he won't be killed. She had not for years been without the hope of a sight of him each day.

They paused at her gate, and he stood looking down at her, bare- headed in the moonlight, her hand in his.

"Well, Tibby—this is good-bye."

"You will send me word sometimes?"

"I'll try to. But it won't be easy, you know."

"I—I'm not so very brave after all," she discovered, and suddenly leaned against him, a hand at her throat.

"Why, Tibby—" He was infinitely touched. "Tibby, you aren't going to cry—I haven't seen you cry since that day at Jamestown—child, will you miss me so much?"

She wanted to sob at him that you must miss the air you breathe and the light of the sun in the heavens, but if he could not see for himself that without him you were beggared and useless and maimed, what was the good of saying anything at all? Tibby set her teeth and stood away from him, breathing through her nose.

"I'm sorry, sir—I was acting like a cry-baby. Good-bye, sir."

"Good-bye." She looked so small under the moon, so straight, so alone and defenseless. He bent swiftly and kissed her cheek. "Good-bye, sweetheart. And God keep you."

"Thank you, sir," said Tibby unsteadily—and then because it was bad luck to watch a person out of sight, she hid her face in her arms on top of the gate while his footsteps receded into the dark.

The Carolinas

1780

I

The hot sun was coming up behind him as Julian rode out of Williamsburg that morning in early June of 1780. In his saddlebags he carried two changes of linen, a warm extra waistcoat, spare stockings and queue ribbons, a bachelor's sewing kit without a thimble, toilet articles including a razor and a cake of soap, a brandy flask, a packet of food, and two small volumes—Dryden and the Earl of Chesterfield, the latter a recent and as yet unexplored purchase.

He took the river road which ran left of the College—the road along which he had set out on another June morning with the twins for a picnic on the bank at Jamestown—that day when they had heard about Bunker Hill. Five years ago—and it seemed a lifetime. This was his seventh Virginia June; the long hot days and sweet sudden nightfalls filled with Negro melody; the mingled scent of dusty pink roses and box hedges and herb gardens in the midday sun; the silent miracle of fireflies before the round yellow moon came up, and the tiny frog choir down by the Creek. Virginia—soft as a woman, stanch as a friend, and always good to look at—he belonged to it now. It was home.

Before long, as he rode beneath the tall cool pines, the turning which led down to Jamestown Island curved away on his left. He passed it with a backward look and kept on his way up the river towards Charles City Courthouse and Richmond. But he remembered the rank smell of the steaming marsh as they crossed it that other morning when the war had not yet really begun, for Virginia—the deep shade of the sycamores around the broken church and Tibby's voice saying, "Tell about the bride-ship"—Tibby laying out the picnic meal on a clean napkin spread on the grass and propping up the doll Julia to look on—Tibby's grief, silent and quivering in his arms, so that he promised to stay in Virginia till he grew a long white beard. . . . And now here he was, riding out to war, with the long white beard becoming somewhat problematical.

Tibby's small brown hands had caught and held his life in a world, no longer new to him, where men did not hesitate to stand on their rights and did not flinch from shedding blood to maintain them—a violent, sore-beset world now, grim and groggy and battered, but still on its legs and fighting mad. Not children playing with fire in Arcadia now, he realized. Not irresponsible rebels who liked the sound of their own stirring phrases. Not two or three sullen cities defying from a safe distance a just and well-intentioned king. This was a new nation, a virile, lion-hearted chip of the old block, determined, as Englishmen always are, not to be browbeaten—much less browbeaten by a rank outsider of limited intelligence and mid-European ideas of government. This was the spirit of Runnymede abroad in a new land. This was a fight Englishmen had fought before and would doubtless have to fight again—a fight to preserve personal liberty and constitutional government from the encroachment of tyranny. As an Englishman, he belonged in this fight himself, on the side of the men who demanded the things England itself stood for, no matter who sat on the throne.

It was not a state of mind he had easily recognized in himself—this strong necessity to go out and hit back at something. But gradually it grew on him. St. John always loved a fight, whether it was a friendly fencing bout in the back garden just to work up a healthy muck sweat, or a thunder of cannon and rattle of cavalry which was war—St. John took fire, he laughed aloud, his quick, hard body braced itself competently to shock and effort, he got something out of it, something which to him was joy. The Days were bookish men, uncombative, slow to anger, patient in adversity—but the iron strain was there, and a dogged sort of courage which never failed them. The fall of Charleston had reached that deep vein in Julian, as the war came home to him. Deliberately, as he did everything, he had made up his mind. Clinton must be stopped. And he personally must go and see that Clinton was stopped, else his life would not be worth the living any more, for he would have

no right to things he was accustomed to think of as his, nor to the
friendship of people he had come to love. *I was a stranger.* . . . But not
any more. I am a Virginian. I defend her soil.

His horse's feet were clumping daintily over a stretch of corduroy
road and he roused to glimpse the mansion called Green Spring through
the pines. When Jamestown was the capital, Green Spring was the
Governor's country home, and old Lord Berkeley, the Cavalier Governor, had held his court there a hundred years ago. It belonged now
to the Ludwells, who were abroad, and like their house in the Duke of
Gloucester Street it was closed, but Julian had been granted permission by the agent to see it in connection with the chapter on the Bacon
Rebellion in his history. That too seemed a long time ago now. The
history, painstakingly documented, lovingly penned, and copied fair
and after anxious excisions and additions and more deletions copied
again, had been bogged down for quite some time, at the chapter on
the Stamp Act. He had stuck there, conscious of a growing difference
between his own opinions and those his father had held. Or would not
his father have changed too by now? During the recent period of inner
turmoil Julian had laid the history aside, for it only underlined his
difficulties. Now that he was clear in his mind again, now that he saw
his way and had set his course, there was no time to finish the manu-
script. When the war was won he could write books. But first . . .

He left Green Spring behind and came to the slashes—a low wet re-
gion covered with pine, slippery to a horse's feet, dismal and lonely
to a rider. After about five miles of it the road emerged on the high
sandy bank of the Chickahominy and there was the cheerful bustle
of the ferry and the usual ticklish business of a nervous horse which
would not trim the boat.

Then he rode on through the slashes, and for the first time in years
he was aware of America as a wilderness again—for this was the
furthest he had ever penetrated into the back country, though he only
followed a route often taken by Jefferson to his home near Charlottesville, and by St. John Sprague on his errands for Mr. Wythe's law practice in the years before the war took him north to his post at Washington's side. Williamsburg seemed already very far behind.

He came at last to Charles City Courthouse, where a chance conversation at the only inn revealed that de Kalb had moved down to Peters-

burg and was there awaiting orders, reinforcements, supplies—he had need of them all. With him was an inadequate army of perhaps two thousand Continentals—veteran Maryland and Delaware troops. Presumably he knew what he was about, but with Charleston fallen his little corps hadn't a hope unless reinforcements came in soon.

Looking very thoughtful, Julian rode without hesitation to the nearest ferry and crossed the James River, bound for Petersburg.

It was a small town, easily swamped by even a small army. Julian dismounted in front of Pride's Tavern, which was swarming with soldiers, and began to tie his reins to the hitching-bar. A rough-looking man in a sort of uniform of faded blue stuff with facings which had once been scarlet eased up beside him and spoke confidentially out of the corner of his mouth.

"Wouldn't leave that horse here alone by itself if I was you."

"Why not?" asked Julian with a level look.

"We need horses. You wouldn't be aimin' to sell it?"

"I might."

The man spat lustily, more from swagger than from need.

"How if I was to get you a good price for it?"

"Who are you?" asked Julian, his tone polite, his eyes watchful.

"Sergeant Appleby, Sixth Maryland."

"How's recruiting, Sergeant?"

"Bad."

"You get me into the Sixth Maryland, and we'll see about the horse," Julian suggested, and the sergeant blinked.

"Mean you figger to enlist?"

"Well, I thought it was about time, yes. Any vacancies?"

"Plenty. Where you from?"

"Williamsburg."

"Ain't Virginia puttin' any regiments into the field these days?"

"Militia. I thought—"

"Mean you want to join *for the war?*"

"Till it's won, yes."

"Glory be!" murmured the sergeant mildly, and something like respect dawned in his hard black eyes. "Young feller, you come along with me—and bring that horse!"

Julian followed him down the middle of the busy street, leading the horse, which drew covetous glances on every side.

"You see, I haven't got a musket," he explained, his long strides easily matching the sergeant's. "So I thought—"

"Muskets are plaguey scarce. Cartridge paper is scarcer still and wagons just *ain't*. That's what we're waitin' for—wagons. And ammunition stores ain't no good without cartridge paper. The Governor of this here state of yours—Jefferson—what's he doin' all this time?"

"He is an able man, I believe."

"Then where's our cartridge paper? Where's our wagons? Heard about Charleston?"

"Yes. That is why I am here."

"Looks like we'll need some help, eh!" The sergeant laughed bitterly. 'Wisht a few more of 'em felt the same way. Never been in the army?"

"No. I can fence, but that's about all."

"Fancy swordwork, eh! Not much good here. We use muskets and bayonets."

"Yes, I know. I have never handled either one."

"God above!" breathed the sergeant.

"Pistols, of course, but—"

"Can't figger you out, quite. What's your trade?"

"I am a schoolmaster."

"That so? I mighta known." The sergeant eyed him with new interest. "Greek and Latin?"

"Oh, yes. And Euclid! That's not much good here either, is it?"

"How's your guts?"

"All right, I hope," said Julian briefly, and the sergeant nodded, for something in the quiet self-possession which walked beside him had caught his rugged fancy.

"Of course we're a Maryland regiment," said the sergeant with significance, and added on a sidelong glance, "You bein' from Virginia puts you kinda out of step to begin with. Now, Baltimore's a nice genteel place—"

"Very well," Julian agreed promptly, "I'm from Baltimore."

"You don't say!" exclaimed the sergeant in pleased surprise, and offered to shake hands. "I'm from Baltimore myself! Funny I never run

into you there! But, say, I dunno, if you've got a family in Williamsburg—"

"I haven't."

"Bein' wrote down from Baltimore, y'see, if anything *happened,* like,
you wouldn't be on the Virginia casualty list, an'—but so long as you
didn't leave an old mother or a best girl back there in Williamsburg—?"
He paused incredulously.

"No," said Julian, anxious only to get the formalities over and set
about the grim business of being a soldier.

"Well, ye're lucky, at that. I got two kids in Baltimore—kinda like
to live to see 'em grow up."

"I hope you will," said Julian simply. "Now, about that musket—"

The sergeant laid a hand on his sleeve and pointed. They had come
to some tents at the end of a lane leading out of the main street. Ahead
of them passed a little procession carrying long bundles, each slung between the shoulders of two men who carried spades and pick-axes also.

"Looks like we might have a spare musket or two," he said, and
gave a dry cough. "There goes the buryin' party."

Thus after a somewhat dim ritual of enrollment rather glossed over
in the circumstances, Julian found himself a private in the Sixth Maryland. With a final pang, he watched his pretty mare being led away,
and because the sergeant had liked him at sight received back almost
half her sale price.

The sergeant had already placed him in the care of a friend in the
ranks, Neddy Blake, for instruction in military life and etiquette, the
common words of command, the drum-beats, and the inner mysteries
of a musket. Neddy had a fine contempt for English shooting—the
regulars were taught to point their muskets horizontally, brace themselves for the recoil, and pull the trigger, hoping the gun would go off
—that way it took a man's weight in lead to kill him, said Neddy,
fondling his own gun and explaining further that she had such a tarnation recoil you had to aim at the knee and let her kick the ball into
their stomachs.

Julian nodded wisely with his teeth on edge, and fingered his unfamiliar weapon patiently under Neddy's guidance. It did not occur
to him at all that the army might have a better use for a man who spoke
three modern languages and wrote them in a fine, fast hand, than to

put him behind a musket he must learn how to fire. In Julian's mind, the
army was simply a place where you shot and were shot at. The nuances
of staff and headquarters appointments were unknown to him.

Neddy was a lean, hard-bitten man with a big nose—twice wounded
but indestructible, nursing a grim and gnawing desire to see the war
out wherever it carried him and however long it took. They sat together in the hot dusk beyond the cook-fires, slapping mosquitoes and
downing mugs of soup, and Neddy's talk rambled on while Julian
listened attentively, storing away facts in his trained memory for contemplation at his leisure.

The army at Petersburg had heard of Charleston's fall only the day
before, and it had been a bad blow. They were too late now, and too
few, but they would keep on southward, hoping for reinforcements,
harrying Clinton as much as possible, but of necessity keeping out of
his reach. The Baron was no man to give up now, said Neddy with
pride, and Julian saw that de Kalb was popular with his men. He had
a French aide, du Buysson, like a son to him, and Colonel Williams
of the Sixth, now acting as adjutant, was a fine soldiering man. And
then there was Armand's Legion, a scant hundred and fifty cavalry-
men, mostly Europeans, a tough, murderous crew, wanting a very
firm hand.

General Gist was all right, the commander of this Maryland brigade,
said Neddy, but General Smallwood, now, who had the First Brigade—
well, *he* thought he knew more than the Baron, which didn't on the
face of it make sense, the Baron having fought the Seven Years' War
abroad, and all. Some people made fun of the Baron for his frugality,
but that was wrong too. The Baron was poor. He had to clothe himself out of his pay and buy his own horses, and he had to pay in Continental money, which was now sixty dollars to one in gold; he had
to feed his orderlies and servants from his own table, he could not
even afford the equipage he was entitled to for travel in the field, and
had to lodge at mean inns and private houses and was pitilessly over-
charged. And now he could not even get cartridge paper out of the
State of Virginia. He'd seen better wars than this one, the Baron
had.

On the following day, what wagons they had were loaded with tents
and a meager supply of foodstuffs, and the army began to move south-

ward towards Hillsborough in Carolina, carrying its own baggage. The first few days weren't bad, though the relentless drums beat *reveille* in the gray light before dawn, and the *general* (strike tents, pack up, call in the guards, and stand to arms) came at six o'clock, and the *march* at seven. Except for shoulders aching from the unaccustomed weight of his musket and pack, and an uncommon amount of thirst, Julian stood it very well. He wore his own boots and tan breeches with a battered blue regimental coat which was a trifle short in the sleeves but otherwise a good fit, inherited like the musket from some Marylander who no longer had any need for it.

They marched through sandy, level country, southwest from Petersburg. Then, as they approached the Nottoway, the roads turned to red clay which rain made paste into which a man sank to his ankles and a horse to its knees. Wagons stuck in it up to the hubs, traces broke, wheels came off, axles gave way, increasing to danger point the loads of the wagons remaining in use. Equipment had to be abandoned, food began to run short, thunderstorms of incredible violence alternated with intolerable heat, and the bites of ticks and chiggers and mosquitoes were slow torture.

By the time they reached Hillsborough, where they hoped for a junction with some militia from Virginia and North Carolina, Julian was walking in a daze of sore fatigue, lightheaded with a permanent hunger, unshaven, caked with the red clay, his sole idea to keep up with Neddy, not to fall out and get left behind, not to think, not to feel, just to keep going somehow.

At Hillsborough they rested, he never knew nor cared how many days. Food was scarce in the barren countryside, but foraging parties brought in scraggy fowls and now and then a lean cow or a bag of corn. And food was less important for a while, if only you could stop walking, and tend your feet, and mend your clothes, and find water for a shave, and feel like a man again.

The militia, when it came, was scanty and ill-equipped and as hungry as anybody. There seemed to be no orders awaiting de Kalb at Hillsborough, and very little news. Clinton was said to have left Cornwallis to finish the job in the South, and returned to New York for another go at Washington. Nobody knew just where Cornwallis was now, but his next in command, young Lord Rawdon, was at Camden, and a makeshift design was evolved to harry his outposts and foraging parties in that vicinity till more ambitious plans could be laid.

During the halt at Hillsborough, while Julian was doing a job of sentry-go, he saw an odd little company ride into camp. There were about twenty of them, of all ages, well mounted and armed, but ragged and variously clad, and among them several big buck Negroes. They all wore black leather caps with a silver badge, and they were led by a thin, dark, frail-looking man with a closed, uncommunicative face. Their appearance was so completely unmilitary and their bearing so diffident that jests and jeers from the almost equally unpresentable Continentals followed them all the way to headquarters, where the thin man dismounted and walked with a noticeable limp into the building. Contrary to general expectations, he remained there with de Kalb a long time.

Neddy was not on sentry duty that day, and Neddy always circulated and got the news. Julian at his post saw Neddy in his characteristically casual conversation with one of the stranger's men while the horses were being watered, and knew a twinge of envy for Neddy's happy faculty of sliding into friendship with all comers. And as was to be expected, Neddy could hand out the facts over the scorched corn bread and watery soup which made up the evening meal.

"Yep," said Neddy with his mouth full, "that there was Francis Marion, as ever is." He affected a mild, indulgent surprise at the lack of intelligent comment from his hearers. "Ain't you heard," he inquired of them maddeningly, "ain't *none* of you dolts ever heard before of this here Francis Marion?" Nobody had. They admitted it impatiently, awaiting exposition. "Why, he's an Indian fighter from down Charleston way, he is. He was with Moultrie in '76 when they beat off the redcoats there, and he was with Lincoln last spring, too, only guess what happened." He paused impressively. No one spoke. "Well, I'll tell you what happened," he obliged then, pleased to see that his audience was growing. "Seems this feller Marion just naturally don't approve of cards and drinkin'. And one night a bunch of his team-mates thought to make him join the party willy-nilly and b'God they locked the door on him, sort of prankin' round, so's he couldn't leave. He left, though. By the window. But he had to jump for it and in doin' so he broke his ankle and had to be invalided out for a spell. Yessir, and

that busted ankle was all that saved him from bein' in Charleston with
the rest when Lincoln surrendered, and b'God that's why he wasn't
captured along with all the other officers!"

"That's a very moral tale, Neddy," Julian suggested affectionately.
"I hope you will let it be a lesson to you."

"That's the way they told it to me," Neddy insisted.

"So where did this Marion get his army?" asked a voice.

"They're all friends of hisn—people who could arm themselves and
live on next to nothin'. Yes, and masterless slaves too—he don't keer
what color you are so long as you've got a horse and can shoot straight.
What's more, if you *can't* shoot straight, you straightway lose your gun
to somebody that can, he don't waste no time lugging around fellers
that can't hit 'em right where the belt crosses!"

"And what did he want with the Baron?"

"Didn't want nothing'," said Neddy. "Came in to offer his services."

"Rode out agin, didn't he?"

"All but one man," said Julian unexpectedly.

"How's that agin?" Their eyes swung round to where he sat.

"He left one of his men here—name of Horry. Captain Horry. Won't
let anybody touch his horse, will he, Neddy?"

"No, *sir,* treats that horse like it was a baby! I offered to rub it down
fer him myself—like to git my hands on a good horse now and again.
He done it all himself, though. Kind of lonesome, maybe, when they
all rode off and left him here with us."

"Left him what fer?" inquired a voice.

"He's to be aide and guide to the Baron on the march. The Baron's
a smart one, and don't you fergit it. He'd ruther have Marion's gang
out in the swamps loose on the British than tied up with us. They're
like foxes, those fellers—once they go to earth nobody can find 'em till
they're ready to show—nobody but another one of the same kind. That's
why we've got Horry—couldn't get no word to Marion without him.
I got an idea we're goin' to need Captain Horry!"

Early in July the exhausted army under de Kalb reached the Deep
River and paused again at Buffalo Ford for recuperation and provisions.
The State of North Carolina had made no arrangement for the sub-
sistence of the troops which had been sent to protect it. The new crops
had not yet ripened and the population itself was living on the rem•

nants of last year. Foraging parties were under orders to commandeer only a reasonable part of each farmer's supply, leaving him something for himself, but though these orders were as a rule conscientiously carried out by the officers in charge there was a widening circle of resentment and hardship round the camp. A strong detachment of Carolina militia under General Caswell had already gleaned from the countryside and would not come in from its private skirmishes and join forces with de Kalb as it was expected to do.

Then in the middle of July news came to the Deep River camp. General Gates had been appointed by Congress to lead the Army of the South against Cornwallis, and was now on his way to take command.

To de Kalb, who had no petty ambition and felt his responsibilities keenly, it came as something of a relief to know that now he could turn them over to a superior officer. To the men, the appointment of the showy victor of Saratoga held out some promise of better communications, increased supplies, a new lease on life. But to Julian it was a depressing outlook.

Under de Kalb they had suffered greatly and endured almost unbearable privations, but always with the knowledge that their commanding officer shared their discomforts and was doing the best any general in his circumstances could do. They had confidence in de Kalb as a soldier, and affection for him as a man. But Julian remembered St. John's rude laughter at the time of Burgoyne's surrender—Gates was a summer soldier, hanging round Congress—Schuyler had done all the work before Saratoga—and now de Kalb had borne the brunt of the march through Carolina. How had Gates got in again?

Julian noticed that Neddy too sat silent among the hopeful speculations of the Sixth Maryland that night. Their eyes met, and Neddy shook his head.

"Don't do any harm to perk up their spirits some," he muttered. "But I'd sooner keep to the Baron. This ain't fair on the Baron, he hasn't had a dog's chance so far. Gates will come swelling into camp, maybe with wagons behind him, wagons full of rum, maybe, and they'll all let out their belts a notch and licker up and Gates will be a hero. The Baron has brought us this far. Why don't they send him more men and rations and wagons, instead of another general? We don't *need* Gates," Neddy summed it up querulously with a glance over his shoulder at his optimistic comrades. "All we need is what any self-respectin' army needs—something in our stummicks that will stick to our ribs, and something to carry our baggage—and maybe some more artillery. And all they send us is Gates!"

II

There were no wagons behind Gates, and consequently there was no rum.

He was full of assurances, however, exuding self-importance and creating enormous bustle. The camp was somewhat hypnotized by this impression of big things just ahead. But their brief enlivenment vanished in blank astonishment when his first orders contained the announcement that they must expect to march direct for Camden at a moment's notice. March on what? They had been served with half rations for that day, and nothing for tomorrow. And yet they were to move forward.

Julian was less surprised than most of them, but he wondered at the acquiescence of experienced officers like de Kalb and Gist and the adjutant, Williams, in so crack-brained a course. He had no way of knowing about the paralyzing over-confidence of the new broom, which left Gates' subordinates speechless and shrugging their shoulders in bewildered resignation. No man could be so wilfully wrong as Gates seemed to be. There must really be something in his loud reiterated promises of wagons loaded with rum and supplies which were to overtake them at any minute—had he not been, he demanded, in touch with the State legislature?

The noon day halt on the first day's march consumed the scraps which remained in the soldiers' knapsacks. For two more days they marched southward past empty houses and deserted fields, through devastating heat and blinding thunderstorms. The terrain got worse as they went, and no supplies arrived from the rear. The men, already weak, were staggering in their tracks, holding each other up, impeding the few overloaded wagons which were left. Still deprived of the soldier's only luxuries, rum and tobacco, the dark, scowling ranks had finally begun to straggle dangerously, to plunder and to steal.

Julian stumbled forward at Neddy's side in a nagging nightmare of being left behind in the wilderness which had at last engulfed him. By now they had come to the pine barrens, vast tracts of sandy waste alternating with swampy areas, where the crowding trees made twilight of high noon and a murmuring wind was never still; and at night the frogs' shrill clamor gnawed at nerves already ragged from the unceasing camp noises of coughing, groaning, belching, cursing men lost to the last decencies in their fatigue and misery. But for Julian there could be no surcease from the disgusting proximity of his wretched comrades, for he knew that in solitude lay oblivion and he was ridden by that dread of being left behind. . . .

From the Carolina militia, who knew the vicinity, a widening ripple of apprehension and dissatisfaction was spreading, picked up at once by the one-man intelligence bureau whch was Neddy Blake. The Carolinians said they were on the wrong road. True, it was the most direct route to Camden, but it led through the endless barrens, already stripped of sustenance by the inhabitants who had starved out and fled, leaving derelict farms and even abandoning livestock. There were wild watercourses here which a few hours' rain turned into raging torrents impossible to cross even if there had been ferries, which there were not in most places. Somebody ought to tell Gates, they said, that there was another route to Camden, longer but much preferable, via Salisbury and Charlotte, which lay through a fertile country, where a road to Virginia could be kept open to the rear in a friendly Whig population, and where hospitals and workshops and magazines could be safely established— and from which the British outpost at Lynch's Creek in front of Camden might be flanked. Neddy put it in a nutshell. In a countryside like this one, said Neddy, a forlorn hope of caterpillars must have starved.

There was no one to inform them, luckily, that somebody had told Gates. Colonel Williams, as an old acquaintance rather than a subordinate officer, had undertaken to remonstrate. But recommendations carefully drawn up in writing and signed by the chief officers of the General's command were ignored by Gates, and the marching order stood unchanged for the most direct route which he himself had hit upon after a summary survey of the inadequate maps spread out and spilling untidily over the edges of the camp table in his tent. Gates asked for no advice and he took none.

Encouraging word went out through the tottering ranks that the fertile regions of the Peedee banks ahead would provide corn from the new crop. They came to the Peedee and found the corn, far from ripe but sweet and tender. There was no bread. The men boiled the green ears with the lean beef and tough pork they foraged day by day, and ate it without salt. They found green peaches and ate those. The results, of course, were disastrous, for colic and dysentery ran epidemic through the column. The officers stuck to a tasteless soup made of the stringy meat and thickened with their hair powder, and remained in somewhat better health.

They came one evening to May's Mill, where they had been promised reinforcements and flour, and they found as usual nothing. When the sunset drums had beat the *retreat* and the roll had been called, Julian lay where he had dropped, half dead with hunger and sickness, blind and deaf to the feeble attempts to make a camp and build fires, over which there was almost nothing to cook, which went on around him. This was worse than anything they had experienced under de Kalb's leadership. For this there was no remedy but to lie still and die. His feet were a mass of sore and running blisters gritty with dirt, his beard was days old, his shirt hung in sweat-drenched, ground-stained ribbons, his hands were filthy and torn, with split black nails. There had been no opportunity or strength to wash, much less to shave, for what seemed to him a lifetime. He felt only a clod among clods, and except for his aching bones and racked insides, dust returning to dust.

Neddy knelt down beside him, speaking repellent words of encouragement and false reassurance. Neddy's hand gripped him, rolled him over on his back. Julian raised a crooked elbow to hide his face from the sky and moaned.

"Pst!" said Neddy in his ear. "Here comes the colonel. Pull up, lad, don't let him find us like this!"

Colonel Williams, who commanded the Sixth when not acting as adjutant, passed slowly among his men that evening, looking as gaunt and ill as any of them, but trying with a well-placed word here and there to avert a rising mutiny with which he could feel only sympathy. To a group which muttered about food he showed his own empty mess-case and canteen with a smile. When he came to a boy who blubbered from pain and homesickness, he paused to lay a hand on the nearly naked shoulder with tact and understanding. At last he stood above Julian, looking down at the guardian scarecrow who crouched beside his motionless friend.

"Ah, Blake," he said, for everyone in the Sixth seemed to know Neddy by name. "Glad to see *you're* still with us! Anything I can do here?"

"He ain't used to it, sir," Neddy explained apologetically. "His feet has gone bad—he's got guts, all right, but he just ain't used to it. Eddicated man, sir," he added confidentially.

Williams bent and laid hold of Julian's shielding arm, and Julian tried instinctively, without opening his eyes, to turn his face into the ground.

"I've took a sort of fancy to him, sir," Neddy went on sheepishly. "B'God I had to *show* him how to fire a musket when he first come in, back at Petersburg! He ketches on, though. He's hell-bent to be a soldier!"

"Had anything at all to eat tonight?" asked Williams quietly.

"No, sir."

"Some corn has been brought in to the mill. It's God's truth, Blake, they are grinding it now. There will be an issue of bread tonight, and something in the morning as well. See that your friend gets his share, won't you—he's not fit to look after himself."

The colonel straightened, and passed on through the groups of sullen, lounging men.

May's Mill thus proved to be heartening, and a night's sodden slumber with a comforted stomach which at last had been given something to gnaw on restored Julian a little. There seemed to be no longer any fixed design in anyone's mind as to the objective, or even a hazy notion of what would be the outcome of the fantastic march on Camden—just a monotonous slogging forward towards an enemy whose strength was unknown and whose position might be almost anywhere.

Caswell did come in at last, scared in by a skirmish with a British outpost; and Stevens with a brigade of Virginia militia caught up on August fourteenth when Gates was at Clermont within a day's march of Camden. The army was still living from hand to mouth, and Stevens brought nothing much in the way of supplies except a stock of West

Indies molasses. Somebody had a brilliant idea—and the molasses was issued to the troops as a treat in place of the rum which had never arrived. It went down on top of the green fruit and scorched bread made from green corn, and most of the army spent most of the night in the bushes.

With Stevens was a tired, road-stained courier who had come all the way from Washington's headquarters in New Jersey, carrying private letters from the Commander-in-Chief for Gates and de Kalb, and commissioned to make a confidential report to His Excellency on the situation as he found it—for it was no secret any more that Congress had appointed Gates, its favorite, without even consulting Washington, who had intended Greene for the southern command. So that when Major St. John Sprague rode into the Continental camp at Clermont that day with Washington's despatches in his saddlebags he was not altogether surprised, though none the less horrified, at what he encountered there.

It was a heartrending hour St. John spent with his friend de Kalb the same evening, bent over a map on the rough camp table in the big German's tent, tracing by the light of a single candle stuck in the neck of a bottle the route Gates should have taken from Hillsborough, to prevent Rawdon's comfortable withdrawal of his Lynch's Creek outposts and to take his supplies. But it was too late now. Even while they discussed in low tones the highly unsatisfactory prospect before them, the summons came to a council of war.

What a granny-looking fellow it is anyway, St. John found himself thinking as the staff grouped themselves rather silently around Gates in the lantern light, and he could not but compare Washington's austere efficiency with the opaque urbanity of Gates. The plan of advance and battle at Camden was all Gates' own, and it was laid down now as an established fact before his dismayed officers. Among them, only de Kalb had the tenacity to raise his voice in objection. But Gates had no use for objections. So long as his subordinates maintained a silence which could be construed as consent, he did not care what they were thinking.

As the meeting adjourned, Colonel Williams remarked that he would give a good deal to know where he would be dining the day after tomorrow. Gates rounded on him, all bluff and confidence. "Dine, sir? Where but in Camden, with Lord Rawdon as our guest!"

With de Kalb's heavy hand resting on his arm, and the young French aide du Buysson walking on the Baron's other side, St. John accompanied the old general back to the tent where the map still waited under the guttering candle, and the three of them looked at each other a long moment, beyond speech. At last de Kalb, seated creakingly on his narrow camp bed, motioned his juniors to stools beside the table—

"Even if we live to tell it," said de Kalb impressively, "no one will ever believe us. He plans an elaborate night surprise, to be executed by exhausted troops like these, and half of them raw militia! And then, to take a British stronghold like Camden unawares, he puts at the head of his column a mounted legion under our friend Armand—!" He wagged his great head wearily, he tried to smile. "It is genius," he admitted generously. "He has a genius to do the wrong thing!"

"Thank God I arrived here when I did!" said St. John. "I've seen enough to clear *you*, sir—no matter what happens! I shall go to Congress myself! I shall ask to make my report in person—"

"Na, na," de Kalb interrupted him with a large vague gesture of a large fat hand. "Congress? Pah! Who fights this war? Washington! I do not like for General Washington to think I am a numskull. That is all that matters. You must tell His Excellency I did what I could."

There was some sort of altercation outside the tent, du Buysson sprang to his feet, and Colonel Armand appeared at the flap, a gaunt, excitable man, white with anger. The sentry's anxious face showed over his shoulder, and du Buysson waved it away as Armand burst into agitated speech.

"Sir—*mon général*—I beg your indulgence—but I must speak with you! The order of march—my legion to head the column—sir, it is not *possible!*"

De Kalb gave his massive French shrug, his rueful, enchanting smile. "It is in the orders, Colonel Armand."

"But it is all contrary to military tactics—a child playing with his wooden soldiers on the nursery floor would not conceive it—it is to say *imbécile!*" cried Armand, quite beside himself. *"Regardez, mon général —je ne sais pas où j'en suis!* An army, warned to silence on pain of death—*sous peine de mort,* it is written in the order!—the men must not speak, they must not cough, *mordieu,* they must not sneeze!—but they are to be led on this *fantastique* venture, through the dark, on an unfamiliar road which runs across a swamp—*by cavalry!*"

"I have just said to du Buysson and the Major here, how no one will ever believe it," remarked de Kalb, with what seemed like satisfaction that his views were corroborated.

"No one will live to *tell* it!" shrieked Armand.

"My words exactly," de Kalb nodded, and glanced with twinkling triumph at St. John Sprague.

"He has done it on purpose—*à quoi bon?*" Armand flung out thin, soiled hands which shook in the candlelight. "He has done it to see me wiped out! He does not believe in cavalry—he does not like me, he never did! *Pas vrai!* I know that—it is a personal spite, he wants to be rid of me! *À merveille! Je suis flambé!*"

"Na, na," said de Kalb soothingly. "It is no time for spite, in the middle of a war."

"I will not do it!" wailed Armand, and his unsteady hands went to his face. "It is certain death—it is to deliver my men to massacre—I will not march—!" He rocked in the candlelight.

"It is in your orders," said de Kalb, and his voice hardened. "I am not in command now. It is no good coming to me."

"But if you only would *speak* to him, *mon général—*"

"I spoke. You heard."

"If you only would try *again,* sir—now, before it is too late—"

"I can do nothing," said de Kalb, suddenly stony. "That is all, Colonel Armand. Good night."

"But *cavalry*—to lead a *surprise attack*—!"

"Dismissed," said de Kalb, and Armand stumbled from the tent, his hands before his face.

There was a silence then, in the flickering light, with the sentry's tread outside.

"*Enfin, ouf!*" exploded du Buysson finally. "God knows it is a bad business all round—but Armand has no better discipline of himself than of his unfortunate men! Well, I do not envy him his post, I confess!"

St. John raised his eyes from contemplation of his boots and found de Kalb's knowing, almost roguish look fixed on him.

"Major Sprague, you have arrived in time to act with du Buysson as
my aide in this—emergency," said the Baron. "If you think His Excellency would permit—?"

"I should be honored, sir," St. John replied simply, and they drew
together over the map without further waste of time, to discuss alleviat-
ing strategies.

The Sixth Maryland was in the Second Brigade, which was posted
to follow the First, which came immediately behind Armand's Legion
in the line of march, with Colonel Porterfield and the Light Infantry
flanking him in Indian file. Behind the Marylands were the Carolina
and Virginia militia and the artillery. Neddy said the militia always
wavered when their officers were killed, instead of going in to avenge
them the way veterans would. And after every skirmish the militia
always wanted to go home and kiss their girls and tell the news and
chuck their weight about, instead of keeping their noses to the grind-
stone. . . .

Julian reeled through darkness as sultry as day, grateful for Neddy's
presence at his side even after the curse of silence was imposed upon
them. The deep sand dragged at his feet, and there was a dull, nauseat-
ing pain in his middle. He had tried more than once to picture his first
entry into battle, but his most gruesome imaginings had never achieved
anything quite like this. And it was altogether uncalled-for that one
should be obliged to endure a grisly stomach-ache along with one's
baptism of fire.

Every now and then he and Neddy jolted together as one of them
stumbled with weakness or staggered on the uneven ground. Julian's
musket had long since worn such a sore place on his shoulder that he
had fastened a clumsy moss pad inside his coat. The musket went on
boring, till it seemed to chafe the bare bone, and at every step the ill-
hung cartouche-box banged his weary thigh. Sand filled his broken
boots, sifted through his mended, worn-out stockings, and made agonizing grit between his toes. In his nostrils was the now familiar stench
of hot, unwashed, sickly men, and the sweating horses of the officers.

The sand deadened footfalls as the army moved forward without
drum or bugle to cheer their courage. Talk was forbidden, but still
there were sounds, under the high bright southern stars—the sound
of a retching man unable to suppress a groan and a curse; the sound

of a man who tripped over a root or stone and fell and could not rise again and did not care; the clink of bit and spur and sabre as an officer eased his horse along the line with now and then a low word of command; the rumble of artillery wheels across a clearing; and always the *sluff, sluff, sluff* of weary marching feet which Julian felt would follow him beyond the grave. The thick southern night made its own sounds too—great frogs bellowed from the swamp either side of the road, unseen things crashed and slithered from under the men's very feet, insects hummed and blundered in their faces, outraged night birds fled screaming through the trees overhead.

After about four hours of this a burst of firing up in front rent the night.

"What's that?" said Julian, jerked from a walking stupor, and felt his queasy stomach turn within him.

"Scouting party, mebbe," said Neddy, sounding very calm. "Or mebbe mounted pickets."

A sharp order to halt and be silent ran back along the line, but the drums broke fiercely into the long roll, sounding the alarm. They waited, leaning against each other, listening to what seemed to be an impromptu battle raging just ahead. Gun flashes were visible in the darkness, there was a growing confusion of drums and bugles and shouted commands.

"They've got Armand treed, sure as you're a foot high," said Neddy wisely. "Yep—I told you—here it comes—b'God, it sounds as though we'd flushed the whole damned British army!"

To his increasingly blasphemous astonishment, Neddy proved to have guessed right. By a monumental coincidence, the British army had been set in motion from Camden at the same hour of the same night, with the same objective—surprise attack. It met the Continental force head on, about two o'clock in the morning, where the road ran along a narrow rise between two swamps in the pine forest.

Some of Armand's troopers, wounded, or shattered by shock, fled helter skelter to the rear, panicking the First Maryland Brigade and spreading terror as they went. The men on the flanks stood firm, and the British, taken no less unawares, soon fell back. As though by mutual consent the shooting ceased, and both armies paused blindly in the dark.

From prisoners taken in the skirmish Gates learned to his undisguised amazement that Cornwallis himself had arrived from Charleston only the day before and was leading the British in person, and that Tarleton's formidable green-clad dragoons had also joined the Camden garrison. Stuttering with self-justification and expletives, Gates called a hasty council. Of the weary, disillusioned men who gathered round him only de Kalb stood out stoutly for retreat under cover of darkness, and Gates' attitude towards the old warrior carried an open slur on de Kalb's personal courage. St. John would have flared up at that, but was checked by the weight of de Kalb's hand on his arm. Stevens of Virginia blurted that it was too late now to do anything but fight, and Gates hastily agreed with him, because, he pointed out, to turn back now would look like flight. So the order to posts was given. The incapacitated, the camp followers, and the heavy baggage were ordered to the rear along the road which ran to Charlotte. No vote had been taken, the meeting broke up in fatalistic shrugs, and the battle lines were drawn before dawn.

On the brink of his first engagement Julian was fortunate in being among veteran troops, for it was a severe trial on the nerves to find your battle stations in darkness and then wait there in your tracks for daylight, and the militia companies suffered acutely from the shakes. Julian sat on the damp ground beside Neddy, his musket across his drawn-up knees. The frogs were still noisy above the smothered sounds of the fumbling army, and fireflies flitted like lanterns everywhere.

Although everyone dripped perspiration in the heavy, stinking air of the swampland, Julian's hands were cold and unsteady, and his heart hammered in his ears. He tried to tell himself that it was physical weakness from the bad food and the endless dysentery, but he knew it was mostly fear; fear of the wilderness he had come to on this frightful march, leaving behind him the merest decencies of life, till hunger became a bestial thing and the will to survive was something less than human; fear of the trained, steadfast enemy they had come up with at last, doubly dreadful in the shrouding dark, making at this moment its own professional disposition of its forces; fear of the first gray streak of a day which might be his last, or worse, might leave him maimed and better dead; fear of his own fear, which at some crucial moment might show in his behavior so that he would disgrace himself under fire. He was starving and sick and less than half himself, and he knew that he was afraid to fight, and he despised himself accordingly, and felt Neddy's arm laid hard across his shoulders.

"Bear up, lad," said Neddy in his ear. "They make a lot of noise comin' in, and they look something fierce, but they can bleed under those red coats, same as the rest of us!"

As daylight came, it could be seen that the lines were very close, and that the position would give the advantage to the British, whose flanks were better protected by marshy land. The Sixth Maryland was on the right wing, which Gist and de Kalb commanded. Caswell's tardy militia had the center, across the road, and Stevens' Virginia brigade was on the left. Smallwood's First Brigade of Marylanders, pulling themselves together after Armand's disaster, were held in reserve, behind the artillery.

Long before the sun was visible the British drums were heard beating to arms, and as the American drums hastily replied de Kalb rode down through the purple haze and took up his position, running a raking blue eye along the lines so that each man straightened himself instinctively to meet it. The Sixth Maryland were ready—they were veterans of the northern campaign, they knew what was coming and how to meet it. Julian's smarting, sleepless eyes slid without recognition over the officer who rode beside du Buysson and fastened themselves on the calm, massive figure of the Baron astride the big horse, and he felt his lurching heart steady itself so that the drums no longer seemed to beat in the pit of his stomach, and his sensations of sheer sickness abated somewhat. Gates, he noticed, was nowhere to be seen.

An aide from Colonel Williams cantered in to say that the enemy were deploying by the right and that Colonel Williams had advised Stevens to attack them at once in hopes of catching them on one foot. Before he had finished speaking, the first British volley crashed in. Stevens was too late. Smoke drifted low on the hot, still air. The battle had begun.

Dry-throated, with the taste of powder already on his tongue, Julian saw to his priming and awaited the order to fire. De Kalb's voice rang out over his shabby ranks as unhurried as though on the parade-ground, while the whole British line moved in on them, the red coats showing dark through the muffling haze. *"Cock firelock!"* The order echoed from officer to officer towards him, and Julian's fingers as he obeyed were clumsy and damp. *"Make rrready!—Take aim!"* And he muttered to himself because the gun barrel wavered in his sight. "FIRE!"

But the British received the volley and came on, noisily, under the order to charge bayonet, during those naked, frantic moments when even an experienced man must fumble with cartouche-box and ramrod in the effort to re-load in time. *"Handle carrrtridge!"* Yes, all right, snatch the cartridge from the pouch—bite off the top—faugh, you're bound to get the stuff in your mouth-*"PRRRIME!"*—give us time, can't you, got to shake some powder into the pan now, don't spill it all, lummox—*"Shut pan!"*—shut it is, too, and no wind to blow the powder into your eyes today, thank God, but don't let's drip sweat into it, that would be worse—*"Charrrge with cartridge!"*—hurry up, powder down the barrel, that's the stuff—shaking like a leaf, you are, but hell, so are the rest of them—*"Drrraw rammers!—Rrram down cartridge!"*—oh, Lord, I nearly forgot that, blow my own head off in a minute—*"Rrreturn rrrammers!"*—you're absolutely right, sir, mustn't lose the bloody rammer, leave us in a pretty fix—God, why can't they make a gun you can fire more than once without going through all these motions—*"Cock firelock!—Make rrready!—Take aim!"*—all right, here we go again—listen to those redcoats yell—yes, I'm all right, Neddy, only it's so damned slow and so many things to think of—has he forgotten the next word?—"FIRE!"

It was a lively corner of hell the Sixth Maryland occupied that day. The smoke would not rise on the dank air, and it was therefore impossible to see the effect of the gunfire on either side, except that it was plain that nothing stopped the British. Now the artillery of both armies was playing furiously, and the din was laced through and through with the rattle of drums beating the long roll and the sharp sweet notes of the bugles. Du Buysson dashed in on a wounded horse to say that Caswell's militia would not stand much longer, and Stevens' men were crumbling under the first British onslaught, and that Singleton's artillery had had to retire from the road. Then Colonel Williams arrived, his horse white with lather, to tell de Kalb that Gates was behind the reserves giving no orders at all, and the whereabouts of General Smallwood, in command of the reserves, were unknown to his officers, who had not seen him since the battle started and who desired to know the Baron's wishes.

With his own brigade firm as a rock at his back, de Kalb ordered Williams to go and bring up Smallwood's men to hold back the British right. And then he actually began to push forward with his own men, step by step, in lively hand-to-hand fighting, his cheery orders still coming with the rhythmic precision of the parade ground, though he was bleeding from two wounds.

"B'God, we ain't doin' so bad!" crowed Neddy, the joy of battle on him. "The Carolina militia always runs, but if those bastards from Virginia, beggin' your pardon, laddie, will only stand up to it a little longer—*wheee,* you *would,* would you, bloody-back, and be damned to you!—come on, lad, the Baron's down! Come on, you club-footed, ham-strung sons-o'-bitches, the Baron's lost his horse—!"

By the time they reached him, the Baron was up on his feet. He had received a sword-cut on the head while he was entangled beneath his horse, and du Buysson was binding his own sash around the wound and imploring him to retire from the field. De Kalb brushed him aside and led a bayonet charge on foot over heaps of slain, and took fifty kilted prisoners from the British Seventy-first, which was a Highland light infantry regiment.

Julian was among the men in a cordon round his commander, who had no remount and was bellowing with berserk courage, his hat gone, his silver hair untied and hanging beneath the startling scarlet sash-bandage which swathed his head like a turban. The excitement of the charge, the savage, grunting, successful use of his bayonet which had saved his own life twice over, and a breathing space in which to realize that he was still alive, had made a soldier out of the schoolmaster. Blood was running down his left arm in a sticky stream, and Neddy made him take off his coat and fashioned a rough bandage from his torn-off shirt sleeve before the fight engulfed them again.

Julian felt no pain now, and no more fear. It was necessary only to keep de Kalb in sight, though you could hardly see beyond the length of your own musket in the powder-smoke and haze, with the sweat in your eyes, nor tell friend from foe until it was almost too late. His cartridges were all gone, and through sheer necessity he had mastered the old soldier's trick of priming his musket by banging the butt on the ground and spitting balls down the barrel, from a supply held in his cheek. Even through the smoke and confusion it was plain even to a novice that the Sixth's casualties were climbing. "B'God, they're thinning us!" cried Neddy angrily. "It's comin' from the left, those varmints aren't coverin' us, laddie, what kind of an army is this! O-*ho*, you with the silver buttons, how d'ya like it, eh?" There was no answer as his bayonet got home.

Just as the British might have wavered and the tide of battle hung, another aide on horseback catapulted in among them calling on de Kalb.

"Colonel Williams says the First Brigade cannot hold much longer, sir—Stevens' men have taken to the swamp, and when the First gives way, Cornwallis will turn your flank—for God's sake fall back, sir, you'll have the whole British army against your left—!"

"Tell Williams he must rally the men once more and we shall have Cornwallis yet! Push the cannon ahead, I do not hear our artillery, where is Singleton? Tell Williams it will only be *minutes* now, till we can begin to throw them back—"

The aide was staring past de Kalb at a bloodstained, coatless, dishevelled figure with the infantryman's black powder smear across its mouth.

"*Julian!*" cried St. John incredulously. "*Julian, for the love of God—!*"

And Julian after one quick glance upwards swung his musket butt-end first at the Highlander's bayonet launched full tilt out of the haze at St. John's back. It took him off balance and he fell with the red coat on top of him, and they rolled against the feet of St. John's horse. St. John, unscratched, fired his pistol point-blank and leaped from the saddle to lay hands on the dead weight pinning Julian down, but de Kalb seized and shook him, bellowing above the musket-fire—

"Get back to Williams, do you hear—tell Williams to rally them once more—"

Du Buysson, hatless, horseless, powder-grimed, flung himself at the Baron from behind, his voice barely audible in the noise of furious fighting all around them.

"We can't do it, sir—they've flanked us and they're sending the cavalry at us—Armand is nowhere—*we can't do it, the Greens are coming in!*"

But the mighty de Kalb, streaming with blood, hauled St. John up from his knees and threw him bodily against the saddle.

"*God damn you, Major, will you ride?* Tell Gist to hold fast and tell

Williams to close up the left and support me with Gist! It's only Tarleton and his cutthroats! Front rank bayonets, rear rank fire! *You know how cavalry hates bayonets!* RIDE!"

A ball caught him in the lung and he sagged coughing into du Buysson's arms, while St. John turned his back on Julian where he lay, and galloped away towards Smallwood's deserted post where Williams was now in command. Behind him he could hear the thunder of Tarleton's dreaded dragoons coming up, and his memory shuddered away from the things he had seen before now in the wake of a cavalry charge. At the same time exquisite pain lodged in his right knee and his horse stumbled, but kept on going, and the silver music of Tarleton's bugles pursued him like delirium.

Further weakened now by loss of blood, Julian was struggling to free himself from the scarlet-clad body which St. John had not had time to drag away. On all sides of him frantic officers laid the flat of their swords to infantrymen who fled like leaves before the wind, and the ground beneath him shivered long before with a roar the charge burst above him in a clanking maelstrom of iron-shod hooves and flailing sabres and spurs and the blood-chilling British huzzah—so that he fell back and lay still where he was, grateful now for the shield of his dead enemy. Even over the rattle and pound and din of the charge he could hear du Buysson's frenzied cry: *"It's the Baron de Kalb! In God's name, spare the Baron de Kalb!"*

Flying hooves kicked dirt into Julian's eyes and struck with a sickening jar on the body beneath which he lay huddled. Then the death scream of a horse shrilled above the battle sounds, and the animal came down heavily in its tracks, its head and shoulders across the legs of the dead Highlander, its rider thrown on top of the heap. Dazed by the impact and gasping for breath under the inert, smothering weight, Julian lay and felt warm blood soaking his legs and could only guess because he had no new pain that it was not his own.

Finally, leaving behind it what seemed an echoing quiet, the charge had passed over him and he was still alive.

Giddily he fought his way to a sitting position, elbowing away the two dead men who had shielded him, and wiped the dirt and sweat from his eyes. Near him on the ground lay de Kalb, with du Buysson spread-eagled face down on top of him as he had thrown himself to protect his helpless commander. There were sabre cuts in du Buysson's back and shoulders, but he raised himself slowly to his knees and bent above de Kalb, loosening the Baron's cravat with dexterous, gentle fingers.

Julian picked up the canteen which was attached to the dead dragoon's belt and shook it, and it gave a pleasant gurgle. He detached it, disentangled his legs from the horse and the Highlander, and found them sore but whole. He crawled painfully on his hands and knees towards du Buysson.

"Here's some water," he said. "Is he still alive?"

"Yes—he is alive." Du Buysson raised de Kalb's head in his arms, unmindful of his own wounds. The bulky sash-bandage had been torn off and the Baron's white hair was stained with his blood. "Can you get a little water between his teeth?"

Together they worked over the prostrate giant, trying to stanch his wounds, using the precious water drop by drop, while the battle raged a few hundred yards beyond them, with spent balls dropping near. Riderless, crazed horses ricocheted here and there, and the brutal August sun burned away the cloaking mist. The Baron writhed under their hands and muttered something.

"It is the name of his wife," said du Buysson. "Always he thinks of her—*mon général—courage, mon général, c'est du Buysson ici—soyez tranquille, c'est du Buysson—toujours—*" Tears were running down his face through the powder stains.

Julian looked about for Neddy, suddenly fearful of what he might see. The ground was strewn with the bodies of men of both armies, some of which moved, or tried to, some of which were no longer human forms. Baggage and precious equipment abandoned in flight littered the trampled earth. Horses lay kicking and thrashing in death throes or still cantered aimlessly with empty saddles till they dropped of wounds or exhaustion. And now that the noise of battle was more distant, other sounds were audible—hideous sounds of agony and terror, the long, awful wail of the wounded and the shrieks of fugitives pursued into the swamp by the merciless dragoons. In the brassy sky above, silent, watchful, waiting, hovered the black shapes of the turkey-buzzards.

For a few moments Julian sat staring through the receding battle haze, wondering why he did not react emotionally to the horrors all around him, astonished at his own veteran calm. Well, there it was, he had fought his first battle, and he hadn't been afraid, except just at first, and he hadn't done so badly, either, and though his wound still bled he was alive, by a miracle, *alive*— Then, without warning a cold wave of nausea rose within him, and the world turned black and blurry and he slewed around just in time and gave up everything but his immortal soul on the ground, retching, blind, and bereft of dignity; emerging spent and chastened in his hasty pride, and very much aware of the mangled horse near by, from which rose a mighty stench to rival the lesser smells of swamp and gunpowder.

But just beyond the carcase one of the twisted human figures sat up slowly, wiping at a cut in his scalp with the tail of his shirt. Julian recognized the inspired flow of language almost before he saw the man.

"*Neddy!*" he cried in relief. "*Neddy, thank God!*"

Neddy pivoted on his seat, his vague gaze found and focused on the man he had taken a fancy to, and his wicked, leering smile broke crookedly.

"Hullo, laddie! The lobsters cut me wide open! Would you give me the loan of your shirt to tie it up with? Or no—b'God, I'll use this one here!" He began to rifle the body of the Highlander St. John had shot.

"Take it easy, I'll help you," said Julian, crawling towards him, and together they tore off the white linen shirt in strips and made Neddy a tidy bandage. Before they had quite finished, Neddy's gaze sharpened on the middle distance, and his grin widened to a sort of canine snarl.

"My, my, look what's come amongst us!" he marvelled.

A group of mounted British officers was bearing down on them briskly across the terrible field, white wigs and scarlet coats and white doeskin breeches all very handsome, the silver half-moons of the polished gorgets above their lace jabots reflecting a blinding glare.

"It's—it must be Cornwallis himself," said Julian stupidly, and saw du Buysson stagger to his feet to face them.

"The Baron de Kalb is severely wounded, sir," said du Buysson, and swayed in his tracks as Cornwallis reined up above him. "I implore you to give him proper care at once by your surgeons."

"Why, yes, it shall be done," said Cornwallis, taking in the situation with maddening deliberation, and his high conqueror's glance ran on to include the bloodstained pair on the ground beyond, who gazed up at him rather spellbound. "I am sorry to hear of the Baron's—misfortune," said Cornwallis courteously, and added in the same tone, "Gentlemen, you are all my prisoners."

Gates was "carried away," as he afterwards put it, from his strong position in the rear, by the flight of the militia. He was mounted on a fleet Virginia horse which brought him to Charlotte by nightfall, a distance of some sixty miles. Caswell somehow contrived to keep up with him. Armand's corps disgraced themselves by looting the abandoned baggage of their own side.

Gates had arranged no rendezvous in the event of a retreat, but Gist, Smallwood, Armand, and a few other officers besides the faithful Williams, found their way to the city, only to learn that Gates had already departed on a fresh horse for Hillsborough. What was left of the veteran companies who had escaped death or capture by taking to the swamps straggled to Hillsborough after him. They were ragged and beaten and hungry, but Gates was all the commander they had, so they rallied to him.

The militia had broken too soon, and the Continentals had stood too long. The colonies had lost an army by capture at Charleston, and another by annihilation at Camden. It looked now very much as though they had finally lost the war, and there was dismay and despair in the Carolinas.

Cornwallis removed his wounded and prisoners into Camden, where de Kalb died of eleven wounds. Du Buysson's were not fatal. Julian and Neddy Blake received a surgeon's care, and were pronounced fit to set off with a hundred and forty-eight others under a strong guard along the hot swampy road for Charleston and the wretched prospect of a British prison ship.

The road they travelled was often only a narrow log causeway running through vine-laced undergrowth at the edge of stagnant brown water. Towering cypress and gum trees bearded with gray moss made what would have been welcome shade if they had not also cut off every breath of air. Mosquitoes swarmed, and slimy furtive things slipped into the water with little whispering sounds on every side, and a man from Delaware died hideously of snakebite.

As a walking wounded case, Julian plodded hopelessly ahead, his arm throbbing and swelling for need of fresh dressings, and hour by hour he felt the threatening fever rising in his blood. They were better fed by the British than they had been for days, but weakness gained upon him, and he lost track of time in the moss-hung twilight of the swamps.

The Wateree became the Santee, which must be crossed to come to Charleston, and the hurry-up order was passed along the line so as to make use of the ferry before nightfall. But they were too late after all, and rather than divide his party the British officer in charge decided to bivouac for the night on the near bank.

At the halt, Julian dropped in his tracks on the muddy ground, past caring to secure one of the evil-smelling blankets which were issued at nightfall, and slid into a kind of coma mixed with delirium, in which his old dread of the wilderness returned and magnified and became a fever-nightmare of trees a mile high, snakes the size of a man's arm, and mammoth disembodied pink-lined jaws which gaped for him on every side—and then, the crowning horror, he heard the long shrill yell of unseen Indians. . . .

Neddy was shaking him awake to pandemonium in the dawn. The yelling he had heard was Francis Marion's famous war-whoop as he charged with a flailing sword on sleepy British sentries, followed by his crew of lethal warriors. Horry had brought the news of Gates' defeat and Marion moved promptly to intercept the British guard with its contingent of prisoners bound for Charleston.

Taken entirely by surprise, the guard defended itself fiercely in hand-to-hand fighting, in which the prisoners soon joined with whatever weapons they could lay hold of.

Neddy sailed as usual into the thick of it and seized the flying halter of a loose horse which a British sergeant carrying a bayoneted musket was trying to catch and use himself.

"Here you are, laddie!" Neddy called to Julian. "Up on his back, now, and ride like the devil out of here! I'll catch me another and be with you in no time—"

The bayonet ran him through. He gasped, and hung on it, and when it was withdrawn he fell without a sound beneath the horse's feet, and the sergeant mounted. Still groggy with sleep and fever, Julian hurled himself bodily at the man on the horse, who had no stirrups, and dragged him down and they rolled together on the ground.

The musket caught by its sling on a stump and was jerked out of the sergeant's hand. Julian recovered it by a lucky twist of his body which put him on top of it, fought for it savagely, edged it slowly out from under him, and struggled to his knees still gripping it. The sergeant, exuding a steady stream of army words which wasted his breath, grabbed out his pistol too late. Julian lunged at short range, his body behind it, for his arms had no strength left. The sergeant yelled once and lay still.

Julian left the bayonet where it was and crawled to Neddy, and there was nothing that could be done for him. Julian crouched above him, sick and shaking and sobbing for breath in his weakness. Neddy's eyes came open, and knew him.

"Did ya get him?" he asked faintly.

"I got him," Julian nodded, and Neddy grinned his crooked, canine grin, and died.

"You there, on the ground! Catch hold of this brute if you want him!" cried a voice from above, and as Julian turned the halter of the sergeant's horse was flung at him by a man who wheeled his own horse and rode into the fight around the wagons. Julian thought he recognized Horry, whom Marion had left behind as a link between himself and de Kalb.

Automatically he mastered the dancing animal, retaining it for his own. The fight was nearly over and the British were in flight, leaving their dead behind them. Some one came and carried Neddy away. Julian started to follow, leading the horse, but a wave of faintness overcame him and when he rallied again the business of sorting out the prisoners taken and the prisoners rescued was going forward cheerfully. Some of the Continentals elected to join Marion's corps and were given British horses and equipment. Others preferred an escort to the North Carolina border with the chance of getting home or rejoining their old regiments.

"And you, my lad—what's your choice?" It was Horry again, swinging his horse up beside where Julian sat holding to his own mount's mane and fighting dizziness and nausea.

"Well, I'm not much good like this—" he got out. "But I'd like to come with you."

"Glad to have you!" said Horry kindly. "You'll be in for some riding yet. But I reckon we can find you a saddle hereabouts."

Some one led the horse finally, while Julian clung to the pommel with both hands, not knowing or caring that he was being carried deeper into the swamp along a track which only Marion's men could find. Clammy water splashed him to the waist—moss-beards whipped his face, mosquitoes settled and filled themselves unmolested; some one held water to his swollen lips, some one laved his temples and wrists, voices spoke encouragement. At last they laid him in the bottom of a boat, and the smooth motion was heaven after the horse, and the air grew cooler.

There was a rustling silence ashore, broken by the grinding of the boat pole against the cypress trunks, and the scrape of the flat bottom along submerged logs. Julian opened his eyes and lay looking up into the tall trees, which were so dense and so festooned with the gray streamers that the color of the sky hardly showed through. A wind moved up there which never reached the water level. Over the edge of the low gunwale he could see dark water, reddish in the flecks of sunlight, dimpled by the zigzag patterns of the waterskaters, cut by the sharp triangular wake of swimming snakes. Narrow streams led off, lost and winding, between clay banks. In some places the moss hung so low that it touched the water and dragged across the gunwale, squdgy and terrible, to wet his undefended face. Over all was the rancid swamp stink.

At last the boat's nose bumped and grounded, and some one jerked it higher. He smelled the smudge-pots of a camp, and some one was urging him to move again. He strove to obey and found his feet under him—stepped out into water ankle deep, slipped on the yellow clay of the sloping bank, felt himself falling, felt himself caught and saved by strong, kind hands, and all was darkness and a beautiful oblivion.

They had brought him to Snow's Island in the midst of the Peedee swamp—dry, high land, covered with magnificent moss-draped trees, a natural sanctuary for the hunted. There were deep cane-brakes and swamp at the edges of the Island, and patches of Indian corn which were tended by the convalescents. Here Marion had established his secret headquarters, arms depot, and hospital, always strongly garrisoned, but almost impossible for an outsider to find. Prisoners or visitors were brought in blindfolded, as though the winding cypress aisles were not confusing enough. He never encumbered himself long with prisoners, they were either paroled or exchanged or—the British rumor ran—hanged.

In securing this fortress Marion had commandeered all the boats in the neighborhood and destroyed all those he did not need. His men had cut away the bridges, preferring unmarked fords, and felled timber across pathways which ran too near. It was a moated keep, with look-out posts in the tree-towers manned by sleepless riflemen. Invalids, lying up between forays with sword-cuts or bullet-wounds, policed the place and kept it tidy. The smudge-pots against the mosquitoes were never allowed to go out. There were few tents, but sail-cloth stretched between the trees gave some shelter from the sun and rain. Laurel and jessamine, palmettos and white cup lilies decorated the primitive door-yards. Tall men must dodge at every turn the same hanging moss which cleared Marion's head. The horses grazed with their saddles on and the bits hung round their necks, their owners' swords and pistol-belts suspended from convenient branches above them.

Here Julian lay for days, alternating between delirium and stupor. There was no surgeon, and medical care, while painstaking and gentle, was inexpert. Horry insisted that it was a good man and could be pulled through—"Dead on his feet, he was, there at the Ferry," he was fond of saying. "But grabbed himself a redcoat and finished him off as pretty as ever I saw. I'm bettin' on that feller, mind you don't go and lose him now!"

It fascinated these simple woodsmen that in delirium Julian could speak a language other than English—with, as it were, his eyes shut. When they discovered that he actually spoke more than one, he became a local curiosity. They would gather in respectful twos and threes under his sail-cloth canopy and try to guess which one it was—"That's French, that is!"—"Was that Greek, or *what?*"—while the one of their

number who was just then acting as nurse swished the flies and mosquitoes from the sick man's face and took a possessive part in the argument.

Marion would come and look down at him and shake his head in
his non-committal way. "An educated man," he said to Horry one day,
with a sort of awe. "I have sent to Hillsborough for the loan of a surgeon. I wish we knew who he is."

"One of the aides, must be," said Horry. "He had lost his coat or
we might have his rank to go by. *I* never saw him, though, all the time
I was with that outfit. Could have come in at Clermont, maybe—"

"He is not a foreigner."

"Bless you, no! But he has sure got the gift of tongues. Listen to that,
now, would you! What do you suppose it *means?*"

"*Omnem crede diem—tibi diluxisse supremum—*" Julian was mutter-
ing now. "Each day that dawns—the last. Must tell that to Tibby. *Pro
patria—pro liberis—*that's too easy—*pro aris atque focis suis—*construe,
Kit, construe—*Fallentis semita vitae—*untrodden paths—of life—Tibby,
forgive me, I am deserting you—*On n'est jamais si heureux ni si malheureux qu'on s'imagine,* Tibby—that's La Rochfoucauld—there on the
top shelf—third from the left—damn, I've lost Chesterfield and never
read it!—no time now—too late—must win the war—oh, damn the
war—*on n'est jamais—si malheureux—*"

"Who is Tibby, I wonder," murmured Horry. "Maybe we oughtn't
to listen any more—"

Marion turned away silently and they departed from Julian's side.

"If he lives," said Marion, "we'll have to send him back up north."

"To *Gates?*"

Marion snorted. But—

"He don't belong here," he said.

"But that feller can fight," Horry argued. "Dead on his feet, but he
wasn't lettin' his friend go to glory without company. That is guts.
We can use him."

"He don't belong here," said Marion, closing it.

A few days after this an excited orderly with a bandage round his
head appeared at the flap of Marion's tent.

"Say, General, you'd better come quick! He's makin' sense! The feller that talks Greek and all. He's woke up all there! They said to fetch you on the run!"

IV

It was a strange, illogical friendship which grew up between himself and Marion during Julian's long convalescence. Each embodied something for which the other entertained respect amounting to envy. Marion's admiration for scholarship and long, straight limbs matched Julian's schoolboy worship of a born fighting man. They discoursed for hours together, the small, limping, taciturn partisan general and the shy, deep-thinking schoolmaster, and each found in the other's society an abiding satisfaction.

Marion wanted to hear about Europe no less than about Williamsburg, which was to him almost as remote. He spoke with a certain pride of his own Huguenot forebears, and of his one ill-fated West Indian voyage and shipwreck as a boy. Julian could see that here was a man as great in his way as the towering Washington, and strove patiently to get him to reveal himself to a sympathetic listener. He sensed Marion's immense loneliness in the task he had set himslf, and wondered at the terrific latent power in the solitary little man's lean frame. Marion on his side was puzzled that so fine a lad, possessing all the conceivable attractions for women, should be so alone in the world, with apparently no one to care what became of him. Each felt the same vague, compassionate impulse to alleviate the rigors of the other's existence with the warmth of his own friendship. And in a measure each succeeded.

Julian was weeks on the mend, more from the fever than the wound. It was some time before he had the strength even to crawl from his cot to a rough log chair which had been fashioned for him, and back again. Meanwhile, the life of the camp went on around him.

From here at Snow's Island, Marion's men went out in small mobile parties to break up enemy supply trains and prisoner convoys, to terrorize the undisciplined Tories and prevent them from organizing. His scouts were both patrols and spies, picking up prisoners, information, and booty. They hid in treetops above the enemy encampments and carried off tethered horses and drowsy sentries to exhibit as trophies. They had to be superb horsemen, dead shots with a rifle or a fowling-piece, firing from the saddle as effectively as from the ground. And they had to have the Indian way of taking their direction from the stars, the sun, the bark of trees, and such natural woodsmen's guides. There was never any waiting for boats or pontoons, the horses were forced to swim like dogs. Marion left no track behind him, if he could avoid it, and was often vainly hunted for hours by his own detachments. He would find them, more often than they found him. All recruits were taught a strange shrill whistle which could be heard at great distances.

His troops consisted of his neighbors and friends and some stray slaves. During the informal councils at which every man squatted on the ground holding his horse's bridle, Marion consulted his officers frequently, listened politely, and silently reached his own conclusions, which were communicated to them only by his future actions. They watched his cook, and by the food prepared for him each day they forecast his intentions.

His preference was to move at sunset, riding all night, as much as sixty miles, until the enemy's watch-fires and grass-guards were in sight. He would strike at dawn, on a sudden bugle blast, yelling like an Indian. During these forays he lived on cold roast sweet potatoes and drank cold water, and expected his men to subsist on the same. In camp they had the roast sweet potatoes hot, and hominy, sometimes a dry hoe-cake, rarely some lean meat or game. They had salt only when they captured it from the British commissariat. If necessary they starved themselves in order to feed their horses. The men were badly clothed in homespun, which gave little warmth in the damp swamp nights unless eked out with captured British uniforms. They often slept on the ground without blankets, and there was a long time that Marion himself did not own a blanket, having lost the only one he had in a fire.

Their equipment was so scanty in the beginning that they had raided sawmills for saws for their forest blacksmiths to convert into swords and bayonets. A new recruit still often had to accompany a foray unarmed and provide himself with the weapon belonging to the first victim of his comrades' fire. They rarely numbered more than sixty at a time, and they often attacked with only three rounds of ammunition apiece, expecting by the time it was gone to have searched the cartouche-boxes of the dead and wounded for more. Sometimes even buck shot was scarce and they used swan shot, which would not kill. There were many complaints from the British officers that the damned Swamp-fox would not come out and fight like a Christian.

His steadfast rule was always to know his enemy's strength and positions ahead of his attack, which was often ambush and always surprise. Once the noise made by his horses crossing a wooden bridge had given the alarm, and thereafter the men were required to dismount and spread their blankets on the boards before taking their horses over a bridge. He taught them to make themselves invisible, like Indians. "Take trees!" was a routine order. And "No quarter for Tories!" and "Mark the epaulet men!"—meaning Get the officers—were often heard, as battle cries. Also he taught them to retire slowly when pressed, re-load under cover, and try a second fire. He was not humiliated or angry when his meagre forces retreated discreetly before the British bayonets. He expected them to retreat in a pinch. But not too far.

He would disappear from camp for days at a time, with a few followers, and return unheralded bringing welcome booty or lacking two or three men. He would be greeted with satisfaction by those who had remained on the Island, and when he had retired to his tent the rest would gather round for stories of the raid—stories to which Julian listened enthralled. It got to be a recognized part of the business of each raid, to bring back a story for Mr. Day, which would be duly recounted at his bedside with colorful embroideries and interruptions and slapping of thighs and raucous laughter—how one of the five James brothers had scattered a Tory troop singlehanded by shouting over his shoulder as he charged them alone, "Come on, boys, here they are!"; how in a Georgetown night raid they had carried off a British general without his breeches and considerately returned him on parole; how MacDonald had thrust his bayonet into a British back so that it stayed there, and the redcoat had galloped off at full speed, and now—heh, heh, heh!— MacDonald was without a tarnation good bayonet; and how, at Black Mingo, Horry, who was subject to a stammer at moments of great excitement, could not get out the order to *Fire* and in desperation yelled, "Shoot, damn you, *shoot!*"

Sometimes pathetic refugees from a plundered countryside, their homes burned over their heads by marauding Tory bands, were picked up half starving by a scout and brought in to the sanctuary at Snow's Island which they were trying to find and could not. Marion would give them a meal of roast sweet potatoes and an escort to some more permanent haven.

Once a British officer from Charleston, under a white flag, was guided in blindfolded to negotiate an exchange of prisoners. His escort contrived to let him step into swamp water above his shiny black spatterdashes as they helped him out of the boat, and led him with loud expressions of regret under the moss festoons into Marion's presence before they removed the blindfold. All the British officers seemed to be big men, and Captain Verney loomed enormous above the slight, limping figure which advanced to meet him with grave courtesy.

It was dinner time before their business was concluded. Julian answered the mess call along with Horry and three or four others who dined in Marion's company, in time to hear Captain Verney from Charleston accept an invitation to the meal. There was no dining table. They sat about informally on log seats under a stretched sail-cloth in a ring of smudge-pots. Marion was a brigadier-general now, but he dressed no differently and required no more punctilio of his men than before.

The young British captain looked around him in some wonderment at the lean, rough-clad men, slouching at ease under the moss-beards, their rifles and sabres standing carelessly to hand against tree trunks or dangling overhead, their grazing horses ready for immediate action—while among them passed a half-naked black servant handing out roast sweet potatoes still smoking from the ashes and served on a piece of bark without a sign of cutlery or even salt. To drink, there was a gourdful each of the "water weakened with vinegar" which was Marion's customary beverage.

"This is, I presume, an emergency meal?" the captain inquired with interest, puzzled as to why this should be so at a permanent headquarters.

"Oh, no," drawled Horry, breaking the potato in two in the middle and biting into it. "We often fare worse than this in—emergencies."

"In fact," Marion added gently, "this is a special occasion because to-day there is a second helping—of the same."

Captain Verney tried to imitate Horry's methods and burnt his fingers and his tongue.

"What pay do you get here?" he inquired when he could speak.

"Not a cent," said Horry flatly, and Captain Verney began to suspect that he was being got at.

"Are you fellows *joking?*" he demanded.

"No," said Horry sadly. "It ain't funny—sometimes."

"You mean you actually live like this, without pay or rations—? But why do you stand for it? Surely you deserve better than this!"

"There is some idea, Captain Verney," Julian began slowly, for Marion seemed embarrassed by what appeared to be almost pity in the visitor's face and made no reply, "there is some idea of achieving liberty —even without pay."

Verney looked at him sharply, for it was the first time he had spoken. "You sound like a Londoner."

"I was."

"Are you a prisoner here, then?"

"Not here, no."

"Your fellows took him at Camden," Horry explained with some satisfaction, "and we got him back again at Nelson's F-Ferry. When he's delirious he talks G-Greek."

"You have joined the rebels—of your own free will?" gaped the captain.

"My dear sir," said Julian pleasantly, "I have the honor to be a rebel."

"But you—if I may say so, this is no life for a man like yourself!"

"Well, that is your opinion," Julian conceded. "Personally, I don't think I would care much for Charleston society just now."

"But I don't understand!" insisted Captain Verney. "You are one of Us."

"No, there you really are mistaken," said Julian firmly, and turned with affectionate deference to the enchanted Marion, who could not have been so blissfully rude to a guest if his life had depended on it. "Did you mean what you said, sir, about that second helping today?"

The captain stared about him again at the hard, unsmiling faces wiped so clean of all expression save a studious courtesy.

"It is epic," he stated simply. "They will not believe it, at home. I do not quite believe it myself." He accepted a second potato with alacrity. "These are roots, are they not? And you live on them, without—without even rum, I take it. All for liberty. England will lose this war," said the captain simply, and burnt his tongue again.

Early in December Marion received a belated reply to his request for a surgeon from Hillsborough, in the form of a letter delivered by his Captain Melton who returned full of news. Marion sent for Julian to hear it, and Horry and some others gathered round.

The letter was from General Greene, who had arrived at Charlotte to replace Gates in command of the southern army.

"Good!" said Julian in relief. "Now you will see a change—if it's not too late."

Marion's dark, secretive face brooded above the letter.

"He sounds like a good man. Do you know him?"

"I had a friend at Brandywine. He says Greene is the next best man to Washington."

"I would have said so myself," said Melton, and a wary sort of hope showed in the gaunt faces which turned towards him as he spoke. "Best man *I've* seen, bar one." And his eyes went doglike to his leader.

"My friend at Brandywine knew nothing of that one," Julian smiled.

"He says we are to go on here as we are until further notice," said Marion, his eyes on the letter. "He says—'Until a more permanent army can be collected than is in the field at present, we must endeavor to keep up a partisan war, and preserve the tide of sentiment among the people as much as possible in our favor. Spies are the eyes of an army,'" Marion read out slowly from the letter, " 'and without them a general is always crossing in the dark, and can neither secure himself nor annoy his enemy. It is of the highest importance that I get the earliest information of any reinforcements which may arrive at Charleston, or leave the town to join Lord Cornwallis. I wish you, therefore, to fix some plan for procuring such information, and for conveying it to me with all possible dispatch. . . .' Judging by the signature, it looks as though the whole thing is written in his own hand," Marion added thoughtfully, turning the page in his fingers.

"Think likely, since he's got no secretary to write it for him," said Melton. "They are mighty understaffed up there, and all the officers work twenty-four hours a day, almost. Colonel Williams is there—he is a good man to have in the field, and what he doesn't know about Camden you could put in your eye. Guess by now Greene has got the rights of that, if there was any doubt in his mind to start with! And Harry Lee has come in with a troop of light horse. They will be a help. 'Pears Gates didn't believe in cavalry—leastways not before Tarleton charged him at Camden. But Greene can't even spare officers for a court martial, that's why Gates is gettin' off so easy."

"You say General Greene wants a secretary," said Marion, without lifting his eyes from the letter.

"I should say he wants two. But he won't get 'em, never fear! He hasn't even got lint and bandages, he says, let alone a spare surgeon, and an action now would mean a terrible loss in wounded, for lack of care. He is moving down to Cheraw soon, for winter quarters."

"So I am to become a not very glorified spy," Marion mused above the letter. "Well, so be it. That is all, gentlemen. Captain Melton, you will be prepared to start back with my reply to General Greene in the morning."

"Any time you say, General."

They rose informally, made for the tent door in a bunch, and jostled through it. As they went—

"Mr. Day," said Marion, and Julian turned back to where Marion sat quietly, holding the letter, looking tired and small and very much alone.

"Is there something I can do, sir?"

"You heard what he said about General Greene needing a secretary."

"Yes, sir."

"You will ride north with Melton tomorrow and report to General Greene for duty."

"But—I'd rather stay here, sir. I'll be fit for active service soon—in fact, I am now if you would only—"

"In an army that is properly run," Marion interrupted thoughtfully, "a good soldier does not express preferences to his commanding officer."

"I'm sorry, sir, but—"

"Nor does he say But to an order."

Julian was silent, wearing a dogged look.

"You are not fit for active service as we perform it here—and you never will be, though your shooting has certainly improved since you began target practice with Horry." There was a silence, and Marion sighed and raised his head. His piercing eyes ran over Julian's splendid height, clothed now in rough homespun and broken boots, but carried with that indefinable air that made him "one of Us" to the son of a British earl. Marion's rare smile broke slowly. "In that army I was telling you about, that is run the way it should be—a good general doesn't indulge himself in friendships in the middle of a campaign either. I shall miss— our talks, Mr. Day. But you start north with Melton in the morning."

"Very good, sir," said Julian stiffly.

"That is all, Mr. Day. Good night."

"Good night, sir."

But in the early morning, with Melton saddling up and a few silent men waiting round for awkward farewells to the stranger who had become one of them, Julian sought Marion's tent again and met the little general coming out.

"Good morning, sir. I—wanted to say good-bye."

"I had something the same idea," said Marion drily. "You see, Mr. Day—" He hesitated and seemed to find it difficult. "You see, I do not need a secretary."

"I know," said Julian, smiling. "And I'm not much of a soldier—yet. I'm no good to you, I can see that. I only hope General Greene can find a use for me. I've—enjoyed myself here, sir. In that army you spoke about, is a rather second-rate infantryman permitted to wish his commanding officer luck?"

Marion made a vague gesture of cleansing his right hand on the seat of his breeches before he held it out.

"I'm not one for speeches," he said, with an effort. "But God bless you, boy."

They were not to meet again.

For his journey Julian had been outfitted with fine whole British doeskin breeches in which it was necessary to lay a pleat at the belt, and a less imposing coat of scarlet regimentals which had been turned a sort of brownish-purple with a streaky vegetable stain. Still, as Horry remarked, it was better than wearing it inside out to avoid accidents, like some. He wore a British tricorne too, from which the cockade had been removed, and a scarlet sash with a pistol in it, and good British boots a size too large. They gave him the same horse—Neddy's horse—which he had ridden away from Nelson's Ferry.

Following the swampy course of the Peedee northward with Melton, he came early in January to Cheraw and what was fondly called by General Greene a camp of repose. It was anything but that, for Greene had come to Carolina not so much to command an army as to create one.

Julian presented his credentials at headquarters and was put to work copying despatches. He had had no idea of the secretarial work involved in fighting a war. Several copies of each letter had to be made, sometimes in order that it might have the benefit of two separate post-bags in the hope of getting one of them through to its destination, sometimes in order that more than one superior or subordinate might know exactly what had been said to the others, sometimes to report progress or relay information in an endless chain. He wrote for hours at a stretch, thankful that his wound had not been in his right arm; wrote until cramp gripped his hand and the cords at the back of his neck rebelled against holding up his head at that angle any longer; wrote until the words danced and blurred on the page in the yellow candlelight. But he was getting a new insight into the war now. He was seeing dimly what lay behind the lack of supplies and the seemingly hopeless muddle which caused the often needless hardships of the common soldiers, as he copied out Greene's persistent itemized appeals for bare necessities—everything was lacking at Cheraw from breeches to cartouche-boxes, and there was no transport at all—and then wrote tactful replies to the disheartening letters from Richmond or Philadelphia on what was being done, and why more had not been done, etc., etc.

Greene himself had an enormous, sleepless capacity for work, and was greatly beloved by his jaded associates. Julian liked everything he heard about his new commander—how he had been read out of meeting in his Rhode Island Quaker community after joining the local militia back in '74—how he enjoyed dancing and a joke, and had married a gay, pretty wife with whom he was openly in love—how he had missed Bunker Hill by a day and had hardly been out of the sound of cannon fire since then—how at Harlem he had seized the drag-ropes of the artillery himself when his men wavered, and how his impersonation of Dr. Slop in *Tristram Shandy* was as good as a play—each anecdote related to the newcomer by an admiring staff added to the general's stature.

He called no councils of war, and confided in no one, and nothing was too trivial for his attention. He was hampered at every turn by the lack of hard money, and few of the local merchants would sell to him for paper money. He paid the country women roundabout in salt for some shirtmaking. It was difficult even to find enough paper money for the express riders' needs. But while Cheraw was no Egypt, as Greene himself was the first to admit, food and forage were more abundant there than around Charlotte, and more easily obtained.

Cornwallis was wintering at Winnsborough west of the Wateree, with strong posts at Camden, Ninety-six, and Fort Granby. In order to worry him, Greene detached General Morgan with nine hundred men including Colonel William Washington's cavalry to work the country beyond the Catawba in Cornwallis' rear.

Before January was out, Morgan sent back word that he had defeated Tarleton at the Cowpens, and the details made cheerful hearing at Greene's headquarters. William Washington, cousin of the Commander-in-Chief, was the hero of that glorious day—for when the British seemed to have carried all before them and were huzzahing their triumph Washington ordered his bugle-boy to sound the charge and his troop of highly irregular horse galloped headlong into the enemy with sabres swinging. In the mêlée which followed Washington and Tarleton met face to face, and although Tarleton's men were already giving ground he turned, with an aide either side of him, for a personal encounter with his enemy. Washington was accompanied only by a sergeant and the bugler—the latter as everyone knew, too small to carry a sword. The sergeant disabled the sabre arm of one of the aides who was trying to cut Washington down from behind while Tarleton engaged him in the center, and the little bugler pistoled the aide who was coming in on the other side. Washington parried Tarleton's thrust and wounded him in the right hand. Tarleton wheeled to discharge his pistol, catching Washington in the knee, and retired in some haste.

It was truly a rout for the British, who had lost over two hundred casualties and six hundred prisoners—Colonel Howard was said to have had the surrendered swords of five British officers in his hand at one time. But—there was always a But to good news—Tarleton had got

away and Cornwallis himself was now within thirty miles of Morgan
with reinforcements, and the Americans were therefore retreating at top
speed eastwards towards the upper Catawba fords with their spoils.
Roads were bad and rivers were swollen with winter rains.

The camp at Cheraw drank William Washington's health in cherry
bounce, and cheered the bugler, who was killed, and had a *feu de joie,*
and found itself under marching orders for Salisbury to the north, with
all detachments called in and all stores to be collected and loaded. General Huger and Colonel Williams were to command the main army on
this march, while Greene set out across country, with only one aide and
a sergeant's guard of dragoons, to meet Morgan in front of Cornwallis.

V

Julian had come up in the world now, and rode his own horse among
the other members of General Huger's official family, on the winter
march northwards along the Peedee. But his knowledge of what the
men in the ranks were enduring was acute. Many of them had only
blankets around their waists like Indians, and their unshod feet left
bloody tracks in the rutted red clay roads. Rain was almost incessant.

Before they reached Salisbury, Greene had joined Morgan and sent
back an express with orders changing the rendezvous from Salisbury
to Guilford Courthouse, as the retreat forced him ever eastward. On
February eighth the two armies, Morgan's from the Cowpens and
Huger's from Cheraw, were united near Guilford Courthouse. But there
was no time to rest, though Morgan's men had already travelled a hundred and fifty miles almost on the run from the other side of the Catawba, and Huger's had hurried a hundred miles from Cheraw over
hideous terrain, with horses so played out they could hardly move the
wagons.

Greene could muster now about two thousand men, including five
hundred militia whose time of service was nearly up, and two hundred
cavalry. Cornwallis had something under three thousand, with three
hundred cavalry, including the punished remainder of Tarleton's fa-

mous dragoons from the Cowpens. Both armies were in bad condition from sickness, lack of wagon transport and insufficient food, and both suffered from the weather. The British were better shod and better clothed and on the whole better provisioned, but at the same time it was not at all the kind of war they were accustomed to.

Cornwallis had failed to prevent a junction between the two American forces, and the only course left to him was to get between Greene and Virginia and compel him to fight at a disadvantage or surrender. The armies were only twenty-five miles apart. Greene was determined to avoid an engagement at present, and on the tenth he gave orders to press on northward—drawing Cornwallis always farther from his bases, crippling his communications, wearing out his drenched and bewildered regulars. Lincoln and Gates in turn had failed. On the bedraggled survivors of those failures and on a leader tireless as fate rested the outcome of the southern campaign, perhaps of the whole war.

Virginia was Greene's source of supply, and was stanchly Whig in sentiment. He had left General Steuben in Richmond as he came south last December—Steuben the Prussian drillmaster, who in 1778 by a potent mixture of patience and profanity had made a disciplined army out of the frostbitten rabble which wintered at Valley Forge. Steuben had not had a word of English then, but he kept an American aide beside him when he exercised the companies, to swear at the troops in words they could take to heart while he relieved his feelings in a sulphurous combination of German and bad French; and he was not too great, either, to take the musket himself and march and wheel the awkward squad off its feet. It was said that when Lafayette once expressed surprise at the orderliness which finally reigned in camp, and the absence of noise in which the troops conducted their daily affairs, Steuben had replied in even greater surprise, "Noise, my lord Marquis? I do not know where noise should come from, when even my brigadiers dare not open their mouths but to repeat my orders!"

Nevertheless Steuben's men all adored him, partly because he took an active and open-handed interest in their private lives—he never had any money because he gave it all away. Greene was happy to know that he had Steuben at his back, and Jefferson got along with him well enough, despite the wear and tear of their respective positions at Richmond. Muhlenberg and Nelson, who commanded the militia in Virginia, had accepted him gratefully as their superior. The only complaints, and they were loud, came from people who had tried to conceal from him their ability to supply the equipment he needed for the destitute army.

Once across the Dan and in closer contact with Richmond, Greene hoped to be replenished from a friendly population hitherto free of British depredations. Marion, Pickens, and Sumter must do what they could with partisan warfare in Carolina until he could return to its defense. Food was already better, discipline was better, spirits were higher among the Americans under Greene's leadership, in spite of the gruelling marches over the red clay roads which hardened at night, went into slime during the day, and were deeply cut with horse and wagon tracks.

Greene had never had his clothes off since he joined Morgan on the Catawba, and he slept in the saddle. At night while the army rested on the frosty ground with one blanket to three men, he wrote and dictated letters by the light of a sputtering lantern. The two armies were so close together that Cornwallis' advance guard under O'Hara and Greene's rear guard under Lee and Williams were in constant skirmishes and the greatest vigilance was necessary on the American side to prevent a night surprise. Patrols had to be so numerous that each man got only six hours' sleep out of each forty-eight. Neither dared to halt long, and so killing was the pace that an early breakfast was the only real meal served during the day. This way the armies covered an exhausting average of thirty miles a day.

By the middle of February Greene's men had won the race and were bivouacked on the far side of the Dan, from where they saw Cornwallis turn back thwarted towards Hillsborough, where he raised the royal standard. He had not captured the American army, but he had at least chased it out of the Carolinas and he now anticipated a general Tory uprising in his favor.

In the camp beyond the Dan on Virginian soil, Julian was sorting out the contents of a newly arrived post-bag when Greene erupted into the tent and fell upon his letters.

"What in the name of the Almighty is all this about Arnold?" he demanded, scrabbling at the seals.

"Arnold, sir? I understood he had got away to the British at West Point."

"That is not news, Mr. Day! But Williams says he has just heard Arnold is in Virginia—and that wants looking into! Ah, here we are— a letter from Steuben!"

Julian waited with only a pretense of occupying himself while the general read with deliberation and sounds of annoyance the letter from Steuben. Then he waited while Greene expressed himself at some length on the black treasonous soul of Benedict Arnold. When he could bear it no longer—

"Did you—did I hear you say something about Arnold being actually in the James River, sir?"

"The fellow has had the brass to burn Richmond!" Greene told him furiously. "Sailed up the James with a flotilla full of Loyalists and regulars like a pirate and burnt the capital because it wouldn't surrender! Steuben had nothing much to defend it with on such short notice, having sent us all his best troops. The legislature scattered and no one was taken."

"Williamsburg?" said Julian, and his tongue was dry. "What happened at Williamsburg?"

"Nothing, so far. Nelson is there, with only four hundred men. Arnold has gone back down the river and begun to fortify Portsmouth, while he awaits reinforcements from New York. There is a price on his head. And while I don't want the money—as God is my witness, I wouldn't *take* the money, but what wouldn't I give just for the *chance* to take Arnold's head!"

"Are we going after it, sir?" asked Julian hopefully, and the bloodthirsty ex-Quaker rose and walked about the narrow tent, round and round the table, in an agony of decision and renunciation.

"Lead me not into temptation!" prayed General Greene. "I cannot turn my back on Cornwallis now. Nay, nay, I have set my hand to the plough in Carolina—no pleasure trips in this war, my boy—our job is still there, beyond the Dan—"

"But with Arnold in our rear—" Julian ventured, in a private ordeal of his own.

"Steuben will have to account for him, from Richmond—while we stray not from the path of duty nor lust for the stolen fruit of vengeance on the traitor. God give me strength," implored Nathaniel Greene, whose boyhood piety of phrase had not left him just because the Quakers had

disowned him, "God give me strength to hew to the line here, where my
duty lies! And at the same time, may God strengthen Steuben's arm,
and bring the sinner Arnold to a meet and terrible end!"

"Yes, sir. But couldn't we just go up to Portsmouth and hang him
ourselves?"

Greene paused and bent upon Julian a look half angry, half playful.
Not many of his military family took the liberties his quiet-voiced secretary was allowed. Not many of them knew to such a hair's breadth where
the general's always perilous patience would come to an abrupt end, or
how to tickle his somewhat undernourished and sometimes unrefined
sense of humor.

"Cornwallis would keep, sir. And we are half way to Portsmouth
now," said Julian, returning the look with eyes which were steady and
anxious.

"Get thee behind me, Satan," said General Greene. "Half way to
Portsmouth from where?"

"From Cornwallis, sir."

"If only my geography was as bad as yours!" sighed Greene, and his
tongue slipped still further into the language of his youth, as it was
likely to do at times of stress or moments of genuine affection. "Thee
cannot hope to turn me from my duty, Mr. Day, by such flagrant appeals
to my baser side, I promise thee. And thee knows as well as I do that
the traitor Arnold is not the real enemy. *He* is at Hillsborough still!—
and thither lies our way. Thee will take down a letter, please, to General
Steuben."

Julian said no more. But it was an odd sensation to find himself here,
in an army bivouac with the surging Dan between himself and the British, while behind him the particular spot he had gone out to fight for lay
defenseless in the path of destruction. There was the Virginia militia,
of course, but the militia had not prevented the burning of Richmond. . . .

He thought of Aunt Anabel, and her airy conviction that if only she
had a couple of good swordsmen in the house she was safe. He thought
for the thousandth time of St. John and what could have become of
him after that brief glimpse at Camden. All his inquiries among the
officers who had gathered at Charlotte and Hillsborough after the battle
had failed to yield any word of St. John, beyond the obvious fact that

he was not among them. And he thought of Tibby, frightened, robbed, or bullied by the soldiery. When he thought of Regina, he hardened his heart. Regina would welcome the British as friends and deliverers, and nothing unpleasant would happen to her.

It was useless to write to them in Francis Street and ask how things were with them, for there was no way to send a letter and no address at which he could receive a reply. The army would soon be on the move again, reinforced and refreshed, southward across the Dan.

VI

But the Tories did not do much rallying round Cornwallis after all— perhaps because Greene lost so little time in taking up the trail again, which was easy enough to follow by the smoking ruins in the wake of Tarleton's raids. Cornwallis knew too that Greene was receiving reinforcements as he came—Stevens, Lawson, Eaton, Butler, each with their fresh contingents. For Cornwallis there was nothing nearer than Wilmington.

Keeping Lee's alert light cavalry between the main army and Cornwallis, Greene advanced warily, shifting his ground daily, until it seemed to the Tories and Cornwallis that Greene was everywhere. At last he felt strong enough to risk battle on ground of his own choosing, and he chose Guilford Courthouse, which his knowing eye had marked down on the way north as a likely spot for a man to make a stand.

Cornwallis, on whom the cat-and-mouse game of dodging about the countryside had begun to tell, recognized the necessity for some conclusive action. His regulars knew how to behave under fire. But these long, aimless-seeming marches through cold and hunger were demoralizing them to the point of desertion. Also, unless he could show a victory soon, a lasting victory, the Tories would never join him. At the same time, a decisive defeat would be his ruin. Cornwallis was cornered at last.

Greene arrived at his battlefield late in the day on March fourteenth, and Julian rode with him and the quartermasters while he surveyed

again the ground which Cornwallis had not been clever enough to occupy before him. Julian was wondering what would happen now if
Cornwallis would not come out and fight. He was noting too the difference between the preparations which went on all around him here
and the bungling, extemporaneous doings before Camden. Sitting his
horse at the general's side, he watched the weary, muddy column swing
on to the camp site to the cheerful beat of their drums and form battalions, dressing right and supporting arms as required by Steuben's
new manual of regulations. Within a remarkably short time the pickets
and grass-guards were out, the drums were beating for wood and water
detachments, arms were piled, and the tents began to go up; the sinks
were being dug, the wagon-park took form behind the sutler's tents and
cook-fires, and the smell of supper was soon in the air.

He had seen it done before under Greene's business-like command but
it never failed to impress him as a sign of the discipline and spirit of
men whose every action was likely to attract the all-seeing eye of the
general. It was Greene's habit too sometimes to go the Grand Rounds
himself at night, giving the countersign and visiting the sentries like any
officer-of-the-day. This made for wakefulness and punctilio among the
guards.

There was no fumbling about in the dark this time in a blindfold
attempt to anticipate the enemy's intentions and positions. Everybody
knew exactly where he was and what was expected of him. Julian felt
a surge of almost schoolboy excitement and confidence, as he followed
the little knot of officers back to the Courthouse building on the brow
of the hill, where headquarters were established. This time Cornwallis
would catch it.

He paused on the steps of the Courthouse and looked back. The field
stretched away below him in the late light like a map—copse-woods,
clearings, and ravines, cut by the road to Salisbury along which the
British must approach. The Carolina militia, which would form the
front line, had a rail fence to act as breastworks with an open cornfield
in front of it. Three hundred yards to their rear in the second growth
oak woods lay the Virginia militia. And on the hill's crest to the right
of the Courthouse were Huger's and Williams' veterans as a strong reserve. Two of the four precious big guns were being tugged into position just in front of him by grunting cannoneers. The other two were

down the road with the second line. Lee's light cavalry and William Washington and his Cowpens heroes would secure the flanks.

While he stood there, the sunset drums began to beat the *retreat* on the right, and all the other drums woke to instant response. The brisk spring air was sweet with woodsmoke and the fragrance from soup-pots. It was a peaceful and orderly scene, he thought with some astonishment. It was hard to believe that by tomorrow night—

"Mr. Day!"

"Yes, sir, coming, sir."

There was a frost during the night, and the morning broke cool and clear. Breakfast was savoury and unhurried. The *general* beat at six o'clock, tents were struck, and the baggage moved to the rear. Lee had gone out with some of his light horse to reconnoitre along the Salisbury road, and soon a courier came back at full gallop to report the British army on the march. Cornwallis had taken up the gage.

The faces round the council table in the Courthouse were grave but confident. The gravity was caused by something other than respect for Cornwallis, and it was voiced by Colonel Williams, as spokesman, just before the council dispersed.

"If you have no objection, sir, I—there is something we wanted to say," he began, and looked nervous as a girl under Greene's amused regard.

"Couldn't you save it till after we get all this out of the way?" Greene inquired patiently.

"No, sir."

"Oh, very well, if you *must* make a speech—!"

"It is only this, sir. We feel—we recognize perhaps more clearly than you can do yourself, sir, how much depends on you—on your continued presence in the field. Without you, sir, the south is lost. And so—I have been asked to say—to beg you on behalf of us all not to expose yourself needlessly in this engagement, sir. We are here to run your errands under fire. There is not one of us who cannot be replaced. But if we should lose *you*, sir, we would have no—no remount." He sat down, rather red around the ears.

Greene was touched. For a moment there was silence in the bleak room while he sat with his eyes on the map-covered top of the table beneath his big quiet hands.

"If you want me to fight the battle from here," he said then, "you should have hung on to Gates, he is your man for that."

"You are worth ten of Gates to us, sir," said Stevens brusquely, and Greene looked up at him under his brows.

"And for why?" he demanded. "Because the men know where to find me—out there amongst 'em! If I am indispensable, and no man is that, the hand of the Lord will cover me. To your posts, gentlemen."

The day was turning unseasonably warm, and Greene took off his hat and wiped his shining brow with a big blue and white handkerchief as he rode down to inspect the front lines. Julian, acutely conscious of a persistent flutter underneath his breastbone, came behind with Major Burnet, one of the aides, and looked with compassion at the poor devils along the rail fence awaiting their first sight of the enemy. They were all good marksmen, he knew, with two brigades of rifles among them, but they were new troops, dreading the British bayonet. Himself the veteran of many bitter skirmishes since his first battle, Julian had not forgotten his own sensations at Camden, and the comfort of having Neddy Blake beside him. He still missed Neddy in a crisis.

Individual faces stood out as he followed his general along the lines —a boy's face, starched with fright, staring enviously at the men on horseback who were not stationed here under the first onslaught; a hard, unshaven, grim face, empty of all but the determination to kill; a mocking, grinning face like Neddy's, at ease and unafraid—what was it doing in the militia? His eyes went back to the terrified boy—he wished that Neddy could be beside that boy today. . . .

Greene's voice rang out strongly—"Three rounds, my lads—three rounds, and then you may fall back!" he said, and the men grinned and cheered him, and he grinned back and raised his hand in a broad gesture full of fellowship and command, and they all felt better for a sight of him, and hitched up their breeches and spat copiously and demanded in loud, truculent tones if his lordship thought they had all day to wait for him and his red-coated bastards—but their laughter was a little too shrill for realism.

Greene's smiling calm was infectious. By noon, when they had made the rounds, Julian had achieved an almost Olympian detachment, so certain was he now that this time the Carolinians would stand, and that with Lee and William Washington instead of Armand to deal with

Tarleton even the famous dragoons would meet their match. Greene on his tour of inspection had arrived last of all at Washington's post on the right behind the second line, and they found him anticipating with zest another chance at the dark-browed ruffian who had contrived personally to give him that wound in the knee at the Cowpens. William Washington had the same powerful frame and modest ways as his relative, the Commander-in-Chief. His sabre stroke was certain death, and his handwriting was small and lacy like a woman's.

Soon after they left him and rode back slowly towards the observation post near the Courthouse, vicious firing began in the distance, as Lee made contact and fell back towards the main army. About one o'clock the British fifes and drums were heard, long before the van swung into view down the road, their banners caught by a light breeze. Moving in blocks like toy soldiers, ignoring a sharp cannonade by Singleton's two pieces in the road ahead of them, they deployed superbly either side of the road and formed their lines, while their artillery came up and began to reply.

It was a beautiful sight and a terrifying one, and Julian's stomach turned over as he watched. Could anything shake them, much less stop them? Cornwallis had not the advantage this time, either in position or numbers, but he was forming a line without reserves, except for cavalry, as though he had no doubt that a single onset would sweep the field. The kilted Highlanders of the Seventy-first, the Guards, and the Hessians formed his right; the Twenty-third, the Thirty-third, some Loyalist Volunteers, and the Grenadiers were on his left.

Tensely the group surrounding General Greene awaited the sound of the Carolinians' fire from the breastworks which were hidden by the trees between. It came unevenly, at random. They were too far away at the Courthouse to hear the British commands, but the woods ended abruptly in bare cornfields which the British had to cross without cover of any kind and the downhill slope was just sufficient for the watchers at the Courthouse to catch glimpses through the cannon smoke as the red lines halted, made ready, and fired into the American breastworks. And then, behind the drifting haze of their own volley, the British threw forward their bayonets and charged at the quick step, with their long huzzah.

There was no reply to the British volley. The Carolinians had panicked, throwing away their muskets, canteens, and knapsacks in a wild stampede to the rear. Butler's aide came tearing up the road on a bleeding horse and gasped out to Greene that there was no longer a front line. "It's an utter rout, sir! They are running like sheep! It's up to the second line now, sir!"

Julian, through his incredulous horror, became aware of a voice.

"The God-damned, string-spined, lily-livered sons of sin, not an ounce of guts in a mile of them!" said General Greene, and drove home his spurs.

"No, no—let *me* go, sir— *General, let me take the order—*" Burnet shot out after him, and both were swallowed up in the smoke.

Julian and the remaining aide, Morris, looked at each other, tight-lipped. "Come on, then," said Morris, and they followed.

No one present on the field, not even Greene, was quite abreast of the battle after that. The Virginians in the second line knew that they opened ranks and let the Carolina militia through, taunting them as they fled, and then faced the British advance bravely, cutting great gaps in the red line with a well-delivered volley. For a while, bayonet to bayonet, they bore the weight of the attack. But it was too much for them, and they fell back from the right, uncovering the Continentals to the Grenadiers and the Twenty-third, while the left still held. The Continentals knew that they had a stirring glimpse of General Greene as he rode among them in the gunpowder murk—"Stand firm!" he cried to them. "Steady, now, and you can finish it, our fire is taking effect!"

These were Williams' men, and Huger's. Coolly they poured in a volley and then went to the bayonet. The British staggered and gave ground. And then Washington's bugles sounded and his cavalry swept in, sabre arms flailing, and it all dissolved into the shrieking, clanking, iron-shod carnage of the cavalry charge. When he had passed, the whole British left rallied doggedly, but the Continentals met them again and fought like men inspired, discipline for discipline, against the regulars.

It was Cornwallis himself who decided the day. Relying on the seasoned men he commanded, he ordered his artillery to open at close range, firing ruthlessly into the Grenadiers and the Twenty-third, in order to check the stubborn advance of the Marylanders. His officers turned away sick at the sight, but Cornwallis called it stern necessity, and stood by grimly while the British cannon spoke again and again, mowing down red coats and blue impartially.

Julian, galloping down to the left on courier duty, arrived just in time to see the Virginians there give way at last, and to learn that Lee, presumably still fighting the Hessians in the woods, had lost touch. He came pelting back along the littered road and overtook Stevens, wounded and being removed from the field by his men in their sullen retreat, their faces still to the enemy. Riding wide to clear a hallooing gang of Marylanders who had found some of Hamilton's Loyalists to deal with, he came to the screaming, smoking, bleeding confusion in front of the British cannon, and almost collided with Greene, who was also riding full tilt into it in an effort to pierce the battle smoke and see for himself where the destructive fire was coming from.

"In God's name, sir—!" gasped Julian, and so far forgot himself as to lay hold of the general's bridle.

"That misbegotten son of Satan is firing into his own men!" shouted Greene, his face white with his un-Quakerish fury.

"Will you please turn back, sir, the cannon are just beyond us—!"

"What an army they have got!" yelled Greene above the din, with a kind of awe. "What *infernal* discipline! Could thee believe it if thee did not *see?* He is slaughtering his own officers in their tracks to stop us! I couldn't do it, boy—I haven't got the black-hearted courage to do such a thing!"

"Stevens has a ball in his thigh, sir—"

"Where is Lee?"

"Out in the woods on the left, sir, engaging the Hessians—hasn't been heard from for some time. Lawson says it is no good now, sir—they have turned our left flank and Tarleton's dragoons are drawn up in the road awaiting the order to charge! Lawson is falling back to the Courthouse—"

"It's these damned raw troops they send me! One half that first line never fired at all! It takes veterans to win a battle, and I haven't got enough of them! If only I had more Marylanders—"

With a glance over his shoulder towards the steady pound of well-served cannon and the whine and crash of the shot, Julian wheeled the general's horse and still holding its bridle started smartly for the high ground near the Courthouse. Greene, with his mind on the inhuman behavior of Cornwallis, was unexpectedly docile.

"Merciful God, he was destroying half the battalion, and they rallied and formed again!" he marvelled. "We cannot win now—he has done it again, damn him. Well, it was very near—we shall have to retreat again, but his losses must be terrible—terrible! Now that you have rescued me singlehanded, Mr. Day, will you be so good as to find Colonel Williams and tell him to prepare to fall back to the old camp at Troublesome Creek! We must leave our wounded."

For Julian, the confident excitement of the morning had now to give way to a disappointment so dire as to amount to despair. They had been so near to winning the battle—the British were groggy and reeling, one more fresh wave of Marylanders would have done the business, but there were not enough Continentals there at the Courthouse to follow up Williams' advantage. It was somehow worse than Camden, because it had been so near. . . .

Unlike Greene, Julian had not been present on the equally heartbreaking day at Brandywine, nor seen Lafayette almost weeping with frustration after Monmouth. He had acquired no philosophy for defeat when victory had seemed possible. He had seen the panic of the Carolina militia coming back from the front line—seen men flee with starting eyes and hoarse sounds of terror while their frantic officers caught at them, actually wrestled with them, cursing, threatening, and pleading. He had seen the gallant stand of the Virginians, who to be sure were well aware that Stevens had posted riflemen behind them to shoot down the first to submit to any unauthorized desire to retreat. He had seen Washington's cavalry reform after the charge, blown and gashed and fewer in number, but quite ready to go in again. And all for nothing. All just to leave Cornwallis in possession of the field again, counting hideous losses it was true, but still technically the victor. Julian took it very hard.

From Troublesome Creek, which they reached after a dreary night march through a cold rain, Greene sent back a surgeon under a white flag to tend the American wounded. And to a return flag from Cornwallis pompously demanding surrender, he replied tersely: "I am prepared to sell you another field at the same price."

The battered American army, which had acquitted itself so much better this time than at Camden, was in remarkably high spirits. Their losses were much lighter, they knew, than those of the British, and they had retired in good order from a stoutly contested battleground. Cornwallis was not beaten, maybe, but he was badly mauled, and they were willing to try again. But the British were retreating towards Wilmington, and once more the short militia term became a factor to an American general. There would be no holding them now once their time was up, with such a story to tell. Regretfully Greene decided to let Cornwallis go, and to turn his attention to Rawdon at Camden, where Marion and Sumter could be of assistance with their partisan troops.

Julian sat at the rickety camp table in Greene's tent where they labored together over the correspondence. The general was writing a letter to his wife, his face gentle and unguarded in the lantern-light. Julian's task was making a copy of a letter to General Steuben which was to be enclosed in the bag which was going to the Commander-in-Chief. *"We fight, we get beat, rise, and fight again,"* he wrote, transcribing from Greene's neat, unhurried script. *"I am determined to carry the war immediately into South Carolina. The enemy will be obliged to follow us, or give up their posts in that state. If the former takes place . . ."*

There was a flurry outside, and the sentry's voice—an orderly came in hastily with a post-bag just arrived by express from Richmond. Eager as he was for news from the north, Julian forced himself to go on writing while Greene broke the seals, until—

"God be praised!" cried Greene, and slapped the table with his big hand so that the ink-horn and lantern jumped. "Thank the Lord, from whom all blessings flow! Lafayette is coming south! He was at Head of Elk when this was written! He is coming to Virginia with an army to cook Arnold's goose! Bless the boy, what I wouldn't give to see him here! Ah, well!" He dismissed that happy possibility with a sigh. "Still, this puts a very different look on things, I promise thee! Wherever he is, the Marquis is worth his weight in wildcats! Mr. Day—never mind that, whatever it is—take down a letter, please, to General Lafayette. *My dear Marquis—To say that I am rejoiced to hear of your appointment to the Virginia command is superfluous. I could wish that your marching orders had included—* No—no, perhaps not, I think thee had better take a fresh sheet of paper. *My dear Marquis . . ."*

Virginia

1781

I

Williamsburg had dreamed on through the summer heat, after Julian left it. There was little news from the north until August, when St. John sent a letter home from Richmond on his way south to de Kalb, which said that the arrival of Rochambeau at Newport with the first contingent of French troops sent to aid Washington had been very heartening at headquarters.

And then, early in September, the first beaten stragglers from Camden began arriving back in Virginia.

No further word came from St. John, and the story of de Kalb's death was not reassuring. Julian seemed to have vanished on his way to Richmond. Had he too been with de Kalb? Dorothea and Aunt Anabel waited, looking pinched and sleepless, through the long, baking days and the endless, sweet-scented nights. There was nothing else to do but wait, and try to hope that St. John had survived the battle and that Julian had not been there at all.

It was not only in Williamsburg that the summer of 1780 took its toll of fortitude and faith. A wave of weariness swept the whole country after Camden, a hopelessness worse than the near panic after the Jersey losses in 1776. It was now four years since the Declaration of Independence had been signed, and the British still had not been driven out. The colonial government, decentralized into thirteen separate units, seemed paralyzed. The army was starving and never paid. Except for Saratoga and the French alliance, little had been gained, and these two happy auguries had scant fulfillment. On top of everything else, came the scandal

225

of Arnold's treason at West Point, and the cause itself seemed to be falling apart.

Then at the end of December the drums were beating the alarm from Yorktown to Richmond as a fleet of twenty-seven sail entered the Capes, and Nelson called out the militia on the Neck while Jefferson and Steuben prepared to evacuate all possible stores from Richmond. The British landed at Hampton, seized small craft, and began to ascend the James. Word ran ahead of them that they were led by the traitor Arnold, and that there was a regiment of Loyalist cavalry under Simcoe from New York. Every effort was going to be made, people said, to take Arnold alive.

Most of the plantation refuges of the Williamsburg families lay on the banks of the James open to plunder by a river-borne army, so that now the town houses seemed the safer place to be, and the women and children were kept there, while the menfolk looked to their weapons and the frightened militia drilled belatedly and took up cautious positions under hastily devised cover to the south and west of the city, as Arnold's flotilla approached the broken church and tide-lapped ruins of Jamestown.

Aunt Anabel said piteously—"Julian needn't have gone to the army, he could have defended us better here at home!"

On the third of January a small fishing-boat piloted by a half-grown Negro boy slid into the Landing on Queen's Creek and made fast. The boy crawled forward and knelt beside a man who lay collapsed against the gunwale quite unaware that he had reached the end of his journey.

"We done it, suh," the boy announced with some pride, and shook the unresponsive shoulder of his passenger. "We slip through pretty as you please. You better be gettin' home now, suh, 'fore they ketch you in that uniform."

The man roused himself and sat up dazedly.

"What's this?" he asked. "Where are we?"

"Capitol Landing, suh—just where we was makin' for."

"Good. That's good." But still the man sat confusedly blinking at the steps and the bank beyond as though he had no idea how to reach them.

"Lemme help you out, suh. Best git under cover in them clothes I'd say, suh. Redcoats all round us fust thing we know."

"Yes—yes, of course—must get home—will you help me as far as Francis Street?"

The Negro boy rolled apprehensive eyes over his shoulder at the empty landscape. He had collected his fee before starting, and was anxious to be rid of all connection with his dangerous cargo.

"Got be gettin' back tonight, suh—stormy weather and all—tain't my boat, I ketch hell if somepun happen to her—"

"Yes, all right—give me a hand, will you?"

Hoisted unceremoniously on to the slippery mud which covered the bottom steps at low tide, he grasped the handrail and dragged himself upward, replying with a vague gesture to the boy's conscience-smitten, "Take keer yourself, suh," as the boat cast off. His right leg was almost useless and would only bear his weight for a moment at a time. The dark blue coat of his uniform was torn and streaked with blood and dirt, he wore no shirt at all because it had long since gone for bandages, his boots were unspeakable. He had not had a shave for days.

He plodded on painfully across the muddy planks of the Landing and into the road which led towards town. Sometimes there were trees or fence-posts to cling to—sometimes for as much as a dozen steps he had to limp forward with no aid at all, watching his feet, absorbed in the all but impossible task of putting one in front of the other.

Tibby saw him from the window and snatched up a shawl and ran down the path to where he had paused, holding dizzily to the crazy fence which separated the dooryard of the cabin from the coarse grass at the side of the road.

"You mustn't go into Williamsburg like that, sir!" she cried. "The British are in the river!"

"Yes, I know they are—damn' near rode straight into them—"

"Mr. Sprague!" Tibby came through the gate and laid supporting arms around his sagging body. "Oh, Mr. Sprague, I didn't know it was you! You're hurt—you must come inside and lie down—"

With an effort, he raised his head and focused on her face.

"It's Tibby," he discovered with satisfaction. "That's luck—I—wanted to see you. Tibby, where is Julian?"

"We don't know, sir. He left for Richmond to join the army after Charleston fell."

"Then it *was* Julian!" he said, and stood holding to the fence and striving for consciousness. "I didn't dream it—afterwards. I saw him!"

"You *saw* him, sir?"

"At Camden." He caught her arm with a grimy, shaking hand. "Before God, Tibby, I had no choice—it was an order—I had to leave him there—"

"At *Camden?*" There was white, fierce terror in her face. "You l-left him—*at Camden—?*"

"With de Kalb. He was wounded—I don't know how badly—" His eyes glazed. "Tibby, I've got to get home—"

"Yes, sir—you ought to be in bed—it's not far now, I'll help you walk, just lean on me—"

"Run on ahead and fetch Joshua, will you? That's best—you can't help me—too heavy for you—please—run—"

She left him without another word, fleet-footed down the road, the shawl streaming out behind her. After a moment he straightened again and began his limping progress in her wake, holding to things as he passed, but somehow keeping on his feet towards that blessed moment when Joshua's powerful black arms would bear him up—the Capitol was in sight now at the end of the lane—and then he had reached the Duke of Gloucester Street—at last—everything was deserted there, the men had all gathered on the other side of town for the defense of Jamestown road—two women coming, though—and he a sight to scare the birds from the trees—

Regina, accompanied by Lucinda, was on her way to the apothecary's shop, for the arrival of the British in the river had brought on one of her mother's headaches. They hurried through the fading winter afternoon, anxious to be home again before candlelighting, for no one knew what would be happening in the streets of the town tonight. . . .

"Look, Regina, there is another poor soldier just getting back. Won't the British take him prisoner if they come? Oughtn't we to—"

"We must ask the apothecary to look after him. He—*St. John!* Oh, my dear love, I've been so miserable— St. John, why didn't you send us any word, you will forgive me, won't you, St. John, you always do forgive me no matter how badly I behave to you, oh, thank God I've got you back safe at last—!"

It was Regina's voice, they were Regina's hands, Regina's arms were round him—smiling, he slid into unconsciousness at her feet.

Joshua and Tibby ran up breathless through the dusk and found them there—Regina kneeling in the winter mud of the Duke of Gloucester Street, her dress a blue velvet ruin, with St. John's head cradled in her arms, while Lucinda stood above them crying, and the apothecary held hartshorn to St. John's nose.

Joshua stooped without a sound and took his master from Regina as though the limp body weighed no more than a child's, and carried him towards Francis Street. At the corner Dorothea met them, a white shawl thrown around her shoulders, and Aunt Anabel awaited them in the doorway. As Joshua passed into the house with his burden, Regina spoke from the gate—

"Please, Dolly—please, may I come in?"

After one look, which saw her for the first time with her muddied skirt and the tears running down her white cheeks, Dorothea held out sisterly arms.

Lucinda followed them into the house, but Tibby turned away unnoticed in the dusk, hugging her shawl about her. She had done what was required of her and fetched Joshua, and now she had time to think again—now she could contemplate the icy fact that Julian had been at Camden after all, with de Kalb, and wounded. Some of them were taken prisoner, she knew. The Charleston prison ships were said to be floating hells. There wouldn't be surgeons, there wouldn't be food, there wouldn't be enough air to breathe. . . .

Faintly, through the winter twilight, came the sound of firing, down Jamestown way. The British must have landed! Tibby began to run towards home, panting, stumbling, blind with tears, seeking the shelter of familiar things in candlelight, and the reassuring presence of her mother, where nothing was ever quite so bad as it might be.

Undressed, and patiently scrubbed clean and shaved by Joshua's careful hands and tucked into his own snowy bed again, St. John found himself drinking broth from a spoon, and looked up gratefully into Aunt Anabel's sweet face.

"Poor soul," he murmured. "Did I give you an awful fright?"

"Now, Sinjie, don't talk. You must drink this, and then go to sleep."

"Tell me just one thing," he pleaded. "I did meet Regina—she was there in the street?"

"Yes, indeed she was, and she is still down stairs, with Dorothea. But you are not to have visitors tonight."

"I thought maybe I was out of my head again," he said, relieved. The spoon was waiting. More broth went down. "Don't let her walk home alone," he said. "The British are coming up the river."

"I know, dear."

"If they have any sense they will go straight on to Richmond. There is nothing for them here."

"The militia have gone down to Burwell's Ferry."

"How many militia?"

"About four hundred, they say. Nelson has them."

"It's not enough." St. John drank more broth, and his eyelids were heavy. "Auntie, how am I going to tell Dorothea that I rode away and left Julian wounded at Camden?"

"Oh, Sinjie—*wounded?*"

"I was riding courier for de Kalb. The men on the left wing wouldn't stand, and de Kalb wouldn't retreat. Julian was fighting in the ranks, all over blood and powder. I thought I must be seeing things—but it was Julian, no mistake, he proved that. Then I had to leave him there with de Kalb— I don't think we had better tell Dorothea there was a cavalry charge coming in."

"De Kalb died," said Aunt Anabel. Her face quivered.

"I'm afraid they both did," he said, and turned his head away from the spoon. "No more, Auntie. You must tell her—I'm too tired—"

"Yes, dear, I'll tell her. Try and get some sleep now."

Before she was out of the room the heavy slumber of exhaustion claimed him. He never knew that they let Regina come and kiss him good-night before Joshua escorted her and Lucinda home through the empty streets, when the firing at Jamestown had stopped.

He never knew either that later that night a scared and shaking black butler knocked on the door of Regina's bedroom and said there was a gentleman demanding to see her. She put on a warm robe over her night-dress, tied her hair back with a ribbon, and descended the stairs.

The candelabra on the drawing-room table had been lighted for the visitor, and it was David Allen who stood over the dying fire, wearing the tight green coat and white breeches of Simcoe's Loyalist dragoons, and black cavalry boots.

Regina's heart lurched like an alarm bell. Only the day before, still nursing her obstinate quarrel with St. John, she might have been glad to see David, she could at least have acquiesced in his presence at Williamsburg in that uniform. But now her one thought was how to get rid of the man in the green coat before he found out that St. John lay helpless in Francis Street. There was the chance, of course, that David already knew that, perhaps had come because he knew. Simcoe could have received word from informers that an American officer had that day returned to Williamsburg. It would be quite a feather in Simcoe's cap to capture one of Washington's aides, and David had what he must consider an unsettled score with St. John since that day at Farthingale. Arrest now would mean a British prison for St. John, where he was sure to die from lack of care. . . .

As Regina paused on the threshold her mind was busy with lies she could tell David, ways she could find to protect St. John—desperate, crazy, hopeless things she might do to keep David away from the house in Francis Street.

He turned and stared at her unbelievingly as she stood there in the doorway.

"Oh, God, I had forgotten how beautiful you are!" was his only greeting.

"David, what are you doing here like this? Have they taken the town?"

"We could have it if we liked. The militia have scattered, as usual. My troop came ashore just to sweep up, and I—I have a few hours' leave." He came towards her with outstretched hands, his dark eyes shining and hungry. "My darling, there is nothing to be frightened about, we're headed up river for Richmond in the morning. Regina—say you are glad to see me, can't you?"

"Yes, David, of course I'm glad, but—what will you do at Richmond?"

"Burn it, if it won't surrender! Hang Jefferson, we hope, and make an end to the war in Virginia as soon as possible!"

"Hang—*Jefferson!*"

"Jefferson for André! Why not?"

"Oh, David, that's murder!"

"I forgot he was a friend of yours. But we are at war, you know. Except for tonight, that is. Sweetheart, I have moved heaven and earth to win this glimpse of you! Come into the light—"

Reluctantly, for she was seeing a great many things differently now, she let him take her hands and draw her into the room.

"You must go," she said urgently. "You aren't safe here."

"Safe?" He laughed. "There is no militia any more! And even if there were—it's worth risking my neck to see you like this!"

"Please go, David." She flushed as his gaze ran over the loose velvet gown and her unbound hair. "Some one might find you here—at this hour—"

"It's not quite the welcome I expected," he said, bewildered. "From what you said before I went north I hoped—"

"I was wrong, David. I have changed my mind."

"Well, upon my word, that's pretty cool! I hoped when I got into the Rangers you would be pleased with me!"

"I—I never thought you would come to burn Richmond," she explained lamely.

"How else can we win wars, my dear, than by burning capitals and hanging rebels? Williamsburg won't be touched, I fancy. We will make our headquarters at Portsmouth, and if things go well while we are there—"

"David, you are not to come here again, do you hear? Not while you wear that coat!"

"But I am wearing this coat because you always said—"

"If I had anything to do with your joining Simcoe's Rangers I'm sorry. Terribly sorry."

"So you have changed sides since I went north!" He looked at her narrowly. "You have turned rebel now! May I ask why?"

She passed him towards the fire, her hands to her face, moving without her usual proud assurance. Perhaps if he realized at once there was no longer the bond between them of belief in the King's cause, he would be offended and go. Perhaps in his anger at her for deserting him he would forget about St. John, or leave Williamsburg without ever finding out that St. John had come back.

"I don't know what I am any more, David, I—have no right to judge anyone. I am rather ashamed of myself all round, I think, and I wish you had never paid any attention to me. What kind of man are you, anyway, to choose the color of your coat to please a woman, instead of having ideas of your own too strong for her to meddle with? It doesn't matter what I said—it is what you yourself believe that counts!"

His handsome, sulky face was bleak.

"I suppose I have St. John Sprague to thank for this," he accused, and her denial came too soon, too anxiously.

"No, no, I—haven't seen him!"

David came to her on the hearthrug and turned up her face to his with a ruthless hand. The Williamsburg Tory who had informed on St. John Sprague naturally had not reported on Regina and one had had to come and see for oneself. It appeared that the thing he had most dreaded had happened in his absence and Regina had found her heart. Regina was lying to him to protect St. John—but wouldn't she perhaps do the same for any friend in the circumstances? Against his better judgment David must needs go on hoping.

"You *have* seen him," he said, her chin held fast between his finger and thumb. "Wasn't he at Camden?"

"No—I don't know."

"And wasn't he sent home wounded?"

"David, you're very frightening like this, I hardly know you!" Deliberately, imprisoned in his hold, she drained her body of resistance, made it soft and helpless against his, gave him her blue eyes full of reproach and appeal. Because, whatever he might know, he was at least on the right track. It might rest with her now, what happened to St. John. Her mind raced and fumbled among the things she might do—keep David here somehow—get word to St. John—but St. John couldn't be moved—keep David here, but how—throw him off the scent—but *how*—persuade him that St. John meant nothing to her any more, and perhaps he would let it go—? "You used not to treat me like a court martial," she murmured and laid warm, coaxing fingers on the hand that held her chin, and saw his eyes take fire while his left arm went round her waist and caught her to him till the butt of the pistol he wore tucked into his sash bruised her ribs.

"And do you really love a man for the color of his coat, Regina, or for the heart that beats inside it?" he murmured, for if her quarrel with St. John was unabated he had nothing to regret in the accomplishment of his errand in Williamsburg, which, once he had taken it on, had weighed a little heavy. "Suppose the green coat I wear says I must arrest St. John Sprague's blue one and escort it to Jamestown tonight—the fortunes of war, Regina! I assure you he would do the same to me. And so to the victor—the spoils!"

She waited, soft and willing in his arms, while his lips descended on hers and her fingers stole towards the pistol which pressed her side. They had found and clasped it firmly before he lifted his head, but still she was in his arms, drawing back from him only a little, loosening his hold only by her own smiling confusion and a belated self-recovery.

"That was very—presumptuous of you," she whispered, putting him from her with a hand against his chest—and then with a sudden jerk she was free of him, the pistol torn from his sash and pointed at him, very level and steady. "You are going back to Jamestown alone, David —or not at all," she said.

He stared at her a moment, and then folded his arms with a smile.

"You wouldn't really shoot me with that thing," he marvelled.

"You must give me your word of honor to ride straight back to James-town and never say a word to Simcoe about St. John if I let you go."

He gave a little sound, half laugh, half snort, but his easy pose, arms folded across his chest, did not alter.

"My dear girl, Simcoe knows. That is why I am here."

"He sent you? For St. John?"

"Somebody had to come for him. And I wanted to see you."

"You used St. John's arrest as an excuse to—to—" She looked at him with real repugnance.

"To see you, yes," he said quietly. "Otherwise they would have sent a sergeant with a mounted guard and hauled him into a saddle with very little ceremony, I assure you. Would you have preferred it that way?"

"You will have to say you could not find him." The pistol did not waver. "Say that he was warned and got away."

"Otherwise you will shoot me in my tracks." His white teeth gleamed.

"I—I would give the alarm."

"To whom? I tell you there is no militia. They ran. So in order to save you from committing murder, I must commit a dereliction of duty, is that it?" He moved towards her lazily and her finger stiffened on the trigger, but he reached for the barrel and twisted the pistol easily out of her grasp. "It would never have gone off like that, you know," he smiled, and showed her how it had not been cocked. "Still, you meant well, didn't you! It was very pretty, and I shall tell him you did it, I am sure he will be—flattered." He replaced the pistol in his sash and swung round with a jingle of spurs and sword-belt to pick up his high crested cap from the seat of a chair.

"David, wait!" She caught at him with desperate hands. "He is badly wounded—he will die if he's moved now—"

"I am sorry. I will try to arrange for him to have good care at Portsmouth."

"You will take him out of this house over my dead body, David. I married him today!"

"You *what?*"

"He is my husband." Regina drew a long breath. The wild lie had tumbled out unconsidered, and now she saw its possible advantages. Now perhaps she could keep David out of Francis Street by appealing to his kindness of heart. "He is in bed upstairs—very ill. M-mother is sitting with him. Do you want it on your soul that you have made me a widow?"

He stood looking down at her while astonishment gave way to comprehension. Truth seemed in every gracious line of her as she strove for the man she loved, and yet he knew that she lied. She hoped that by claiming St. John as her husband now she could save him from arrest, so long as it hung on the chivalry of a rival. And it made very little difference to David now whether the marriage ceremony had been performed or not, for he saw that she was already lost to him. He was conscious only of a swift desire to get away quickly, back to the war, back to battle and sudden death.

"It would certainly weigh heavy on my conscience," he admitted wryly, "if I made you a widow before you were wife! Very well, Regina —I leave you your bridegroom. Do you want my blessing as well?"

"Oh, David, I am grateful to you! You won't—get into trouble?"

"I shall certainly get into very serious trouble, my dear, if anyone bothers to prove that the bird had not flown before I got here. However—" He set the Ranger's leather cap with its glossy bearskin crest on his head and somehow became a foot taller. "—we have a few other things on our minds just now! I began the war in a green coat," he said, standing stiffly before her, "and I shall see it out in one. Even for you, I don't fancy myself as a deserter. But now that you are against us too, I might as well confess that this Arnold affair stinks rather high in my nostrils." A moment more he stood there, filling his sight with her beauty. "I find I wish you happiness in spite of myself," he said ruefully. "God bless you, Regina."

And he was gone, with his heartbreak, down the road to Jamestown at a gallop.

II

Bit by bit, when he was not too tired to talk, they pieced together St. John's story. He had got to Charlotte after Gates departed for Hillsborough, and he collapsed there from loss of blood. But Cornwallis pressed close on the Camden fugitives, and St. John fled just ahead of the British entry and managed to reach Hillsborough, where Gates had set up headquarters.

The wound was in the same leg as before, near the knee this time, but fortunately not in the joint. The hospital at Hillsborough hardly deserved the name, and was cruelly over-crowded. St. John's horror of amputation made him prefer a hazardous journey to an army surgeon's care, and he applied for discharge, which Gates granted in his usual vague hurry. St. John set out from Hillsborough with a raging fever, and got nearly as far as the Virginia line and then collapsed again, outside a farmhouse where he had stopped to buy food. They took him in and nursed him with simple country remedies through weeks of fever and dysentery. The wound healed meanwhile in a sort of way, and early in December he was on the road again, riding a much restored horse which had profited by the rest but had to be coddled for lameness. Just as he approached the south bank of the James the British flotilla under Arnold began to move up the river, and he turned downstream, hoping to cross behind them. The horse had gone very lame and he left it, buying passage around Point Comfort in the fishing-boat with his last piece of hard money.

Regina came to sit with him a little while each day, and their happiness shone round them like a second sun—and no more nonsense, please God, said Aunt Anabel. As soon as he was able to be propped up and hold a pen he got off his report to Washington's headquarters by a responsible courier. Then he sent for Tibby and told her the story of Camden. She listened silently, without tears. When he had finished—

"I don't think he is dead," said Tibby.

"I hope you are right," he sighed. "But why don't you?"

Tibby turned her eyes out the window to the winter sunshine.

"I just don't *feel* as though he is dead," she said.

"The sun goes on shining, child, no matter who dies."

"Not in my heart," she told him. "If he couldn't ever come back—things would feel emptier. He is some place—he is alive—or I would know."

"Sometimes I wish you didn't love him quite so much," St. John said very gently, so that she hardly realized he had put her secret into words.

"I think perhaps if you love a person *enough,* it can come between them and harm," she explained earnestly. "But if you are going to do that, you can't save out anything for yourself. It mustn't matter what happens to you—so long as they are all right. That is what I have tried to do for Mr. Day," she added simply. "I am his ransom out of the pit. I never ask God's mercy for myself—only for him."

"Tibby, I am fond of him too. But no man deserves all that."

"He won't know," she said, as though that excused it.

"Well, he ought to know!" St. John cried impatiently. "He ought to be able to see—!" And then he remembered Dorothea, and fell silent.

"He never sees things like that. He doesn't even know about your sister," said Tibby, and he stared at her.

"Good God above, Tibby, are people made of glass, to you? I suppose you must know too that he is in love with Regina!"

"Oh, well," said Tibby apologetically. "She is so beautiful. Miss Dorothea is beautiful too, so it doesn't seem fair, but I don't think he has ever realized how beautiful she is. Perhaps he will when he comes back and finds Miss Regina married to you."

"And are you resigned to that?" he queried curiously.

"Miss Dorothea wouldn't mind if I see him sometimes. So it wouldn't be very different than it has always been." But her eyes filled as she said it.

"Tibby, come here to me." St. John leaned towards her impulsively, and held out one hand. "Isn't there something I can *do?*"

She looked back at him gravely, her hand in his—the girl who never asked mercy for herself.

"Don't mind the way he feels about Miss Regina," she entreated. "Don't hold it against him."

"I know what you mean," he said solemnly. "And I promise not to let it make any difference at all."

When she had gone he sat a long time with his pipe, turning things over in his mind. In spite of himself he was somehow surer than he had been that Julian would come back. And then what?

As spring came on, it was very evident that the British intended to try and finish the war in Virginia as soon as possible, and that Washington meant to eliminate Arnold from his Portsmouth stronghold. In April Lafayette began his southward march, and almost simultaneously Cornwallis left his base at Wilmington with a recuperated force to join Phillips, who had superseded Arnold in the British command in Virginia.

Williamsburg was always delectable in May, and Tibby felt a lift to her heart which no amount of alarms and anxiety could quite dispel Her mother was ailing and frail, and Tibby had taken over most of the laundry and the making of the fine myrtle-wax candles and the scented soap which brought in enough money to keep the little household running. Kit took such odd jobs as slave labor left to him, and received in payment bits of food or some garden seed or a nearly worthless piece of paper money, from people who mostly just wanted to be kind. Mawes did a day's fishing or carpentry now and then, and drank the proceeds.

She had not known how to tell St. John the half of her belief in Julian's safety. What had begun as a pathetic sort of game, played to stave off desolation after his departure, had now become an article of faith. For years she had never walked down the Duke of Gloucester Street without the hope of meeting him. And now out of her need she contrived the comforting pretence of living each day as though he was just around the corner. Each day she learned from the books he had given her, and set herself new tasks of memory and penmanship and needlework. And not a flower bloomed or a sunny morning shed glory but she called his attention to it in her secret way, holding him fast at her side in his absence as she had never done in reality. It brought him nearer, it kept him safer, if she never, for a single twenty-four hours, acknowledged to herself that he was not there. If she loved him *enough*. . . .

On a warm afternoon in May she went scuffing through the dust of the Duke of Gloucester Street with a basket on her arm—she had delivered three beautifully laundered fichus and a gauze apron and some caps to Mrs. Greensleeves, whose personal maid was ill, and besides the payment in coin she had received a small sponge cake which was for her mother's supper. Sarah had felt too faint to finish the ironing and Tibby had done it for her, and put the corn bread in the oven to bake before she left the cabin.

As she passed the Raleigh on her way home, Mr. Southall looked round from a conversation with a couple of friends at the hitching-bar and shouted at her in his genial way—

"Hey, you with the basket! What's your name?"

She smiled back at him with her usual self-possession, for all three of them were known to her and had teased her ever since she could remember.

"I'm Tibby Mawes," she answered gaily. "It's 'bout time you learned that, isn't it?"

"You are, are you!" said the inn-keeper with affection, and winked at his cronies. "Well, suppose I was to have a letter come addressed to Mistress Tabitha Mawes—would you have any idea who it was meant for?"

"A letter?" she said, rooted.

"From Richmond, as ever is. It's right on that table inside the door, you might look and see if it would be for you."

She hurried into the tavern and found the letter—addressed in the fine, ornate hand of the schoolmaster. The world was rocking round her as she carried it out again and blindly passed the grinning group at the hitching-bar and turned back to the churchyard where she could be alone.

She set the basket on a table-tomb just inside the gate and broke the seal of Julian's letter with fingers that shook. *Mistress Tabitha Mawes* on the outside just like a lady. But inside—*Dear Tibby*. She steadied herself against the cold tomb—even her knees were shaking now—he was alive—he was safe—and he had written to tell her so.

Dear Tibby—

This is the first time I have had an opportunity to send off a letter which had any hope of reaching you, and I am not sure about this one, but a post-bag is leaving and I must try to let you know that I am not lost entirely. You were very nearly rid of me forever after Camden, Tibby, but thanks to General Marion I am alive to tell the tale, which I shall do at pitiless length when next I see you. But I wasn't much good to him after he had gone to all that trouble, so he passed me on to General Greene, under whose wing I witnessed the battle of Guilford Courthouse last March.

But General Greene didn't have much use for me either, if you can believe such a thing, and he sent me to General Lafayette, who was then coming down towards Richmond. Although the Marquis speaks English till all is blue, General Steuben still has some difficulty, and they allege that an aide who can be as intelligent in either French or German as he ever is in English is not to be sneezed at. The Marquis is short of aides and secretaries in any language, so it looks as though he might be able to bear with me till he can get something better, especially as a great deal of his correspondence is with General Greene and they both believe—without much cause—that I understand conditions in Carolina, etc. You would be surprised at the amount of letter-writing it takes to fight a war.

We have gone into a sort of headquarters at Wilton, which is a plantation a few miles outside of Richmond—this is no military secret, Cornwallis knows all, I assure you, and will soon be in our midst, and I trust most cordially received. I saw him once, think of that—at Camden it was, when he did me the honor to name me his prisoner, along with General de Kalb and other members of the Quality. He is an impressive man, and was most polite about it too, but he carries a little too much weight for this climate.

The idea now is to amuse him and await reinforcements. We

have got so we can do that sort of thing in our sleep. I don't know how you could get a letter back to me, but I would like one very much, my dear, you may be sure of that. It is nearly a year since we said good-bye that evening at the Landing, and I have thought of it many times—*Thou shalt not be afraid,* you said, but I have been, bless you, I have been frightened almost out of my boots more than once since then. I am no hero, Tibby, I always suspected that and now I know!

Sweetheart, I have saved the worst till the last, but I don't see how I can dodge telling you that I saw your St. John at Camden, and since then I have not been able to find out what became of him. Perhaps you know by now, and I pray that you do, and that he is safe. I shall send a letter to Francis Street in this same bag, but in case it should never arrive there you had better go round and tell them this much if they have not heard from him. I wish I could add something for your comfort—and my own. Try not to hate poor Miss Regina out of love for him. They were made for each other, and in her heart she knows it.

Sometimes I think the army has made a philosopher out of me at last. Perhaps it is because we never have quite enough to eat. Please present my affectionate regards to your dear mother, and believe me, Tibby, always your devoted servant,

JULIAN DAY

When she had read it ravenously for the third time, some of its less obvious implications began to penetrate the roseate haze which enveloped the churchyard. What, in fact, was all this about Mr. Sprague? She read it again, and it failed again to make any sense whatever.

Tibby straightened her hat, picked up her basket, and set out for Francis Street.

She found St. John alone in the drawing-room, and saw by his face as soon as she entered that the other letter from Julian had arrived safely.

"You have heard from Mr. Day too," she said, and her eyes were radiant, for his smile confirmed her own boundless relief and joy.

"Yes, thank God! Dorothea and Aunt Anabel are upstairs crying over the letter." He had risen, still with some effort because of his wound, to greet her—there would be a halt in his step all the rest of his life, but he hoped soon to rejoin the army in the north—and he offered her a chair with his usual exquisite formality.

But Tibby stood in front of him, the letter clasped to her childish bosom, looking puzzled and embarrassed.

"Mr. Sprague—may I speak to you about a very private matter, please?"

"Why, yes, my dear, anything you like, of course."

"One time when I was here you sort of took me by surprise and I—told you how I loved him."

"Yes, child. But I had known that for some time."

"You had?" She was surprised. "Have you ever spoken of it to him?"

"Why, no—not really. Why do you ask that?"

"Well, I don't think he knows. Because you see—he seems to think it is you!" she blurted and grew pink before his astonishment.

"But that is ridiculous!" cried St. John, and then was a little hurt at her prompt agreement, because after all, at least before he had got this game leg—

But Tibby unfolded the letter and read aloud to him very fast the paragraph which ended with the injunction not to hate Regina. "There, you see?" she added. "Now, why should he think I mind what you do?"

"Certainly, why indeed!" said St. John with just a trace of bitterness. "It is perfectly plain you would boil my head to make soup for his supper any day! The man is a fool! Would you mind letting me read that again—slowly?"

She let him take the letter, pointing out the place on the page. He read it in silence, and—"*Fool!*" he said vehemently again as he handed it back to her. "Oh, how like him that is! Why do we put up with him, Tibby? Why do you *bother* with such half-wittedness? Shall I write down a piece of my mind and send it to him?"

"There is no way to reach him," she said absently, for something else had occurred to her. "I remember now—the night before he went away, down by the Landing—even that night he must have thought it was you. Because if he hadn't—" She stopped, and folded up the letter in fingers that were quite steady now. If he hadn't thought she suffered from the same malady as his own he would never have leaned against her there on the bridge for mutual comfort. It was his belief that her need of St. John matched his for Regina in hopelessness that had brought him into her arms. She folded the letter again and again, and gave a little sigh, and then smiled up into St. John's troubled face.

"Oh, well," she said, "it wouldn't matter anyhow, if he knew the rights of it. I don't mind if you don't."

"I am going to try to get a letter through to him somehow—just to say that I am still here, and all that. Would you like to enclose something in it?"

"Yes, thank you, I will bring it round this evening. But I would rather you didn't say anything to him about—about this. It wouldn't do for him to know that I told you what was in his letter."

"He wouldn't have to know. I could say—"

"I would rather you didn't," she said again with her quaint dignity, and the door opened before Dorothea, who had obviously been crying and was nevertheless a little more radiant than anybody.

Tibby beheld Dorothea's translucent happiness with an almost maternal smile, and said yes, it was wonderful news, and she must go now because of the sponge cake and her mother feeling so poorly and the corn bread in the oven—and then escaped into the street.

But as she walked home, with the folded letter warm in her fingers and the sun hanging low and golden over the treetops, there was no room after all in her heart for anything but thankfulness that he was alive and quite himself and safe with Lafayette and had taken the trouble to write to her. Before she had got as far as the Capitol she was trying not to run, because she was almost grown up now, but she hurried so there would be time to read the letter to her mother before Kit got home—Mr. Day sent his affectionate regards to her mother—that was because of the time she nursed him through the fever, and the time he paid for the doctor when she had it so bad herself, and the time she hadn't been too proud to ask him to buy the cough mixture for Kit, and the mending she did for him, going through his things when he wasn't there so he wouldn't have a chance to offer to pay. . . .

As Tibby reached the cabin door the smell of burning corn bread met her, and she ran to the oven and jerked out the pan—the loaf was a blackened crisp. With a sudden sharp presentiment she called and got no answer. And then, through an open door, she saw the blue dress skirt across the bed.

Sarah Mawes lay flung down on the white cotton counterpane, her full skirt and one work-worn hand trailing to the floor.

"Oh, mother, I shouldn't have gone out, you said you were feeling better—!" She went to the bedside, picked up Sarah's hand, pressed Julian's letter into the cold fingers. "Mother, we have heard from Mr. Day at last, he is safe with L— *Mother!*" The letter slipped to the floor. A chill from the hand she held ran up Tibby's arm to her heart. She had never seen death before, but the feel of death was unmistakable to her young flesh. She dropped the hand, which no longer had any familiarity to her touch. "Oh, Kit, come quick—*Kit, get the doctor!*"

But at the door she paused, and hung there an instant, undecided— for Kit was down the Creek that day after birds' eggs, and could not hear her call. Besides, it was too late for the doctor. Her mother was dead—quietly as she would have wished it, without making anybody any trouble—but just too soon to hear the letter, and it would have made such a difference to her to know for sure that Mr. Day was safe. . . .

The room was darkening as the sun went down, shadows were closing in around the lonely figure on the bed. She stood looking down at her mother from the doorway, trying to realize that it was not a stranger who lay there, and therefore not a frightening presence. She must not run for Kit now, she must stay here till he came. Her mother, who had died alone, must not be left again, now that she had no further need of company.

The house was very still in the twilight—very empty, for Tibby was alone in it as she had never been before. She turned back slowly to the bedside. Slowly her knees bent beneath her till she knelt with her face against the blue skirt beside that cold hanging hand, and slowly the tears came.

At last, spent with sobbing that seemed to her to reverberate through the darkening room, she strove again for composure, for Kit's sake, and to steady herself began to try to think clearly—

"I should have waited till Kit got back before I went to Mrs. Greensleeves—" she whispered, forcing her stiff lips to form words again. "I should never have left her alone like that—I thought she felt better —she said she did—Mrs. Greensleeves gave me a cake for her supper— I should have brought it straight home— Oh, mother, the letter was at the Raleigh, I wanted you to know—I was going to read it to you, every word, before Kit came—I should never have gone back to Francis Street, or I might have been in time—in time to tell you his message— listen to the letter, mother, I'll read it to you now—oh, please, God, let her hear—"

On her knees beside the bed, her wet cheek resting on the blue skirt, she reached for the letter, where it had fallen and unfolded it tenderly in the dimming light, and began to read it aloud—unevenly, with gaps between the words where her breath gave out—because wherever her mother was now she might still hear and be comforted that they had been right all along, and nothing had happened to him. . . . *Dear Tibby—This is the first time I have had an opportunity to send off a letter which had any hope of reaching you, and I am not sure about this one—but a post-bag is leaving and I must try to let you know— that I am not lost entirely. . . .*

There was a little silence in the drawing-room in Francis Street when Tibby had gone, and then Dorothea said—

"Sinjie, has it ever occurred to you that Tibby might be in love with Julian when she grows up?"

"Well, yes, it would be only natural," he admitted doubtfully and turned away for his pipe, but Dorothea never needed to see his face clearly to read his mind.

"It has happened already," she said, and caught her breath. "Why, of course—I might have known—she *is* in love with him!"

"Well, even if she is, he hasn't an idea."

"He thinks of her as a child still. And of course she is—but by the time he comes back from the war—"

"My dear, don't let's cross bridges."

But she stood there, staring towards his voice, which was as though he had failed to meet her eyes.

"How old is Tibby now?" she asked quietly, and he sighed.

"Tibby is sixteen. I seem to be the only one who can see it."

"Yes—sixteen—of course she is," repeated Dorothea, stricken with revelation at last. "And she belongs to him. She always has, she owes everything to him, and he has always been all wrapped up in her. Some day very soon he will realize that."

"Dorothea, you are borrowing trouble, child, we don't know yet how things will work out. On the last reports it was Regina he was in love with, don't forget that!"

"Yes, but then, everybody is!" she smiled bravely. "Sinjie, when are you and Regina going to be married?"

"When the war is over."

"But Regina is ready now. She would go to the church with you tomorrow. Especially if you are going back to the army—"

"When the war is over, I said," he reiterated firmly. "When I am sure to keep all my arms and legs. Not before."

She saw that his mind was made up, and not even Regina could change it then. And soon she slipped away to her room upstairs and sat by the window while the sun went down. I must learn to do without Julian, she told herself quite steadily, shedding no more tears. I must learn to stop wishing and hoping. The quicker I learn, the easier it will be. And I *will* learn not to think about him. . . .

Julian had chosen in his letter to belittle his appointment to Lafayette's military family, but actually he had been received into it with open arms, after a roundabout journey to avoid Phillips at Petersburg and Arnold at Chesterfield Courthouse, joining Lafayette a day's march above Richmond. He carried letters from Greene, whom Lafayette loved next to Washington, and one of them spoke highly of the courier who brought it, which naturally predisposed the Marquis in Julian's favor. A few minutes' conversation in French made them friends.

Julian was still wearing the disgraceful remnants of the British coat and breeches in which he had left Snow's Island, and had to be clothed by donation from Lafayette's officers. Only the Marquis had legs long enough to provide him with breeches, but a spare coat and waistcoat, linen, lace *jabot* and black *solitaire,* stockings, boots, and even a queue ribbon that was not all frayed, were requisitioned from the family and Julian stood at last in respectable Continental blue and buff, left

over from the lavish outfitting which Lafayette had done the year before at his own expense for his own corps. They even found him a
sword, and when his captain's commission came through, to match
the single epaulet on the right shoulder of the coat, he felt that now
he was really a soldier. The aide's green ribbon slanting across his
breast, fastened in place by Lafayette himself, crowned his satisfaction.

"And now," said Lafayette, banging him on the shoulder with affection, "we shall win the war!"

But for the time their chief concern was to keep out of Cornwallis'
reach till General Wayne could join them with his Pennsylvanians.
Lafayette remarked that he was at the moment not even strong enough to
get beaten. He had all the Richmond stores moved up river to the Point
of Fork camp, with Steuben to guard them, and the Virginia legislature
had already removed to Charlottesville. Cornwallis had received further
reinforcements from New York, and now commanded about seven
thousand men, outnumbering Lafayette more than three to one.

In order to prevent himself from being cut off from his rendezvous
with Wayne or from the stores, Lafayette kept falling back in a more
or less parallel line to the north and west of Cornwallis' advance, destroying bridges and felling trees across the roads behind him. Tarleton's inevitable dragoons were often uncomfortably close on his heels.
The old cat-and-mouse game which Cornwallis and Greene had played
through the Carolinas had begun again, this time with Lafayette as
the American quarry. And while the Marquis maneuvered with great
skill from river to river, the British burned warehouses and took civilian
prisoners and stores almost at will.

Then, as before, there came a point where Cornwallis must abandon
the chase and become the pursued, as he in turn retreated towards his
coastal communications and supplies, with an eye on Williamsburg as
headquarters. Augmented now by Wayne and Steuben to the total of
two thousand Continentals, not including militia and a rather informal
cavalry corps of Virginians riding their own blood mounts, Lafayette
followed warily across the Chickahominy and down the Neck, never
coming near enough for battle, never quite losing touch.

Williamsburg sat there in the glory of its June heat and roses, and
watched Cornwallis approach. He was at Bird's Tavern on the twenty-
fourth, Cooper's Mill on the twenty-fifth, Spencer's Ordinary on the

twenty-sixth—there was nothing to stop him, and Lafayette drove him nearer each day. Williamsburg remembered the shelling of Norfolk, and the hangings at Charleston, and the fires at Manchester and Richmond, and its residents looked at each other with tense, blanched faces. Those who could began to send their womenfolk out of the town by water from the College Landing on Archer's Hope Creek, where fishing-boats could be hired.

After some hesitation, Regina's father decided that his wife and daughters would be safer at Farthingale, up the river near Westover, than directly in the British army's path, especially as, if Lafayette kept on coming, there would have to be a battle on the Neck. St. John had gone north again at the end of May, before Cornwallis turned back towards the coast, and supposedly he was with Washington in Connecticut. Mrs. Greensleeves implored Aunt Anabel to remove Dorothea from the neighborhood of the soldiery by accompanying her own family to Farthingale, and insisted that St. John would never expose his sister to the horrors of a British occupation of Williamsburg.

On June twenty-seventh, with the spectacular scarlet column bearing down on the town from the north like conquerors, drums beating and banners flying, while a fishing-boat waited at the College Landing with the Greensleeves' luggage already on board, Aunt Anabel suddenly gave in. But first she sent Joshua with the coach full tilt to the cabin by the Queen's Creek Landing to collect the twins, declaring that she could never look Julian in the face again if she left them behind.

Tibby came to the door and stood silently while Joshua explained that there was no time to lose, and she wasn't to bring any baggage, they were just to come in whatever they stood up in.

"I can't go," she said, when he had finished. "Kit is sick."

"How sick? I carry him," said Joshua efficiently.

"He has been in bed two days—he can't eat, and it hurts him to move —he could never stand a journey."

"Fever? Lemme look." Joshua bent his massive form to pass beneath the cabin lintel and stood above the bed. He laid a gentle black hand on Kit's head, while Kit looked back at him blankly, without recognition.

"It can't be the smallpox, because Mr. Day had us inoculated," said Tibby from the other side of the bed. "We ate some berries yesterday

—maybe they weren't good for us. I feel kind of queer myself. He can't keep anything down."

"Could be fever," said Joshua. "Lots of folks awful unhealthy right now."

"He had been doing so well," she sighed. "He hadn't been sick since March. And then this had to happen. We can't move him."

"Don't look like it," Joshua conceded doubtfully. "Coach awful full. He was supposed ride up on the box with me."

"You will have to tell them I can't leave him," said Tibby. "And thank them very much for thinking of us. I was going to ask Dr. Graves to come and see him—"

"Dr. Graves done gone to the army. Don't know who you could git now, to doctor him."

"Then I must just pull him through myself," she said resolutely. "We'll be all right here, there is nothing the British want of us."

"Mebbe so," said Joshua unhappily. "Sure is too bad. Here—you take this." He fumbled in a secret pocket and brought out a hoarded piece of hard money and pressed it into her hand. "You take that, case food is hard to git."

"Thank you, Joshua—I will pay it back some time."

"Don't need worry about that. I won't have no call for it, don't suppose." He stooped again under the low lintel and out into the sunshine. "Boat can't wait no longer, I'm 'fraid. Just you lie low," he said comfortingly. "Gineral Lafayette chase 'em out again, you wait! Gineral Lafayette at Tyre's plantation now—less'n twenty mile up the Neck, that is, beyond Spencer's. You wait!"

Kit was calling for water as she turned back from the doorway. She laid the money on the table and went to the well to draw a fresh bucket. He held to her with hot dry hands and begged her not to leave him again. She was still sitting beside the bed when Mawes burst into the cabin, wild-eyed and sweating with terror. He had, as usual, been drinking.

"The British are coming!" he cried. "They just keep on coming, bloody thousands of 'em! They'll be in the town by morning! Pretty soon we can't get past 'em on the road to the other Landing!" He began fumblingly to gather together a few things into a bundle. "You know what Tarleton does? He pins you to your own door with a bayonet and

burns the house over your head! Gimme some food, whatever there is
—I'm gettin' out of here!"

"There is corn bread on the dresser," she said tonelessly. "Kit is
sick."

"Sick, eh! Been stealin' fruit again, no doubt! What's this?" He
snatched up the coin from the table.

"Joshua left it for Kit. You can't take it, it's for Kit!" She flew at
him as he pocketed the coin, but he flung her off and dumped the half
loaf of corn bread into the bundle on top of a spare shirt and some tools.

"Now, listen, you—I've hid the horse down by the Creek, where
those willows are—you know the place. I'm goin' by water, three of us
got a boat. But I want you to see to the horse, understand? Go down
and let him drink and tie him to a different tree each day, so he can
graze. Mind nobody sees you go, leave it till dusk. Then the British
won't find him and when the bastards are gone we'll have a horse but
nobody else will! Don't forget him, now. I'll be back when those lobsters have left."

He was off at a shambling run, with his bundle.

Drearily she got out the bag of corn meal and began to make up
another loaf of bread. Kit couldn't keep it down. She would try to
beg a little milk for him when the cows were driven in, and make some
gruel.

All night she sat beside Kit, wringing out cool cloths, patiently answering his random talk, while her own sickness held off and finally
receded as though by sheer effort of her will. Whatever it was, Kit had
got it worse than she had, as usual. Whatever it was, her own hardiness
fought for her, while she ministered to him.

The British marched in next morning, down the road past the College, not with fire and sword after all, because Cornwallis needed the
town, and there was no resistance. But they took possession very
thoroughly and made themselves at home without any consideration
for the townsfolk.

As evening fell there was a tramping of feet down the path outside
the cabin door, and a big sweating man in a red coat with blue facings
stepped without ceremony into the kitchen.

"Hulloa, the house!" he bellowed. "Look sharp, now! Who's at
home?" Receiving no reply, he stamped on into the cabin and came

upon Tibby kneeling beside the bed where Kit tossed and moaned. She looked back at him, rigid with fear, but silent, her chin out. For a moment he stood staring at her, and then said, "Somebody sick, missy?"

"My brother."

"You all alone?"

"Yes, sir. What do you want?"

"Something wet to drink. Buckets of it."

"There is a well at the back. You can help yourself."

He leaned his bayoneted musket against the doorjamb and came to the bedside. Tibby shrank back protectively, covering Kit as best she could.

"Now, now, we don't make war on children," the soldier said brusquely. "I won't hurt him. Might be I'd know what to do." He turned back the sheet and felt Kit's hot body, forced open his black, swollen mouth to look at his tongue, and shook his head. "It's bad," he said. " 'T ain't just the fever. Did he eat rotten food maybe?"

"I don't know. He may have got something. He can't hold anything on his stomach any more."

"That's weakening," said the soldier. "Tell you what, missy, I'd ask the apothecary for something to stop the vomiting if I was you."

"I haven't any money. And the doctor is gone. And I didn't dare go into town for fear I might not get back."

"Because of us?" The soldier seemed hurt. "Bless you, we'd never harm a bit of a thing like you, minding her own business, and that. Tell you what, missy, I just finished me sentry-go at the bridge and I've got an hour or so. You fetch me a nice drink of cold water and I'll set here as a kind of hostage, you might say, and cool off, while you run along to the apothecary and tell him about your brother. Here's a penny, it's all I've got left, but he'll give you something for that if you tell him how it is."

Tibby accepted the penny with astonishment.

"You are very kind, sir. I never knew—"

"Oh, we ain't such a bad lot, us Fusiliers. I had a boy of me own, once. Get along, now, but fetch me that water before you go. And if you have any trouble, look for these blue facings, see—and tell 'em you're a friend of Phineas Jones."

"Thank you, sir. I'll come back as fast as I can."

But the apothecary's shop had been stripped of its remedies by the British quartermaster, and the clerk who sat among the ruins was unable to help her, though he was hysterically full of tales of the disasters wrought by the British on the town. The streets were crowded with red-faced, swaggering soldiers, and hardly an inhabitant was in sight. She returned emptyhanded, breathless from running, just at dusk, to find Phineas Jones dozing beside the bed and Kit in a stupor.

"Here is the penny back, sir." She held it out in a damp little palm. "There was nothing left in the shop."

"Tck-tck," said the Fusilier and rose and stretched himself. "Well, that's how it is. No, you keep it, missy, I'll have more coming to me soon. Might come in handy to you."

"That's very good of you, sir," she said forlornly, trying not to cry for sheer weariness and despair.

"Where's all your menfolks, missy? With the army?"

"I have a—a friend with General Lafayette," she told him with a certain pride.

"Oh, my, that's bad, that is," said the Fusilier sympathetically. "Lafayette don't have a hope now. You might as well make up your mind to that."

"Nothing has happened to him so far." Tibby's chin stuck out.

"Well, we ain't really got round to it yet, that's all. Remember Camden?"

"Gates wasn't any much of a general, they say. But Lafayette is different."

"Oh, pshaw, missy, I could take the Marquis over my knee any day! You'll see!"

"W-will there be a battle here?"

"Think likely, hereabouts. Tell you what, missy, if you want that feller of yours to live to marry you, best you get him away from Lafayette any way you can, and the sooner the better. Just you take that as a friendly warning, so to speak, because I happen to feel kindly towards you. Once we get squared around and really start in on those dirty, half-starved scarecrows the Frenchman calls an army, we'll eat 'em alive, and it won't be a pretty sight, I'm tellin' you straight. And it might come sooner than you think, at that! Good night, missy, and good luck to you, I'm sure!" he added benevolently, as he collected his musket from the doorway and clumped out.

The cabin was very still when he had left it, except for Kit's breathing, which had become heavy and uneven. She sat beside him steadfastly in the light of a single candle, bathing his wrists and temples, fanning his flushed, feverish face, fighting panic and a cruel loneliness—with the persistent, piercing, sweet song of the tree-frogs in her ears. She never heard them now that she did not remember that evening on the bridge above the Landing, and Julian Day leaning on the rail with his face against her shoulder and her cheek against his hair. It didn't matter any more why he had come to her, or what he believed her to be suffering too—it only mattered that once he had been there, in her arms, and nothing could ever take that away from her in a hundred years. . . .

About midnight Kit died, after a sort of spasm which left her faint and shaking as she tried to hold him. When he was gone, she knelt a long time beside the bed, dry-eyed and exhausted, her forehead resting against the mattress. She tried to pray and found that she was praying less to God, who was nebulous and far, than to Julian Day, who was as near as Lafayette. And then the tears came, and she wept hopelessly, not so much for the loss of her brother as from need of the man who might never love her as a woman but whose presence in her sight was all that held the sun in the heavens.

At last she was quiet and heard the first sleepy bird-notes before the summer dawn, while the obsession grew and grew that she must see him somehow, that if only she could tell him—tell him what? That with her mother dead, and now Kit, she stood alone and in desperate need of his protection? He would take care of her, of course—he always had, and he was too kind ever to refuse her anything. But he was a man, and unmarried, and how would it look, now that she was grown? If she had been Kit it would be different. A man could adopt a boy without embarrassment. Kit could have lived with him forever, unquestioned, and not made him any trouble. But it was Kit who had to die. . . .

The candle had guttered down into a pool of wax and was sputtering and smoking feebly. She raised her head, trying to see out of eyes which were puffy from weeping and lack of sleep, her head ringing with fatigue, her body racked and gnawing with hunger. Automatically, she wet finger and thumb with her tongue and reached to snuff the candle—her hand paused there in mid-air, short of its mission—she knelt, giddy and incredulous, staring at the chair beside the bed where Kit's clothes lay folded in a neat pile, while her numb brain fumbled at a dazzling idea. . . .

While she contemplated the idea, believing herself detached and calm now as though it was not her own, the candle gave a final gasp and went out. The window pane was barely grey, the birds had not really begun, but the British drums were sounding *reveille* in the town.

Tibby rose from her knees. With quick hands, suddenly competent and steady, she lighted another candle and began to do the things she had to do.

The sun was not yet over the treetops when a figure which might have been Kit rose from kneeling beside a mound of freshly turned earth at the rear of the cabin, shouldered a small bundle, and turned away towards the bank of the Creek where Crowsmeat was hidden. Behind her, without a backward look, she left Kit's body in the shallow grave she herself had scratched out with a pick-ax and shovel. It wore a sheet for a shroud, and above it was a makeshift wooden cross into which she had burned her own name with a hot poker: *Tabitha Mawes*.

IV

They were changing the guard at the bridge—she could hear the corporal's voice rasping, *"Prrresent arms!—Rrrecover arms!—Frrront face!"*—as she crawled through the bushes on the bank until a bend in the Creek hid her from their sight. She found Crowsmeat among the willows and he whickered with pleasure at her approach. The saddle was still in the woodshed behind the cabin, and it was too heavy for her to handle alone anyway, but an old blanket which sometimes protected him from flies and rain was folded on the ground under the trees. She laid it across his bony back as a pad—it would be more comfortable than riding him bareback—and climbed on to a fallen log and mounted with difficulty from there.

The woods on that side of the town were well known to her, for she and Kit had always quartered them several times a year in search of myrtle for candlewax and edible berries and wild fruit and birds' eggs. The Creek was wide there, and her way was soon blocked by a marshy stream which joined the larger one just beyond. She had to waste precious time waiting for the tide to go down before she could ford it, and then bore westward, intending to intersect the road from the east somewhere beyond the last British picket at the College end of the town. Joshua had said that Tyre's plantation was beyond Spencer's Ordinary, which everyone knew was on the north road to Richmond.

The going was very rough, and sometimes she had to dismount and lead or coax the unwilling Crowsmeat through the tangled undergrowth. When she was on foot branches caught at her bundle and hooked the blanket from Crowsmeat's back so that she had to go back and search for it. She had no way to carry water, and suffered from thirst as the long hot day passed its meridian. She had brought corn bread in the bundle, and she ate what fruit she could find along the way to make her own provisions last.

It was slow work, with many rests for Crowsmeat and a hunt for drinking water, and darkness found her somewhere north of the town and still short of the Richmond road. She slept exhaustedly on the ground with the blanket wrapped around her against the damp, and Crowsmeat tied to a nearby tree, and woke in the dawn to the recurrent problem of mounting him on top of the slippery blanket without stirrups.

She nearly encountered a picket on the road after all, but his back was turned and leading Crowsmeat a step at a time she retreated breathlessly through the undergrowth and escaped his notice. The next time she approached the road it was empty, and she turned into it with relief and pressed on northward up the Neck. Twice during the day she dodged into the bushes and held Crowsmeat's nose while small parties of British horsemen went by, and once she circled out into the woods to avoid passing through the little settlement around Chickahominy Church.

The detours ate up time, and Crowsmeat's pace was always stately, so she spent a second night in the woods beyond Spencer's Ordinary

and made a breakfastless start in the dawn. By now she had had leisure
to contemplate the various aspects of the thing she had done in such
haste lest the kindly Fusilier should come back to see how Kit was.
If he found the cross behind the cabin he would be confused, but to
anyone else the story of Tibby's death would pass muster. Luckily she
had mentioned to Joshua that she felt queer—so when Aunt Anabel
must be faced again it would only be necessary to say that Kit had got
better and Tibby had got worse and died—with a little uncertainty as
to the exact day when it happened. Of course Kit, if he had lived, would
have been a man soon—he would have had to shave, that is, and his
voice would have got deeper. It was easy enough to counterfeit Kit
now, but how about when he should have come of age, what would be
expected of him, and how long would it be before—

Well, it was no good worrying about that now. The British army was
in Williamsburg in all its might and glory—big, swaggering, confident,
beery men in red coats and white crossbelts, clanking with accoutre-
ment, cleaning out the shops, taking over people's houses for officers'
quarters, able in their magnificent stride to toss a penny to a sick boy—
they didn't make war on children, the Fusilier said—no, but they made
war on Virginia, and what chance had gentlemen like Julian Day or
St. John Sprague, or even General Lafayette himself, against these burly
conquerors who laid out their horse lines all through the town and
overran even the churchyard and the College? This was the army which
had taken Charleston and hanged people right and left, the army that
had burned and pillaged and murdered through Georgia and the Carolinas. And now it came to a stand at Williamsburg, with Lafayette
moving towards his fate. Perhaps she would be in time to tell Mr. Day
what the Fusilier had said, and he could tell Lafayette—but Lafayette
must already know. There would be a battle on the Neck, everybody
said. Cornwallis expected the British fleet to come into Yorktown at
his back, and Lafayette would hurl his ragged men against the British
bayonets till they all died, and then it would be Washington's turn,
up north.

The world was on fire, the world might be coming to an end, but in
the meantime she would see Julian Day again, and if there was a battle
she would be in it too. Because if Julian Day had to die that way, she
must die too, beside him, where she belonged.

She tried to plan what she must say to him, as she rode. Neither she nor Kit had ever lied to him before—unless you could count those other three times she had worn Kit's clothes and nobody had noticed till she broke the ewer. Tibby is dead, she must say as soon as she got to him —and she had brought along the doll in her bundle to prove it. Tibby is dead. The words had a queer taste on her tongue. I am dead, and this is my brother, who never felt about Julian Day quite the way I do. I must be careful, I must remember I am Kit when I see him. Kit would be fairly off-hand about it, if he had left me under the cross and come to Tyre's plantation. Kit was so ashamed of his own weakness he always pretended to be much more off-hand than he felt. He wanted so much to be manly and strong—but the least little thing always made him cry. I should have been the boy, they said—they said I had all the guts. Reckon I'll need them now. . . .

Tibby is dead, Mr. Day. How would Kit have said that? Not too off-hand, he could never have managed it. And mother too—he would have to say that mother died in May. Mr. Day had never answered the letter Mr. Sprague sent, and Aunt Anabel said it obviously had never got to him. He will be sorry about mother, he sent her his affectionate regards. Can I tell him about mother without crying? Well, anyway, I don't think Kit could.

What happens when I come to the pickets at the plantation, will they want to look in my bundle? I can say it is my sister's doll—but a girl has to have things in her bundle that a boy doesn't need—if they look in the bundle I'll never get to him—if they find out I am a girl before I get to him. . . .

She avoided Cooper's Mill and returned to the road beyond it, and with her heart in her mouth rode boldly up to the American picket outside Tyre's plantation.

"Whoa, there," he said, and eyed the small straight figure atop the decrepit horse with friendly amusement. "Where might you be bound for, sonny?"

"Please, sir, I want to see General Lafayette," she announced.

"Ye don't say! Anything special, or just a social call?"

"It is very special, sir."

"Cornwallis send you?" he grinned.

"No, sir. But I come from Williamsburg all the same."

"Don't tell me!" marvelled the sentry, only half believing. "Ain't they got no pickets out?"

"There was one in the road but he didn't see me. You wouldn't have a bit of breakfast left over, would you?"

He looked at her pale lips and sunken eyes, and the horse which stood splay-legged with fatigue.

"Well, no, I wouldn't, I et it all, such as it was," he confessed regretfully. "But I tell you what you do, son, you go on into camp and tell 'em you're hungry and see what happens. Tell the fellow at the gate Jim said you could go in. He's a friend of mine."

"Thank you, sir."

She rode on, smiling back at him over her shoulder, for the encounter had raised her confidence. He hadn't suspected anything. It was going to be all right.

Roll call and inspection were over and the camp was proceeding about its daily business. Smoke from the cook-fires hung low on the still, hot air, and there was the smell of soup-pots and horse lines, as well as a whiff from the sinks at the rear. Blacksmiths were musically at work, and a drummer-boy was practicing his roll under the colors planted in front of an adjutant's tent, while a couple of his fellows looked on critically. It was all surprisingly peaceful-looking, for a war.

Instead of turning Crowsmeat's head towards the smoke of the fires on the left, she followed the wide, tree-lined avenue which led from the gate to the brick mansion whose stout pink chimneys were visible through the trees. Half way up the drive she slid to the ground, adjusted the blanket tidily on the horse's back, and took the halter. No one had yet accosted her bundle.

Leading the aged horse, walking close against his nose for the courage his indifference to his surroundings lent her, she approached headquarters. General Lafayette was somewhere behind that handsome white-painted doorway, and with him was Julian Day. After two nights in the woods, she looked mussed and shabby and sparrow-like enough to pass for Kit anywhere, though they were his best clothes she wore —a brown holland coat and breeches, a tan-colored waistcoat, white cotton stockings, black shoes and a black tricorne. The white linen shirt had been fresh when she put it on but it needed laundering now, and the starched frill and cravat were limp and soiled. She had cut her straight dark hair to shoulder length and tied it back with a black ribbon into a queue like Kit's.

A sentry paced up and down in front of the house along the gravelled drive, and a Negro groom sat on the bottom step with the reins of two waiting horses dangling in his hands. On the scarred and trodden lawn at the edge of the drive a group of lounging riflemen wearing buckskin hunting-shirts with fringes, like trappers, watched with idle interest while the forlorn little figure paused in the sentry's path as he came towards her.

"Is this General Lafayette's headquarters?" she inquired of him politely.

"Run along, bub," said the sentry, and passed her without breaking his step.

"You got an appointment with the general, sonny?" a rifleman called to her, and raised a laugh among his friends.

"Is he inside the house?" she demanded hopefully.

"Sure, so is General Washington! We're waitin' to see the parade go by!"

She knew they were fooling her, because General Washington was in Connecticut, as anybody could tell you. The broad white door of the house stood open to the summer heat. Tibby's eyes measured the distance between it and herself, between herself and the sentry. Then she dropped Crowsmeat's halter and the bundle and made a dash up the steps.

The sentry reached for her with an oath, the Negro groom grabbed at thin air too late. On the threshold she crashed into the waistcoat of an officer who was coming out. He plucked her out of his buff facings and sword-belt and held her, his fingers biting deep.

"What's this?" he said sharply, and glanced at the sentry.

Tibby talked fast.

"I'm looking for Mr. Day, sir, he is with General Lafayette," she got out all in one breath.

"How do you know he is?" The officer's grip relaxed a little, and he stood looking down at her keenly.

"He wrote my sister a letter from Richmond."

"Oh, you have brought him a message—from your sister?"

"Yes, sir. I come from Williamsburg."

"From—!" The officer eyed her more closely. "How on earth did you get here?"

"I rode." She gestured towards the ancient horse in the drive.

"And what about the British? Weren't you afraid of them?"

"No, sir. I came through the woods most of the way."

"Well, I'm damned," he said, not letting go her arm. "You come inside."

"Is Mr. Day here, sir?" she persisted as he pulled her over the threshold.

"Just you stand there. Don't move. I'll see about it."

He left her in the square white hall, its polished floor all scarred with spur-marks, its wide stair soaring upwards—and went to open a door on the right.

"Captain Day?" he called into the room, and a voice said, "He is inside, with the general."

The officer looked back over his shoulder at Tibby.

"Wait there," he said. "Don't move." The door closed behind him.

Tibby waited, her heart pounding. The sentry paced up and down in the drive, where Crowsmeat stood drooping in the hot sun. The riflemen's voices rose and fell and their laughter was free. There was a tramping on the stairs and three more officers in blue and buff came down with a clank of swords and spurs. They beheld a white-faced lad in their hall with surprise.

"Hullo!" said one of them genially. "Where did we get this?"

Tibby stood her ground, her chin out.

"By George, he has come to enlist!" cried another, and made as though to clap the new recruit on the back. Tibby's instinctive dodge seemed to him the wince of a child which anticipated a blow. "Here, here, did you think I was going to clout you, then?"

"Ducks like a nervous maid," said the first man. "Who beats you at home, boy?"

The three of them stood over her in a grinning semi-circle, friendly but terrifying. Tibby swallowed her heart and took a step backward in spite of herself.

"Cat's got his tongue," said the third man. "Who let you in here, son?"

"I'm waiting—for Captain Day."

"Day? Good God, he belongs to Day!" they exclaimed, and glanced at each other, and then looked with increased interest at her worn and dusty shoes and stockings, her skimpy sleeves, and the crumpled shirt-frill. "Brother, perhaps?" they suggested incredulously.

"No, sir. N-no relation, sir. I have a message for him—from Williamsburg."

"From Williamsburg!" Again they glanced at each other.

"That is my horse out there," said Tibby, seeking to distract attention even a little from herself. "He needs a drink pretty bad."

Through the open door they could see Crowsmeat, trailing his halter, the bundle on the ground beside his forefeet.

"Where is Day?" they asked each other, and their faces were grave and curious now.

"He's in there, I think." Tibby pointed at the door on the right. "I am to wait here."

"I should damned well think you are!" said one of them, and started towards the door just as it opened before Julian, who stood a moment sorting out the several figures in the hall.

"Kit!" he said then in astonishment, and came forward, very tall in the unfamiliar blue uniform with the aide's slanting green ribbon, and a sword at his side, but kind as ever, and—oh, thrice merciful God! —*safe,* with both his hands held out to her. Tibby caught at them blindly, feeling dizzy and near to tears now that she had done the impossible and found him. "How did you get here?" he was saying. "Did Tibby send you? Is Tibby all right?"

It was upon her. She raised her face to him slowly, met his eyes, and told her lie with a steady voice.

"Tibby is dead," she said.

His lips parted as if to echo the words, but he stood rigid and silent, while the three officers melted tactfully out of the door. Watching him fearfully, she saw that he cared a great deal about Tibby. Exultation strangled her compunction. The news had hurt him—because he held Tibby dear.

"Come up to my room—and tell me about it," he said quietly, but she resisted the arm he laid across her shoulders.

"Crowsmeat is outside. He ought to be fed and watered. And may I please get my bundle?"

"Yes—get your bundle." His arm released her. He followed her to the doorway and told the Negro groom to care for the horse.

Tibby rejoined him, carrying her bundle, and preceded him silently up the broad staircase and along the upper passage as he guided her to a room at the back. It was just big enough for a narrow bed and a high chest of drawers, a table full of papers and pens, and couple of chairs.

"Have you had anything to eat?" he asked, and she shook her head. "I'll send for something." He went to the top of the back stairs, where she could hear him calling to a servant.

She crossed the room and laid her bundle on the bed and took from it the doll Julia. Her palms were damp with nervousness but it was all right so far. He hadn't questioned which one of them she was.

When Julian came in, closing the door behind him, she held out the doll to him, carefully clinching the lie.

"Tibby sent you Julia," she said. "To remember her by."

His face was a little frightening as he took the doll from her. For a moment she knew a wild impulse to tell him that he was not to grieve, that Tibby was not really dead, that Tibby was here, beside him— She clenched her teeth against it. If she told him that, he would only send her back to Williamsburg. If she told him that, she might never see him again, especially if there was a battle— Looking up at him as he stood silent, the doll in his hands, she knew that the one thing she could never do was to leave him, to be without him, ever again.

"What happened?" he asked at last, with an effort.

"Well, you see—mother died in May."

"Your mother too? Oh, Kit, I'm sorry, I—that must have been dreadful for you both. Was it the fever again?"

"We don't know. Dr. Graves said her heart was tired. Tibby came home one day and—found her. It was along about the time your letter came from Richmond. We—Tibby wrote to you, and Mr. Sprague sent the letter."

"It never reached me. I didn't know."

Her eyes were brimming. He laid a hand on her shoulder—the hard, restrained gesture of man to boy, and she braced to meet it as Kit would have done, and wiped away tears with the back of her hand in his unfamiliar gesture.

"Poor Tibby," he said gently, and his eyes were on the doll. "She needed me then. When did she—how long after—?"

"Only a short time ago, sir. I was sick first and Tibby nursed me when she was feeling very queer herself—then whatever it was got worse and she died."

"Alone?"

"I was there. Father had left town on account of the British—and the Spragues went up river to Farthingale with the Greensleeves. Even Dr. Graves was gone. We took care of each other. We were used to that."

He turned away from her silently and sank into a chair at the table and put a hand to his head. She watched him a moment, her conscience writhing that she must distress him so, and then laid a hand on his sleeve.

"You mustn't feel so bad," she said. "She didn't suffer. She just—didn't wake up."

"It seems impossible—it seems as though I would have known—I can't quite believe it yet—" His voice died away.

Incredulously she recognized the same sort of thing she herself had said to St. John Sprague when Julian's own death was in question. And now he seemed to know that she was so much a part of him that neither of them could die and the other not feel it in the air they breathed. She had never dreamed that he could not be altogether deceived about Tibby so long as he felt her still in the same world with him. Self-preservation demanded another turn of the screw.

"She said you would let me stay with you, sir—if she died."

"She told you to come to me?" He turned to look at her from behind his shielding hand. "She didn't know how it is here, Kit, or she wouldn't have done that. You are too small for the army. You will have to go back home, I am afraid."

"I could be very useful to you, sir. She said I could look after your horse—and your boots—and she said perhaps I could help you with the letters, sir, because you taught us both to write a neat hand, you always say that yourself, sir."

Julian rose, moving heavily, and went to set the doll Julia on top of the high chiffonier, where he left it with a long look.

"St. John Sprague—you said he sent me a letter?"

"To tell you he had got back from Camden, sir."

"Thank God for that. I didn't know what had become of him."

"As soon as the wound healed he went to General Washington, up north. His aunt wanted to take us to Farthingale too, but I was sick then and Tibby had to stay with me."

"It's a relief to know they are not in the town. I have been very worried about all of you since Cornwallis went in." He seemed to pull himself together, to come into sharper focus. "Sit down, and tell me about Williamsburg. What is going on there? Tell me all you saw—all you heard."

"I didn't see much, sir—with Tibby sick, and all. I only know what the apothecary's clerk said—and of course the town was full of soldiers drinking, and that. It is full of flies too—like the plague—I suppose because of all the horses that came with the British. They bite like anything, everybody is nearly crazy with them. The British have smallpox too."

"Yes," said Julian attentively. "Go on."

"Cornwallis has his headquarters at the President's house at the College, sir. They turned the Madisons right out, and won't even let them draw water from their own well. They have taken all the ammunition and stores down to Yorktown, and pretty well stripped the shops. There is a cannon down by our bridge, and a sentry. And outside the Raleigh—"

"*Captain Day!*" It was a bellow from the foot of the stairs, and Julian rose.

"I have to go. Stay here. Don't go out and get yourself lost, I won't be long. Here is some food," he added, from the doorway, as a Negro boy arrived with a tray and set a plate with a hunk of bread and a chicken leg and a glass of milk on the table before Tibby.

She ate hungrily, using her fingers. In a few minutes Julian was back, looking brisk and alert.

"Come on," he said. "You can finish that later. The general wants to see you."

"General *Lafayette?*" Tibby stared, one cheek bulging.

"Hurry up, Kit, don't keep him waiting!" Julian pulled her out of the chair, wiped her mouth with his own handkerchief, and then wiped her grimy, greasy paws, one after the other, efficiently. "He wants to hear about Williamsburg, we have had no word out of the city for twenty-four hours, and anything you know may be important. Don't be nervous, now, just tell him anything you would have told me."

He whisked her down the stairs and through the white door in the hall. A room full of orderlies and secretaries looked up to see them pass, and a second door closed behind them.

General Lafayette sat at a large desk facing the door. He had brilliant searching eyes, and a captivating smile. His reddish hair, already thinning, was brushed straight back from his high forehead into a black queue ribbon, and there were traces of powder in it. His uniform was the smartest she had ever seen, not excepting St. John Sprague's new ones after Brandywine. His epaulets were magnificent, his linen foamed with lace, his buttons and gold braid shone like jewels. He would be a difficult man to lie to.

Tibby crossed the room with Julian's reassuring hand on her shoulder. He fronted her up to the desk and then stood back, leaving her to face Lafayette alone.

"This is the lad, sir," he said.

Tibby met the brilliant eyes bravely, wondering if she could hear the general speak above her own heart's thumping.

"What do you call yourself?" he asked kindly, stroking a white quill pen between his long fingers.

"Kit, sir. I mean Christopher."

"What is your age?"

"Fourteen, sir."

"You are rather small, are you not, for fourteen?"

"I am a twin, sir. We were both small. My sister died last month."

"Oh—you had a sister." It was as though light broke over him. And the way he said it, with a long *e* for the short *i* and the syllables evenly spaced, made the word beautiful and somehow significant. "I see," said Lafayette, and the words fell small and clear from his lips. His gaze rested thoughtfully on the place where the frantic pulse was beating in her thin throat, dropped with deliberation to where the wilted shirt-ruffle vibrated visibly to the pounding of her heart.

Tibby stood helpless before him while the betraying blood flamed upward to her hair, and she thanked God as Lafayette's eyes again met hers that her back was towards Julian and that Lafayette's face showed his discovery less than her own. How he had got the first inkling she could not guess. The fact remained that he knew.

"I see," he said again, stroking the quill, his eyes holding hers. "*Alors,* you joined the army, eh? And you came through the British lines to do it. That is a thing my spies seem to find rather difficult. Well, now that you are here, what can you do to earn your keep if we let you stay?"

"I—write a fair hand, sir. I could help with the letters."

Lafayette dipped the quill in the ink-pot and held it out to her, flicked a sheet of paper towards her across the polished wood of the desk between them.

"Write," he said, with his French *r.*

Tibby bent above the desk. Her fingers were cold and shaking. *Sir, I beseech you—*, she wrote unevenly, and stopped.

He glanced at it cornerwise, accepted back the pen. His eyes went beyond her to Julian who stood composed, at ease six feet away. His skeptical French mind wrestled with this backwoods innocence and then accepted that. Captain Day was deceived. But how? For how long? On the face of it, the thing could not be done. It was, of course, none of his affair.

"Well, Captain Day—his writing is at least as legible as my own—" The sheet on which Tibby had scratched her plea was crumpled casually in his long fingers and truly aimed at the already littered fireplace on his left. "Give him a pen and set him to work. But first—"

"M-my lord—" Tibby stammered, her green eyes swimming. "*Mon général—que le bon Dieu vous bénisse!*"

"French?" exclaimed Lafayette, with a surprised glance at Julian.

"A little, sir. His sister's was as good as mine."

"*Tant mieux!*" cried Lafayette, and his smile flashed. "That is, of course, very useful! But first—" He leaned towards her across the desk. "Tell me about Williamsburg."

"Oh, sir, you must please turn back, he said you hadn't got a hope, sir!"

"Who said?"

"The Fusilier. He came to the cabin for a drink of water. He was very kind, sir, he said they didn't make war on children, and he gave me a penny to buy medicine for—for Tibby." Small grimy fingers went to her mouth in an unconscious gesture. She had nearly let it out that time. She must be careful or this man would surprise the truth from her yet, before she knew it.

"What else did he say?" Lafayette inquired with interest.

"He said there would be a battle on the Neck, sir—and that once they got started they would eat you alive—and they can, too, you never saw such an army, they—they aren't gentlemen like you, sir!"

"Bless you, child, we are a rough enough crew in the ranks, I promise you! Have you seen my riflemen?"

"Yes, sir. But the British are all dressed alike, and their bayonets—there are so many of them, sir, and they are all such *big* men, and—oh, please, sir, it's a *terrible* army!"

"*J'en suis sûr!*" agreed Lafayette cheerfully. "And how was your friend the Fusilier dressed, *par exemple?*"

"He was a redcoat, sir."

"His facings?" Lafayette tapped the buff which turned back his own blue coat with silver buttons.

"Light blue, sir."

"That would be the Twenty-third, sir, what's left of 'em after Guilford," said Julian.

"Webster's, eh!"

"Webster was killed, sir."

"Who was your Fusilier's commanding officer—did he say that?" Lafayette asked Tibby.

"No, sir."

"Did you hear the names of any officers?"

"There is a General O'Hara quartered at the Raleigh, sir."

"That means the Guards, sir," said Julian.

For another ten minutes Tibby underwent a stiff cross-examination as to the doings of the British—where she had seen big guns, where sentries were posted, what color facings she had seen in the town, and a great deal more to which she did not know the answers. She replied steadily, keeping her head, gaining composure during the ordeal. At last she was dismissed to Julian's room to write down everything which occurred to her about the occupation, while Julian himself remained behind at a table near the General's desk to finish a letter to General Greene.

V

That evening Tibby sat eating her supper off the end of the kitchen table, while the maids washed up after the meal which had been served to the officers in the dining-room. The yard door stood open to the sunset.

Suddenly a tall officer in the blue Continental uniform crossed the threshold, his back to the light. For a second she thought it would be Julian. Then her heart stopped, and black Phoebe dropped the crock she held and curtsied above the pieces.

Lafayette stood in the doorway, smiling at their astonishment.

"Good evening," he remarked gently to the buxom cook, who recovered to place a wooden chair and wipe it off with her apron. "I wish to ask this lad some questions—privately."

Tibby had struggled to her feet and stood stricken beside the table. Lafayette waited against the light, while the cook gathered the two maids with a compelling glance and they all three retreated respectfully to the yard. Then he removed his three-cornered hat and approached the table easily, his handsome sword ajingle.

"Please don't have any fear," he said, "I am no ogre to eat you." Tibby stood mute, enduring his searching gaze. "It was Christopher who died," he said.

"Yes—m-my lord."

"And Captain Day still does not suspect?"

"No, sir. I brought him the doll he gave me—I said Tibby wanted him to have it as a keepsake. He never doubted. How did you—" The words died away before his small French shrug, his broadening smile.

He tossed his hat to a chair and sat down on the edge of the table near her, swinging a booted leg.

"Americans!" he marvelled. "I will never learn. Always they amaze me. You wonder what affair it is of mine," he added, amused. "Captain Day is a member of my military family. A member in very good stand-ing, I assure you. Therefore I have an interest. Believe me, a *friendly* interest."

She caught at the word.

"You mean you won't give me away?"

"Is there no one else to do that?"

"No one in Williamsburg, sir. We were alone when Kit died. I did everything for him, and made the cross myself." Her eyes were fixed on the moving, polished boot. "It says *Tabitha Mawes.*"

"*Mon Dieu,* but why should you do such a thing? It is to me a hor-rible thing to do!" he cried with a little shudder, and waited. She was silent. "You have buried yourself alive. Why have you done this thing?" he persisted.

"It was the only way I could come to him. I had to see him. I just had to—see him," she repeated helplessly.

"Does he matter so much to you as that?"

"Nothing else matters to me," said Tibby, unconscious of pathos.

"Fourteen," mused Lafayette, and there was doubt and query and amusement in the word.

"I am sixteen, sir."

"Ah!"

"I took something off our age when you asked me, I was pretty sure he wouldn't remember how old we were, he never could."

"And is he then blind?" murmured Lafayette.

"It has been over a year since he has seen us. I look just the way Kit did then—he was always the smaller one—and Mr. Day never took much notice of how I looked anyway, you see, on account of Regina Greensleeves."

"*Comment?*" queried Lafayette.

"Regina Greensleeves. She is the most beautiful woman in Virginia." It was stated as a fact.

"Who says so?"

"You should see her, sir. Like the moon walking."

"The moon is cold," he reminded her, his French heart enthralled by this tragi-comedy being played under his very nose in the middle of a war.

"I don't think—" she began, for she was vaguely aware that Regina, for all her lily-aloofness, was anything but cold.

"Does she love him, then?"

Tibby frowned, searching for the right answer, unwilling to admit, lest it diminish the stature and prestige of Julian Day, that Regina Greensleeves was not his for the asking.

"There are so many others in love with her," she explained slowly. "Especially Mr. Day's best friend. In the end perhaps she will see that no one else can hold a candle to him, but—it looks as though she would marry Mr. Sprague."

"*Eh, bien, alors*—?" Lafayette spread his hands, but she shook her head.

"Then it will be Miss Dorothea," she said. "She is in love with him, I know, and she is very beautiful, and a lady. Kit and I—we just went to school to him."

"But, *mon Dieu*, this is of the theater!" Lafayette rose from the table-edge and strode about the room, his sword and spurs clanking. "This is not the sort of thing one anticipates to encounter in a wilderness! This is—*incroyable!*" He stood over her, and she wilted against the table, looking up at him, her small chin set. He nipped it between his finger and thumb, raking her face with his bright, knowing eyes. "What has this fellow Day done, to deserve such love?" he demanded.

"You m-mustn't call it love, sir—"

"What must I call it, then?"

Tibby stood with her chin imprisoned in his fingers while her green eyes filled. She tried to blink them clear again, and her tears dripped warm and wet on his hand. Pity and concern caught him up and he laid his other arm across her shoulders, and she wept convulsively against his coat-sleeve, undone by his sympathy.

"Little one," he soothed, patting her. "Little one, this cannot go on. You cannot stay here."

Instantly her sobbing ceased.

"Oh, please don't send me away, sir!"

"Not I, my dear. He will see for himself how impossible it is."

"Are you going to *tell* him?" She jerked away from him, outraged and at bay.

"If he cannot see for himself, he must be told. This is no life for you."

"I thought you were kind," she said dully, without reproach, accepting betrayal, and her knees gave way so that she dropped back into her chair at the table.

Lafayette looked heavenwards.

"And I with Cornwallis on my hands as well!" he cried. "I am trying to fight a war—and now *this,* in my own household! Why do I concern myself? Child, I *am* kind. Believe me, I do what is best for you—some day you will thank me that I see so clearly for you now, and you will say to me, 'Ah, yes, it was foolish, to think I could take the field like a soldier!'"

She seemed not to hear, sitting motionless, her head against the back of the chair, her eyes closed. There were no tears now.

Lafayette bent and took the small soiled hands in his big warm ones. She did not appeal against the sentence he had put upon her. She merely sat, without dramatics or design, looking helpless and half dead. Lafayette was wrung.

"*Petit ange,*" he murmured above her. "Poor misfortunate infant, my little lost one—do not look like the end of the world! Surely this life is too hard for you—surely you cannot be content in these circumstances—what is the good to you here, like this?"

"I can see him every day," she answered literally, through white lips.

"And where, if you will allow me, are you going to sleep?" he inquired with Gallic simplicity.

"He has given me a blanket in the store-room. No one goes there but the cook. She says I can eat in the kitchen if I wash up my own things. I think he gave her some money to arrange it. He said himself that the drummer boys would be too rough for me. That is natural, you see, because poor Kit was always delicate."

"And when we are on the march again? We shan't be here long, you know. How when we have no roof over our heads, and the rain comes down? What then?"

"I could—lie near him, on the ground."

"*Parfaitement,*" he shrugged, and she would not meet his eyes. "Child, the man is not utterly an *imbécile.*"

"It is different for you, sir, because you are not accustomed to see us together, Kit and me. Captain Day does not question which one of us I am, because dressed like this I look exactly like Kit."

"You are defending his stupidity," he nodded. "But you do not convince me."

"It doesn't show on me!" she pleaded. "No one else has seen, but you!"

"It shows in the way you lift your chin," he said. "It shows in your wrists, in the position of your feet when you sit—" His eyes rested briefly again on the frill of her shirt. "Most of all, it shows when you look at him."

"He will never see that. He is used to it," she promised doggedly.

"Some one else will see it, soon enough. Some rough soldier or sniggering drummer boy will discover it first, maybe, and then the word will run between the camp fires that Captain Day has got his doxy with him at headquarters, and how would you like that?"

To his admiring surprise, she laughed outright at a thing so far from the probabilities.

"Do I look like a doxy, sir? Or does he look like a man who wants one? The worst they could think is that he is stupid—as you do. But they won't get the chance, I will keep out of their way."

"I cannot allow you to remain," he said firmly. "We shall get a battle soon, and you will be very much in everybody's way then. I realize that Williamsburg is not fit for you at present, so I think I shall send you to Charlottesville with the next courier. Mr. Jefferson will have to look after you, he has nothing else to think about!" He watched her face close in again, pale and set, with tight lips. She would never whimper. He went on one knee beside her chair—the French Marquis, Washington's general, the magnificent Lafayette—on one knee, holding her cold paws in his long brown fingers. "Tell me again, what is that strange name of yours—the one on the cross above your brother."

"Tabitha."

"Tabitha—" (That difficult short *i*. That all but impossible *th!*) "Tabitha, some day you will forgive me." It was a plea.

"May I see him once more before I go?" she asked, motionless between his hands.

With one of his broad, impulsive movements he left her and took a turn around the room, moving in a stirring jingle of metal.

"Am I Herod, commanding a slaughter of innocents?" he queried of the rafters. "Am I a bowelless Hessian, a red-skinned scalper of babes?" He whirled on her from the end of the table, stood contemplating the still triangle of her face with its closed eyes and rigid mouth. *"Enfin!"* he said quietly. "I know nothing. Are you listening, Tabitha? I was not here tonight. It is none of my affair, I will henceforth concentrate on Cornwallis. Do as you please, in God's name!"

"You mean—I can stay?"

He gave her his French shrug, his open hands, in a gesture of defeat.

"And you won't tell him *anything?"* she persisted.

He came to her, cupped her chin in his big palm.

"How can you so love a blockhead who must be told?" he marvelled.

She caught the warm, caressing hand in both hers and pressed her lips to it.

"And may I be there to see," he added piously, "when our incredible Captain Day comes to his senses!"

His spurs were loud on the stone floor, his long shadow passed across the threshold, he was gone into the fading sunset light.

Tibby rubbed grimy fingers across her eyes as though awakening from a nightmare. And then, because one gets very empty in the army, she returned philosophically to her cold, unappetizing supper.

When she had cleaned her plate and cup, she went to report for secretarial duty in Julian's room.

Candles were burning on the table, a pile of newly opened despatches had just arrived from Lafayette's own desk and awaited copying, sometimes in triplicate, sometimes in translation. Notations in Lafayette's own hand were pinned to some of them.

But Julian sat by the window where twilight still lingered, with the doll Julia in his hands, staring out into the trees—idle and sad. Tibby came towards him rather timidly.

"Will you—m-miss Tibby very much?" she suggested.

"Miss her?" His eyes went back to the doll. There was no life in them. His long body sagged, drained of its splendid vitality. "Well, yes, I suppose you could put it that I will—miss her."

"D-did you think so much of her, sir?"

"That is a silly question, Kit. You know I loved Tibby very dearly."

"But I thought it was Regina Greensleeves you loved!"

Julian rose with a sigh and set the doll Julia back on the chiffonier and arranged her skirts decorously.

"That was a very different thing," he said. "Tibby was—was a child."

"Well, but—she would have grown up some day. She would have been a woman."

"Will you for God's sake not chatter about her?" Julian requested sharply. "It will be bad enough to see your face every day!" There was a strained silence in the room. Tibby stood biting her knuckles, between hysterical laughter and hysterical tears—she had had a long day, and a hard one. Then Julian moved heavily towards the table and sat down. "I'm sorry, Kit. It is not your fault you look like her. Come and get to work. There is enough here to keep us at it all night. I will do General Greene's first, and you may make a copy of Lafayette's letter to General Washington. I can't offer you better than that, can I!"

Tibby received the closely written pages reverently, dipped her pen, bent above the blank paper, and (remembering to imitate Kit's *y's* and capital *I's*, almost the only difference between her script and his) began to write: *My dear General: By the utmost care to avoid infected grounds we have hitherto got clear of the smallpox. I wish the harvest time might be as easily got over. But there is no keeping the militia into the field. Many and many are daily deserting, but it is next to impossible to take them in their flight through the woods. On the other hand, the times of a great number are daily expiring and you might as well stop the flood tide as to stop militia whose times are out. Under these circumstances, it would perhaps be better to go and fight Lord Cornwallis, but exclusive of the diminution of force I have already experienced, I confidentially will tell you that I am terrified at the consequences of a general defeat. The ennemy have been—*

"He has put two *n's* in *enemy*," she remarked into the silence.

"Then you will do likewise," said Julian, without looking up.

"Yes, sir."

—The ennemy have been so kind as to retire before us. I thought at first Lord Cornwallis wanted to get me as low down as possible on the Neck and use his cavalry to advantage. But it appears he does not yet come out, and our position. . . .

They sat together, the candles between them, while the night closed in. Sometimes a paper changed hands, sometimes he spoke low-voiced directions, sometimes they paused to stretch cramped fingers. *Tattoo* was sounded, and gradually the camp sounds died away outside. The white curtains at the window moved in a hot breeze which brought the scent of jessamine and roses. The candles dripped and guttered and were snuffed and finally had to be replaced with new ones. They toiled on, relaxed in the brooding intimacy of mutual fatigue, and complete absorbtion in a task.

At last Julian looked up to find her slumped against the back of the chair fast asleep, the quill still drooping from her hand, which was none too clean.

"Go to bed, Kit," he said gently, and laid his hand on her arm to rouse her, and found the bones under his fingers pitifully small—as small as Tibby's. "You must be worn out, with travelling. Go to bed, I'll finish the job."

She rubbed swollen eyelids with a mumbled protest, but he rose and took a candle from the table to show her the way to the storeroom, where her blanket had been laid on a pile of clean straw in a corner beneath rafters hung with bacon sides and herbs and corn, in an atmosphere redolent of salt meat, spirits, and molasses. She pitched forward into blackness, drugged with exhaustion, and was asleep again before his footsteps had died away.

Julian returned to his room and paused before the chiffonier where the doll Julia sat. His impulse was to shove it out of sight into the top drawer so that possibly he could forget its presence and work in peace. Instead, he stood a long time with his arms folded on top of the chiffonier and his face hidden against his sleeve.

VI

She saw very little of him, after all, in the middle of a war. But it made the deception easier, and at least she knew where he was, and could feel that she was of some use to him, when she spent long hours alone at his table copying the pages which he sent up from Lafayette's room—pages usually drafted in his own fine hand.

On the fourth of July, two days after her arrival in camp, Lafayette gave a dinner to his officers in celebration of Independence Day. She could hear the laughter and the toasts dimly from the kitchen where she sat over her own bowl of savoury chicken soup with dumplings. But before the meal was finished an orderly came with a message for the Marquis. There followed a sudden scraping of chairs across the floor as everyone adjourned to urgent duties. Cornwallis was moving out of Williamsburg.

His destination was reported to be Jamestown—and probably from there across the river to Cobham and Portsmouth, which was held for him by General Leslie down from New York—and possibly he would go from there to the north again, to join Clinton against Washington and Rochambeau. Lafayette was not strong enough to prevent him. But at least the British could not be allowed to go unmolested, and an attack on the rear guard at the ferry was feasible.

Lafayette's army moved forward to Chickahominy Church on the fifth, and Wayne was sent on with five hundred of his brown-coated, hard-fighting Pennsylvanians by forced march to Green Spring, which brought him to within a mile of where the enemy seemed to have paused on the riverbank. When on the march, Julian's place was near Lafayette, and he left Tibby riding Crowsmeat in the surgeon's care, with orders to be useful to him if possible and to stay back out of the way if there was fighting. The surgeon said obligingly that he could always use an extra lad to sit on their heads.

When Lafayette arrived at Green Spring early on the sixth, Wayne's advance guard was already in action with the enemy outposts, and his information was that the bulk of the British army had crossed the river, though one or two of his officers were inclined to think it hadn't. Wayne, whose headlong courage and willingness to storm hell itself had been famous since Brandywine, wanted to attack in force (with five hundred men) and find out that way where the British army was.

Lafayette was more cautious. He had learned to be, since Brandy-wine. He ordered up the rest of the army to Green Spring and stationed two battalions of his best troops under Barber and Vose half a mile to the rear of Wayne's position, leaving Steuben in reserve near the mansion.

Meanwhile Wayne's men had driven in Cornwallis' mounted outposts and were firing persistently on his pickets, causing heavy casualties among the officers, who were replaced with such promptness and obstinacy that Lafayette became still more suspicious. The pickets did not behave like rear guard pickets, which should fire and fall back. These pickets were covering something. Lafayette rode out alone towards the riverbank, to reconnoitre.

The owners of Green Spring were still abroad and the house was in the hands of the agent, with a quota of slaves. Everything was placed at the disposal of the surgeon and he began his grisly preparations for an engagement, arranging his instruments on a kitchen table set out on the lawn. Under his directions, Tibby brought blankets and linen and rolls of lint, and the servants from the quarters joined in building fires and heating water. There was a fierce sun by late afternoon and the firing had increased.

Tibby had not seen Julian since breakfast. She watched her chance and slipped through the surgeon's fingers—found Crowsmeat and rode him cautiously towards the gunfire, avoiding the notice of officers, and keeping to the trees except where the marshy land on either side drove her back to the corduroy road. She needed to know where Julian was, and if that took her into the battle she was dauntlessly prepared for even that, though Crowsmeat was not, and had begun to jerk at the bridle in a nervous way, and she had to kick him unmercifully in the ribs to urge him forward.

Her palms were cold and wet on the worn leather reins, her heart beat thickly. This was the thing she had dreaded so, this was one of the reasons she had come out of Williamsburg to find Julian Day —so that if there was a battle she needn't sit helplessly miles away waiting for second-hand news; so that if anything happened to him she would be there, she would know about it at once; and if he fell she would be the first to reach him and see to it that the surgeon tended him in time. . . .

The guns were making a lot of noise now, and the acrid taste of powder was in the heavy air, and a smoky haze had settled. Through it she could make out a knot of men on horseback near the causeway, and set a roundabout course towards them. A lone horseman shot out of the woods on her right at full gallop, and swerved at sight of her.

"*Nom de Dieu,* go back!" he shouted. "Go back to the house at once, do you hear? Wayne is charging the whole British army down there!"

It was Lafayette, returning from the riverbank. He galloped on towards the group of officers. As he arrived they scattered before him, carrying his shouted commands to front and rear, and Tibby was able now to pick out the tall rider with the easy seat which was Julian Day. Lafayette had sent him forward into the action—"Find Wayne!" were his orders, if she had known. "Find Wayne and tell him for the love of Almighty God to fall back! It is Cornwallis entire! I could see clearly from the shore—they are all there! It is *embuscade!* Wayne is to fall back *instantly* on Barber and Vose! Du Bréon, tell Barber to open ranks and let Wayne through and keep firing! Gimat, tell Vose—"

She was not near enough to hear, but she saw that Julian was riding straight for the worst of it. Tibby dug in her heels and Crowsmeat danced forward reluctantly. She broke a branch from a bush without dismounting and began to beat him ruthlessly, her one idea to keep that slim receding figure in sight as long as she could.

Lafayette had spurred out on a somewhat parallel line to the one taken by Julian when a ball caught his horse in the chest and it went down in a heap. Lafayette rolled clear and his groom dashed up with a remount. As he reached the new saddle, he saw Crowsmeat headed for the front line at his ramshackle gallop, with a small bowed figure riding him at the whip like a jockey nearing the post.

Lafayette paused to swear at her in all the languages he knew, though she was far beyond his reach now, and even while he did so something knocked her from Crowsmeat's back and the old horse turned and fled for the rear at a better pace than he had made in years. Lafayette swore harder, and then saw a wounded soldier crawling towards her where she had fallen. From then on, other matters occupied his mind.

Wayne's drums began to sound the retreat now, though he would have to abandon his cannon because all the horses which drew them were dead. Wayne as usual had overshot discretion and was paying for it.

Having delivered Lafayette's order and grinned at Wayne's blasphemous acknowledgments, Julian cantered back towards where he had left his commander, and as he rode he heard behind him the triumphant huzzah of the British infantry charge. A wounded Continental rose from the ground almost under his horse's feet and caught at the bridle.

"Get to the rear, you fool!" Julian shouted, trying to control his rearing horse. "The surgeons are at Green Spring, you know that as well as I do! No, I can't help you, make for the rear, man, there is a bayonet charge coming!"

The soldier went on shouting back something which was inaudible in the battle din, until Julian's glance followed the man's pointing finger. With an exclamation he swung out of the saddle to kneel beside the crumpled thing on the ground.

"How did this happen, I left him with the surgeon—he had no business to follow me—" Speech died in him. Under his hand, as he pushed back the open waistcoat and shirt to expose the wound, was the small white breast of a girl, with a slow crawl of blood across it.

"The ball is high in the shoulder, sir—nice and clean," the soldier was saying. "She'll be none the worse for it, if it's seen to."

"Tibby!" Julian gathered her into his arms and stood up, holding her against him. "Oh, my Tibby, I should have known—!"

Wayne's retreat flowed all around them now, panting, swearing, sweating, coughing blood, but guiltless of panic and sometimes turning to fire as they came, making for the Continental lines which would let them through and close protectively behind him while they got their breath and re-loaded.

At that moment Lafayette arrived against the stream, alone, without even a groom beside him.

"Name of a name, Captain Day, find me du Bréon! I sent him to Barber and he vanished!"

Julian raised dazed eyes to the man on the horse.

"It's Tibby," he said. "It's not Kit, it's Tibby."

"I know, I know, but must I ride courier myself?" demanded Lafayette, with an exasperated glance over his shoulder, searching the battle haze for another aide. He was always short-handed and this was a most incoherent battle, worse than Monmouth in its small way, and he had been left high and dry there more than once. The trouble was to keep them mounted, there were never enough spare horses, and that meant tragic loss of time— For only a split second he hesitated while the retreat eddied about them, filthy, bloodstained, cursing men, trying gamely to fire as they ran—and the British drums were coming closer. *"Sacrébleu,* then give her to me and find du Bréon!" cried Lafayette impatiently, and reached for the limp little body in Julian's arms and laid it across the saddle in front of him, held firmly in his bridle arm. "Now, *ride,* and tell Barber he must go on firing till Wayne can re-form behind him! And send me du Bréon, for the love of God, on the way!"

"Yes, sir. Thank you, sir." Julian mounted with a set face, and pelted off towards the left, where Barber was.

For several minutes, while Lafayette tore through the smoke and gunfire rallying Wayne's men, encouraging them to re-form behind the steady lines of veterans who were meeting the British charge, Tibby lay unconscious in his bridle arm, and Wayne's men stared as at an apparition while they hastily obeyed his blistering commands. Then du Bréon appeared suddenly beside him, having been unhorsed and delayed to find another mount.

"*Mon Dieu,* is that Day's lad, sir?"

"Can Barber hold?"

"For a time, sir. But Galvan's men are done."

Gimat dashed up from the front on a horse flecked with blood and foam.

"Their cavalry are making ready to charge, sir!"

"Hell and damnation!" said Lafayette. "We'll run for it—darkness will save us, with any luck. Du Bréon—take this to the surgeon and report back at once. Gimat—come with me!"

Du Bréon received Tibby across his saddle bow with annoyance, pushed back the shirt to glance at the wound, and let out an expletive of surprise—paused to wad his handkerchief against the bleeding, and rode off rather gingerly towards where the surgeon worked on the lawn in front of Green Spring.

Meanwhile Julian was pounding over the field in search of Lafayette, whom he finally tracked down again among Wayne's men.

"Barber has been flanked, sir! He is falling back on the causeway!"

"We are all falling back, as fast as we can!"

"Where is Tibby, sir?"

"Du Bréon has taken her to the surgeon. Kindly ride to Vose and say we are falling back to Chickahominy Church, firing as we go. Tell him there may be a cavalry charge."

"Very good, sir."

Twilight had already begun to close in on the causeway under the trees. The hot, battle-stained troops poured along the narrow road, most of them in good spirits still. They had not won a victory, but then, they never did, and they had kept their heads and their muskets, even if they had had to leave some precious cannon behind. And the cavalry charge never materialized, for the engagement had been so hot and bold, thanks to Wayne, that Cornwallis suspected a trap and held off from the risk of pursuit in the fading light.

Lanterns were swaying on the wagons of wounded which moved back along the road from Green Spring when Julian arrived there, hunting the surgeon. For an agonizing space of unmeasured time he wove in and out among the wagons, peering at their groaning, bloody cargoes. She couldn't be here. She couldn't have been laid in with the rest on the hideous straw. . . .

"Captain Day! Oy! Here you are, sir—over this way!"

He turned to see a grinning soldier with a bloody rag around his head at the side of the road, pushing a wheelbarrow in which Tibby was propped against cushions brought out from the Green Spring parlor. Her eyes were closed, she had sagged a little sidewise; her shirt and the rough field bandage were stiff with blood. Julian flung himself from his horse and dropped to his knees in the dust beside the wheelbarrow, while the wagons rumbled on in an unceasing stream behind him.

"Tibby—" he whispered, and laid an anxious hand on her heart. "Tibby, are you all right?"

Very slowly she roused under his hand. Uncertainly she opened her eyes again to the pain and the terror of being alone among the army in the middle of a war. Dimly in the wavering lantern light of the retreat, she saw the one face in the world, bending above her.

"Sweetheart," he said, and held her hand to his lips—as though she was a lady—as though she was a woman.

"You didn't get k-killed—" she noted contentedly, and fainted again.

Leading his horse, he walked through the dark beside the wheelbarrow which the wounded man trundled patiently in the wake of the dreadful wagons. Lanterns bobbed round him, mounted men brushed past him with a clink of hoof and bridle, the wagons creaked and the jolted, tortured wounded groaned and cursed. Once he answered to his name cried out of the dark and passed along the line by a man on a horse.

It was Gimat, with the Marquis' compliments, and had he found the lad? Yes, thank you, he had found him. Excellent, and would he kindly report to the Marquis for special duty as soon as they reached camp?

Gimat was gone again, into the blackness which crowded the road. And that would mean another night of copying despatches, he supposed

—another grind of endless penmanship, the endless explanations and courtesies and appeals which made up a general's correspondence—*The Major-General Marquis de Lafayette has the honor to present his compliments to General Nelson, and begs him to recollect,* etc. . . . He wondered if the ball had been removed from Tibby's wound. He wondered how she had borne it without his arms around her. He wondered how he could have been so blind. . . .

A thought struck him, so hard that he stumbled. Lafayette had said, "I know!"

VII

By midnight Lafayette's army had regained the camp at Chickahominy Church, and most of the men desired little but a chance to throw themselves down where they were and sleep.

When he had seen Tibby laid on his own blanket on clean straw in an empty wagon, with the good-natured soldier on guard, Julian sought out the exhausted surgeon and exacted a promise to see to fresh dressings before another hour had passed. He then presented himself at Lafayette's tent, and found the Marquis lying on the cot in his clothes, an arm across his eyes. There was a lighted lantern on the rough camp table, and writing materials.

"You sent for me, sir?" Julian spoke quietly from the tent-flap.

Lafayette sat up, and swung his booted legs to the ground. He looked tired, but calm.

"Well, Captain Day—that was a close call, however you look at it!"

"I am afraid it was, sir."

"Wayne is crazy," said the Marquis, almost with admiration. "Cornwallis showed him a cannon, did you hear?—just its nose, all alone, looking out of the bushes—helpless and shy, like a piece of cheese in a mousetrap! And Wayne must have it, he cannot resist—he says he thought it would be so simple to send out and take just that one tempting cannon! And what happens? The whole British army happens to Wayne! If Barber and Vose had not been exactly where they were, General Wayne, to say nothing of you and me, might be *en route* for a Charleston prison tonight! I do not understand, even now, quite how we got away. When Gimat said the cavalry might come in—!" He shrugged off nightmares. "Ah, well—*c'est fini!* And mademoiselle—is she comfortable?"

"The ball has been removed. She seems unconscious most of the time."

"Shock," nodded Lafayette. "It should pass. You have friends in Williamsburg, I presume, who would nurse her?"

"They have left Williamsburg, sir. They are at a plantation near Westover."

"Ah. Then if we can be sure in the morning that Cornwallis will continue in the opposite direction, you may have leave to convey her to them."

"Thank you, sir. That is more than kind of you."

"I cannot spare a man to go with you. If you take her in a wagon you will have to drive it there and back yourself."

"I will, sir."

"And you will of course rejoin me as soon as possible."

"Certainly, sir."

"Good night, Captain Day." Lafayette stretched himself again on the cot.

But Julian lingered.

"May I ask, sir, how you happened to know she was a girl?"

"*Mon Dieu,* I *looked* at her!" groaned Lafayette, supine, his arm across his face. "*Once!*"

"I—well, I wonder that you did not tell me, sir."

"At first I could not believe that you had to be told. After that, she convinced me that it was none of my affair. And now, *mon ami,* if you will be so good as to go away—I am composing a letter to General Washington."

"Good night, sir."

Julian slept the rest of the night beside the wagon where Tibby lay, and by sunup he was washed and shaved and brushed off and tidy, and bribing the quartermaster for the best team he could scrape together. She roused vaguely when he bathed her face with cool water, and he got her to swallow a little soup, when all she wanted was more water.

The surgeon came, and said she would do for the journey, but her fever was rising.

Spies had brought in word that Cornwallis was crossing the James in earnest now, leaving prisoners and wounded on the Island, and Lafayette's intention was to advance and claim them on the following day.

And so Julian found himself bound for Farthingale after all these years, carrying Tibby Mawes to sanctuary. By one excuse after another, he had always avoided staying under the same roof as Regina, dreading the risk such intimacy involved—the risk of St. John's discovering the true state of his feelings, first, and then the risk that her wilful wiles would betray him into something regrettable.

He found this morning that he viewed with entire equanimity his first meeting with Regina in more than a year. And he knew why. He had got Tibby back again, as it were from the grave, and it was Tibby that he wanted, and nobody else. She was still too young to understand, of course, but he told himself that he could be patient. Other men would fall in love with her sweetness and courage when they had a chance, when the war was over, and life was normal again—he must wait, he must give Tibby a chance to choose, it was any girl's right to choose. But no one, he was sure, would ever desire her with such a passion of tenderness and cherishing as had come upon him now that he had so nearly lost her—no one would ever labor so hard as he would to keep her safe and happy and unafraid, and she trusted him, she always had, she loved him, he was sure, in her way, and if he was careful, and deserving, perhaps some day St. John would mean as little to her as Regina quite suddenly had come to mean to him, without heartbreak, without regret—if he was patient, and careful, and deserving.

Amid which humble reflections he crossed the Chickahominy by a leaky scow hardly long enough to accommodate the wagon, and drove along the Charles City Courthouse road which he had followed the year before on his way to join the army—through the little town, where he stopped at the inn to bathe her face and hands and hold a cup of water for her to drink—out into the fertile, smiling country beyond, where the plantation mansions began.

It was nearly dinner time when he arrived at Farthingale by the lane at the rear of the house, which faced the river. He climbed down from the wagon in the stable yard and went round to the back of it. Tibby opened her eyes and smiled at him wanly.

"May I please have a drink of water?"

"Yes, my dear, it's all over now. Aunt Anabel will soon make you comfortable in a nice clean bed."

As he lifted her out of the wagon Joshua and the Greensleeves' coachman came running towards him across the yard.

"Jesus Gawd, somebody done brang that pore sick boy!" said Joshua. "Where 'bouts lil missy, suh? Mr. *Day,* suh," he added, recognizing the man in the uniform with increasing astonishment. "Ladies round on the lawn in the breeze, suh. Sure is a hot day," said Joshua, who never forgot the amenities. "Jes' follow me, suh, Reuben tend to yore team straight off."

With Tibby lying limp in his arms, Julian crossed the mown green turf after Joshua and turned the corner of the house, where Regina and her mother sat with their guests in a picturesque group with books and needlework in the shade of a tulip tree. They rose in alarm at sight of a soldier who obviously could not be St. John, but Aunt Anabel's eyes were quick.

"It's Julian!" she cried and started towards him. "We thought you were with Lafayette! Is that Kit? Where is Tibby?"

"Tibby is here," he said. "We were both with Lafayette."

"Tibby is *where?*"

"This is Tibby. Kit died, and she came to me for protection. Will somebody put her to bed and try to find a doctor, and let me explain later?"

Under Aunt Anabel's supervision, and with a minimum of fuss, it was accomplished. Dinner was a little late, but at the table Julian told the story as briefly as possible to a highly sympathetic audience which was also gratified to learn that Cornwallis had left Williamsburg.

"I never meant to desert them like that, Julian," Aunt Anabel apologized. "I did send Joshua after them, when I should have gone myself—"

"I know, she told me."

"There were so many things to think of—we decided very suddenly, and we had to drive almost *into* the British to get to the Landing—it was terrifying—"

He laid his hand on hers.

"Don't blame yourself," he said gently. "Just get her well now and keep her safe for me."

"It just shows you," said Aunt Anabel, and wiped her eyes, "how the poor child will follow you to the ends of the earth—"

"It is pretty flattering, to have her count on me like that," he said, and refrained in the nick of time from the churlishness of remarking that she had had no one else to count on when Aunt Anabel had gone.

"Aunt Anabel means that Tibby has always worshiped the ground beneath your feet, Julian," said Dorothea gently, for there was no sense now in pretending not to notice, and the sooner it was settled the better, she told herself firmly.

Julian glanced at Regina and forebore to explain to them in her presence his conviction that Tibby admired St. John first and foremost—it was Tibby's secret, after all, and he respected it. Perhaps if he was successful in his own plans, no one need ever know except, of course, St. John, who seemed to be already aware of it and could always be counted on to be tactful.

He asked to say good-bye to Tibby before starting back towards the army beyond the Chickahominy, and Aunt Anabel led him up to her room just after sunset. Tibby lay very white and small in the high four-posted bed. Her hair had gone back into pigtails. Her eyes were fastened on the doorway.

"You are not supposed to talk," he said, smiling down at her from the foot of the bed. "And all I am allowed to say is good-bye."

Her chin quivered. The tears started, and she was too weak to check them now. She turned her face sidewise into the pillow.

"Now, now," cautioned Aunt Anabel, and went to lay an anxious hand on her forehead. "You will only make the fever worse if you cry."

Julian bent over the bed on the other side.

"Don't cry, sweetheart. You are quite safe now. I'll come back to see you as soon as I can get leave—and I want to find you getting well." He kissed her cheek, and left the room abruptly with the taste of tears on his lips.

Tibby had been hardly a week at the plantation when an army courier arrived down the lane with a letter from Julian. It was all her own, nobody else got anything. Very flustered, she opened it awkwardly

with her left hand—her right was still tied to her side on account of the
wound—and read:

My dear Tibby—
   Today I shall pass by going towards Richmond, but with no hope
of getting away from General Lafayette to see you for even a minute.
It is not that I am so valuable, but he has nothing better at present to
help with his correspondence, which is larger than ever, if possible.
   The army, such as it is, is on its way to a rest camp at Malvern
Hill, which lies between you and Richmond, and might as well be
at Fredericksburg, for all the good that does you and me. We caught
one of Tarleton's men the other day, and he seems to think Cornwallis is bound for the north by sea and a combined attack on
Washington with Clinton. The Marquis is so afraid he will miss
something, he is ready to start for Baltimore at the drop of a hat—
but at least for a time we are to be at Malvern, guarding the Virginia
stores and ready to move the minute Cornwallis shows his nose out
of Portsmouth.
   The man is waiting for this, so there is no time for me to turn
phrases, even if I knew how. He has orders to bring back a reply,
as I must know how you are. If you are strong enough to write me
a line yourself it will be treasured. But if not, please ask Aunt Anabel to send me a report on your progress. I assume there is progress
because I must, or go out of my mind. Always your devoted
                                                     JULIAN DAY

   Tibby drew a rather unsteady breath, and looked up from the letter
into Aunt Anabel's smile, where she sat at the bedside, dying of curiosity.
   "Well?" queried Aunt Anabel. "What does he say? Is he coming to
see us?"
   "They are on the way to Malvern, but he can't get away. He wants to
know how I am. Do you think I could write with my left hand?"
   "Can't you tell me what to write?"
   "I would rather do it myself."
   So Aunt Anabel, on whom things had begun to dawn, brought a big
book with a sheet of paper on it, and dipped the pen while Tibby wrote
laboriously:

Dear Mr. Day—

Thank you for asking, I am much better but I never learned to write left-handed. Can you read it? Aunt Anabel is holding the book. It is nice to know you are near. I hope you are well.

Ever your most obliged and loving,

TIBBY

And it had to go like that, with never a word to him about what it meant to have such a letter from him to keep under her pillow—a letter from whose ending the customary word "servant" had been omitted, so that it made him without formalities her devoted Julian Day. Each time she looked to make sure it really read that way, she reminded herself that he was in a hurry and had probably left out the "servant" by mistake. But if he ever did it again—then she would know he had meant to.

Meanwhile the fever receded and the clean wound healed and she got better, and began to take a rapturous interest in the dress of Dorothea's they were altering for her to wear when she was able to be out of bed again. It was a rose-colored tabby silk with white lace and a white petticoat, and for the first time in her life she was going to have a hoop, and Dorothea had promised to do her hair up over a roll and curl the ends where she had cut it for Kit's queue. She was not only getting well, she was growing up. In that household of gentle, loving women, Tibby bloomed with a new confidence and learned to stop saying "ma'am."

Julian's next letter arrived early in August. *Sweetheart,* it began—but of course he had called her that sometimes before, it didn't really mean anything—

Sweetheart—

Your lefthanded letter was most gratefully received. This comes to you roundabout by a courier on his way to General Greene via Petersburg, so there will be no way to send a letter back to me. It is only to say that we are moving in the wrong direction, north to the Pamunkey. Blame Cornwallis for that, he has got into Yorktown, confound him, and no one knows which way he will jump now—north to New York, south to Charleston, your guess is as good as mine. Meanwhile, we hope to be joined by some more Maryland troops. If only we could also be joined by the French fleet things might take a very satisfactory turn. Such a possibility has doubtless occurred to Cornwallis too.

I shall write again when I can, my darling.

J. D.

My darling. Tibby lay looking out the window with a very odd feeling in her stomach. It should have been in her heart, she thought, but it wasn't.

Then for a long time there was no word from him. Mr. Greensleeves wrote from Williamsburg, where he had remained during the occupation, that Cornwallis was digging himself in at Yorktown as though for a siege, though he was doubtless hoping the British navy would come and rescue him any day now. If only the French navy could get there first, Mr. Greensleeves pointed out, then, with Lafayette's army across the Neck, *then* they would see something! Lafayette, he heard, was moving down from New Kent Courthouse. *"In short, my dears,"* he concluded, *"we who sit midway in this forsaken capital have a tremendous sense of things brewing."*

During the first week in September his presentiment was clarified. He wrote jubilantly to say that French troops under the Marquis de Saint-Simon had been landed at Jamestown by Admiral de Grasse, who had at once put out to sea again to look for the British, and there was a rumor that Washington was in Philadelphia, headed south. Wayne's troops were actually in Williamsburg and quartered at the College. *"We are the center of an armed camp here,"* he added. *"It is like watching the last moves of a long chess game. I cannot convey to you the growing sense of excitement in the very air we breathe these days. Everyone asks the same question: What about the British fleet? Without it, Cornwallis is a dead duck!"*

Two weeks later, a neat little sailing vessel arrived at the Farthingale landing and an orderly presented himself at the front door with letters —letters from Mr. Greensleeves and from St. John and from Julian.

Deaf to the exclamations and cries of joy all around her, Tibby read her own:

My darling—

Are you well enough? Can you be moved? It is difficult to be coherent in the few minutes at my disposal. St. John has arrived here —Williamsburg—with General Washington, as you may know by now. General Rochambeau is here, the French army is here, the French fleet is hereabouts, having driven the British admiral back to New York. We are closing in on Cornwallis for the kill. He is outnumbered and there is no danger now that he can erupt suddenly up the Neck, and St. John has contrived to get a boat sent to bring you all back to town. There will be coaches waiting at Jamestown, and you will have a fine view of the French army encamped there as you drive in. They are very beautiful!

I only wish I could promise to be at Jamestown myself, but poor Lafayette has been laid low by an ague and I am nearly crazy with extra work. He would have it that he is dying of old age, having just turned twenty-four. Dying or not, he can still dictate letters by the hour!

It is all beside the point, which is that at last I shall see you again. St. John says you are to have my old room in Francis Street, and you will find my blessing in it. Theoretically du Bréon and I have tucked in at the schoolhouse, but neither of us ever sees a bed any more. You will like du Bréon, he is one of the aides, and I will bring him to call as soon as you are well enough—I have promised him you will speak French with him as long as he likes! Why do I run on so? All I mean to say is just—Make haste, my Tibby, and come home!

J. D.

VIII

They arrived at Jamestown on the twenty-sixth of September, shepherded by St. John's orderly, and drove through the French lines in the coaches provided for them, admiring the tall, white-clad troops of the Marquis de Saint-Simon, which seemed to swarm. The orderly preferred not to guess how many of them there were.

St. John was not at the Francis Street house, and there was no sign either of Julian, except a note on Tibby's pillow in his old room: *This is a big bouquet of red roses to greet you. There aren't any in town. I will come as soon as I can. J. D.*

"Well!" said Aunt Anabel, much gratified. "Julian *is* coming on!"

Tibby's stomach felt queer all the time now, and her hands were cold and had a tendency to tremble. Aunt Anabel said she was overtired and made her lie down on the sofa and have her dinner off a tray.

In the late afternoon St. John was suddenly amongst them—still limping, as he always would now, but brown and laughing and exhilarated, and kissing everybody. They knew that he had already seen Regina, just by the look of him. When he caught sight of Tibby he let his jaw drop.

"Holy Je*ho*-saphat!" said St. John slowly. "Introduce me, somebody!"

Tibby made him a curtsy. One of Dorothea's prettiest dresses had been made over for her, with a trim boned bodice above the high, flaring hoop and a soft lace fichu at the V-shaped neck. Dorothea, schooling herself towards a day when she must prepare Julian's bride for her wedding, had dressed Tibby's dark hair over a roll, with a bunch of curls at the back. The bandage she still wore was not visible. Small as she still was, open-faced and without airs, Tibby was not a child dressed up. She was a young woman waking to love, with stars in her eyes and that first fleeting blush and bloom that can come only once and is gone too soon.

"Tibby!" said St. John, allowing himself to stare. "Tibby, I am—overcome!"

"Was I so dreadful before?" she asked anxiously, and he laughed and gave her a brotherly hug.

"You were always adorable," he said. "But this is mighty sudden! Have you seen Julian? Or perhaps I should say, has Julian seen you?"

She shook her head, looking worried.

"Maybe he won't like me to be different than I was," she worried, her eyes going from one to the other of their proud, pleased smiles. "Maybe he had got used to me the way I was."

"Maybe he had," nodded St. John with satisfaction. "Maybe it is time he got a surprise. Why isn't he here, anyway? What is keeping him?"

"General Lafayette is sick," said Tibby.

"But good Lord, he's up again! Still wobbly in the knees, but he gets about. Julian is a stick-in-the-mud if ever I knew one, I wouldn't stand for it, Tibby—"

"Sinjie, that will do," said Aunt Anabel crisply. "Sit down and tell us what is going on."

But before he could more than begin to do that, a starchy orderly arrived from headquarters to say he was wanted there as soon as possible.

"Damn," said St. John, rising. "I asked for two hours, and it is not half gone. Come and walk down Gloucester Street with me and see the pretty Frenchmen in their pretty white uniforms!"

"Oh, Sinjie, I don't think that would be quite—?" said Aunt Anabel, and raised her eyebrows at him.

"Oh, stuff, Auntie, whose army do you think this is? Besides, it will give us ten more minutes to talk. It is entirely the thing, I assure you, to take a stroll in the cool of the day, and flirt with the officers!"

They got their hats in a flutter of anticipation, and St. John gave Aunt Anabel his arm while the two girls followed, and he told them which houses had the honor of sheltering which generals, and pointed out evidences of the British occupation.

"Washington is in Mr. Wythe's house," he was saying as they turned into the Duke of Gloucester Street, which was full of bustle—trim orderlies hurried to and fro, colored grooms led groups of saddled horses, liveried slaves out on errands loitered on one foot to pass the time of day with each other, express riders pounded up to the Raleigh's crowded hitching-bar and dismounted stiffly and disappeared within. "And the Comte de Rochambeau is lodged in Peyton Randolph's house. Cornwallis left the President's house a total wreck when he moved out, and the well was roiled, they had to have it cleaned. A lot of slaves have disappeared—scared away, probably, as much as carried off or deserted. Mr. Greensleeves says the flies were simply incredible—worse than the smallpox. We are using the Palace as a hospital, and the French will have the Great Building at the College for theirs. Apparently the British —There you are, Tibby, look what has just come out of the Raleigh!"

But Tibby had already seen, and felt her stomach sink again, while her throat went dry and her hands turned cold and there was a sort of dizzy singing in her ears. Julian had emerged from the tavern with two other officers—one of them in Continental blue like his own, and one in the French white with purple pipings and powdered hair. They were

making their way through groups of lounging townsfolk and soldiers
towards their horses at the hitching-bar.

"Let's just walk straight at him and see what happens," said St. John.
What happened first was that Julian caught sight of Aunt Anabel,
and with a word to his companions, turned aside to greet her warmly
and then bent over Dorothea's hand. St. John, who had deliberately
screened Tibby at first, now took a step to his right and Julian stood
looking down at her. It was a moment before he came to. He had not
expected to see her out taking a walk, for one thing, and no one had told
him about the charming made-over gown with a hoop, and the fashionable dressing of her hair under a wide hat with pale green ribbons.

Speechless, she made him her curtsy. Julian held out his hand, palm
up, and she laid hers in it, and he kissed her fingers. So, except for the
way his warm lips lingered, nothing very much happened after all.

St. John meanwhile was presenting Julian's companions to his aunt
and sister—Captain du Bréon—Vicomte de Vioménil. Julian turned in
time to finish the introductions, to Tibby.

"You and Captain du Bréon have met before," he added gravely.
"At Jamestown. But I don't suppose you recognize each other."

Du Bréon blinked vaguely. This exquisite little creature—Jamestown—?

"Ah, no!" he cried in comic amazement. "It is not the same one!"

"I am pretty much confused myself," Julian admitted, with another
long look at Tibby.

"Yes, we can see that!" remarked St. John with satisfaction.

But du Bréon's gaze had gone back to St. John's sister, resting en-
tranced on the damask rose coloring and soft dark eyes—the small, delicious throat and the young curve of her breast under the gauze fichu.
Du Bréon had seen nothing in America so far that he could not take or
leave with equanimity—the hardships of the northern campaign, the
languor of the southern nights—the modest Boston maidens, the spoilt
Philadelphia belles—but now, he stood transfixed before Dorothea
Sprague, his hat in his hand and surprise in his heart, for here was a
creature to adore, soft and kind and unaware, with a beauty still in the
bud which could be made to flower. . . . He plunged rather wildly into
words, just for the sake of holding her attention to himself.

"But how the war is embellished daily!" he exclaimed. "Your arrival in Williamsburg, mademoiselle, brings out all the roses like June again!"

Dorothea turned up her face towards him with frank laughter at so impetuous a compliment—that confiding lift of her round chin, so that she might really see his face—the *début* of her dimple—and du Bréon was utterly undone. As his handsome, smiling face came into focus above her, Dorothea was swept by a strange excitement which she had somehow thought never to know again. She had given Julian up, in her steadfast heart. She had said good-bye to first love. Except for one hasty proposal of marriage, the war years had deprived her of courtship and balls and flirtations, all. She was hungry for the admiration her beauty deserved, cheated of the compliments and ardent glances which would have come her way if all the Virginia gallants had not been gathered up into the army. And she had lived for years in Regina's shadow, with the chastening knowledge that both her brother and the man she most admired were Regina's property. Now, under du Bréon's fascinated eyes, something revived in Dorothea which had been drooping. For once, in a new stirring of pride and gratification, she had no automatic impulse to refer at once to Regina Greensleeves as more worthy of admiration than herself. Instead, she basked in du Bréon's homage and became more beautiful by the second.

News had just come in that General Greene had fought another battle in South Carolina, at Eutaw Springs—not an out-and-out victory to be sure, but the British were withdrawing towards Charleston, leaving Greene intact and confident. Both sides had suffered heavy losses, however, and Julian was dreading the casualty list, for these were the same men with whom he had shared the hardships of the long retreat across the Dan. William Washington's corps was badly hit and Washington himself had been wounded and taken prisoner of war. Marion was said to be still harrying the British rear guard—"And I can just about hear him yell from here," Julian added with a smile.

"Glory be, did you see *Marion* down there?" cried St. John, for Marion was something of a legend in the army now.

"I was weeks at Snow's Island," Julian said quietly.

"Well, I'm damned!" marvelled St. John in real envy. "Tell us the story of your life, grandfather!"

"Not today," said Julian, embarrassed by their large, respectful eyes upon him. "We are on our way to Jamestown camp. I hope to get

back this evening, Aunt Anabel—may I come to Francis Street then?"
"If you aren't *late,* dear. Tibby has had a tiring day and must go
to bed after supper."

"How late is late?" inquired du Bréon of Dorothea's brown eyes.
"And may I come to Francis Street too?"

For a moment more her wide, defenseless gaze met his. Then she
flushed and glanced at Aunt Anabel, who said, "Tibby has been ill and
is still under orders, Captain du Bréon. The rest of us will be receiving as
usual until a reasonable hour."

"Alas that war, as a rule, is so unreasonable!" said du Bréon, and they
all three made handsome military bows with their heels together and
their hands on their sword-hilts, and were off to the French camp at
Jamestown.

Tibby walked home in a trance. The tall schoolmaster with his
grave, gentle ways had become this gilded figure of romance in epaulet
and sword who kissed her hand in front of the Raleigh as though—as
though— Imagination reeled.

"What a good-looking boy!" said Aunt Anabel, who knew one when
she saw him. "How strange it is to have Williamsburg full of real live
Frenchmen!"

"You mean the Vicomte?" murmured Dorothea perversely.

"No, silly, I mean the Captain! Julian's friend."

"Oh," said Dorothea faintly. "I thought—I thought the white uniform
was so impressive."

"Did you, indeed!" smiled Aunt Anabel. "You never looked at it once
the whole time!"

Dorothea found that evening unusually long. A little after ten, when
Aunt Anabel had yawned three times, they went upstairs to bed. The
French, Dorothea reminded herself in the mirror, brushing out her dark
curls, always say the charming thing. By tomorrow he will have forgotten. And later, on her pillow in the dark— It was the accent, perhaps,
that made him seem so *different.* And later still, just as she fell asleep—
An accent is always bound to seem attractive. . . .

Tibby lay awake till midnight, listening for the beat of horses' hooves
in Francis Street, but Julian did not come. In the morning there was a
note on her breakfast tray: *Returned after midnight, hoping you were
sound asleep. This evening. I promise. J.*

J. Was she to call him Julian now? She had always longed to say his
name out loud.

The hours of that day were endless.

It was after candlelighting, while they sat in the drawing-room listening to Dorothea's harpsichord, that Julian and St. John arrived together.

"Hold tight," said St. John at the doorway. "We are leaving for Yorktown at dawn, and we haven't got five minutes between us. Tibby—God
keep you!" He kissed her cheek. "Dorothea, you have made a conquest,
my dear. Our friend du Bréon sends you his compliments, his regrets, his
kindest regards—in fact, his heart! But he cannot come to say good-bye."

The old Dorothea would have stammered that he had seen her but a
few minutes in the street. But this Dorothea raised her chin a little, and
her dimple showed.

"Give him my l-love," she said.

"Well, I don't mind if I do," St. John remarked surprisingly. "He
seems to be rather a nice fellow, with eyes in his head!"

And then, by some talkative sleight-of-hand about a glass of wine all
round before they were due back at headquarters, he had spirited Aunt
Anabel and Dorothea out of the room and left Julian standing there,
beside a closed door.

Tibby looked at him piteously. Her heart beat to bursting, for it was the
first time she had seen him alone since she had begun to feel herself a
young lady, and since he had written those increasingly informal letters.
In all the seven years since he had come to Williamsburg she had never
felt so strange with him, as though now they were two different people
from the ones who had picnicked on the riverbank at Jamestown and
said good-bye on the bridge above the Landing. Age was no factor between them any more—she was grown up. Regina Greensleeves no
longer stood between them either—he said himself he had become a
philosopher about that. Was it possible that nothing at all stood between
them any more, and that he meant to claim her for his own? The face
she lifted to him as he crossed the room towards where she stood rooted
was a mixture of radiant expectancy and lingering doubt.

"You have always been full of surprises, Tibby," he said slowly as his
eyes went from her high-dressed hair to the silk-draped hoop she wore
so proudly. "But I confess this is a real shock."

"You mean my clothes?" she queried anxiously. "I said perhaps you wouldn't like me to be different than I always was, and they said—" She broke off uncomfortably. *Maybe it is time he got a surprise,* St. John had said.

"I like you this way very much," he assured her gently.

"It is only one of Dorothea's dresses made over." But her fingers touched the stiff rose-colored silk with wonder still, and she stood straighter than ever in the coveted hoop.

"I didn't mean the dress, my dear. It is Tibby herself who is—strange. We shall have to get acquainted all over again."

"I'm just the same," she assured him. "Dorothea showed me how to do my hair, and it does make me look taller, doesn't it! And I am wearing heels, too. But that is all the difference, really."

He reached out for her left hand, and stood a moment looking down at the place on her arm where the break had been, his thumb caressing the honey-colored skin.

"What a long time ago it was, after all—the night I picked you up outside the Raleigh with a broken arm—"

"It—doesn't really show any more—"

"And that day at Jamestown, on the riverbank—that was years ago too, wasn't it—"

"I was terrified you would go back to England—"

"I meant to go—if you hadn't cried—"

"Are you sorry now that you didn't?"

"No."

"You—you said that day you would stay in Virginia till you had a long white beard," she reminded him shakily.

"It was a promise, Tibby."

"If anything—happened to you now I'd feel it was my fault," she whispered.

"Nothing is going to happen to me—now."

"W-will there be another battle—at Yorktown?"

"It looks that way."

"You will be careful, won't you—and not get killed?"

For the first time since he had taken her hand he raised his eyes to hers. It was still Tibby who looked up at him, an inch taller in her heels, her dark hair brushed back over a roll from her small, eager face, with a knot of rose-colored ribbon holding the cluster of curls at the back. The filmy lace fichu revealed the line of her slender throat into her straight shoulders, and the sweet swell of her little bosom. She had grown quite out of his knowledge over night, so that he felt almost shy of her, as though he had not held her in his arms more than once, as though she had not sat by his bedside with a book when he had fever—as though they were not linked by years of small intimacies and the secret, coded words and signs of old acquaintance. But it was still Tibby's greenish gaze, swimming with tears, which sought his with that dear defenselessness he knew so well, the look which said so plainly that what he said would be, and what he wanted was law. A wave of apprehension passed through him, not for his own skin but for Tibby, if anything should happen at Yorktown so that he could not cherish and protect her all the rest of her days. And so she found herself in his arms, held close against him, her face in the fresh lace at his throat.

"Sweetheart, you are not to worry—Cornwallis can't get away now, we have got him bottled up."

"And then will the war be over?"

"I hope so," he sighed. "My dear, I hope so."

She felt his hand move on her shoulder, felt his strong, heavy heartbeat as she leaned against him, felt herself dying for him, in his arms.

"Did the wound heal?" he was saying, and she nodded with his face against her hair. "You are so little, Tibby," he was saying, while his arms cradled her. "How can anything so small as you are raise a man's heart so high? I will come back to you, my darling, never fear—it is only the poor devils who have no one to say them pieces who get killed. Let me have that magic spell of yours once more—the one that brought me safe out of Camden."

And though she was half smothered in his lace and strangled with her own tears, and his arms were crushing the breath out of her lungs, she found the words he wanted.

" 'For He shall give His angels charge over thee, to keep thee in all thy ways,' " gasped Tibby. " 'They shall bear thee up in their hands, lest thou dash thy foot against a stone.' "

"My dear, my dear, how can I bear to leave you in tears again!"

"I'm s-sorry, sir, I'm trying not to," she sobbed, and put a hand to the agonizing ache in her throat.

"I have a name," he whispered. "But I have never heard you say it."

"Oh, Julian, may I really?"

Tears shone on her cheeks and the war seemed very far away as he held her. Resolutely he put from him the longing to kiss her lips and ask to take with him her promise to be his wife. When they had finished at Yorktown—then he would have the right to make love to this enchanting creature his Tibby had become.

"If I don't go now," he said with an effort, "they will catch Cornwallis without me and I shall miss the fun."

"Will it take long?"

"Not with Washington here, you'll see—and the French as well. Promise not to cry while I am gone."

"I'll try. Will you send me word?"

"If I can. You mustn't fret if you don't hear. Good-bye, sweetheart— and all my love."

"Good-bye—Julian."

He left his kiss on her hair, unclasped her clinging fingers from his coat, and made blindly for the door.

The army marched out of Williamsburg at five the next morning, down the Duke of Gloucester Street and along the Yorktown road. The town turned out in its shift to see them go. The music of the fifes and drums could be heard in Francis Street, so that Tibby woke and lay shivering and sobbing in Julian's bed, and Aunt Anabel came in with a cup of hot chocolate and sat beside her till she slept again exhausted.

IX

Yorktown was under siege.

The Continental forces lay in a wide semicircle on the landward side of the town, the French on the left, the Americans on the center and right. When Washington arrived at Williamsburg with his army from the north, Lafayette had made the gracious gesture—he had voluntarily resumed his position as major-general in command of a division of

Light Infantry in the Continental army, so that General Lincoln, who had long since been exchanged at Charleston and returned to Washington's fold, was second in command now.

The French fleet under de Grasse walked up and down off Cape Henry, cutting off rescue or retreat for Cornwallis. But the British fought on behind their fortifications, and within a week's time the wounded began to come back to Williamsburg in wagons from the field hospital. Casualties were for a time considered surprisingly light, but after the night of October fourteenth, when Lafayette and de Vioménil in a joint action took the British Redoubts Nine and Ten, they were suddenly worse.

"If only one could do something at Yorktown oneself, the waiting wouldn't be so bad!" said Dorothea, trying not to pace the floor, for Tibby had had a relapse and lost her dinner and had been ordered to bed for a few days. "If only one weren't so helpless, being a woman!"

"I was thinking about what Mrs. Greensleeves said this morning," said Tibby from her pillows. "About the French."

"What was that?" Dorothea paused. She had tried not to think about the French too much, but one had to keep talking about something.

"She said things were much worse at the College, where the French wounded are, than at the Palace, because the French haven't got enough servants. She said Regina wanted her to lend one of their maids to the French surgeons for a few hours each day, just to change the beds and things, and help with the food. And Aunt Anabel said she would send Jerusha over there each afternoon, if that would help. But Jerusha doesn't speak French. It must be pretty lonesome, not to be able to make anybody understand what you want. I was thinking I could go and interpret for them, as soon as I am well enough."

"Why, yes!" said Dorothea, catching at it. "Yes, that's a very good idea!" She stood a moment, grieving for the French captain's countrymen who had never learned to speak English—there must be quite a lot of them, poor dears—it wasn't every Frenchman who spoke English like Captain du Bréon. "A man could ask Jerusha for a drink of water all day, and she wouldn't know what he wanted," she said slowly. "But I would. Tibby, what a splendid idea! I will go with Jerusha this afternoon and see if they will let me help too!"

Aunt Anabel was not much taken with the idea herself, but she consented because of a wish to occupy Dorothea's mind. Jerusha was scandalized, for no lady in her experience had ever done such a thing as to approach a strange man in his bed, let alone a whole army of them, and foreign at that.

Shocked and disapproving, she followed Dorothea to the College and up the steps of the Great Building. There was no doubt as to the use the College was being put to. All around them were the odors and the sounds of sick and suffering men.

"T'aint no place for you, honey—best you go home—I can come back myself later on. T'ain't no place for you—"

"Be quiet, Jerusha—I must do something, or go mad—" She peeped in at the door of the nearest room, and a wave of foetid air caught her nostrils and rocked her back on her heels. There were rows of cots and pallets with narrow aisles between, an occasional chair or stool, and a large table against one wall which was full of basins and bedclothes and bandages both fresh and soiled. There was a ceaseless mutter of men's voices, some of them in aimless delirium, some in sharp, agonized cries of pain. "This is dreadful!" said Dorothea, and caught at the door-jamb. "They—they can't be left like this!"

"Best you go straight on home, now, honey, and I better see can I find somebody that will lemme start right in. I got plenty to do here." Jerusha's capable fingers were itching to begin.

A surgeon with his sleeves rolled up, gray-faced with fatigue, came out of another door and paused to look at her in a weary daze.

"Yes, mademoiselle? You were looking for somebody?"

"Well, I—I came to ask if I could do anything to help, I—we heard you were short-handed."

"We are short-handed, no mistake." He spoke with a strong French accent, but no fumbling for English words. "In fact, the surgeons' mates go to sleep on their feet, but I am afraid you— Is your maid trained to nursing?"

"Oh, yes, Jerusha will do anything you ask of her. But I want to be of some use myself."

His mind seemed to work slowly in a fog of fatigue.

"I suppose you could help with the feeding," he said. "Some of them cannot manage alone, and I cannot spare anyone— Can this girl help me in the operating room without screeching and fainting?"

"Yes, of course." Dorothea held fast to her purpose. "Where do I start
—feeding them?"

He jerked his head at the ward behind her.

"Anywhere. Their next meal will come up soon—soup. Just go round
and spoon it into them if they need help. There is a man in there with
both arms off—" He turned away, his shoulders sagging. "I have got
three of them in the operating room—come with me, girl."

Jerusha followed him obediently, with a last anxious glance over her
shoulder, and Dorothea, feeling faint, was left alone in the hall. She
drew a long breath and approached the door of the ward again and
looked in, determined to find the armless man and be of assistance to
him. On the third cot down the row on her right, a dark head moved
restlessly from side to side, and a thick, protesting voice spoke blindly
from behind closed eyes in semi-consciousness.

"*Maman,*" it was saying. "*Maman, où est-tu? A boire—de l'eau,
maman—à boire—par pitié—à boire—*"

A half-empty pitcher of stale water and some mugs stood on the table
among the mess. Dorothea filled a mug and carried it to the bedside of
the man who called for his mother. Trying to remember how it was
when Sinjie was so bad after Camden, assuring herself that anything
she had done for Sinjie she could do for this nameless French soldier, she
slid her hand behind his head and said distinctly—

"*Voici de l'eau, monsieur.*"

The fretful words died on his lips. He lay very still, as though afraid
to move again. Dorothea leaned over him, holding her breath in disbelief
—yes—yes, it *was*—unshaven, parched with fever, breathing heavily,
wounded and suffering alone, it was Julian's friend du Bréon. Slowly his
eyes unclosed, and she was surprised to see that they were dark blue—
and it was his mother he had called on, not some woman's name—

"Try and drink a little water," she said impulsively, forgetting all her
French. "I'll hold it for you."

He went on staring up at her, his blue eyes dull with pain—regarding
incredulously the petal-pink cheeks, the tender chin, the soft, nearsighted,
compassionate gaze of St. John Sprague's beautiful sister.

"*C'est un ange,*" he stated with sudden conviction. "*Je suis mort.*"

"*Ce n'est pas une ange,*" she assured him patiently in her pretty school
girl French, supposing that he did not know her. "*C'est une Américaine.*"

"America," he murmured. *"C'est le paradis."* His eyes closed again, and he added on a long sigh, "Except for the pain."

Dorothea was pinioned, one hand under his head, the other holding the mug of water. He seemed content to leave her so indefinitely. Sinjie had never behaved like this.

"You are in the hospital at Williamsburg, sir," she said firmly. "You were asking for water and I have brought it. Try to drink a little. I will help you."

But he lay still, his eyes obstinately closed.

"It is a delusion," he said. "I dare not look again."

After a moment's thought, she withdrew her hand from behind his head, intending to dip her handkerchief in the mug and bathe his lips and temples. Quickly his own hand came up and caught hers in a hot, fierce grip.

"Ah, no—don' go away! *Je vous en supplie—restez—restez—ici—*"

"I am not going away," she told him matter-of-factly. "I am trying to bathe your face with cool water, if you will let go my hand."

Reluctantly his fingers released their hold and hers slipped away from them, and returned to raise his head from the pillow.

"Won't you drink first?" she coaxed gently.

"Drink—yes, very thirsty—till you came—wanting water—till you came—" The brim of the mug met his lips, they fumbled a moment, and then he drank greedily, still voluntarily blind, his lashes long and black against his pale cheeks. He was, she decided, much younger than one would think. His left arm was bandaged to the shoulder in a clumsy sort of way, and the bandage was not clean. His right arm was uninjured, and the hand now held hers on the mug, tipping the last of the water down his throat. She let his head go back carefully against the pillow. She remembered with compunction the man who had no arms—

"Don' go—!" he said again anxiously, imprisoning her fingers between his and the mug with feverish strength.

"I am going just as far as that table to get some more water and make you as comfortable as I can." She gently freed herself and filled the mug again.

A glance at the dirty linen roundabout doomed her handkerchief. She soaked it in the mug of water, carried them back to du Bréon's cot, and went on her knees beside it in a rustle of lilac taffeta skirts. The

blind face on the pillow turned towards her, and his breath came with a
little hiss between his teeth.

"They want to take off my arm," he whispered. "It is not gangrenous.
I have said I will die first. Stay here, and watch—I might fall asleep—
I am afraid to sleep—they might come and take off my arm—please stay
and watch—don' let them—"

"No, I won't let them," she promised soothingly, and began to bathe
his face with the cool, wrung-out handkerchief.

Slowly his eyes opened again—to find her face almost on a level with
his now. Slowly they explored its delicate beauty, wonderingly, as though
it were mirage. She endured the scrutiny bravely but her color rose.

"Could you—take off your hat?" he whispered.

With one hand she pulled the end of the lilac ribbon and laid the hat
on the dirty floor beside her. His gaze plunged into her dark curls,
seemed to memorize their last detail, and returned to her face.

"I was afraid to look again," he whispered, "for fear you were not
really as beautiful as I thought—when I first saw you, there in the street."

"Oh, you—you remember that," she breathed, for she had not been
sure.

"Remember it, mademoiselle? Remember the most beautiful face in
the world? And now that I see it again—I am afraid ever to stop looking
—for fear I miss something."

"You will miss your sleep," she said, as though she spoke to Sinjie in
a fractious mood, but her dimple showed.

"I—asked your brother to say good-bye—"

"Yes—he told me."

"He said you sent me your love," he repeated incredulously, and waited
for denial.

"It is a phrase we have," she explained, and the cool handkerchief
came down across his eyes for a moment. *"C'est à dire—mes amitiés—*
but perhaps a little friendlier than that."

"It was my shield at Yorktown," he said with conviction. "I saw
Barber fall—then I got this—and I saw your face in the light of the
Bengal fire—as clearly as I see it now—were I blind, I should see it still—"

"You must rest now," she reminded him rather unsteadily. "You will
tire yourself with talking."

"Was Barber killed?"

"I don't know. I haven't heard."

"We took the redoubt in ten minutes," he told her with pride. "We did it all with the bayonet—never fired a shot—" Laughter shook him briefly. "Day carried the message—if only I too had seen de Vioménil's face—!"

"Captain Day? What message?"

"Lafayette was furious because de Vioménil swore his Gâtinois were better trained and would take their redoubt before we got ours—he was wrong—in ten minutes we were successful on our side—and there was still hell's delight going on over at Number Nine—so Lafayette sent Day with his compliments and did they perhaps require some help from us —from where I lay I could see that he and Day were roaring with laughter as they framed the message—de Vioménil would not see that joke— he got the redoubt, though—the Gâtinois took Number Nine in the end—"

"Did you see Captain Day after the battle?"

"It was not a battle, mademoiselle, it was only a pair of redoubts— which caught us with enfilading fire—too much to be borne—so we took them—"

"And—Captain Day—?"

"Last I saw—he was off to twit de Vioménil! I would have liked that chance myself—"

"I am a bad nurse to let you talk so much. Go to sleep now, and—"

"But when I wake up you will be gone!" He caught at her hand, the wet handkerchief between their palms.

"No. I promise to stay. You can trust me." She removed the handkerchief deftly, leaving her fingers in his. "See, you can hold me here, even in your sleep." She smiled at him, the smile of a mother above a crib, and touched his matted hair. "Go to sleep," she whispered, and against his will his heavy lids came down.

She knelt on the floor beside him, her fresh skirts swirled in the dirt and bloodstains and spittle on the unswept boards, the odor of dying men heavy on the breathless air. She had a great deal to think about. He had given her in a few gasping, vivid words the sight and sound of war—Julian and Lafayette roaring with laughter in the light of the Bengal fire—the schoolboy jest carried through gunfire to de Vioménil in the midst of wounds and death—but *it wasn't a battle, mademoiselle, it was only a pair of redoubts*—Julian must be safe, or he would have been

sent back to Williamsburg by now—no news was good news, as near
the battle line as this—Captain du Bréon had remembered the meeting
in the street—he had seen her face as he fell, at Yorktown—he said it
was the most beautiful face in the world. . . . It was a serene face now,
full of a brooding peace as she knelt beside the cot with du Bréon's hot
fingers clasping hers, while her arm began to ache and her feet went to
sleep beneath her. He was far from home, and a little out of his head
with fever, and he wanted his mother. . . .

A slovenly colored servant arrived with a trayful of bowls of soup. He
cleared a space on the table among the dirty rags and began clatteringly
to hand round the ward's dinner. Du Bréon slept on without moving,
and Dorothea, quite numb now from the waist down, beckoned the
Negro towards the cot when the tray was empty.

"I want a surgeon," she said. "Will you ask one of them to come here,
please."

"Doctors awful busy right now, missy."

"I know. But this is urgent. Please ask some one to come here."

Doubtfully the Negro left the room, and in a few minutes returned
with the same surgeon she had seen in the hall.

"Captain du Bréon is worried about his arm," she said. "Can it possibly
be saved?"

The surgeon shrugged non-committally. It was a suppurating wound
—it must be continually cleansed, the dressings must be constantly
changed—there were not enough attendants—there was no time for just
one man among so many—therefore—

"Could I do it?" asked Dorothea.

The surgeon's bloodshot eyes took in her youth, her daintiness, her
destructible lilac silk gown, and he compared them to the ghastly sounds
and smells of the ward. He shook his head.

"Can't you show me how to do it?" she insisted, and unclasped du
Bréon's hand from hers and rose painfully, trying to find her feet in
what seemed to be nothing but cottonwool filled with pins and needles
between her and the floor.

Rather impatiently the surgeon began to unwrap the bandage, reveal-
ing a shattered elbow beneath a dressing long in need of changing. A
stench rose from the wound. Dorothea flinched, and stiffened.

"It wants bathing," she said through white lips.

The surgeon nodded and brought a basin of water and some clean cloths. She watched while he sponged away dried blood and pus, and then she held out her hand for the rag.

"It must be kept clean," she said. "I can do that, you are busy, I know. As soon as you can spare Jerusha send her in here to feed the man who has no arms. I will take care of this. How often does it need to be done?"

Succumbing to her air of cool self-possession, the man made further explanations, handed over the hideous basin and cloth, and went away. Dorothea set to work, gingerly at first, then with more confidence. Du Bréon had stirred and groaned under the surgeon's hands. Now he seemed to wake with a start and lay looking up at her.

"You are still here," he wondered, his face rigid with pain.

"I am here, yes. You aren't going to lose your arm, they have shown me what to do."

"You will—disgust yourself—" he gasped, sweating.

"I'm sorry if it hurts—I am doing the best I can—you can rest soon, while I help some of the others to eat their dinner."

"Ah, yes—the others—some of them are very bad—"

"You mustn't be frightened if you don't find me always here beside you. I shan't be far away and I will come back."

"Always—come back—*toujours—restez—toujours—*"

He drifted into merciful unconsciousness.

Darkness was falling when Jerusha came to the ward, her white apron stained with blood, and together they fed the cold soup to the men who had not managed to handle it alone. Once as they passed between the rows of cots, Jerusha gave a little moan and drew up the blanket. Dorothea did not look back, but bent above the next man.

When that was all accomplished, and the wound tended again, Jerusha said it was time to go home, but Dorothea shook her head.

"I promised not to leave him," she said. "Tell Aunt Anabel I need her here. Ask her to come straight back with you, please."

Jerusha perceived the futility of protest. She went away mumbling to herself, and the ward grew darker as a lantern was lighted in the hall. Two shadowy forms came in and carried away the man who had died. Dorothea spoke to them, asking for candles and some warm water, and more clean cloths. The strangeness of her situation in the stinking ward never penetrated her absorbtion in the task she had set herself—she was oblivious of everything except du Bréon's need of her, and her answering need of the promise she read in his eyes. This man was hers, if she could save him. And she knew that she could save him.

Aunt Anabel arrived breathless at the College and entered the ward to find her niece still kneeling on the filthy floor, tending the ugly wound by the light of a single candle which had been stuck on to the seat of a stool beside the cot. This was their fragile Dorothea, who hated spiders and turned faint at the sight of a sick dog. Aunt Anabel was somehow not surprised.

"I want to take him home," Dorothea was saying as she laid on a fresh dressing. "He can have Sinjie's room. Do you think we can move him tonight?"

"Well, dear—" Aunt Anabel began uncertainly, wondering what Sinjie would think of all this.

Du Bréon roused as though conscious of a new presence, and opened his eyes.

"You have come to take her away," he said simply to Aunt Anabel. "Are you her mother, madame?"

"I am her aunt—all the mother she has now."

"Ah, yes, I remember perfectly—Aunt Ana-belle. Are you going to take her away now?"

"I am afraid she won't come away."

"So kind—" he murmured. "For hours now—each time I look, *mon Dieu*, she is still there—to save my arm—madame, you must forgive me, please, if I seem to you *un peu précipité*—but if I do not lose my arm, have I your permission—pay my addresses to your niece?"

"You have my permission to get well as fast as you can, and then we shall see," said Aunt Anabel, and laid her hand on his hair.

"Mademoiselle Dorothée—he did say Dorothée—?" His anxious, pain-filled eyes sought her face, and Dorothea leaned above him, her own eyes very bright in the light of the candle.

"Dorothea—we say."

"Dorothée-a—adorable—" His French *r*'s tripped him up, the stress fell on a broad *a*.

"You mustn't try to talk any more now," she said, and obedient as a child, he went off to sleep.

Aunt Anabel saw that arm or no arm, this headlong French lad would possess Dorothea's mothering heart from now on, saw that she had found salvation if not the first rapture she had once craved from Julian. Without any more ifs, buts, or ands, Aunt Anabel tracked down the driven surgeon and got his permission to remove Captain du Bréon to Francis Street that same night, pointing out to him—as though he was not only too glad to be rid of even one sufferer—that it was the accident of du Bréon's speaking French that had caused some one to bring him to the College hospital anyway, instead of to the Palace with the other Continental wounded, where he belonged.

The surgeon, who didn't really much care where du Bréon belonged, agreed politely to everything. Joshua and the Greensleeves' Reuben carried the French captain on a stretcher through the dark streets, and Joshua put him to bed in St. John's room with as much loving skill as though he handled his master. It was midnight before Dorothea could be persuaded to let Jerusha take her place at his bedside, and Aunt Anabel led her away to her own room.

"You promise to call me if he wakes and seems the least bit confused?" Dorothea insisted.

"Yes, dear, I promise."

"I don't think he quite understood where he was going—it is the pain and the fever—but he speaks beautiful English, doesn't he!"

"Beautiful."

"Do you think," pursued Dorothea diffidently, brushing out her hair, "do you think he might like to live in America?"

To St. John's observant eyes, as the Yorktown siege went on, the change in Julian was almost as miraculous as Tibby's blossoming. They met fairly often on their lawful occasions as staff officers, and sought each other out in the scanty leisure their duties left them, and St. John saw that the shy young schoolmaster had become a competent, experienced officer, cool under fire, steady in emergency, with no more misgivings as to his place in the world and his ability to carry through whatever

he undertook to do. Self-reliance underlay his habitual modesty like a
rock now. And perhaps only St. John could appreciate what it had cost
him in fortitude and resolution to arrive at his present degree of cheerful
efficiency under any conditions the fortunes of war might impose upon
him.

Here was a man Virginia needed, St. John thought, noting the unassuming ease with which Julian coped with the volatile Lafayette, the
almost insulting ease with which he exchanged personal witticisms in
their own language with the French officers, the obvious respect and
affection in which he was held by the men who had shared the arduous
five months' campaign in Virginia's summer heat. There were no limits
now to Julian's future in the world after the peace. And in Tibby he had
found his own soul.

St. John was still somewhat staggered by the conversation which had
taken place between himself and Julian after they had left the house
and started back on foot to headquarters that last night in Williamsburg. At first he had waited with some impatience for Julian's news.
And Julian had made chat about the prospect of rain and the outlook
for Cornwallis. At last St. John could bear the suspense no longer.

"Well, be that as it may, am I to congratulate you?" he inquired.

"Not yet," said Julian uncomfortably. "You see, I don't want to hurry
her into—that is, it will take a little while, I suppose, for her to—"

"To what, in heaven's name?"

"Well, shall we say to assimilate your marriage to Regina, and to
learn to think of me as something besides the schoolmaster—"

"Now, don't tell me you are still in a fog about that!" cried St. John
sharply.

"I don't know quite what you mean by fog, you surely guessed some
time ago that Tibby had formed a—an attachment for you—"

"Oh, God above!" ejaculated St. John. "She never cared tuppence for
me! How did you ever get that ridiculous idea in the first place?"

"Why, she was jealous of Regina, I told you that, and you said—"

"But it had nothing to do with me! She hated Regina because of *you!*
Tibby knew you were smitten with Regina, make no mistake! And
Tibby was always in love with you!"

Julian stopped dead in his tracks.

"All this time?" he said, and his voice went high with incredulity.

"All her life, more or less! Why do you think she came to you at Tyre's?"

"Because she—she had no one else, when Aunt Anabel had gone—"

"Because she loved you, fool, and was dying for a sight of you!"

Julian had stood there while the street eddied about him in the last bustle of an imminent march. Light from the Raleigh spilled out of its many windows and caught the expression of stupefaction on his face, as evidence rolled up in his memory, evidence full of new meaning no longer obscured by his own obstinate misapprehensions.

"You can't—are you sure about this?" he asked.

"Oh, Julian, ask anybody, man! I had no idea you had brought her all the way from Jamestown to Farthingale without getting things straightened out! Didn't you write her letters? What on earth did you say to her tonight? Why do you think I left you alone with her just now?"

"I must go back to the house," said Julian suddenly. "I won't be long, please say that I—"

"Are you two discussing the weather out there?" cried du Bréon's exasperated voice. "The Marquis is waiting, Captain Day, I would advise you to report at once!"

It had been too late to go back to Francis Street then.

Cornwallis knew the game was up, but he held out until the seventeenth, with smallpox and camp fever raging in Yorktown and the fortifications crumbling under the allied cannonade. He tried a gallant sortie against the Soissonais section of the French line and was beaten off. He tried to escape by boat across the mouth of the York River to Gloucester Point, and was prevented by a storm. Finally, even as Washington and Rochambeau laid plans for a general assault, a red-coated drummer boy mounted the only piece of whole parapet remaining and beat the *parley,* which went unnoticed in the noise of the guns till an officer stood beside him and waved a white handkerchief.

The terms were hard, the same as those imposed on Lincoln's beaten army at Charleston in 1780—complete surrender, colors cased, bands forbidden to play tunes belonging to the victors. And General Lincoln, who had made the Charleston surrender to Clinton, was present now to see it done the other way round.

On the afternoon of October nineteenth, the ragged, excited American army was drawn up a mile long across the barren field between the lines. Lafayette's veteran Light Infantry in their battle-worn blue with white facings and plumed caps had the post of honor on the right, and Julian, who had suddenly remembered that he had a book to finish, was among the glittering group of aides which surrounded the Marquis. Here was history in the making—and he realized with some astonishment that he himself had had a hand in its making, and his heart beat faster under the well-brushed blue coat he wore now with such an air of unconscious authority and dash. For months he had been caught up in the day-to-day intricacies of army life—perspective opened suddenly before him there on the field of surrender. This was a war, and they were winning it. This was a great day indeed. I must remember this day, he thought with pride, sitting his horse behind Lafayette at the right of the line. I can tell my grandchildren that I saw Cornwallis give up his sword. . . .

Facing the Continentals stretched the long white ranks of the French, the Comte de Rochambeau, glittering with gold braid, at their head. Each regiment bore two flags, its own and the King's white and gold *fleur de lys* banner. Then General Washington arrived at a canter on a white horse, followed smartly by his well-polished staff, and they took up their position at the middle of the lines, and Julian observed that the Commander-in-Chief's granite-faced composure contrasted impressively with the ill-concealed jubilation of his troops, who had been forbidden to cheer. St. John's eyes caught Julian's as the staff swept in, and his left eyelid drooped for an instant in a schoolboy wink. Julian himself watched the odd details of the ceremony unfold before him with a growing desire to chuckle.

The British marched out of Yorktown superbly, spruce and shining and contemptuous, and the tune they had characteristically chosen to play was an old English air called *The World Turned Upside Down*. Cornwallis, in fact, was so contemptuous that he did not appear at all. General O'Hara came in his place, carrying his commander's sword, which he singled out Rochambeau to receive, as a surrender less humiliating than one made to the backwoods rebels.

Rochambeau, quite equal to any occasion, bowed slightly in the saddle and indicated Washington, to whom, perforce, O'Hara then made Cornwallis's excuses. Washington, very grave, hoped that his lordship's indisposition was nothing serious. O'Hara, no doubt grinding his teeth, had no choice but to proffer the sword to the American Commander-in-Chief. Washington, his face still immovable, waved him on towards General Lincoln, and Cornwallis' sword changed hands at last, deputy to deputy. The massive Lincoln, who had never officiated at this end of a surrender before, had the tact to return the symbol to O'Hara at once, before leading the way between the double lines of victorious troops and across the field to where the British army was to lay down its arms in a circle formed by French hussars in tall hats and braided coats mounted on handsome, well-groomed horses.

There another delicate point of military etiquette arose.

Twenty-eight British and Hessian captains with cased colors to surrender found themselves facing twenty-eight Continental sergeants detailed to receive them. This they considered infra dig, and hesitated to advance the two paces when the order was given. Alexander Hamilton, as officer of the day, solved the *impasse* by designating the youngest commissioned officer in the American army, one Ensign Wilson, aged eighteen, to receive the colors one by one from the captains and pass them on to the sergeants. The ceremony of capitulation then proceeded, and the sullen British regiments entered the circle of hussars one by one —"*Prrresent arms!—Lay down arms!—Put off swords and cartridge boxes!*"—the last command to the defeated army was given by its own officers, and the cheeks of some of them were wet with real tears as they marched back between the watching lines of the allies to their battered quarters in the town.

Washington despatched a note to Cornwallis inviting him with all the courtesies of war to dinner at American headquarters that evening. Cornwallis declined, preferring to confer his presence first on the elder de Vioménil.

The war was not over, of course. The British were still in possession of Wilmington, Charleston, and New York. Julian held his breath when it was suggested that Lafayette join Greene with reinforcements at once, and with the aid of de Grasse and the French fleet repeat the Yorktown maneuver at Wilmington. But de Grasse was unwilling, being due back in the West Indies, and anyway the year was drawing to its close and it was time to think of getting into winter quarters, and the idea was soon abandoned. Lafayette consoled himself by planning an immediate trip to Philadelphia, where he could apply to a grateful Congress for leave to spend the winter in France. He would not need an American aide in France. . . .

Meanwhile the etiquette of surrender continued, and the British, Hessian, French, and American officers all dined each other in turn with the utmost civility. The high-ranking British officers would of course soon be exchanged, the rank and file would be marched off to a prison camp to be established near Winchester. Washington planned to return at once to the problem which still awaited him around New York. But there was a general feeling on both sides that the end, however delayed, was near.

About midnight of an autumnal day late in October, a lone rider swung from his horse in Francis Street, and Joshua, wearing his livery coat over his nightshirt, opened the door a cautious crack—then threw it wide, crying—

"Lawd be praised, it's you, Cap'n Day, suh!"

"I'll thank you to remember I am a major now, Joshua," Julian grinned as he crossed the threshold.

"You don't say, suh! Mm-*mm*, reckon we all got step lively now, suh! You fixed to sleep here tonight?"

"Well, I—"

"Make you up a nice bed on the sofa, suh. Miss Dorothea's Frenchman done got the master's bed, and Miss Tibby sound asleep in yourn!"

"Miss Dorothea's *what?*"

"Yes, *suh,* she done cotch herself the nicest French boy you ever did see! Brang him back from the hospital, we did, and sure looks like weddin'-bells at last, suh!"

"Joshua, what on earth is going on down there?" Aunt Anabel spoke softly from the top of the stairs where she stood in a house-gown, holding a candle.

"Major Day come home, ma'am."

"Julian! I'm so glad, dear, we've been expecting you for days! Is Sinjie all right?"

"He's getting a night's sleep, for once," said Julian, mounting to the landing and bending to receive her kiss on his cheek. "I couldn't come until Lafayette made up his mind about things and we had gone through all the motions to assure Cornwallis there were no hard feelings. Everybody has been very polite to everybody else, and even his lordship seems resigned now to his surrender. May I see Tibby?"

"*Tonight?*"

"Tonight. In fact, this minute." He drew her on up the stairs with a hand under her elbow. "Why else have I ridden twelve miles on a road as dark as your pocket?"

"Now, Julian, she is fast asleep at this hour, it has been very hard on her, I really think if anything had happened to you—"

"May I just look at her?" he pleaded.

"Well—come very quietly."

She led the way with the candle, turned the knob of Tibby's door without a sound, and they tiptoed to the bedside.

Tibby wore one of Dorothea's nightdresses, which had a ruffle at the neck and full sleeves with a ruffle at the wristband. She lay with her cheek turned to the pillow, one arm thrown above her head. Her hair was tied back like a queue in curls.

"Would it be all right if I just sat here for a few minutes?" Julian laid his hand on the arm chair drawn up beside the bed. "I promise not to wake her."

Aunt Anabel opened her mouth to say that it wouldn't do at all, and then saw his face as he stood looking down. Aunt Anabel closed her mouth again and set the candle on the bedside table and went away, leaving the door open behind her. He never missed her.

The light shone across Tibby's face on the white pillow. He pulled the chair nearer and sat down with his chin in his hand, half smiling, unable to tear himself away, as though fearing to lose her before the new day could break. Finally, though he had not moved, her eyelids quivered and lifted half way. He did not speak, and her eyes closed again, so that he thought she had dropped off without fully regaining consciousness.

"If I look again," she said softly, "will you be gone?"

"Try it and see," he whispered, motionless, and for a long moment they looked at each other in the candlelight.

"It is really you!" she cried, and sat up to make sure.

"Sh! Lie down quick, or I'll catch it from Aunt Anabel!"

With a guilty glance at the door she dropped back against the pillow. "Does she know you are here?" she whispered.

"Yes, but I wasn't supposed to wake you," he whispered back.

"How long have you been here?"

"Only a minute."

"How long can you stay?"

"Not much longer than that. I'll come back in the morning, though. They have given me a week's leave."

"Only a week? Isn't the war over?"

"Not exactly. We have still got to win back New York and Carolina."

"Oh, don't let them send you away!"

"Sh!" He leaned forward and took both her hands in both his on the coverlet. "I have arranged everything very nicely—I think! Lafayette is off to Philadelphia, and I am to stay here with Rochambeau and talk French."

"Right here in Williamsburg?"

"Yes, right here. Rochambeau is going into winter headquarters here, and I shall be in my old room above the school, will that do? Tibby —how long must I wait for you to grow up enough to marry me?"

"M-marry—?"

"I know it is too soon to speak of it, but—now it is too late not to! You are mine, Tibby. I want you." He laid his face against her palms.

"Oh, Julian, I—I never thought you'd ask me!"

He moved from the chair to the edge of the bed, and she felt his arms slide between her and the pillow. She lay back against them confidently, looking up at him with shining, unembarrassed eyes. Oddly enough, her stomach wasn't acting up at all, now that he was here and all the uncertainty was past. She wasn't nervous of him any more. She belonged to him. He said so. It was a feeling full of warmth, and comfort, and security she had never dreamed of—with an irresponsible fringe of sheer joy.

"You are sure nothing will cure you of this?" His own eyes were grave. "You are quite sure you won't just wake up some morning able to see that I am a very ordinary sort of man, no better than a lot of others, and maybe not so good?"

"I shall never see that, as long as I live." She laid a small warm hand along his cheek. "What is it?" she whispered. "You look very queer."

He drew in his breath.

"I feel very queer," he said. "I am going now, Tibby. You must get your sleep."

"Did you *mean* that—what you said about marrying me?"

"Yes. I did. We will talk about it in the morning." He rose reluctantly from the edge of the bed, and she held him by one hand.

"But if we are really going to be married, couldn't we begin now?"

"My dear child—!"

"Couldn't you kiss me good-night?" she entreated, and he caught her to him recklessly and found her lips with his. It was no child's kiss she gave him, it was warm and yielding with a knowledge beyond her years. Much shaken, he forced himself to release her, and she nestled into the curve of his shoulder with a sigh. "I thought you never would," she sighed.

"Tibby, I don't know what to do about you, I—you have rather knocked the breath out of me."

She leaned against him contentedly, running experimental fingertips up and down his sleeve, straightening the lace beneath his chin, exploring delicately her new rights and privileges.

"When can we be married?' she inquired into his silence, for he sat rather like a man on whose hand a wild bird has perched. "I am almost seventeen now."

"Well, how did that happen? I thought—"

"I lied to General Lafayette about my age that day. I had to. Kit's voice had changed."

Julian rocked with quiet laughter, cradling the thin, eager body in his arms.

"Tibby, I can't live any longer without you! There is no use even trying. Do you remember the first piece you ever said for me, from the Book of Ruth—*thy people shall be my people*—"

"I know a better one than that, for us."

"Tell me."

" 'As it was in the beginning,' " said Tibby, pressing closer to his shoulder, " 'is now, and ever shall be—world without end—amen.' "

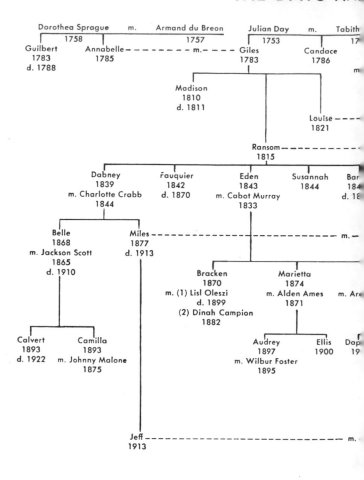

Dorothea Sprague   m.   Armand du Breon   Julian Day   m.   Tabith
        1758   1757   1753   17
Guilbert   Annabelle — — — — — — — m.— — — — Giles   Candace
1783   1785   1783   1786
d. 1788   m

Madison
1810
d. 1811

Louise — — —
1821

Ransom — — — — — — — — — —
1815

Dabney   Fauquier   Eden   Susannah   Bar
1839   1842   1843   1844   184
m. Charlotte Crabb d. 1870   m. Cabot Murray   d. 18
1844   1833

Belle   Miles — — — — — — — — — — — — — — — — — — m. —
1868   1877
m. Jackson Scott   d. 1913
1865
d. 1910

Bracken   Marietta
1870   1874
m. (1) Lisl Oleszi   m. Alden Ames   m. Ar
d. 1899   1871
(2) Dinah Campion
1882

Calvert   Camilla
1893   1893   Audrey   Ellis   Dap
d. 1922   m. Johnny Malone   1897   1900   19
                1875   m. Wilbur Foster
                                          1895

Jeff — — — — — — — — — — — — — — — — — — — m.
1913

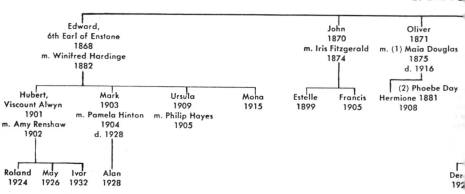

Edward,   John   Oliver
6th Earl of Enstone   1870   1871
1868   m. Iris Fitzgerald   m. (1) Maia Douglas
m. Winifred Hardinge   1874   1875
1882   d. 1916

(2) Phoebe Day
Hermione 1881
1908

Hubert,   Mark   Ursula   Mona   Estelle Francis
Viscount Alwyn 1903   1909   1915   1899   1905
1901   m. Pamela Hinton m. Philip Hayes
m. Amy Renshaw 1904   1905
1902   d. 1928

Roland May   Ivor Alan
1924   1926 1932 1928

Der
192